NO ORDINARY MUGGING

Two men appeared out of nowhere and stood in front of the dumpster, blocking my way. In New York people die every day because they fight to hang onto their wallets. "Here." I thrust my bag at the man closer to me. "Take whatever you want."

The guy on the left impatiently pulled off his gloves, yanked the zipper open, and pulled my wallet out.

"Not much here." He threw the money in a slushy puddle at my feet. "Maybe you should find another job."

"I like my job."

A hand flashed and struck my face. A heavy college ring caught my lower lip, and blood rolled down my chin.

"I said maybe you should find another job. It's good advice—take it."

A switchblade clicked open—my cue to get the hell out of that alley. I elbowed the man behind me, feinted to the right, and spun to the left.

Nice move. It might have worked—if the alley wasn't coated with snow-covered ice. And if I hadn't tripped. The sensation of my unprotected head smashing against the pavement was the last thing I remembered. . . .

"The private eye yarn doesn't get any better than Sharon Zukowski, and the cooler than cool Blaine Stewart."
—Gloria White, author of *Money to Burn*

JUNGLELAND

A BLAINE STEWART MYSTERY

Sharon Zukowski

A SIGNET BOOK

SIGNET
Published by the Penguin Group
Penguin Books USA Inc., 375 Hudson Street,
New York, New York 10014, U.S.A.
Penguin Books Ltd, 27 Wrights Lane,
London W8 5TZ, England
Penguin Books Australia Ltd, Ringwood,
Victoria, Australia
Penguin Books Canada Ltd, 10 Alcorn Avenue,
Toronto, Ontario, Canada M4V 3B2
Penguin Books (N.Z.) Ltd, 182–190 Wairau Road,
Auckland 10, New Zealand

Penguin Books Ltd, Registered Offices:
Harmondsworth, Middlesex, England

First published by Signet, an imprint of Dutton Signet,
a division of Penguin Books USA Inc.

First Printing, July, 1997
10 9 8 7 6 5 4 3 2 1

 REGISTERED TRADEMARK—MARCA REGISTRADA

Printed in the United States of America

PUBLISHER'S NOTE
This is a work of fiction. Names, characters, places, and incidents either are
the product of the author's imagination or are used fictitiously, and any resemblance to actual persons, living or dead, events, or locales is entirely
coincidental.

To Peter Meyers, Sr.

ACKNOWLEDGMENTS

Special thanks to Sarah Lacey for allowing Leah Hunter to appear in this book, to Kay Mitchell for making the introduction, and to Joseph Guglielmelli for patiently answering my legal questions. Extra special thanks to everyone in the Z-Cult—the most loyal fans in the world.

The street's alive
As secret debts are paid
Contacts made, they vanish unseen
Kids flash guitars just like switchblades
Hustling for the record machine
The hungry and the hunted
Explode into rock 'n' roll bands
That face off against each other out in the street
Down in Jungleland

—Bruce Springsteen
"Jungleland"

Chapter 1

There should have been some sign, some warning that my life was about to be bounced around in directions I never imagined, not even in my wildest nightmares, but there wasn't. The day started the same as any other day. The alarm rang, as it does every morning, except it went off an hour earlier than usual. I slammed the snooze button, as I do every morning, and burrowed under the covers to sleep for ten more minutes.

But on this particular morning, Dennis, my husband, wouldn't let me sleep. He gently nudged my back. "Quit stalling, Blaine. Getting up early was your idea, remember?"

He was right, but I would never admit it. The cold and the darkness waiting outside didn't make getting out of our warm bed any more appealing. The queasiness in the bottom of my stomach could have been caused by the early hour, or it could have been a premonition—I was too sleepy to decide. Another—less gentle—nudge from Dennis convinced me to move; I rolled out of bed.

My running clothes were at the foot of the bed, where I had left them the night before so I couldn't use missing clothes as an excuse to skip another morning's exercise. Dennis watched me dress and laughed at my grumbling. As I walked out of the room, he turned over to go back to sleep.

I stumbled down the stairs, wondering why I had thought that running at six a.m. could possibly be good for me. Why another hour or two of sleep wouldn't be just as healthy.

If I were in a mood to be honest, I would have admitted that a silly, unvoiced fear about not living long enough to get old pushed me out of bed, made me start taking vitamins, and left me vowing to eat the three to five daily servings of vegetables the nutritionists recommended. In the dark morning, it's easy to pooh-pooh those fears and go back to bed—but I didn't. In my business, if you don't stay sharp, worrying about getting old can be a waste of time.

I laughed at the gloomy thoughts, did a few stretching exercises in the hallway, opened the door—and found a man sprawled facedown on the stairs. Cursing Bobby and Ryan, owners of the RiverView Bar & Grill—the View as it's known in the neighborhood—I hopped over him. The guy had been sober enough to stumble the half block from the bar to my front door before pausing for a rest. Why couldn't he have stumbled a few more feet to one of my neighbors'?

I gently shook his cashmere-clad shoulder. He didn't move. Mild irritation turned to anger. I shook harder and said, "Come on, buddy. Rise and shine. If I can't sleep, you can't sleep."

He still didn't move. I uttered another soft curse and rolled him over onto his back. The man's unbuttoned jacket fell open; blood seeped from a chest wound, staining his crisp white shirt. Lifeless blue eyes stared at me.

Chapter 2

I pulled my hand back and cursed. The body slowly rolled facedown again. I froze and stared at the corpse; the shock of stumbling across him lasted for only a few seconds. Then, automatic pilot took over. I wheeled around and looked up and down the street—it was empty. I cursed again, louder this time, and climbed over the body to get back inside the house.

After stopping in the hallway to call the local precinct, I ran upstairs to the bedroom. Dennis was still in bed. He opened his eyes and squinted at me. "That was fast, Blaine. Did you break the two-minute mile or did you wimp out when you hit the street?"

"Change of plans." I grabbed a jacket from the closet and pulled it on. "You're not going to believe this, Dennis, but there's a body—a man—on the front stairs. I just called the cops."

Dennis sat up. With professional calm, he asked, "Anybody we know?"

"Not this time." I zipped the jacket and slipped a small camera from my briefcase into my pocket. "I'm going to wait outside for the cops. I already touched the guy and I don't want anyone else messing with him. Want to join me?"

"How romantic. We can watch the sun come up

as the morgue boys cart away the corpse." Dennis pushed himself out of bed and grabbed a pair of blue jeans from the dresser. "I'm right behind you."

I didn't wait; I hurried back outside. The body was still lying undisturbed on the stairs. An early morning dog-walker, carefully bundled up against the chilly autumnal air, strolled past. She glanced at the man and then at me, shook her head in disgust, and hurried by. Quickly, before the police arrived, I stood over the body and snapped a few pictures. I walked to the middle of the street and slowly turned in a circle, taking shots of the neighborhood. The dog-walker stopped at the end of the block and watched. Shaking her head even harder than before, she yanked on the dog's leash and dragged the sleepy animal away. I clicked off the last frame as they disappeared around the corner.

Most people would think taking snapshots of a body is a ghoulish act, but it's my job. No, I wasn't going to sell the pictures to Geraldo or a supermarket tabloid. I'm a private investigator and I knew what to expect when the police arrived. They'd push me away, check to be sure that the corpse was indeed a corpse, and make the calls that would bring detectives, the Crime Scene Unit, and the rest of the team that would eventually remove the body. I'd never have another chance to get near him, to satisfy my curiosity about how and why he chose my doorstep as his final stop.

A royal blue-and-white NYPD patrol car pulled up to the curb. Dennis, dressed in jeans and an old sweatshirt, arrived at the same time. We stood side by side on the sidewalk and watched the red tape unfold. After a few minutes, Dennis started fidgeting. He pulled away from me and said, "This is like the busman's holiday. I'm going to have breakfast. You coming?"

"Not just yet. I'm going to hang out here a little longer."

Dennis gave me a quizzical look, then walked through the narrow alleyway that separates our house from our neighbor's. One of the cops, a young woman, trotted back to her patrol car with a rookie's enthusiasm. As she made radio calls, the other cop, a tall black man who looked like he'd been through a long, hectic night, walked over to me. "Where'd your friend go?"

"Inside. Want me to get him?"

"Nope, not yet." He shook his head sympathetically. "You called this in?"

I nodded. "That's my house. I damn near tripped over him when I came out."

"Don't suppose you have any idea of who he is, do you?"

"Never saw him before. To tell you the truth, I wish I'd never seen him at all."

Luck had sent me a talkative cop. He shook his head again. "He's awfully well-dressed for a bum, don't you think? How much do you think that coat cost?" He supplied his own answer. "Cashmere, hand-tailored. I tell you, it cost a bundle. And that tie. It probably cost sixty or seventy bucks." The cop shook his head. "Well, don't go anywhere. Somebody will want to talk to you sooner or later."

I promised to stay put and leaned against a light pole to watch the action. The curtains on the house across the street moved slightly. I felt my neighbors' stares as they wondered just what I'd done to cause this latest ruckus. I wanted to shout, *This*

one's not my fault, but I didn't. No one would believe me. Too many other disturbances—bombs,
gunshots, and police cars in the middle of the
night—had been my fault.

A tall, husky man joined the crowd around the
body and quietly gave directions. If you took away
his worn, full-length leather coat and replaced it
with a flannel shirt, he could be taken for a lumberjack from the Pacific Northwest. But he wasn't a
lumberjack, he was a cop.

He walked over and smiled in an attempt to put
me at ease. My house was his last unlucky stop
before the night shift ended, and his face showed
it. His eyes were bloodshot and sleepy. His dark
hair was rumpled and he desperately needed a
shave. "So you found the body? Hell of a way to
start your day."

I liked his low-key approach. I smiled and answered, "Hell of a way for that guy to end his day."

"Poor bastard." He shook his head; a lock of
hair fell over his eyes. He impatiently tossed it
back. "Chris Hutchinson. Forty-ninth Precinct."

"Blaine Stewart."

"You found the body?"

I nodded and repeated my story of tripping over
the body. The detective scrawled in his notebook
and asked, "Did you see anybody on the street
when you came out?"

"A lady walking a dog." I shrugged and immediately volunteered, "We didn't hear anything, either.
But we don't usually hear the noise after the bars
close down."

"You think this guy was on his way home after
a night on the town?"

"It looks that way to me. We have problems with

drunks every so often. Mostly noise and puking in the street. They don't usually try to sleep it off on the steps."

"Drunks from the RiverView Bar & Grill? That's right down the street, isn't it? We found a pack of their matches in his pocket."

Quickly, so my statement couldn't be interpreted as a complaint, I said, "It's been a while since we had trouble with people from the View. The owners have been working hard to keep their customers under control." I abruptly turned the conversation in another direction. "That didn't look like a gunshot wound. It's from a knife, right?"

A suspicious light settled in the detective's eyes. He nodded. "Whoever stabbed this guy was good, or lucky—if you want to call it luck. One stab; caught him right in the heart. Have you ever seen this guy before?"

"No. I saw you take a wallet from his pocket. Did it have any identification? I don't want to keep thinking of him as 'the dead guy.'"

Without glancing at his notebook, Hutchinson said, "George Walden. He lived in Hoboken. According to his business card, he worked on Wall Street. Probably came to the Village to party and attracted too much attention."

"Too much attention?" I shook my head. "He doesn't look like the flashy type to me."

"You're wrong. It happens all the time to guys like that. They get loaded, flash a wad of cash, and brag about their latest deal or a bonus that's a hundred times more than I'll ever see in my lifetime. They totter outside and *BAM!* Smacked in the head by some asshole who's tired of being a have-not. It's Walden's bad luck that he decided to wobble down Barrow Street at the same time someone decided to play trick-or-treat."

I blurted out, "But he's wearing a Rolex. That's an expensive watch; don't you think a mugger would have grabbed it? And why didn't the mugger take his wallet? Or did the bad guy empty the wallet and then put it back in the guy's pocket? Neat, civil-minded mugger. He should get an antilittering award instead of a jail sentence."

The detective frowned. I stopped and grinned, slightly embarrassed by my outburst.

"Hey, Sherlock, you ask a lot of questions. You want my job? You go pound the pavement and look for somebody who saw this poor bastard get walloped. I'll go home and get some sleep."

I backed away and smiled apologetically. "Sorry, I didn't mean to be pushy. Thanks for the job offer, but I don't want it. I've already done your job. I don't want to do it again."

The detective looked at me with a questioning eye. I said, "I joined the force when I was fresh out of college. I left after eighteen months—it didn't agree with me. After a few years of trying to work for other people, I realized that I had to be the boss. So, I started my own company."

"Pay must be a lot better." He nodded at my house. "Brownstone in the Village. I never could afford that. Not on a cop's salary."

"The pay's better but the hours are just as bad—worse, sometimes. Are you going to need me any longer? I really should get ready for work."

"A few more minutes and you're outta here, I promise." The detective nodded at our living room window. "That guy who keeps peeking out the window—he your boyfriend?"

"Husband."

"He an ex-cop, too?"

"FBI."

The detective whistled through his teeth. "Holy shit. Walden picked one of the safest places in the city to get murdered. Now, is your husband an ex, or is he still collecting a government check?"

Normally I would have bristled at the personal tone of the questions, but the detective's rumpled, sleepy air captivated me. I smiled. "He's still on the job. It's been a while since he talked about quitting."

I couldn't keep myself from smiling again. It's amazing what a new boss can do. Dennis used to do a lot of talking about quitting. After many hours of talking and agonizing, he wrote a letter of resignation and stuck it in his breast pocket. On the day Dennis planned to present the letter, a new boss miraculously appeared. Since then, I've found myself married to a born-again FBI agent.

Hutchinson pulled me from my daydream. "Did your hubby see or hear anything?"

"Nope. Like I said, we didn't hear anything."

"Maybe I should ask him myself."

I shrugged. "Doesn't matter to me. If you've got the time to waste, be my guest. Do you want me to get him?"

"Don't bother. I'll come back if I have to talk to him." The detective snapped his notebook shut and pulled a business card from beneath the rubber band that held it all together. He passed the card to me and grinned. "If you stumble across a bloody knife in the mailbox or have a midnight revelation, give me a call. Otherwise, have a nice day."

He walked away and joined the crowd around

the body. I stood near the curb, watching the men wrestle George Walden's uncooperative body into a bag. They closed it up and lugged it down the stairs. I shuddered and glanced away. George Walden, who lived in Hoboken and used to work on Wall Street, had undoubtedly envisioned a more dignified end to his life. Did anyone wonder where he had spent his last night?

The police caravan drove away. The morning theatrics were over. The small group of bystanders slowly drifted away. Early morning quiet returned to the street. Curtains dropped all over the block. My neighbors stopped staring out their windows and resumed their daily routines. I went inside and found Dennis sitting in the kitchen, eating oatmeal. Nothing like a nourishing breakfast to start the day—hot cereal instead of a cold corpse.

I sat beside him and cradled my head in my hands. "Well, it's all over. The cops packed up and went home."

"I was beginning to wonder how long you'd stand out there. Blaine, aren't you beyond the stage of curious bystander? Haven't you seen enough bodies?"

Dennis got up and poured a cup of coffee. He put the mug down on the table in front of me and examined my face as if I were a stranger. Avoiding his eyes, I wrapped my hands around the steaming mug. "Too many, Dennis. But I couldn't drag myself away from this one. I feel responsible."

"You feel responsible because he had the misfortune to die on our doorstep? Come on, Blaine, you can't be responsible for everyone in this city. It's coincidence and bad luck that led him to us—nothing else."

"Coincidence." The word felt strange on my tongue. I let it roll around in my mind for a moment, then asked, "Do you really think it's coincidence?"

"Yes. I do." Dennis's eyes locked on my mine for a few seconds—long enough for me to see that he hadn't been entirely convinced by his own words. We both know believing in coincidence can be a fatal mistake. He glanced away. "Drink your coffee before it gets cold. You want some oatmeal?"

I shook my head. I had enough trouble swallowing coffee; oatmeal would have formed a thick, impassable lump. I couldn't swallow the feeling of responsibility, either.

Chapter 3

The depression that settled over me was no surprise. Even Dennis, the most cheerful morning person alive, seemed subdued. He halfheartedly tried to lighten the mood, but I ignored his efforts. I preferred to morosely nurse my coffee—and my unearned guilt.

Dennis finally gave up. Despite my claim of having no appetite, he gave me a bowl of oatmeal, kissed my cheek, and went to shower and dress. I sat at the kitchen table, pushed the oatmeal around the bowl, and thought about George Walden.

By the time Dennis returned, the oatmeal was cold and I hadn't reached any conclusions. Dennis wore a brown, double-breasted Dior suit that was the same color as his hair. As always, he looked more like a *GQ* model than an FBI agent. Dennis leaned down and kissed me. Happy to have such a pleasant interruption, I smoothed an imaginary wrinkle in his shirt and said, "You're looking exceptionally handsome this morning."

"I'm not feeling very handsome." Dennis pulled out a chair and sat beside me. "You said the detective talked about a mugger. You know what that means."

I sighed. Having Dennis confirm my dark thoughts didn't comfort me. "The case will disappear into the open-but-not-working-very-hard-on-it file. Hutchinson seems like a nice guy. But I bet he's too swamped to do much more than file a report."

"Then the investigation is over."

"You're not cheering me up, dear." I sighed again, louder this time. "But you are right. The investigation is over—unless something turns up."

"Or someone turns it up."

We sat quietly for a few seconds. I stared at the bowl, hoping to find an answer in the swirls of oatmeal. I dropped the spoon. It clattered against the bowl, highlighting my resolve. "There's only one thing to do."

"Look into it yourself." Dennis smiled and rubbed my bare leg. "But before you do anything, Blaine, you'd better get dressed."

With that, he kissed me again and headed to work. I turned into a madwoman. I took a quick shower and dressed—I might not make the *GQ* cover with Dennis, but at five-nine with flaming red hair, I'd do. I ran downstairs and grabbed my coat and briefcase. For the third time that morning, I rushed out the front door.

The police had been thoughtful. They hadn't roped off the stairs with their yellow tape. They hadn't even left the chalk outline of the body that television-watchers and moviegoers expect. I didn't need chalk marks; I knew exactly where George Walden's body had fallen. I hopped over that spot and landed on the sidewalk—just as one of my less-than-friendly neighbors walked by.

I nodded at him; he scowled at me. Slightly balding with a beard recently grown to make up for the lack of hair on top of his head, he appeared much

older than the thirty-five years he claimed. One of
Barrow Street's newer residents, the man, whose
name I could never remember (and frankly, didn't
want to remember), had quickly gained the reputation of nonstop complainer and constant
troublemaker.

Traffic, the noise from the View, kids throwing
cigarette butts on the walk: everything in the neighborhood displeased him; everything made him fret
about his real estate investment. Dead bodies on
the sidewalk tend to lower property values—I wondered when he'd start a petition to drive me out
of the neighborhood.

Brad Carlson, my closest friend since kindergarten and my second-in-command for the past six or
seven years, was sitting in his office. I waved as I
walked past. Brad jumped to his feet and ran
around his desk. He chased me down the hallway.

"Hey, Blaine. I've been waiting for you. We
gotta talk about . . ." He looked at my face and
grimaced. "What's wrong with you, Babe? You
don't look so hot this morning."

"Thanks, Brad, I appreciate the compliment." I
ran my fingers through my still-damp hair and said,
"I am having one of those days. Blame it on the
dead man on the doorstep."

"That sounds like a mystery. Who wrote it?"

I pulled the lid from the cup of coffee I'd carried
in from a deli and took a gulp. The hot liquid
scalded my mouth; I cursed softly and said, "You
mean, who left him there? I didn't stay up late
reading a book. When I went out to run this morning, I found a corpse on my front stairs. The guy
died right there in front of my house."

Grace Hudson, who'd been my st
at least a dozen years, has been a
as long. As we struggled to b
businesses, we'd gotten into
lunches and frequent tel
strategies. Lately, as th
mid-nineties faded a
Grace had been ca
frustration at th
trial Average
could mo
have p
I

time ... in the door.

Eileen didn't feel quite the same satisfaction. At her insistence, the entire place, including my office, had recently been redecorated. I liked my comfortable old desk and chairs, but Eileen said they looked shabby. She said that even though I sometimes look shabby, she'd let me stay, but the furniture had to go. I missed my shabby furniture: the new desk was too big and shiny, the leather chair too stiff.

I dropped my briefcase on the floor, sat in the uncomfortable chair, and smiled. At least the mess on top of the desk hadn't been replaced by shiny new in-baskets. The ringing telephone interrupted my self-congratulations. I grabbed it and was greeted by Grace Hudson's unhappy voice.

"You so rich you don't need to talk to your broker? Three calls to you. None returned."

ockbroker for
friend for almost
uild our respective
the habit of monthly
ephone calls to discuss
raging bull market of the
d the stock market tumbled,
ling more frequently to vent her
e uncooperative Dow Jones Indus-
and her nervous clients. If willpower
e the market, Grace's ambition would
shed it to new heights.

pologized and tried to explain that we hadn't
tten home until well past midnight—too late to
return phone calls, even to my night-owl mother.
"What's up? Do you have a hot stock for me? One
that can't—"

Patience is not one of Grace's virtues. She cut
me off. "I have, make that had, business for you.
Too late now. Man's dead."

Grace's habit of not using sentences with more
than four words can be annoying. This was one of
those annoying times. I snapped, "What are you
talking about, Grace? Who's dead?"

"A friend. Your would-be client. Come to my
office. We'll talk."

In my most threatening voice, I said, "Grace,
don't hang up without explaining, or you'll be talking to an empty office. I'm not running downtown
just because you want to see my pretty face.
Who's dead?"

"You don't know him."

I slipped into the pattern of Grace's abbreviated
sentences. "Name?"

"George Walden."

My stomach contracted and squeezed bitter acid into my mouth. I swallowed and managed to say, 'George Walden? He was a friend of yours?"

Before I blurted out how I'd stumbled over his body, Grace answered, "Good friend. Known him since we were training to become brokers."

"Grace, there's something you should know—"

Grace kept talking as if I hadn't spoken. "George called last night. Said he needed help. Your kind of help. He wouldn't tell me more. Said he didn't want to drag me into it. I said you were the best. George was afraid someone would see him going into a private investigator's office."

"That's not unusual. A lot of my clients don't want to be seen anywhere near my office. It's too embarrassing to explain why they're seeing a private investigator. What did you do?"

"Gave him your home address and phone number. Tried to call to warn you."

The censure in Grace's voice annoyed me. "I know. Three messages. You said to call when I had a chance and I haven't had a chance. You never said it was urgent. When did George call you?"

"Nine-fifteen, exactly. I looked at my watch. It was Monday. The Giants were playing. I wanted him off the phone before the game got going."

So we both had something to feel guilty about. Even though I told myself the guilt was irrational—irrational because I hadn't been home when Grace called, irrational because I had no way of knowing George Walden was on his way to see me. Irrational, but still, the guilt twisted my stomach and fogged my head.

Grace's stomach was twisting too. I heard it in her voice. All the warmth had been frozen out and replaced by ice. She sounded like the principal coldly saying she would call your parents, or a cop ordering you to step out of the car. Grace's guilt was just as irrational as mine, but I didn't waste time telling her. She wouldn't have listened.

On the surface, Grace appeared to be unfazed by the tumultuous days on Wall Street. She never mentioned the stress, but I knew that her desk's top drawer was filled with Pepto-Bismol, Rolaids, Pepcid AC, and other panaceas to a stomach on the verge of burning out. Now that Grace had been granted the lofty status of a partner in the firm, she relied more and more on her antacids.

The tight sound of Grace's voice worried me; she was closer to the edge than usual. I decided to deliver the news about finding George in person. News like that shouldn't come through the telephone.

Gardner Norvill & Burnett is on Broad Street, directly across the street from the New York Stock Exchange. Gardner has been in business for nearly a hundred and ten years. Some people, including most of those who worked there, thought the firm wouldn't survive a woman partner—but it did. The firm survived, but lately I wasn't sure Grace would survive the added pressure to prove herself worthy.

The receptionist, an elderly woman who brought back memories of my first-grade teacher, smiled kindly and invited me to sit in one of the plush armchairs. Ms. Hudson would see me in a few moments. I thanked her and took a seat across from an oil painting of Henry Norvill, the firm's founder. He glowered at me. I glowered back.

Grace didn't keep me waiting long. I'd barely

settled in the uncomfortable chair when she came to greet me. No more than five feet three inches tall, Grace looked like a petite cheerleader, but a fierce, at times vicious, competitor's heart pounded beneath her silk blouse, Giorgio Armani suit, and pearls. After coolly shaking my hand and thanking me for coming downtown, Grace led me through a maze of waist-high cubicles filled with young men and women earnestly talking into their telephones. I followed her, watching the glances cast at us by the rookie brokers who sat elbow-to-elbow in the large, open room.

Since my last visit, Grace had moved to a larger office. One large enough for her new partner status, and to fit her oversized desk, credenza (with not one, but three computers that flashed quotes and other financial information), a sofa with two chairs flanking it, several bookcases filled with textbooks called *Security Analysis, The Dow Dividend Theory,* and other equally dull subjects, and an oval conference table with four chairs around it. As usual, vases of exotic flowers covered the tops of the bookcases.

A window ran the length of the office, giving a clear view of the entrance to the New York Stock Exchange. Grace pointed to the conference table near the window. "Sit."

Two mugs of steaming coffee waited on the table. I sat and looked down on the strip of pavement known as the Street. The heart of the center of world finance had very little activity on it. Cabs and trucks impatiently wove through the narrow street. Tourists straggled into the building; stock exchange clerks huddled in doorways out of the wind and the slight rain that had started falling.

They would sneak a quick cigarette, then rush back inside to their posts.

Grace had surfed ahead of the rising market, taking her clients with her to the top. When the market fell, she tumbled faster and harder than most— but without complaint. Before she sat, Grace glanced at the flickering screens that monitored the market's progress. As she turned to me, something flickered through her eyes. Grief? Annoyance? Desperation? I couldn't tell.

"You and George were good friends?"

Grace nodded. "It's like losing a member of the family. . . ."

"There's something I didn't tell you when you called." The words cemented themselves into a hard lump in my throat. I swallowed hard and said, "George did come to my house last night." Knowing my next words would extinguish the hopeful look in Grace's eyes, I said, "He never made it inside. I discovered his body this morning."

Grace turned to look out the window. I followed her gaze and watched the rain fall. After a few moments, Grace cleared her throat and shoved the mug aside. I took it as a sign that she was ready to talk.

"Tell me about George Walden. Why did he need to see me?"

"Don't know. I can guess." She reluctantly said, "George worked for Kembell Reid."

"Kembell Reid." The name had a familiar sound. "I remember seeing something about them on CNN the other night. They're having problems, right?"

"Problems." Grace snorted. "They lost five hundred million dollars. One of their hotshots made fake trades. Inflated profits—and her bonus. Girl wonder turned out to be girl blunder."

"Was Walden involved?"

"Not George. He was too honest. But it happened in his department."

"Did he think he was being followed? Was that why he wouldn't come to my office?"

"Don't know. You're wasting time."

According to Grace, wasting time is a sin. She never wastes time—at least not during market hours when there's always another order to fill.

"So what do you want me to do?" I closed my notebook and slumped down in the chair to wait for the answer I didn't want to hear. Despite my curiosity about Walden's death, I didn't want a paying customer. I wanted to look into the death on my own terms, not according to a client's wishes. Besides, I was emotionally involved, and that's a huge mistake in any investigation.

"Stay on top of things. I want to know what the police do. I want to be sure someone's looking out for George."

"I don't know, Grace." I dragged my words out reluctantly. "The police don't like private investigators tagging along and peeking over their shoulders."

"Don't care. I want to know what's being done. George was my friend. I want to know if the cops shrug this off as just another murder."

"I'm expensive, Grace. One hundred seventy-five dollars an hour, plus expenses—and that's with a discount."

She shrugged. "Doesn't matter. I'll pay."

I tried several other excuses, but Grace wouldn't listen. Finally, I gave in. If I was going to look into Walden's death, I might as well have someone pay for my time. "Fine. I'll start at Kembell Reid. Can you get me in? Securities firms are always skittish when private investigators ask questions about their employees—especially when the company just lost five hundred million dollars."

Grace nodded and grabbed the telephone that sat in the center of the table. As she punched in a phone number and started talking, I sat back and furiously tried to think of a way out.

". . . great. Seven-thirty. She'll be there. Thanks, Gary. I owe you."

Grace hung up and scribbled on a small notepad. I barely noticed the sound of the sheet being torn from the pad. She held the page out to me.

Cases dragging the emotional anchors of family or friends are as welcome as the winter storms that would soon be dumping snow and ice on Manhattan. The hopes and fears of the people you love pile on, weighing you down and threatening to smother you. I looked at the paper in Grace's hand and had a quick change of heart. The thought, *not again,* ran through my mind. This case had too many anchors. I needed a quick, clean job. Turn the bad guys over to the cops and go home. Not this.

Grace impatiently snapped the paper under my nose. "Don't back out. I need you."

Reluctantly, ever so reluctantly, and only because I considered Grace a friend, I reached for the note. Grace had taken to writing with a purple Flair pen. I glanced at the big colorful letters. *H. Gary Preston,* and an address. I tried to joke. "Did you have to tell him seven-thirty? Do you know what time I'll have to get up?"

Grace didn't smile. "Don't screw this up. It's my friend that's dead."

Chapter 4

"Why don't you assign this to someone else?" Eileen took her glasses off and tossed them on my desk. She had come into my office to ask about my schedule and frowned when she heard my answer. "I have a big case starting next week. I'm going to be spending a lot of time in court. I'd rather have you stay around to keep an eye on things here."

"No way, Eileen."

I glared at my older sister and business partner. A few strands of gray lightened her brown hair. Overnight, tiny lines had appeared in Eileen's forehead and at the corners of her eyes. Worry lines?

"Eileen, I promised Grace I'd handle it myself. You can't expect me to pass this job off because you think I need to play babysitter. I trust my people—don't you trust yours?"

Eileen rubbed her forehead, a sign of a recurring headache from an old injury, a nearly fatal souvenir of a past case. She sighed. "Blaine, it's not a matter of trust. We're still rebuilding; we lost so many clients last year. I think one of us should be here."

Being the firm's chief financial officer has its benefits. With a faint smile on my face, I pulled a spreadsheet from the folder on my lap and slid it across the desk to Eileen.

"We've made a remarkable comeback, Eileen. A

lot of those old clients came back—at higher rates. And we brought in a lot of new clients, too. Business is better than it was a year ago. Not to rub it in, but my investigative staff billed more than your lawyers did this quarter. If you can go play in court, I can go play in the field."

Eileen laughed and shook her head in mock disgust. "I should know better than to argue with you. You'd think that after all these years—"

"—you'd stop pulling the big-sister routine and let me—"

"—do your job." Eileen laughed again. "Isn't it time to find a new argument? This one's getting old."

"That shouldn't be too difficult. I'm sure we can find new things to fight about."

I relaxed, lit a cigarette, and studied my sister's face; those worry lines made her look years older. Concerned, because Eileen always manages to look unruffled by the events swirling around her, I softly said, "Why don't you tell me what's really bothering you?"

There's a large window behind my back; if you crane your neck you can see the tip of Central Park. Eileen stared out the window. In her calmest courtroom voice, she said, "Nothing."

My stomach lurched; I didn't believe her. Eileen's voice clearly said that I should stop prying. As usual, I ignored her unspoken warning. "Is something wrong with Sandy?"

"No."

"How's Don?"

My question made Eileen's blood boil. "I *said* nothing's wrong." She grabbed her glasses and stomped out. I watched her go and wondered what had upset her.

By the time the cab stopped in front of my house, it was dark and the lights were on inside. The taxi driver got a bigger tip than he deserved because I didn't want to wait for change and hurried into the house. The smell of garlic led me to the kitchen. I dropped my briefcase on the floor, leaned against the door, and watched Dennis toss bok choy into a wok.

"I knew you wouldn't be able to resist the aroma." Dennis, dressed in jeans and an NYU sweatshirt, tasted his latest creation. He nodded with satisfaction and flashed a wicked grin in my direction. "Burning the midnight oil? You should ask your boss for a raise."

A touch of foresight made me say, "Compared to the hours I'm going to be keeping, this is an early night."

"That sounds ominous, Blaine. Are you going to turn into my redheaded stranger?"

I wanted to say no, but didn't because I knew I'd be lying. Instead, I said, "I hope not." My stomach tightened; even that noncommittal answer sounded false—and I didn't know why.

Dennis rested the spatula on the edge of the stove and gave me a quick—but hearty—kiss. Then he helped me take off my coat and tossed it on a chair. "There was a message on the machine from Grace Hudson. She said you should call her at home. It doesn't matter how late you call."

"Then she won't be upset if I don't call until tomorrow morning. I'm too tired to listen to Grace ask if I've made any progress when I've only been on the job for a few hours. All I want is a normal, quiet evening with my loving husband, who thoughtfully cooked dinner."

"As he does every night." Dennis threw some shrimp into the wok and stirred energetically. "It's self-defense. I'd rather cook than starve."

Insults about my nonexistent cooking skills don't bother me anymore. I laughed. "Thank God you're good at it. Do you need help?"

My efforts to help usually end with blood dripping from fingers, smoke detectors sounding, and calls being made to get pizza delivered. Dennis displayed remarkable self-control; he didn't laugh hysterically. Holding back a grin, he said, "Nope, everything is under control. Just stay out of my way and we'll be fine."

I let Dennis push me into a chair. I rested my head in my hands and watched. He bustled around the kitchen, stir-frying vegetables and mixing sauces.

We tried to have a normal, quiet evening. We ate dinner, discussing the events of our day just like any couple. Except we talked about corpses, kidnappers, and cults—bizarre talk for most couples, but not us. It was a normal end to a normal day.

Chapter 5

After dinner, Dennis found a basketball game on TV and I went upstairs to our study and switched on the computer. Computers. I complain about them all the time. I say that I hate them. I certainly don't understand how they work. But the keyboard sings beneath my fingers.

Like the baker who doesn't understand why the bread rises or the Indy car driver who can't explain internal combustion, I don't know RAMs from ROMs or bytes from bites. But I do know that the Pentium processor with "intel inside" sitting on my desk instantly connects me to worlds that used to take days or weeks to penetrate.

I started to light a cigarette, but stopped when I realized how many I'd smoked since morning. Too many. Sooner or later, I was going to have to stop—again. Instead, I instructed my modem to dial my Internet connection. Once all the connections were made, I started searching my favorite databases and soon lost track of time.

Dennis came in. He rested his hands on my shoulders and peered over my head at the screen. "You've been up here for hours. What are you doing?"

"Getting ready for tomorrow morning's meeting.

I want to know a little about Kembell Reid before I visit them. Is the game over?"

"Yeah, but don't ask me who won. I didn't pay much attention. Find anything interesting?"

I pointed at the stack of articles I'd printed out. "Two dozen variations of the same story. Trader screws up; the company loses a fortune. They're hanging on by a thread while the lawyers and the SEC try to figure out who's to blame and who's going to pay. Half the stories say she's guilty. The other half say she's not guilty. The company says the trader is a thief and a liar. The trader insists that she's a scapegoat, an innocent victim of sexism and corporate greed. Mismanagement, too."

"The victim defense. My favorite."

"Well, I'm glad that's not my headache. Someone else will have to straighten out the stories."

I reached behind me and grabbed Dennis's hand. "I did a bit of research on George Walden, too. He lives—lived—on Washington Street in Hoboken with his wife, Carol. I ran a credit check on him. Nothing unusual. They made a lot of money. They spend a lot, too. Expensive trips. Fancy restaurants. Credit cards from a dozen stores."

"And?"

I shrugged. "Nothing sinister there. I can find millions of people with the same profile."

"Still, I'm impressed." Dennis flipped through my printouts. "Hell, soon we won't have to pound the pavement. We'll be able to conduct investigations from the comfort of our home. Couch potato P.I.'s. Blaine, you could be on to something wonderful."

I sighed. "Yeah, but I'm still going to have to show up for tomorrow's seven-thirty meeting. I don't think Gary Preston will do an on-line interview."

Dennis gently massaged the back of my neck. "It's getting late. How much longer do you think you'll be?"

"I'm just about done." Stretched; the kinks in my neck twisted and pulled. "I'm going to turn into a hunchback if I sit here another second."

"Bed?"

Dennis's fingers promised more than sleep. I tipped my head back to look at him; the sexy glint in his eyes confirmed my suspicions. I grabbed his hands and squeezed them gently in answer to his unspoken invitation. "Bed. You go ahead. I'll be there as soon as I shut this thing down."

The sad experience of losing a hard drive—and all its data—had taught me to back up every session at the computer. I finished my chores, turned off the computer and the lights, and went to the bedroom. Dennis was curled up on his side, asleep.

Disappointed, I gently slid into bed so I wouldn't disturb him. I settled on my side, with my back to Dennis, and closed my eyes. If I took deep breaths and concentrated on relaxing, I'd be able to fall asleep.

I rolled over on my side and closed my eyes.

Dennis's fingertips brushed against my back. Bumps immediately rose on my skin. His hands slid over my shoulders and across my breasts. Dennis doesn't own pajamas. I don't own a night gown. There was no fumbling with clothes.

He whispered, "You weren't planning on sleeping, were you?"

I tried to answer but could only manage a husky *ah*. I pushed back against Dennis and guided his hands lower. His fingers probed and rubbed until I couldn't wait any longer. I flipped over and wrapped my arms around him.

We kissed hungrily, as if we'd been separated for years. I pulled him closer, as close as two bodies can get. Dennis rolled on top of me; his weight pressed me down into the mattress, giving me comfort. Beneath him, I could hide from the world. I could hide from everything—everything but Dennis. I put my arms around his shoulders, urging him closer. I lifted my head and eagerly sought his mouth. My grip on his shoulders loosened on his moist skin. Desperate to not let him get away, I linked my fingers together and raised my hips to meet his body. An explosion shook me. For a too-brief moment, the world disappeared.

I felt Dennis's heart pounding against my chest, in perfect sync with my own heart. He nestled his face against my neck and gently kissed my cheek. I raked my fingers through his sweaty hair and fought to catch my breath.

Dennis fell asleep; I couldn't. Every time I came close, my neck twitched, my legs ached, my stomach churned, and my eyes flew open wide. I got out of bed once for a drink of water, once to open the window, and once again to close it. The fourth time, Dennis reached for me and grabbed a handful of air. In a sleepy, irritated voice, he asked, "Where are you going now? Can't you spend an entire night in bed without getting up a half-dozen times?"

"The phone. We left it downstairs." Years of late-night emergency calls had left me unable to sleep unless the telephone was within reach. "Damned cordless phones are a nuisance. It was easier when we didn't have to go on a scavenger hunt for it."

"Try the kitchen. And don't curse at the phone. You're the one who left it there." With that, Dennis rolled over and buried his face in the pillows. He didn't like me waking him up—again. "Just don't expect me to get it. I don't give a damn about where the telephone spends the night."

That's the difference between owning a business and being a civil servant. Dennis could afford to miss a call—I couldn't.

Regretting my nasty thought, I walked down the stairs, wondering why I couldn't sleep. It's not unusual for me to suffer from sleepless nights when I'm involved in a troublesome investigation. It is unusual for the insomnia to strike so early in a case.

The phone was on the kitchen table, exactly where Dennis predicted I'd find it. I grabbed it and headed back upstairs. When I got back to the bedroom, phone safely in hand, Dennis seemed to be asleep. I put my wayward phone on the nightstand and tried to climb into bed without disturbing him. I carefully punched the pillow and pulled the comforter up to my ears. Dennis rolled over and mumbled, "You okay?"

"Yeah." I kissed his cheek. "Sorry, it's been a hell of a day."

"Umm . . . ," Dennis whispered. "Let's hope tomorrow's better." Then he fell asleep.

Of course, retrieving the phone invited it to ring in the middle of the night.

Chapter 6

Ring it did.

I grabbed the phone before it rang a second time. With eyes closed, I put the receiver against my ear. If I could get rid of this caller, maybe, just maybe, I'd get back to sleep before the sun rose.

Hoping the noise hadn't disturbed Dennis, I whispered, "Hello?"

"Is this Blaine Stewart? I am looking for Blaine Stewart."

"Well, you found her. . . ." Groggy from sleep, I couldn't place the voice. "Who is this?"

"Dani Dexter. I must speak with you."

I opened my eyes and squinted at the red numbers on the alarm clock. "At three-thirteen in the morning? Can't this wait until later?"

Dennis shifted uncomfortably. Rather than risk waking him again, I slid out of bed and walked into the bathroom. Without turning on the light, I closed the door and leaned against the sink.

"I apologize for the late hour." Dani Dexter's voice didn't contain a hint of an apology. "I'm in London. The time difference always confuses me."

I didn't feel any need to be polite. "A woman smart enough to stack up five hundred million dollars in fake trades should be smart enough to understand the concept of time zones." Dani didn't protest, so I continued being rude. "I would think a person with your abilities could figure out that London is five hours ahead of New York. Why don't you call me in the morning—at my office? I might be more inclined to talk to you then."

"I have to see you. Today. I'm taking the Concorde. I will be back in New York in time to meet with you late in the day."

The Concorde didn't impress me as much as an uninterrupted night's sleep would have. I said, "I don't sleep with my appointment book. Call my office in the morning. My secretary will be thrilled to schedule a meeting. The first one's free."

"Wait—you don't understand. I have to talk to you now, not later. I'll be on the plane later."

"I understand that you woke me up in the middle of the night for no reason. I'm sure the Concorde has telephones. You should get something for all the money they charge for a ticket."

"Please listen to me. There is a good reason . . ."

I shifted my bare feet on the cold tile floor. "Ms. Dexter, don't try appealing to my sensitive, understanding nature. I'm not very sympathetic at the best of times, and this isn't close to being one of those times. You have thirty seconds before I hang up. So make it good."

"I'm being blamed for something I didn't do. I'll do anything to clear my name; it's all I have left."

Dani tried to sound cool, but her soft voice couldn't hide an undercurrent of anxiety. I wanted to challenge her soap opera script, but giving in was easier than arguing. At least it would be faster.

I said, "Look, I'm tired and I want to go back to bed. Call my office in the morning. I'm sure I can find some time for you in the afternoon. After all, you are flying on the Concorde. I'd hate to have you waste your money. Good night, Ms. Dexter.''

Before Dani could respond, I turned the phone off. Let Dani spend her time on the Concorde fuming because I'd hung up on her. I left the phone in the bathroom under a stack of towels. I didn't care if it rang all night long—I wanted to sleep.

Dennis barely stirred when I climbed back in bed. I glared at the digital clock. Three-fifteen. In less than three hours the alarm would sound, forcing me from my warm bed. Dennis reached out and lazily draped his arm across my shoulder. I grabbed his hand, glared at the clock one last time, and closed my eyes.

I wondered briefly how Dani had managed to find my unlisted phone number, then I fell asleep. I slept through the alarm. I slept through Dennis reaching over me to turn it off. I couldn't sleep through Dennis shaking my shoulder, although I tried.

"Blaine." Dennis kissed my cheek. I grunted and tried to push him away. Dennis persisted. "You've got to get up, darling. Can't be late, you know." Even with my eyes closed, I knew Dennis was smiling.

Muttering, "I hate people who are cheerful in the morning," I stumbled to the bathroom. Dennis started to say something lighthearted. I slammed the door so I wouldn't hear it.

I tried hot water, lukewarm water, and icy cold water. Nothing worked—I was clean but half-asleep when I stepped from the shower. By the time I staggered from the bathroom, Dennis had gone downstairs. As I pulled on pantyhose and a dark suit, the aroma of coffee drifted upstairs. I was in the bathroom trying to keep my eyes open long enough to put makeup on when Dennis walked in. He was carrying a steaming mug of coffee.

"Coffee is served. I didn't think you'd want breakfast."

"I don't. I'd rather have two or three more hours of sleep." I kissed Dennis. My aim wasn't very good; I smeared my lipstick all over his cheek. "Thanks. I might take back those obscene things I was thinking. How can you be so happy so early in the morning?"

"You'd be happier if you had spent the whole night in bed." Dennis stood in the doorway and watched as I fixed my smeared lipstick. "Did I hear the phone ring last night or was it a dream?"

"Nightmare." I picked up the mug and squeezed past Dennis to the bedroom. "Shoes."

Dennis turned to watch me. "Shoes? You had a nightmare about shoes?"

"I need comfortable shoes. I can't go traipsing around Wall Street in sneakers. The call was from Dani Dexter, the nefarious trader who single-handedly brought down a mighty brokerage firm. She has to see me. And she had to call at three in the morning to tell me so."

I sat on the edge of the bed and sipped the strong, hot brew. "I have the feeling this is going to be a long day.

A wide grin stretched across Dennis's face. "Made longer by the fact that you spent half the night bouncing in and out of bed." Then he pointed to a pair of shoes, navy blue with a low heel, that sat in the corner next to the closet. "Shoes."

Rush hour starts early on Wall Street, but seven o'clock was early even for Wall Street. It took less than fifteen minutes for the cab to reach Kembell Reid's headquarters at the foot of State Street. H. Gary Preston's office was on the top floor.

. Kembell Reid didn't let just anyone inside. It took two phone calls and a careful examination of my identification, "with photo, please," to satisfy the guard in the lobby. He pointed me to an elevator and watched to be sure I didn't scoot off in some unauthorized direction. When the elevator glided to a halt at the top floor, another guard awaited.

That one didn't take any chances either; he escorted me through double oak doors and down a long corridor. A thick green carpet covered the floor; canvases colored with wild slashes of paint brightened the dark walls—I felt like Dorothy approaching the great and powerful Wizard of Oz. We stopped outside another double door. The guard opened it and stepped aside so I could enter Preston's inner sanctum. Corporate security is my specialty. I endured it all without complaint—until Gary Preston glared at me.

"You're late." H. Gary Preston was probably a handsome man, but the frown hid any attractive features. "I expected you ten minutes ago. You may have the luxury of wasting time—I don't."

Bullies, especially bullies in fancy suits, infuriate me. I snapped, "I would have been on time if you had bothered to alert your security force that I had an appointment to see you. I didn't get up at six o'clock to come here to be harassed by a jerk with a tin badge who did everything but check my fingerprints and then have you snarl at me for being a few minutes late. If you have to get to your very important business, I'll leave. Or you can continue to waste time by trying to make me squirm. Or we can get down to business. Which would you prefer?"

"You're very insolent. You know I run this company, don't you?"

"So?" I shrugged. "I run a company, too. I have clients who run companies much larger than Kembell Reid. And if you think I've been insolent, you just wait. I've barely started."

Preston's face took on an unhealthy purple hue. I walked over to the full-length windows next to Preston's desk. The view of New York's harbor was breathtaking, but I wasn't interested in the view. I was hoping Preston would catch his breath and calm down. I faced the Statue of Liberty, gleaming in the morning sun, and shook my head.

"Your company's being put through a grinder. One of your employees was just murdered. It's amazing that you're holding it together. All I'm trying to do is find out who killed George Walden and why."

I turned around. Instead of cursing and pushing me out the door, Preston grinned. "I like you. You want a job?"

"No, thanks." The battle over for the moment, I abandoned my spot at the window and slid into a seat at Preston's desk. "I already have a job. I like it too much to quit."

"No," Gary shook his head impatiently, "I don't want you to sell for me. I can find thousands of hungry kids to do that. I want to hire you. Hire your company."

"That's a pretty quick decision, isn't it?"

"Quick decisions made me rich. I need someone sharp, someone who's not involved in this mess, to figure out what the hell went wrong here. I think you're that person. Those bastards at the Securities Exchange Commission are after me. My board is after me. My shareholders are after me. Everyone's after me."

"Don't you have your own people working on this? I don't see how I'd help."

"Everyone who works here is too busy covering their asses and pointing fingers at each other. They're too busy to figure out how that bitch almost succeeded in running us into the ground. They tell me no one else was involved, but I don't believe them. She's not smart enough."

I wasn't convinced. Preston didn't want the truth. He wanted an easy way out and thought maybe I'd be able to find one. "Sorry, I already have a client. Working for you would be a conflict of interest."

Preston wasn't used to hearing no. His eyes narrowed to angry slits. "What's the matter? Do you have something against people who make money?"

"Not at all. I do have something against murder. Aren't you interested in finding out who killed George Walden?"

"Don't insult me with such a ridiculous question. I'm more than *interested.* I want answers. I promised Carol . . ." Preston hesitated just long enough to make me wonder about what he was leaving out. ". . . George's wife, that I'll do whatever I can to see that justice is done." Preston shook his head. "Christ, I sound like a Superman comic book. Grace gave you a fabulous recommendation; I trust her judgment."

I nodded my thanks, but didn't say anything to interrupt Preston's rush to convince me—of what I didn't know.

"Here." Gary grabbed a thick cream-colored file and slid it across the desk to me. "It's a copy of George's file. I'm sure you'll have questions after you finish reading it. Call me. I'll do what I can to answer them."

I flipped through the file and caught sight of account statements. I glanced at the list of George Walden's investments and raised my eyebrows. The account balance was a few thousand dollars shy of seven digits.

"What about confidentiality? I don't like thinking that my broker would wave my statements around in front of anyone who wandered into her office."

Preston's response was as heated as my question. "I don't like murderers and I don't give a shit about confidentiality. I'm required to collect this stuff. I might as well put it to good use. Call me if you have questions."

I ran my index finger over the embossed K/R on the front of the file and carefully chose words that wouldn't start another disagreement. "I'm not letting you send me away with nothing but a stack of papers. I want to talk to people who knew George. I want to talk to the people he worked with."

"His coworkers have been through enough." Preston's voice sizzled with barely contained anger. "My employees are decent, hardworking people. Do you have any idea of how they feel? They're demoralized. They can't take any more. I won't let you or anyone else stir them up again. Give it a few days. Let them recover from this latest shock. In the meantime, call me if you have questions. As I said, I'll do my best to answer them."

He opened another file and picked up his pen.

Gary Preston clearly felt that his sermon had ended the meeting. I didn't. "While your staff regains its composure, maybe you can answer a few questions. Was George Walden involved in your company's trading problems?"

Preston shifted uncomfortably. Or was it nervously? "I can't say. We're still trying—"

I impatiently snapped, "Come on, Mr. Preston, don't pull that shit on me. You must have an idea of what's been going on around here. If not, take a wild guess."

Preston growled a curse at me. "Don't you ever give up?"

I smiled and waited. Preston could figure out the answer without any help from me.

"We have a problem here. I'll be the first to admit that." Preston leaned forward so I would be sure to see the sincerity in his eyes. "A trader stole from us. George Walden worked in the same department. Shit, you'll find out soon enough—Walden ran the department. But he wasn't involved. I guarantee it."

"How can you be so sure?"

Preston's self-assurance deflated. He sat back and let his hands drop into his lap. His brown eyes lost a bit of their hard edge. "Three years ago, George Walden wandered into my office. He'd been kicking around Wall Street for years, never a failure, never a success. I hired him because Grace Hudson recommended him."

Preston watched the surprise that flickered through my eyes. He smiled. "So Grace didn't tell you that, huh? Well, it's true. And I never regretted my decision. George was the most decent and honest person I ever met."

I shrugged. I've lost count of how many times dead people have been described to me as decent and honest. Loving spouses. Model parents. Patriotic, law-abiding citizens. Honest employees. Saints—after they were dead. What they were while alive is usually a different story. Grief or guilt quickly turns live sinners into dead saints.

"Maybe he knew something."

Gary barely controlled his anger. "If George knew anything, he would have come to me."

I couldn't hold back a sarcastic laugh. "I suppose you're gonna guarantee that."

"Damn you, I will guarantee it." Preston rose from his chair and shouted, "George Walden was part of my family. He was my son-in-law. I want to know why he's dead!"

Chapter 7

During the evening rush hour, the PATH trains from New York to Hoboken are packed door-to-door with commuters. But at ten o'clock in the morning, only a few people with the discouraged look of unsuccessful job hunters going home to polish their résumés shared the train with me. I resisted the urge to examine Walden's file and took a quick nap instead.

The train lurched into the station, gently waking me. I followed the handful of passengers from the train out to the street. A lopsided sign pointed me around the corner to a taxi stand. I followed the arrow and found a row of battered cars and a small group of men standing on the curb, smoking cigarettes and trading insults. One man held himself aloof from the crowd, alertly watching for approaching customers. He waited until it became clear that I wanted a cab, then he smiled.

I gave him the address. Instead of pointing to a cab, he laughed. "Lady, I'd be cheating you if I sent you off with one of these guys. Really cheating you. If you walk that way," he pointed across the street, "you'll find Hudson Street."

Residents of Hoboken will undoubtedly disagree, but to me the town looks much the same as Manhattan or Brooklyn. The people on the streets have the same big-city rush to their steps, the shops look the same, the traffic is just as heavy. There was one unusual thing: instead of seeing a bar or restaurant on every corner, I saw real estate agencies. Brownstones for sale, brownstones for rent. The entire town seemed to be for sale.

As the dispatcher promised, Hudson Street was easy to find. I walked along the street, counting off the numbers until I reached the two-hundred block. Walden's house was in the center of the block. The squat, boxy duplex with its brick facade disappointed me; I expected Gary Preston's daughter and son-in-law to live in more palatial surroundings. The view of a row of high-rise apartments and a parking garage added to my disappointment. I climbed the stairs and rang the bell.

From the moment I saw the tear-stained face of the woman, I knew I'd made a mistake. A big mistake.

Her long dark hair was tousled, her face streaked with the tracks of tears that had been running down her cheeks when the doorbell rang. I didn't want to intrude on her grief, but the old adage that the first twenty-hours after a murder are the most important melted my reluctance. It didn't matter, however. The woman didn't let me open my mouth. She folded her arms across her chest and looked at me with contempt.

"I don't have any comment for you. Leave me alone. Why won't you people leave me alone?"

Her voice sounded harsh from crying. I swallowed the impulse to walk away so she could mourn in peace and said, "You're Carol Walden, aren't you?" She nodded reluctantly. "I know this isn't a good time, but I have to ask you a few questions. I'm not a reporter. I'm investigating your husband's death."

"Are you with the police?"

I decided to tell the truth—something I instantly regretted. "I'm a private investigator. I've been hired to look into your husband's death."

"I don't understand. . . . Did Daddy hire you?"

The thought of spinning a lie ran through my mind. The thought that she'd check anything I said followed along behind it. Even though it wasn't working very well, I went with the truth again.

"I'm not working for your father, but he does know what I'm doing. In fact, I just came from his office." I hesitated; Grace hadn't given me permission to use her name. "Some other people who worked with your husband hired me. I'm sorry to bother you, but I have to ask you a few questions. I know you don't feel like talking."

"You know how I feel?" She spat the words at me. "I'm sick of that damn lie. Everyone uses it. Everyone says they understand. Everyone says they know how I feel. Well, they don't. You don't."

I stood my ground and quietly answered her. "I do. My first husband, Jeff, was murdered six years ago."

"You're not just saying that to get inside, are you?" Carol carefully studied my face for signs of the truth.

"No." Surprised to find tears filling my eyes, I quickly blinked them away. Even after a half-dozen years, they still come without warning. "I wish it were a story. I'd give anything for it to be a lie."

"What happened?"

I took a deep breath and blurted out a condensed version of Jeff's death. It's still hard to talk about that night and the troubles that followed. "I got the call at four-seventeen in the morning. Jeff had been shot. He died before I got to the hospital."

Instead of offering sympathy, Carol challenged me. "So you don't like talking about it, do you?"

"No, I don't. But—"

"Then you'll understand why I'm not talking. Not to the newspaper reporters. Not to the television reporters. Not to anyone. And that includes you."

Carol's anger didn't surprise me. "After Jeff died, I fought anyone who came near me—even those who wanted to help. For years, I refused to answer questions from even the most well-meaning friends. Forget reporters; I wouldn't let them ask a single question. My skin still crawls every time a reporter gets near me. But I'm not a reporter hounding you with the self-righteous excuse that the public needs to know. I'm trying to find out why your husband was killed."

Carol was not impressed. "I don't want your help. I'm not talking to anyone but the police. And you're not the police. So just leave me alone."

A glaze fell over her swollen eyes. Another push, no matter how gentle or well-intentioned, would push her into hysteria. I didn't want to be the person doing the pushing. I smiled sympathetically and said, "Maybe later."

"Don't count on it."

For a petite woman, Carol had a lot of strength. She slammed the door in my face, rocking me back on my heels.

With more optimism than was warranted, I scribbled a note on the back of a business card and slipped it through the mail slot in the door. I waited for a second, hoping she'd fling the door open and invite me inside. Nothing happened. At least she didn't tear the card up and shove the confetti out through the slot.

I trudged back to the train station and thought about my next move. I could always go back to the office and wade through Walden's file—or I could do something more active. Suddenly, the View seemed like the right place to be. If the trains ran according to schedule, I'd get there in time for the lull between the late-lunchers and the happy hour drinkers.

The RiverView Bar & Grill is a convenient place to drink. The owners, Bobby and Ryan, run a tab for regulars and call cabs for those who can't be trusted out on the streets alone. I wasted too many years as one of those patrons who needed an escort home. I live too close for a cab, so Bobby or Ryan would personally walk me home and wait until I was safely inside. When I quit drinking, Bobby and Ryan led the cheering. Since then, they pour me endless mugs of seltzer and gently turn me away when the wild-eyed look of someone needing a drink comes over me.

I did hit the lull. Only a few of the bar stools were occupied; the booths lining the outside walls and the tables in the center were empty. I sat in my usual spot, the stool that's wedged between the wall and the cigarette machine, and waited.

Bobby had his back to the door as he washed glasses at a sink behind the bar. Without turning around, he pulled a mug from the freezer, filled it with ice and seltzer, dropped in a thick lemon wedge, and slid the glass down the bar.

"It's been a while, dear. Ryan and I were afraid you'd found another place to hang out."

I grabbed the mug and laughed. "There is no other place, Bobby. There's just never enough time. Dennis and I hardly have time to see each other these days. When we do manage to be around at the same time, we try to stay home."

"And why are you here now, Blaine, sweetie? Don't tell me you took the afternoon off and decided to spend it with me."

I spun the mug around, watching the wet circles it left on the bar. "Unfortunately, this isn't a social call, Bobby."

"What a surprise."

"I want to talk to you about a customer you had in here the night before last."

Bobby wiped his hands on the towel that's always hanging from his hip pocket. He walked to where I was sitting and leaned against the cash register. "The dead guy?" I nodded. "The cops were here already. Why are you interested in him?"

"Professional courtesy. The guy died on my doorstep. I'd like to know why." I gulped a mouthful of soda in an attempt to wash away the bad taste left from my trip to Hoboken. "I was wondering if you remembered anything about him."

"Blaine, I remember every customer who makes a fuss because I don't stock fancy French wines, sips one glass of house wine and one club soda in four hours, pesters me for change for the phone, keeps on dialing the same number but never gets an answer, and then has the balls to stiff me on the tip. Sure I remember him."

Bobby pointed to a stool at the opposite end of

the bar. "He sat down there. We were kinda slow. I had plenty of time to keep an eye on him."

"Who else was here? Anybody I know?"

"Sure, most of the regulars were here. The basketball guys were here, too."

"The basketball guys? Who are they?"

Bobby stroked his beard and scowled at me. "My, my, it has been a long time since you spent an evening in the View. And to think it took a corpse to get you to remember your old friends. Blaine, dear, Ryan and I decided to give something back to our community." Bobby grinned wickedly. "You know, help the public relations campaign. We're sponsoring a basketball team. Not bad; we're in second place. Soon as I get my three-pointer working, we're in first."

"Bobby, you'll never have a three-pointer. Hell, you don't even have a two-pointer."

Waving my insult away, Bobby stepped back and looked at my long legs. "How tall are you?"

"Five-eleven."

"You play?"

"Not since college. Why?"

"The league's talking about making us put girls on the team next year. You interested?"

I gave Bobby the finger and said, "Call me when you're ready to let women play. Did your cheapskate customer talk to anybody while he was here?"

"He asked Ryan for change for the cigarette machine. He asked me for matches. He said no every time I asked if he wanted another drink. That's about all the talking he did."

"When did he leave?"

Bobby folded his arms across his chest. "Well,

it's like I told the cops. Ryan and I got to talking with the guys about the Giants and those bum Jets. The party went on a little longer than usual. We did the last call around three. Took till nearly four to get everyone out." He shrugged. "You know how those wild nights drag on forever around here."

"Used to—it's been a long time since I took part in a wild night in a bar."

"And thank God for that. You were a wild one, dear."

I ignored Bobby's comment—and his smirk. "Did George stay until the end of your closing ceremonies?"

"Yep. He wouldn't leave. We practically threw him out."

A thought struck me. "Wait a second, Bobby. You said George kept calling the same number. How do you know that? Did you stand behind him every time he dialed?"

"Honey, you're not the only private eye in the neighborhood. I'm pretty observant myself."

"When you want to be," I muttered.

"And you'll thank me for it."

"If you ever finish this story." I twirled the mug and watched the bubbles rise to the surface and burst. "How do you know Walden kept calling the same number?"

"He had a routine; I couldn't help but notice. It went like this." Bobby tore a piece of paper from his order pad, crumpled it up, and stuffed it in his pocket. "George paws through his change till he finds a quarter. Then he takes the paper from his pocket and smoothes it out on the bar." Bobby carefully unfolded the paper and used the tips of his fingers to push the wrinkles away. "Next, he picks it up and goes to the phone. Then"—Bobby held his hand up and dropped an imaginary quarter into an imaginary phone—"the money goes in. He dials. He wants to be sure he has the right number." Bobby held the paper up and squinted at it. "No answer." Bobby crumpled the paper in anger, or nervousness, and stuffed it back in his pocket.

I couldn't keep from smiling. "If the bar business ever goes bad, you have a great future as a mime. He did the same thing over and over again all evening?"

"Until four."

"What happened at four?"

"I told him to clear out. Before he left, he gave it one last try. Went through the same routine. Slammed the phone down when he didn't get an answer, crumpled the paper, and threw it—"

"He made a phone call at four?"

"That's what I said, Blaine. Four o'clock in he morning. And guess what? He didn't get an answer. Why?"

"Nothing." Our telephone hadn't rung in the middle of the night. I felt a bit of relief that was quickly followed by curiosity. Who had George been trying to call?

Bobby rapped on the bar to get my attention. "Let me finish before you start asking questions. He slammed the phone down, dropped the quarter in again, and punched in a number. Bam, bam, bam!" Bobby's index finger punched the air in a rapid-fire motion. "He had that number memorized, all right. No need to consult any ragged paper."

The ice cubes were melting, but I didn't complain

to Bobby about his lengthy story. "Tell me, you wise and handsome bartender, was our friend successful?"

"I think so. He said something. Raised his voice and said something else. I don't think he was cursing at an answering machine. He slammed the phone down and stormed out. So fast that he didn't even have time to leave a tip."

"Did he leave alone?"

"Yeah, he didn't make any buddies here. That's about it. The noon news said the guy got drunk and rolled. Course, Ryan threw the reporters out, but if they'd asked, we would have told them that guy wasn't drunk. Shit, not unless you can get drunk on one glass of chardonnay and a seltzer chaser."

"And I'm living proof that seltzer won't do it." I lit a cigarette, took an unsatisfying drag, and let it smolder in the ashtray. "So he was just a guy killing time, waiting until his date got home."

"Or something. He looked kinda nervous. Too nervous to be waiting for a date. The guys noticed and started making jokes. I had to shut them up. That poor bastard was nervous enough without them making wise-ass comments."

"Who else was here? Any strangers?"

Bobby shook his head with false pity. "Blaine, dear, you must get your sweet husband to take you out more often. This is a bar, remember? Strangers come in, have a few drinks, and leave. More strangers take their place. Thank God for strangers; you regulars don't spend enough to keep the place open."

"And to keep you and Ryan living your jet-set lifestyle."

He laughed. "That too. We've grown so accustomed to eating breakfast, lunch, *and* dinner every day. The place was filled. Mostly regulars, but there was one other loner. A bushy-haired guy with a phone fetish all his own. He sat in a booth, drank a pitcher of beer, and left about half an hour before we closed."

"What do you mean, a phone fetish all his own?"

"He had one of those cellular phones. Used to be just the yuppies that had them; now everybody does. They walk around jabbering about nothing. Me, I don't want one. How about you?"

Rather than tell Bobby about the phone nestling in the bottom of my bag, I shrugged. "Did this guy have any luck with his calls?"

"Yeah. He'd talk for a while, whispering so no one could hear him—like we wanted to listen to him. He'd hang up, drink some beer, and make another call. He did that four or five times before he left."

"Did he leave a tip?"

"Yep. Not a big one, but a tip." Bobby glanced down the bar and saw an empty mug. "Be right back. Got to take care of the paying customers."

Bobby walked away to draw a beer for a glum-looking man who'd been staring at his empty mug. I watched the amber liquid flow into the glass and turned away as a creamy layer of foam formed at the top. The seltzer in my mug suddenly seemed flat and lifeless.

"Thinking about trading that in for something else?"

Startled, I opened my eyes and blurted out the truth. "Yes, I am. What would you suggest, Bobby?"

Bobby leaned down and rested his forearms on the bar. He whispered, "Don't let this get out; it wouldn't be good for business. I suggest that you go home. Too many temptations in here for you today."

"Not even a cup of coffee while I smoke a cigarette?"

Bobby shook his head. His normally cool blue eyes were warm—and sad. "Not today. If I hear anything about the dead guy, I'll give you a call. Go home. Better yet, go back to work. You need to keep busy."

I got off the stool, grabbed my coat, and started for the door. I stepped out on the sidewalk, whirled around, and darted back inside.

Bobby frowned at me. "Now what? I thought I got rid of you for a while. You know, Blaine, too much of a good thing—"

I impatiently brushed his joke aside. "You said George crumpled the paper with the phone number on it and threw it. Where did he throw it?"

"He threw it at the wall by the jukebox." I quickly walked over to the machine. Bobby called after me, "Are you insinuating that we don't sweep?"

"I used to be a steady customer, remember? Clean floors are not a priority here. Well, did you sweep?"

"No—"

"Did Ryan?"

"I doubt it."

"What a surprise." I crouched in front of the jukebox and pulled a small ball of paper out from among the dustballs. "I'd say there's an excellent chance that it's still sitting in a pile of dust." I stood up, triumphantly waving the paper. "Right?"

Inadvertently mimicking George Walden's actions, I put the paper down on the bar and smoothed it out. There was a phone number scrawled on the paper—but it wasn't mine. George Walden had not spent his last night on earth calling me.

Chapter 8

Dani Dexter, Kembell Reid's infamous trader, floated into my office with the regal air of a 1940s movie star making a grand entrance at the premiere of her latest triumph. Dani's blond hair had been carefully pulled back, highlighting her gaunt face. Careless slashes of blush on her cheekbones added a bizarre touch of color to Dani's pale face. The sweet gardenia smell of her perfume turned my stomach.

Trying to brush aside images of Joan Crawford and her garish makeup, I stood and held out my hand. Instead of the weak, moist handshake I'd expected, Dani grasped my hand and gave it a strong, confident shake. Even though she was only an inch shorter than me, Dani made me feel big and gawky.

As I motioned for her to sit, Dani said, "I want to apologize for that brutally late call last night. I'm surprised you didn't tell me to fuck off."

"The thought crossed my mind. Lucky for you, I wasn't awake enough to get the words out. Why the urgency?"

Dani sank into the chair and stifled a weary sigh. "What would you do? The company I work for— used to work for—says I faked trades worth hundreds of millions of dollars—just to make myself a star."

I dryly said, "And inflate your bonus."

"That's a bundle of bullshit."

Her icy composure annoyed me. "Did you?"

Dani's hazel eyes sparkled with anger. "I most certainly did not. I want you to prove it. I want to hire you."

I repeated my favorite phrase of the day. "I already have a client. Working for you would be a conflict of interest."

"I'll pay whatever you want. Talk to your client and get a release."

Not at all unhappy to turn Dani Dexter and her outlandish makeup away, I shook my head. "Can't be done."

"Why not?"

"My client's dead."

"Dead." Dani relaxed. She sat back and crossed her legs. "I'm afraid I don't understand. If your client is dead, there is no conflict of interest."

I snapped, "What don't you understand, Ms. Dexter? Dead is dead." The blank, uncaring look on Dani's face infuriated me. "What's the matter, don't they have newspapers on the Concorde?"

"Newspapers? Do you know how I start each and every day?" Dani didn't wait for an answer. Suddenly tense, she leaned forward and snapped, "I run to the door, grab the papers, and dart back inside before anyone sees me. I examine the front page of the *Wall Street Journal* to see if my name is there. Then I open to the business section of the *Times* to scan that front page, hoping the name Dexter doesn't jump out at me. Once I'm satisfied that I'm not headline news, I go back to the *Journal* and carefully read it. Then I do the same with the *Times*."

"So you must be up on current events."

Dani was not amused. "Do you know what it's like to do that every morning before you take a shower or have a cup of coffee? To hope that you won't have to spend the day dodging calls from reporters and so-called friends who want to gloat over your decaying reputation? Or how about hoping your parents haven't seen the articles and wondering how you're going to keep them from worrying?"

She paused to take a breath. I waited, too fascinated by her performance to interrupt. Dani drew a loud, ragged breath and said, "Some days I don't think I can go on."

The image of George's crying wife popped into my mind and stayed there. I didn't feel a whit of sympathy for the harsh woman sitting across from me. "Most of the people I've talked with say you asked for your troubles."

"Well, fuck them. I didn't ask for anything."

"What about George Walden? Was he one of those so-called gloating friends?"

"George?" Dani's forehead puckered. "What's George got to do with this?"

"He's my client."

"But you said—" My words suddenly made sense to Dani. "George is dead?"

"He was killed the night before last."

Dani's eyes widened; her face lost even more color. "Who'd kill George? I don't understand. Who'd kill George?" Shock spread across Dani's face. I watched and wondered: a terrible surprise, or good acting?

"What happened?"

"When did you last talk to George?"

"I don't remember." Her eyes darted away from mine. "A week. Yes, a week. I talked to George the day before I left."

"You've been in London for six days?" Dani nodded. I asked, "Why were you there?"

"I needed to get away."

"You took a vacation—"

Dani's temper flared. "You don't understand. I had to escape the glare of publicity. I thought I'd lose my mind if I had to face another TV camera or another reporter."

"A good way to establish an alibi." Angry sparks shot from Dani's eyes. I wasn't impressed. "Save it for the police, Dani. But I should warn you, they're going to think even less of your story than I do. What did you and George talk about?"

"Nothing special. George and I talked nearly every day. He wanted to see how I was holding up."

Since I didn't have any reason to argue, or believe her, I nodded and asked, "You worked with George?"

In a dry, matter-of-fact voice, she explained. "I worked for George. He was my boss. Although it wouldn't have been long before I was in charge. George was on his way down."

The quick return of Dani's composure irritated me. "That sounds rather cold. You said you talked to George every day. Wasn't he a friend?"

"Friends? You must be kidding. You don't have friends, real friends, on Wall Street. You have acquaintances. People you work with. People you go to lunch with. People you have drinks with after work. People you make deals with. No friends."

Dani shook her head sadly. "You don't have real friends."

I looked at Dani's cold face and wondered, *Who are your real friends? What do they know about you?* Hoping to push her into telling me more, I made up a story based on the newspaper reports I'd read.

"People in your department say George Walden was a nice guy who was in over his head. He didn't understand your trading. No one did, but they were afraid to ask you to explain because they didn't want to sound stupid. As long as you made money, no one, not even George—your boss—would ask how."

"That's bullshit. George was very bright." Dani noticed my raised eyebrows and snapped, "I don't give a fuck what those assholes say. George knew my trades were good. We talked about them all the time."

"Then why is Kembell Reid missing five hundred million dollars?"

"Mismanagement. I'm the scapegoat."

I sat back and folded my hands behind my head. "Dani, I can't tell you how glad I am that you're not my client. If you stick to that line, I'd have a hell of time proving your innocence."

"George knew I was innocent. He had proof."

"You keep putting words in a dead man's mouth. Tell me something you can prove. Or something I don't know."

"Did you know that Gary Preston has been losing millions of dollars at the track? That he's been looting the corporate cash register to pay for his exciting life? That I'm nothing more than a convenient cover-up? George figured out what was going on."

I made no attempt to keep a frown from spreading across my face. "Are you suggesting that George Walden was murdered to hide Gary Preston's gambling debts?" I paused as if I were seriously considering her allegation. "At least your story is getting more interesting. Keep talking."

Dani shook her head impatiently. "It's not just gambling. It's encouraging his brokers to churn clients' accounts to increase commissions. Bribing officials to get muni bond deals. Buying cocaine for traders—and getting reimbursed through his expense account.

"And always the horses. Betting on every nag that hobbles up to the starting gate. Last year, Gary chartered a 707, filled it with traders and brokers, and flew us all to the Kentucky Derby. He lost a hundred thousand dollars when Julie Krone didn't become the first woman to win the Derby. He laughed it off, bragged that it was chump change."

"A vice for all seasons. So?"

"So!" I thought indignation would make Dani fly out of the chair. "Isn't that enough? George knew enough to close Gary down for good."

"Didn't he recently marry Preston's daughter? Why would Walden try to put his father-in-law out of business?"

Dani waved my objection aside with the back of her hand. "Everybody who worked for George hated him."

"More motives than a barrel of monkeys."

"It's true." Dani insisted. "A lot of people at Kembell Reid had good reason to kill George."

"Name one." When Dani didn't answer, I shook

my head. "You go through motives faster than I go through cigarettes."

"I heard things. Things about people who hated George. I never gossiped; that's why I don't have any names for you. But there are a lot of people who had reason to want George dead. Better reasons than mine." Dani's voice took on the fervent tone of a sales pitch. "Reconsider my offer. Work for me."

Dani stared at me, trying to gauge if she had swayed me. I met her gaze and firmly said, "I already have a client."

I had never felt more lighthearted about turning business away. Without realizing it, I smiled. "If anything changes, I'll give you a call. In the meantime, if you'd like a referral—"

Anger leapt from Dani and smashed into me with the force of an angry surf pounding the beach. "I told you what I want."

Smiling still, I withstood her anger. "And I told you my answer. I guess we don't have anything else to talk about."

I held my hand out across the desk. Dani swatted it away. "You'll be sorry. I won't make this offer again."

Feeling an unexplainable thrill of pleasure at witnessing the meltdown of her composure, I murmured, "That's a chance I'll be happy to take."

Dani flounced out of the room. The door slammed behind here. I watched her grand exit and wondered why she'd bothered staging that show for me.

Eileen walked into my office seconds later. She sat on the edge of my desk and cocked her head to make it easier for her good eye to focus on my face. I glanced away so I wouldn't have to watch.

"You look tired, Blaine. Where have you been? I haven't seen you all day. And who was that woman? She was in such a rush to get away from you, she nearly knocked me over. What did you do to her?"

"Whoa." I held up my hand. "Stop with the questions, Eileen. I didn't do anything to that woman. She told me that half the people on Wall Street wanted to kill George Walden and the other half wanted to frame her. Then she practically ordered me to work for her." I grinned. "I told her I was busy."

I tossed my pen on the desk and realized I hadn't eaten anything except a cup of coffee and a hot dog at the Hoboken train station. "I'm tired and hungry. Eileen, in the past twenty-four hours, I picked up one new client and said no to two others. That woman who nearly stomped on you was one of the two I turned away."

"That's not like you, Blaine. You usually take every case that comes your way. Couldn't someone else in the office handle them?"

"No." I got up and paced around the office. "It's damn confusing. Why me? They all want me to work on the same case . . . and they're falling all over themselves trying to convince me I should be on their side. Everyone except the victim's widow. She slammed the door in my face."

Eileen shrugged. "What's wrong with turning away would-be clients?"

"It scares me. . . . I'm being set up for something and I can't begin to guess why."

Chapter 9

Eileen said good night and started for the door. I stopped her. "Eileen, sit down. Over there." I pointed to the new, uncomfortable sofa in the far corner of the office. "We have to talk."

"I'm busy."

"No, you're not. Sit down. I want to know why you've been avoiding me. What's wrong?"

Eileen turned to me. I didn't notice the apprehensive look on her face; my attention was focused on her clenched fists. "Don't you believe me?"

My sister is supposed to be the levelheaded one, not me. Finding myself in the unfamiliar position of being the logical one, I quietly said, "Eileen, it's not a question of believing or not believing. I only want to know what's wrong."

"Nothing."

I stood and grabbed Eileen's arm. As I dragged her over to the sofa, I laughed. "You're not getting away from me until you share your unhappy secrets. If anyone's going to mope around this office, it's going to be me. Not you. You're not allowed to mope."

Eileen didn't laugh. She sat and stared at the carpet so she wouldn't have to look at me. "I'm worried about Sandy."

I expected more. Shaking my head because I

didn't know what else to do, I said, "Sandy seems fine to me."

"Well, she's not fine."

Despite Eileen's earlier intention to hide her problems, the words rushed out. "When Don comes home from a trip, Sandy either hides or tip-toes around the house, trying to be perfect so Mom and Dad won't yell at each other. Sandy thinks we fight because she's bad. She thinks that if she's perfect, or if she hides, we won't argue. She has stom-achaches and nightmares. They miraculously disappear whenever Don leaves on a trip."

"And reappear when he returns?"

Eileen nodded sadly. "Which only makes Don madder. . . ."

Silence flooded the room. Eileen hung her head again and looked miserable. I regretted forcing her to give voice to her worries. That regret didn't stop me from asking another question. "What are you planning to do about all this?"

When Eileen didn't answer, I repeated the ques-tion. The sound of my voice roused her. She whis-pered, "Get a divorce."

With that, Eileen stood and walked out the door. I let her go; chasing after her and de-manding answers would only push her deeper in-side her shell. When Eileen felt ready to talk, she'd come back.

I left the office shortly after seven—not the first to leave, but not the last. The subways ran on time; the streets weren't crowded. I made it to Barrow Street in record time. But I wasn't fast enough, Dennis had gotten home before me.

He was in the bedroom, changing out of his work

clothes. He was standing bare-chested in front of the closet, reaching for a worn flannel shirt. His pleated trousers had been replaced by a pair of baggy jeans. His white dress shirt was on the bed. I walked up behind Dennis and wrapped my arms around him.

Lacing my fingers across his chest so he couldn't get away, I said, "Don't say a word. Just let me hang on for a week or two."

Dennis kissed my hand and rubbed my arm. "Tough day?"

"Yes." I rested my head on his shoulder and closed my eyes. "A long, tough day. I'm glad it's over."

"You want to talk about it?"

"No." I hugged Dennis tighter and tried to melt into his body. If I disappeared under his skin, maybe, just maybe, I'd escape the day.

"Are you hungry? Do you want dinner?"

I smiled. A good meal was Dennis's answer to every problem. "I don't want anything to eat. I want to stand here all night. Just like this."

Dennis gently rubbed my hands and quietly asked, "What happened, Blaine?"

"I stood outside on the sidewalk for a few minutes before I came in. I couldn't bring myself to climb up those stairs. I kept thinking about George dying there."

"George? So you're on a first-name basis now. You're not going to let this eat at you, are you?"

The touch of his fingers on my skin invited the truth. "It already is. You know, I told Grace I'd investigate the killing. But it's not just George that's bothering me, it's Eileen."

"What's Eileen done now? Are you two fighting again?"

I sighed. "No. We didn't have time to fight." I
rested my head on Dennis's shoulder and quickly
gave him a condensed version of my conversation
with Eileen.

Dennis rubbed my arms. I stood quietly for a
few seconds, enjoying the warmth of his touch. The
comfort didn't last long; I sighed and said, "I went
to Hoboken this afternoon."

"Hoboken's a nice town. How did going there
add to the ruination of your day?"

"I talked to George's wife."

"And . . ."

"Too many bad memories. I talked to her about
Jeff. About the days after he died."

"Blaine, why put yourself through it all again?
You and Jeff had enough good times to remember.
Forget the other crap."

Dennis twisted around and kissed my cheek.
"My dear, you are in serious danger of drifting
away on a bad mood. Is that all, or is there more?"

"There's more."

"You poor thing." Dennis groaned in mock horror. "How did you ever make it through the day?
I'm exhausted. I can't take any more."

I agreed with Dennis; my complaints were getting tiresome. I said, "Take this, buddy," and
pulled Dennis backward until we ran into the bed.
We collapsed on the mattress, giggling and tickling
each other like two teenagers who had just discovered sex—and their parents were gone for the
weekend.

Tickling quickly turned to more serious play.
Dennis had an unfair advantage—he already had

half his clothes off. With precise movements, no fumbling allowed, we pulled our clothes off. My freshly cleaned wool suit landed in a crumpled heap on the floor. My silk blouse, pantyhose, and the rest of our clothes quickly followed.

Chapter 10

The next morning, Eileen was back in hiding. I left her there and headed to my office. I grabbed George Walden's file and settled down to pull apart his financial life. It didn't take long to find something that made me sit back and whistle softly.

$575,000. That's how much George Walden paid for his boxy little house in Hoboken.

$575,000. Cash. Withdrawn by check from his money market fund.

I looked at the statement again and whistled again. After writing that little check, Walden had another four hundred thousand sitting around collecting interest. There was more, much more. About a million and a half in stocks. I was adding up the other investments when Eileen tapped briskly on the door.

She strode in with a manila folder in her hands and a fake smile gleaming on her face. "Got a minute?"

Eileen didn't fool me; she had more than business on her mind. I shoved my papers aside and nodded. "Sure, you can have a minute. Hell, you can have five minutes. After all, you're family."

I snagged the pack of cigarettes on the corner of the desk and quickly dropped it. I'd been absent-mindedly smoking cigarette after cigarette at work and at home. Dennis had been making pointed comments about the smoky perfume clinging to my hair and clothes. It seemed to be a good time to cut down.

Eileen cleared her throat. "This is going to sound silly."

I said dryly, "Try me."

With that slight bit of prompting, the words tumbled out. "I want you to assign a team to guard Sandy."

"Sandy?"

My stomach lurched. My niece was too young, too innocent, to be dragged into our frequently slimy business. Even though we took precautions to keep our families safe, I still worried. Some nights I snap awake, convinced that the phone is about to ring with horrible news about Dennis, Eileen, Sandy, or my brother, Dick.

My mind churned out thousands of gruesome images. I tried to sound calm. "Has someone threatened Sandy—or you?"

"Does it have to be in writing?" Eileen snapped. "Can't you just take my word?"

My fingers itched to grab a cigarette. I clenched my hands together and stared at Eileen. She looked miserable. Dark circles ringed her eyes; worry lines streaked across her forehead. "What's going on, Eileen? Why does Sandy need protection?"

"It's Don."

"Don?" I thought I had lost the ability to be surprised by anything, but Eileen managed to surprise me. "I don't understand."

"He wants to take her for dinner tonight. He wants her for the weekend, too."

I squinted at Eileen and didn't see any trace of

hysteria. I gently reminded her that Don had every right to see his daughter. Before Eileen snapped that I didn't understand, I asked, "Has Don ever said or done anything to make you think he'd harm Sandy?"

"He's said things. Dropped little hints." Eileen shook her head. "But he hasn't said anything that would hold up in court. He's too smart to make real threats."

Divorce. I was letting that ugly word roll around in my head when Eileen blurted out, "He has a plane, you know."

Eileen's curt outburst unnerved me. Instead of saying, *Have you lost your mind?* I cocked my head and said, "So . . ."

"So, he and Sandy could be halfway across the country before I even knew they were gone. They could disappear forever. We'll never find them. . . ." Eileen took a deep breath and in a shaky voice said, "You must think I'm nuts."

I shrugged noncommittally. "You haven't given me much to go on."

"Then talk to Don yourself. He's at the airport, Teterboro, working on that plane of his. He'll be there all day. Please—as a favor to me."

Sometimes it's easier to give in than argue—it must be a sign of the wisdom that comes with age. "Okay, I'll talk to Don. I'll have someone stick close to Sandy for a few days, too—just to be safe."

"Who?"

Thinking as fast as I could, I came up with the name of our newest associate. The one with the lightest caseload, who wouldn't be missed while she played babysitter. "Jeannie."

"She's too new. I want someone with more experience."

"She'll do just fine, Eileen. Trust me. I won't let anything happen to Sandy." My stomach rolled. Blaming too much coffee and too many cigarettes, I brushed the queasiness away. I'd let Jeannie follow Sandy around for a week, maybe two, until Eileen—and my stomach—calmed down.

At the moment, Eileen was far from calm. She leaned forward and anxiously asked, "When can she start? This afternoon?"

Jona tapped on the door and stuck her head in, saving me from having to answer the question. Overnight, a dozen new strands of gray had appeared in Jona's hair; I wondered when she would finally make good on her daily threat to retire. It was a day I dreaded.

"Sorry to bother you, Blaine, but you have a call. It's Gary Preston; he says it's vitally important." Jona smiled. "That's what he said, *vitally important*. Do you want to talk to him?"

I glanced at Eileen. Her body was tense and coiled; she seemed ready to spring from the chair without warning. "Can you wait a few minutes? I have to take this call."

Eileen nodded at me. I nodded at Jona. Jona smiled at me. I smiled at Eileen and Jona. Everyone was happy—for the moment.

Knowing that the happy feelings wouldn't last long, I picked up the phone and cheerfully said hello. Gary didn't waste time being polite. "We have to meet. I'm not in my office right now. . . ." Gary's voice faded for a moment, leaving me to wonder about where he was. "I'll be back this afternoon. We can meet then."

The man obviously felt he could order me around like one of his employees, so I stubbornly refused to give in to his demands. "Sure, Gary, but my schedule's packed today. I can find some time for you tomorrow morning."

"That's too late. I must see you today. It's vitally important."

"My secretary already told me that. Listen carefully, Gary. I can meet you tomorrow morning—not this afternoon. Is nine o'clock okay with you?"

"Nine? Can't you make it earlier?"

"No." I was not going to agree to another crack-of-dawn meeting.

He groaned. "Okay, nine o'clock. Don't be late."

"If I am, you'll just have to wait."

I hung up and looked at my sister. Eileen sat, quietly shredding the corner of her folder, not paying any attention to my conversation. I watched until my silence roused Eileen. I had her write down Sandy's schedule. Once that was done, I chased Eileen out, called Jeannie in, and gave her the assignment. After I was certain things were under control, I headed out of the office.

In order to justify the trip as more than running off to check on Eileen's story, or maybe her sanity, I decided to make Hoboken my first stop. With luck, I'd find a nosy, talkative neighbor who'd be happy to fill me in on the details of George Walden's homelife.

When I drove out of the tunnel, I was rewarded with a sparkling view of the New York City skyline that momentarily distracted me from my worries. My short-lived pleasure ended when I hit the Hoboken traffic. I wove through the double- and tri-

ple-parked cars lining the streets and found the
Waldens' brownstone. As I drove, I rehearsed poi-
gnant lines that would make George's wife and
neighbors talk to me—if I got lucky. My stomach
rolled, reminding me that my luck quotient has
never been very high.

As if to disprove my luckless thoughts, a minor
Hoboken miracle occurred: I turned the corner and
found a parking space at the foot of Hudson Street.
Okay, it was an illegal spot, too close to a fire hy-
drant, but I took it anyway. After all, tickets could
be written off on my expense account.

I locked the car and crossed the street as a
hearse, flower car, two limousines, and a dozen cars
crept by. The cars slowed to a crawl, paused in
front of the Walden house, then picked up speed
and disappeared.

Some people think a black cat crossing their path
brings bad luck. I watched the taillights of the last
car and wondered about the bad luck that follows
someone who has a funeral procession cross in
front of her. No one, not even the most talkative
neighbor, would gossip with the memory of the de-
ceased so fresh in their mind. I hurried back to my
car and drove away—in the opposite direction—as
fast as I could.

The Turnpike was clear. No traffic. No cops in
sight. Rather than take advantage of the opportunity to see how fast I could get the Porsche going,
I kept the car at the speed limit and forced my
mind away from George Walden to Eileen.

Before she'd met Don, Eileen hadn't dated
much. She'd go on a date or two with a man and
then break it off. The excuse was always the same:

studying for her law degree, then the bar exam, required all her attention. Eileen shrugged away questions about her love life with a smile and a joke about not having time to concentrate on men. All that changed when she met Don.

The fateful meeting took place a few months after Eileen started her career in the Manhattan District Attorney's office. She flew the People's Express shuttle to Washington to depose a potential witness. An ice storm closed Washington's National Airport, grounding her return flight. Eileen, being Eileen, sat and fumed at the weather for wasting her time.

Don, dressed in his flight uniform, sat beside her. Eileen complained to him about the delay. They started talking about the weather. As the cliché says, the rest is history. Ignoring our teasing about her blue-eyed, blond-haired flyboy, Eileen and Don married a year after that ice storm. Their wedding day had been beautiful and sunny with no ice in sight. It took years for the ice to form.

The exit from the Turnpike starts innocently enough. It's a wide, curving exit that, without warning, sharply doubles back under the Turnpike. The driver ahead of me misjudged the steep curve and slid off onto the grass. His car fishtailed as it fought its way back to the pavement. Tire tracks cut in the grass were proof that other drivers had made similar miscalculations. I grinned and pressed down on the accelerator; the Porsche gripped the surface without hesitation.

I merged with the traffic on Route 46 and drove past old, slightly threadbare houses and a bridge that went over the Hackensack River. Typical highway scenery began at the bottom of the bridge. Used-car lots, gas stations, fast-food restaurants. Everything looked the same as any other city in any other state in the country. The roar of a jet engine gliding across the highway to a perfect landing at the airport on the opposite side of the road added the only slightly novel touch.

I swung into the left lane and barely beat the light that let me cross the highway to the airport road. The entrance to the first parking lot was blocked by a locked gate in a chain-link fence. I looked at the barbed wire on top and knew I'd have to find another way inside—hopping the fence was out.

Although I'd been told that Teterboro Airport was one of the busiest in the area, I had trouble believing it. Only three small jets were in line to take off. Tufts of grass sprouted through cracks in the concrete. A few planes, some covered by flapping canvas, were parked inside the fence. No one moved around outside.

I drove past a beige hangar with unsightly rust patches dotting its walls and pulled into a parking lot. I stopped in front of a tiny guard booth and took a deep breath. What story would I use this time?

A guard stepped out of the booth and sauntered over to the car. His skinhead haircut, the clipboard, and the *Soldier of Fortune* magazine tucked under his arm added to his menacing appearance. Wondering if he'd be interested in hiring on to guard Sandy, I lowered the window and waited.

Being around jets all day gave the guard an appreciation for powerful engines. He tucked his clipboard and magazine under his arm, looked at the car—not me—with admiration, and whistled. "A Porsche 911 Turbo. Brand-new, right?"

"So new that I haven't even gotten a speeding ticket yet."

"And it almost matches your red hair. You win the lottery or something?"

I ignored the guard's lame comment about my hair and smiled. "No need to win the lottery. I always wanted a car like this, so I've been saving my allowance since I was three."

The befuddled expression on the guard's face shamed me into telling the truth. "Actually, it was a wedding present to myself. I traded in the old one just before I got married. I didn't want my new husband to complain about wasting money."

"This is not a waste of money. This is a thing of beauty. How could anyone think a Porsche 911 is a waste of money?" He shook his head. "Man doesn't have any sense."

I didn't find it necessary to defend Dennis. Instead, I smiled and shrugged. "We don't have the same taste in automobiles."

"Let me guess—he's a Toyota kind of guy. Right? Am I right?"

"Volvo."

"Volvo." The guard shook his head in disbelief. "Lady, if your husband complains about this baby, don't you listen to him. Come by and pick me up. I'll never complain—as long as we have this beauty."

How romantic. I laughed. "Thanks, I'll keep you in mind. Listen, a friend of mine keeps his plane here. I want to drop by and say hello."

He reluctantly dragged his eyes away from the car to look at my face. "Yeah, maybe I can help.

Do you know if it's in a hangar or out on the tarmac?"

"The Executive Air Services hangar." At least that's what Eileen told me when I innocently asked where Don kept his plane.

"What's your name?" The guard took the clipboard from beneath his arm. "If your name's here, it's A-OK. If your name's not here—" He shrugged. "Nothing I can do about it, 'cept call to see if it's okay. I'm not supposed to let anyone in without clearance."

"My name's not on your list. But, please, don't call." I pushed my sunglasses up so he could see my eyes and flashed a sexy, embarrassed smile. I touched the guard's arm; he flinched but didn't pull away. "You see, I was hoping to surprise him. He's a special friend. If you call, it'll ruin my surprise."

The guard scratched his clipped hair and thought. Who was more worthy of a woman in a brand-new Porsche? A man with a powerful plane at his command or a fuddy-duddy hubby with a Volvo? It didn't take long for him to reach a decision.

"Okay." He pointed to an empty space next to his tiny booth. "Park over there. The Exec hangar is to the right of this one in front of us. Now, watch yourself. Don't go walking into a spinning propeller. You'll get both of us in trouble. You look like you can afford to be out of work—I can't; I got bills to pay."

I didn't mention that walking into a spinning propeller would leave me with problems worse than unemployment. *Walking into spinning propellers.* What an attractive thought. I parked the car and walked toward the hangar, feeling the cool breeze of imaginary propellers at my head. I made a wide,

lazy circle around one jet. Even though it didn't
have spinning propellers, the high-pitched whine of
the engines promised death and destruction if I
came too close.

The Executive Air owners were on a rejuvenation
campaign. The rust patches on the outside of their
hangar had been carefully scraped and painted, giving the metal walls a freckled appearance. The tarmac glistened from a fresh coat of sealant.

I stood in the hangar's entrance and sniffed the
mechanical mixture of fuel and grease, and looked
around. There were eight planes inside, four on
one side, four on the other. Two slots were empty,
waiting for the wanderers to return.

The mechanics must have punched out for a
group lunch—the hangar was deserted, except for
a man working on a plane in the deepest, darkest
corner of the building. Too intent on his work, Don
didn't notice me approaching. I wasn't trying to
sneak up on him, but I didn't find it necessary to
give him advance warning. I kept in the shadows
and listened to the clank of his tools. The red plane,
with its white and black trim and large black propeller, looked capable of transporting my niece to
thousands of places where I'd never find her—if
Eileen was right about Don's intentions.

The dashing pilot that had first caught my sister's
eye was a bit heavier, a bit grayer, but still dashing.
Even in greasy, torn coveralls, Don looked capable
of making an eight-hundred-thousand-pound jet
obey his commands at thirty thousand feet in the
air. Was he capable of kidnapping his daughter?

I cleared my throat and said, "Hey, Don."

Don glanced up. He smiled, at least I think it was
a smile, before turning back to the plane's engine.

"Blaine, nice to see you. How did you sneak in here? Security is supposed to keep people from walking in off the streets. Wandering around here can be dangerous." His voice was understandably cool. After all, I came from the enemy camp.

I ignored the cynical voice inside my head that said, *I bet*. "The guard was too busy drooling over my car to notice that the hall monitor hadn't approved my pass. It's not his fault; I convinced him that I was here as a well-meaning surprise."

"Well, it's a surprise all right." No comment about it being a pleasant surprise. "Hand me a wrench, please." Don nodded toward the toolbox at my feet. "There's one in the top tray."

I bent and pulled a shiny Craftsman wrench from the box. I balanced it in the palm of my hand and held it out of Don's reach. "Why don't you take a break? I want your full attention for a few minutes."

He impatiently snapped his fingers. "Come on, Blaine. We can talk while I work. I can do both."

"I can't. Eileen's worried about Sandy. I want to hear what you have to say."

"This is stupid. Tell me you're not going to believe everything Eileen tells you—no matter what I say."

"That's a chance you'll just have to take." I shrugged and slapped the wrench into his waiting palm. "Let's talk about your daughter for a few minutes, Don. Eileen's worried that you might do something stupid."

"Like kidnap Sandy? That's Eileen's latest fantasy, you know." Don wiped a spot of grease from the wrench and carefully examined it for more spots. "Look, Blaine, our marriage is over, but I don't hate Eileen enough to pull a stunt like that. Eileen's upset. She's seeing problems that don't exist."

Don's boyishly handsome grin did nothing to melt my heart. But to my surprise, the logical part of my brain nodded in agreement with him.

Chapter 11

Without warning, another personality took over. An unreadable expression glazed Don's eyes. I caught a glimpse of the stranger Eileen feared. "What's the matter, Blaine? Don't you believe me?" He smacked the wrench against his palm. The menacing sound highlighted his anger. "Are you thinking that maybe Eileen's right?" *Splat, splat, splat.* The wrench bounced against his skin. He inched closer to me. "That maybe I could do something to her—or Sandy?"

I put my hands on my hips and casually moved my jacket aside just far enough for Don to catch a glimpse of my pistol comfortably nestled in its black shoulder holster. "My gun beats your wrench. I started using my old faithful Smith and Wesson again, Don. It's a sturdy American gun."

"Are you threatening me?"

"No more than you're threatening me. I don't want trouble."

"You have a funny way of showing it, Blaine. Listen to me. Eileen and I are getting divorced. That's it. I don't want to hurt Eileen. I certainly wouldn't hurt Sandy."

"Then why is Eileen so worried? Eileen doesn't overreact without cause. Especially not when Sandy's involved."

Don studied the wrench and calmly asked, "Why should Eileen be worried? I'm the one with the worries. Eileen's trying to destroy my family. She's taking everything away from me. What would you do if you were in my place?"

"I know what I wouldn't do—"

"Don't give me advice." Don spaced the words so that each one came out as a full, bitter sentence. His eyes turned coldly brilliant. "Sandy's my daughter too. I won't let Eileen take her away from me."

With a quick flick of his wrist, Don tossed the wrench to the ground. The clatter of metal landing on concrete echoed through the quiet hangar. He grinned. "Had you going, didn't I, Blaine? Now who's overreacting?"

My temper snapped. I lashed out. "That's not funny—"

"You're damn right." Don's voice sizzled with anger. "I wasn't trying to be funny. I'm serious. I don't appreciate you busting in here to accuse me of God knows what. I care about my daughter."

My brother-in-law took a step back and leaned against his airplane. He grinned sheepishly. "Pilot, heal thyself. Now I'm the one who's overreacting." Don stared at me, meeting my eyes with a forthright gaze. "I'm not trying to do something horrible to Eileen. All I want is a fair custody agreement. What else can I say?"

Despite my desire to be on Eileen's side, misgivings stirred timidly. Even though they were faint, they were there. I shrugged.

Don's eyes didn't waver, but my resolve to give him a tongue-lashing did. His next words melted the last of my resistance. "Blaine, I love that little girl more than anything. But I'm not going to steal her away. You have to make Eileen understand that."

He was convincing, but not convincing enough. I retrieved my car from the lustful guard and drove away, filled with misgivings about Don—and Eileen. I called Jeannie and warned her to take extra care with her guard duty.

Chapter 12

Instead of going to the office to face Eileen and taking the chance of having my frustration about wasting time—time that could have been spent investigating George Walden's murder—spill out, I went home. But not to goof off. I planned on spending the rest of the afternoon searching my databases for more information on George Walden.

As I approached the house, I saw a man bending over my front stairs, carefully examining the concrete. With every suspicious nerve tingling, I hurried over and snapped, "Looking for something?"

The man straightened up and grinned. "Nope. Everything's under control. Guess you're not used to coming home and finding cops on your doorstep."

More used to it than he'd expect, but I wasn't going to tell him that. I held out my hand. "Chris Hutchinson. Sorry; I thought you were looking for a way to break in. Is something wrong?"

The detective shook my hand. "Nothing's wrong. I decided to take another look around."

His hair was a little more rumpled than the first time we met, the shirt a little more wrinkled, the eyes a little more bloodshot. But the easy grin was still the same. If I hadn't been so suspicious about the real reason for Hutchinson's visit, I would have relaxed.

"Looking for anything special?"

"Nope. Don't know exactly what it is I'm looking for." He pointed his worn pencil at the faint blood-stain on the stairs. "The autopsy says the bleeding was internal. That's why there wasn't more blood."

Clinical discussions of how a person died make me fidget; it's too easy for me to imagine someone I love being the object of the conversation. I shivered and asked, "Do you think he was stabbed here?"

"You mean, right here on your stairs?" Hutchinson didn't expect an answer. "Don't know. The medical guys will calculate how long it took him to bleed out. If it didn't happen here, it was pretty damn close."

"So you're out looking for blood?"

"You could say that." The slow, easy grin spread across the detective's face. "Kind of a ghoulish way to spend the day, isn't it? You want to know what else I've been doing?"

Sensing that I wouldn't like the answer, I shrugged. "Haven't got a clue. But I bet you're going to tell me. Right?"

Chris shook his head; his smile slowly faded. "I've been talking to your neighbors. At first, I canvassed the neighborhood, hoping I'd get lucky and find an insomniac who glanced out the window at the right moment."

Suddenly, Barrow Street seemed dark and forbidding. Feeling my neighbors' eyes peering out at me, I slowly said, "And then . . ."

"And then I started to hear people say they weren't surprised to hear that a dead man turned up on your doorstep. I hate to tell you this, but your neighbors don't like you. You scare them. You disturb their peaceful neighborhood." He grinned. "Can you beat that? A peaceful neighborhood in this city?"

I didn't laugh, I flushed. "Are you telling me that my neighbors think I'm a nuisance?"

"No. I'm asking you if George Walden was on his way to see you the night he got murdered."

I usually lie to cops without a whit of remorse. But I liked Hutchinson; I didn't want to lie to him. I didn't want to tell the truth, either. Feeling like a politician at a press conference, I blurted out an answer that was neither truth nor lie.

"I didn't know George Walden. We didn't have an appointment."

"I didn't ask if you knew Walden. I didn't ask if Walden had an appointment." Hutchinson sounded exasperated. "Was Walden coming to see you?"

"George Walden and I never talked. I'd rather not speculate on his reasons for being in the area."

Hutchinson blinked. In a flash, the friendly demeanor evaporated. I looked into eyes that brimmed with suspicion. "Try. What are you working on now?"

"I hate to disappoint you, Chris, but I won't discuss my clients with you. They expect me to keep their private business private."

"You can't hide behind confidentiality."

I crossed my arms and leaned against the wrought iron banister. "Is it time to call my attorney?"

"No need to do that. We won't accomplish anything except to get mad at each other." The detective stuck his pad and pencil in his jacket pocket and rubbed his hands together. The sound of flesh rubbing against flesh grated on my nerves. "It's chilly out here. Don't suppose you'd like to offer me a cup of hot. coffee, would you?"

I glanced at my watch and shook my head. I had work to do, work that didn't include entertaining cops. "On any other day, I would—because you're so smooth at fishing for an invitation to get inside and snoop around. But I'm running late."

The wounded look that came across Hutchinson's face was familiar. It's the same one I use when I'm trying to talk myself in where I'm not wanted. I laughed—and lied again. "Sorry. You'll have to take a rain check—I have an appointment."

My detective friend didn't move. "Walden got into trouble at work. I think Walden came to talk to you about that trouble and someone killed him. The question is, did George Walden get killed on his way in or his way out of your house?"

Hutchinson had taken the first step on a trail that could lead to implicating me. Even though I had no reason—that I knew of—to worry, I had to push him back. If not, he'd start examining everything I did. "My doorbell never rang that night. As for the rest of your theory, it's a great plot for a movie. Who told you a story like that?"

The detective's grin appeared more sinister this time. "The infamous unnamed source."

My temper flared and threatened to erupt. I put my key in the lock and calmly said, "I'm going to be late, so if you're done . . ."

"Okay, okay. I get the message. You're a busy lady. Humor me for another minute or two. Are you working with me or against me?"

The man wouldn't give up. I shook my head in annoyance. "I can't answer that."

"Try."

The clipped word annoyed me. Hutchinson stared at me as if I had just become his chief suspect. I shot back, "Ask me again. In English this time."

"Working with me means answering my questions. Working against me means avoiding them. Which is it?"

"I hate multiple choice questions." I unlocked the door and stepped inside. "Have a nice day, detective." I smiled sweetly—then I slammed the door in his face.

After tossing my keys on the small table in the hallway, I picked up the mail. Mortgage, car, insurance, credit cards, pitch letters—bills and junk mail. I tossed the envelopes on the table so Dennis could pick out the important ones, then ran upstairs to my computer.

After a few hours of surfing databases, I had a two-inch stack of papers. I knew when and where George Walden attended school and the credit limits on his VISA and MasterCard. I knew how much he paid American Express in January when the Christmas bills hit. I knew Walden liked to eat at Manhattan's hottest restaurants, drive foreign cars, ski in Utah, and shop by catalog. I knew the statistics. I didn't know the man.

I impatiently pushed those printouts aside and grabbed the file from Kembell Reid. I flipped through Walden's monthly account statements. He'd made it easy for me by writing checks for everything. I wrote down the names of dry cleaners, churches, liquor, grocery and hardware stores, and bookstores. I made a list, cross-referenced the entries against the Internet Yellow Pages, and found addresses for most of the list.

I sighed and looked at my watch. Two trips to Hoboken in one day—not my idea of fun. But if I hurried I'd have just enough time to get there before the businesses closed. After scribbling a note to Dennis, I grabbed my coat and headed out the door. Some might have said I was running in circles; I preferred to think of it as following my instincts.

I heard the same answer everywhere I went: George Walden was a nice guy, friendly, easygoing, and wasn't it a shame about the way he died. With a shake of a head, the conversation faded and I'd move on. Guided by the unrealistically optimistic belief that the next stop would bring success, I kept going. When I reached the end of my list, my optimism had dimmed.

I backtracked to the bookstore parking lot to retrieve my car and drove to Hudson Street. It was time to meet 'George Walden's neighbors.

A Hoboken miracle occurred: I found a place to park. True, it was at the end of the block, but it was a place, a legal place, to park. After locking the Porsche, I started ringing doorbells. Those who bothered to open their doors abruptly turned away when I asked about George Walden. I learned nothing—except to dodge slamming doors. Standing at the bottom of the stairs of the last uncooperative neighbor, I turned my collar up against the cold and headed down the street to my next target.

A church spire at the distant end of the block caught my attention. I reluctantly forced myself toward it. It's not that I don't like churches, it's the people who run them that bother me. When they look into my eyes, they see the things I try to keep hidden. Or maybe they just sense that I'm not good church material. Whatever the reason, the priests, the nuns, the rabbis, and the ministers purse their lips and scowl at me with barely veiled disapproval.

The priest at this church, St. Andrew's, didn't disappoint me. Suspicious from the moment he cracked the door open wide enough to peek out at me, he didn't invite me inside. Instead, he slipped out and closed the door behind him.

Even though it was well past eight o'clock, the priest still wore his work clothes: black slacks, black shirt with a stiff clerical collar, and shiny black shoes. The bright porch light made his face look waxy, almost dead. The tattered maroon sweater and shaggy black hair brushing his shoulders gave me a bit of hope that he might bend a few rules.

The priest's first words took that hope away. His nonconformist outlook didn't extend beyond his unshorn hair. "You're wasting your time. I may be a priest, but I'm not a soft touch. I'm not interested."

"Well, Father, if you're not interested, I hope you're curious."

"About what?" He folded his arms across his chest and waited, daring me to soften him up.

Remembering the entries on George's account statements, I took a wild guess. "About how one of your church's biggest benefactors met his Savior." The priest's frown was deeper than the Grand Canyon. Before he could admonish me for being flippant, I rushed on. "Come on, Father. If that's the worst thing you've heard this week, then Hoboken must be heaven."

"Who are you?"

For the twentieth, or possibly the thirtieth, time that evening, I pulled my ID from my coat pocket and flipped it open. "My name's Blaine Stewart. I'm a private investigator from New York City."

With a voice that rumbled with sarcasm, he said, "And what brings you across the river? Have you run all the criminals out of New York State?"

I held back a sarcastic reply. Wondering if this was divine payback for the way I'd treated Chris Hutchinson, I rubbed my hands together, and said, "It's too cold to stand out here and hurl insults back and forth. Do you think we could go inside before I freeze?"

He looked at me dubiously and seemed to be thinking about telling me to just go away. I quickly promised I wouldn't waste his time and slyly moved up a step.

The priest knew the reason for my visit. He also knew I wouldn't leave. He grudgingly opened the door and motioned me inside. I stepped into a tiny vestibule. The inside of the rectory was even more threadbare than the outside.

The priest pointed to the left. I followed his directions and found myself in a tiny room that was meant to be the parish office. Two filing cabinets, a desk, and a few chairs filled the space. Without waiting for an invitation, I gingerly sat on a rickety chair and waited for the priest to take his seat behind a battered desk. I smiled. "A desk that's covered with more papers than mine. I didn't think one existed."

The harsh lines of his young face didn't change. I

was dealing with a totally humorless man. "You're Father . . . ?" I paused so he could fill in the blank.

"Conrad." He didn't offer his first name; I didn't ask. He didn't try to hide his contempt for me. In fact, he seemed to be regretting his decision to let me inside. "You're here about George Walden."

It wasn't a question, just a simple statement of fact. I nodded. "Believe me, I'm not here to pry secrets from you. I'd rather be at home in bed with my husband."

Father Conrad frowned again. Whoops. I bobbed my head and muttered, "Sorry."

The Stewart charm didn't work—the frown stayed on the priest's face. Ignoring his uncooperative demeanor and icy stare, I recited my law-and-order speech. I used to believe it, but lately I wasn't sure.

"I want to find out who killed George Walden and bring him to justice. To do that, I need to know everything about the victim—about George. I understand he was a member of your parish."

The priest nodded. "He was."

I started with an easy question, hoping to lull the priest into answering the more difficult ones I had in mind. "He recently moved into the area, right?"

"Yes." Father Conrad nodded again and reluctantly supplied me with a thimbleful of information. "But George has been a member of St. Andrew's for several years now. He attended services here for years before his marriage."

"Then you must have officiated at the wedding."

I was rewarded with another suspicious nod. Despite the lack of encouragement, I pressed on. "Did George Walden discuss any work or marital problems with you?"

"I can't answer that."

"Why not?"

"Ms.—"

"Stewart."

The priest nodded his thanks and started his lecture again. "Ms. Stewart, I don't know if you are familiar with the Catholic religion. Even so, you must be aware of the confidentiality of the confessional."

My patience blew. "Cut the crap, Father. I'm not asking you to tell confessional tales. I'm a good guy; you can talk to me."

We stared at each other. I saw the rigid set of his jaw and thought, *Strike out, Stewart.*

His blue eyes finally showed a spark of kindness. "I could make this easy for you."

"If you were a charitable man."

My words tweaked a nerve. He smiled slightly and said, "Still, the Church has rules."

The priest had no reason to help me—and he knew that. Uncomfortable at being in the all-too-familiar position of pleading with a stranger for help, I quietly said, "Rules can always be broken. Do you believe in justice?"

"Divine justice, yes."

"George Walden's family could use a bit of earthly justice," I soften my voice and murmured, "Perhaps you can tell me something that won't violate any confidences."

At least the man made quick decisions. He put his hands together, fingertip to fingertip, and peered over them. "I did have a conversation about their marriage. But it wasn't with George. It was Carol. That's why I'm surprised to hear that she's pregnant. You see, Carol Walden wanted to have her marriage annulled."

Lost in thought, he barely heard my soft question. "Why?" I repeated it in a voice loud enough to get his attention.

The confidentiality curtain fell again. When the priest looked at me, his eyes were veiled. "George had changed. That's what Carol said. That's all I can say."

I wanted to know more. Father Conrad, however, was a man of his word; he turned my questions away with a resolute shake of his head. Being a lifelong practitioner of stubbornness, I admire an expert. I thanked him and left.

I hate walking down desolate streets; too many ghosts try to accompany me. No matter how fast I move, they trail behind. In the cold, dark night, the Hoboken streets lost their small-town feel and took on the sinister quality of Manhattan's worst alleys—fertile ground for my ghosts. The ghosts and questions about dissolving marriages followed me back to Manhattan.

Chapter 13

I went to Gary Preston's office in the morning, expecting another plea for me to sign on with his side. He surprised me. Before I had a chance to sit, or even say good morning, Preston slammed the door shut and whirled around to glower at me.

"George Walden was in on it. That bastard fucked me harder than he fucked my daughter on their honeymoon."

Lovely thought. I took my coat off and carefully draped it over a chair. Not that I cared about my coat; I wanted to give Preston time to sit and catch his breath. "You told me that George was your loyal, trusted son-in-law, and friend. Why the sudden change of heart?"

Gary tossed a thick manila envelope on the desk. It skidded to a halt an eighth of an inch from the end. He pointed at it with his middle finger, inadvertently, or maybe purposely, giving it the finger.

"I just got this. That fucking bastard knew what was going on. He approved that bitch's requests to exceed her trading limits."

Preston was on the edge of losing control. To slow things down, I said, "Wait a second. Are you saying George approved Dani Dexter's trading?" Preston nodded. I undid the clasp on the envelope and shook out a thick sheaf of papers. "Is this the complete report?"

Preston shook his head again, harder this time. A lock of gray hair fell across his eyes; he impatiently brushed it aside and snapped, "Yes, it's complete. Take it. It'll be all over the damn TV tonight. Every time I fart it shows up on the *Nightly Report.* Then it shows up in the *Times* and the *Journal* in the morning. That fucking Bramble. I liked him better when he was on Channel 7 making happy talk about the subways or the zoo."

I stopped leafing through the papers and glanced at Preston. "Bramble? Johnnie Bramble? He's not on Channel 7 anymore?"

"Don't you watch TV?" I shook my head. Preston growled, "That's fucking un-American. He's not Johnnie Bramble anymore. He's John Thurston Bramble, the fucking Third. From PBS."

A year earlier, Johnnie Bramble had been nothing more than a smiling, talking head on the evening news. Bramble had been a glory-seeking anchor, hot on the trail of a multimillion-dollar scandal. I'd been trying to protect my investigation—and my business—until I went for my final revenge.

Preston was so intent on cursing Bramble that he failed to notice my daydreaming. I stuffed the papers into the envelope and tapped my fingers against it. "Did you drag me down here to tell me that Johnnie Bramble is a pain in your ass?"

The CEO of Kembell Reid, one of the country's largest privately owned investment banks, blushed. "My wife said that if I didn't call you, I shouldn't bother coming home. Carol's three months pregnant. We don't want her to lose that baby."

Gary's words sent my stomach rolling and twisting. Years ago I'd been the young, pregnant widow when Jeff was killed. Weeks later, the baby was gone too. I spent years trying to slowly kill myself with alcohol. I no longer mourn the lost lives with the same intensity, but still feel a faint, empty ache whenever I dare to let myself think of what could have been.

I considered saying, *Aw, shit, I wish you hadn't told me that.* Instead, I asked, "And you expect me to—?"

"To get to the bottom of this. Fast. Go talk to whoever you want. Go wherever you have to. Tell me what you want. You've got it."

Instead of seizing the opportunity to roam the halls of Kembell Reid, questioning everyone in sight, I said the first thing that came to mind. "Fine. I want to talk to your daughter." I had a few questions to ask. Questions like why she wanted to have her happy marriage annulled.

"Absolutely not." Gary slammed his palm on the desk, making it sound like a slap across the face. "Carol has been through enough. I won't let you make it worse."

My temper flared. "You just begged me to make things better for your daughter. Now you're jerking me around. Why?"

We stared at each other. Preston blinked first. "I'll try. I don't know if Carol will listen to me. She doesn't take my advice these days, but I'll try."

I gently picked at the suspicious threads of Gary's statement. "I'd think that at a time like this, a daughter would rely on her father's strength. Why won't Carol follow your advice?"

"Because she blames me." I raised a quizzical eyebrow. Perhaps it went a bit too high; Gary noticed and stopped short. "Shit, she blames everybody—not just her old man. Wouldn't you?"

I nodded. I had. When Jeff died, I blamed everyone from Jeff to the bastard who'd set him up. I even blamed myself for letting him go to work that night, as if I could have stopped him. Anyone who came near me got blamed for something. But none of the blame ever brought him back.

In a very soft voice, I asked, "Does Carol seem to blame you more than the others?"

A loud snort that escaped before Gary could cover it up said more than the bland expression in his gray eyes. He shook his head.

"Carol blames me for hiring George. She blames her mother for not insisting that George join us for dinner that night. She blames herself—I don't know, she blames everyone."

"Does Carol work?"

The coarse skin on Gary's face reddened. "Yes, she does."

The defensive tone pushed my eyebrows up again. I murmured, "And just where does your daughter work?"

"Here. Personnel."

"And what does she do in Personnel?"

"She runs the department."

I frowned. "Why didn't you tell me that? Makes me wonder what else you're trying to hide."

"Don't you go jumping to conclusions and scream about nepotism. I hear enough of that from people who think she coasted her way into a cushy job." Gary almost succeeded in keeping a defensive tone from his voice. "Sure, Carol's my daughter, but that kid works her ass off. She knows what people say about how she got her job, her promotions, her bonus—"

I let his defense of his daughter's job go and interrupted with a one-word question. "Bonus?"

It's a common Wall Street practice to divvy up the profits and hand out bonuses, some fat, some lean. Secretaries might receive a few hundred or a thousand dollars; hotshot traders could find checks for millions of dollars on their desks.

I'd spent enough time in these companies to know the jealousies that bubble and threaten to erupt at bonus time. Some say the system rewards effort. Others say it rewards more unspeakable character traits. The speculation on the size of the bonus pool begins months before the year ends and lasts until bonuses are announced. Months later, when checks are distributed, an anticlimactic calm settles in.

Despite the wild tales of outrageous spending, most use the money for braces on the kids' teeth, college tuition, or down payments on new homes. It doesn't matter how the money is used, the rumors and the jealously still fly.

The purposely blank look on Gary Preston's face annoyed me. "So, were people speculating about the bonuses George and Carol received?"

"People always gossip. This business runs on rumors and gossip. I don't see what this has to do with George—or my daughter."

Neither did I, but it seemed worth pursuing. Putting on a confident smile, I said, "What if someone was jealous enough to do something about it? Convince your daughter to talk to me."

Preston reluctantly agreed. "I'm supposed to have dinner with Carol tonight. I'll see what I can do. Call me in the morning."

Saying I would, I stood, grasped the envelope of papers tightly, and shook his hand. I was halfway out the door when Preston shouted, "Hey, Stewart!" I paused and looked over my shoulder. Preston grinned at me. "Do something about that fucking reporter, okay?"

I laughed. "You get your daughter to talk to me. I'll get Bramble to stop talking about you."

Before Preston had a chance to ask how I'd do that, I walked out. John Thurston Bramble the Third owed me. It was time for him to pay up.

I didn't wait until I got to my office. I stopped in the lobby and dug my little phone out, dialed information and got the number for the television station. I dialed that number and asked for Bramble.

Luck was with me. Bramble answered. His cheerful voice sounded even more cheerful when I told him my name. "Blaine Stewart. You're not going to believe this, but I was just talking about you."

People rarely sound so happy to receive my call. Suspicion tainted my response. "You're right, Johnnie. I don't believe you."

"Still cynical. That's what I like best about you, Blaine. You have a healthy disrespect for authority."

"Not just authority, Johnnie. I also have a healthy disrespect for bullshit—and I think I'm getting an earful of it now."

"Never!"

Johnnie's enthusiastic voice buzzed in my ear. When I sensed a slowdown, I asked, "How did you get to PBS? I thought your goal was to be your generation's Walter Cronkite."

Bramble didn't laugh. "With all due respect to Walter, I'd rather be known as my generation's Edward R. Murrow. That's why I moved to public broadcasting. The networks aren't interested in serious journalism. That and the crow's-feet circling my eyes made me move. I didn't want to get booted to a third-rate station in a third-rate market because I wasn't pretty enough for the big time."

"I thought that only happened to the women. Aren't you men allowed to age gracefully and become distinguished?"

"Not anymore, Blaine. It's all about ratings. We're competing with cable, pay-per-view, videos, and satellite dishes. The networks want a Fabio with brains. I thought it was time to set myself up in a new job where I could do some good work. When I got the chance, I jumped."

Bramble sounded pleased, so I tried to sound sincere. "Congratulations. I hear you've been beating up on Kembell Reid."

I pictured Bramble leaning forward, suddenly interested in more than a reunion. "Why? Do you have information about what's going on down there? Are you working for them?"

"Maybe, maybe not. Maybe you should buy me lunch."

"I'm free today. I can meet you anywhere you'd like. Name the time and place. I'll be there."

"Don't get your hopes up too high, Johnnie. I'm not handing you a story this time. I want to trade information, not give it away."

Johnnie hadn't strayed too far from his roots; the smooth-talking television anchor instantly reappeared. "Now, come on. We've worked together before. You know—"

I cut him off so I wouldn't have to hear about the last time. "Forget lunch. You can buy me a cup of coffee instead. There's a coffee shop on the corner of Eighth Avenue and Forty-sixth Street. Meet me there in half an hour. Bring your Kembell Reid file or it's going to be a very quick cup of coffee."

I hadn't seen Johnnie Bramble for almost a year, but he hadn't changed. The hair was still blond, the eyes still blue, and the hair still firmly shellacked in place. When Bramble dropped off the evening news, I hadn't noticed his absence. But I didn't tell him that. Bramble looked too sincere, too pleased with his new status as a serious journalist for me to make snide comments.

Strangely enough, Bramble seemed at ease in the grungy coffee shop. He didn't wrinkle his nose at the grimy linoleum floor, the stale odors of frying onions and cigarettes, or the gum-cracking waitress who slammed two mugs of coffee down in front of us. Little waves of coffee slopped over the rim and landed on the table.

Johnnie pulled a napkin from the dispenser, dabbed at the greasy puddle, and smiled. "Charming. I assume you chose this dump for reasons other than the ambience. Or is this one of your usual hangouts?"

"Coffee's good. Stella may not be the best waitress in town, but she keeps refilling the mugs. Food's not bad. Want to order a burger?" I slid a menu across the table to Bramble.

The stricken look that floated across his face was too much. I couldn't hold the laughter back.

"Sorry, I couldn't resist." Bramble's attempt to look nonchalant made me laugh again. "I've never been here before. I wanted to make it clear that this isn't a social call."

"I didn't call you, Blaine. You called me, remember? I gave up after two months of unanswered calls." Johnnie used the back of his hand to slide the mug of coffee aside. "You used me just as much as I used you. You got your business back; I got my own show. It just went national, you know."

"Congratulations." I fingered the pack of cigarettes in my pocket. "Tell me about Kembell Reid."

Bramble smiled. "Tell you the truth, Blaine, that's the reason why I came. I thought you might want to work together again, be partners."

I nearly choked. The waitress took a half step toward us. Afraid she would attempt the Heimlich maneuver on me, I waved her away. I caught my breath and said, "A partnership?"

"A partnership." Bramble's eyes narrowed to determined slits. "I'm not going over that ground again, Blaine. And if you think I owe you, you're fooling yourself. We're even."

He looked at his watch. A Hermes. Bramble may have left the networks, but he wasn't pinching pennies on a nonprofit salary. "What's it going to be? I can't sit around in this dump much longer. I have a show to run."

"Gary Preston thinks you have an inside line to what's happening in his company."

Bramble smiled at my backhanded compliment.

"Are you telling me that he's hoping you would stop me?"

"Doesn't matter. That's not why I called you, Johnnie. I want you to give me some background on Kembell Reid."

Information does not flow from Johnnie Bramble's mouth. He snapped, "Why?"

"None of this is for broadcast, right?" Bramble nodded. "I'm investigating a murder. George Walden."

Bramble leaned across the table. A casual observer might have thought we were lovers, making plans for a romantic encounter. It wasn't love that sparked across the table between us, it was the tension a hunter feels when closing in on the prey. "Why George Walden?"

"He died on my doorstep. I'd like to know why."

Bramble let that information slide by without comment. It was either old news or he had more important questions in mind. "So who are you working for? Preston?"

"Not Preston. I'm working for a third party who's not involved in the mess at Kembell Reid."

"Not involved and paying your rates?" Disbelief colored his eyes and his voice. "I find that hard to believe."

I twirled the mug and smiled. "Don't be so suspicious, Johnnie. Someone who's upset about a friend's murder hired me. I met with Gary Preston, twice. He's not very cooperative."

Bramble absentmindedly crumpled a napkin and rubbed the tabletop, leaving behind faint coffee streaks. "I'll say. Preston won't even say *no comment* when I call."

"That's why I want to talk to your source."

"Why should I give up a source to you?"

Bramble's ambition was the only leverage I had. "Because a huge story like this one can get you to network prime time. You know, a really big show. A special. Blurbs in *Newsweek* and *Time*. Surely Sam Donaldson, Dan Rather, or one of those guys on *60 Minutes* is going to retire soon. John Bramble could be a natural replacement—if he blows the doors off a major Wall Street firm, exposes a huge scandal, and makes a national name for himself. *Money and Murder*. Makes a great title for an investigative report, don't you think?"

"I'm not sure that's enough."

"Not enough? What, you want me to get Oliver Stone to direct?" I grinned and shook my head. "It's all I can offer, Johnnie."

"Do I get an exclusive?"

"Do you see any other reporters in here?" I turned to look over my shoulder. "Nope, don't see anyone from the *Times*. Don't see anyone from NBC or CNN, either. You're it, Johnnie. You get an exclusive—just like last time."

I was done talking; Johnnie had to decide without any more prompting from me. I sat back, finally lit a cigarette—and waited. It wouldn't take long. From the moment Bramble had rushed in the door, wearing a casually rumpled trench coat and every blond hair in perfect alignment, I knew he wouldn't be able to resist.

"Same ground rules as last time?"

I nodded.

"You were damn good last time."

I smiled slightly. "I'll be even better this time."

"Mariah Becco."

The name was new to me. "Who is Mariah Becco?"

"My source. She's black. She's flamboyant. She's a rising star at Kembell Reid. She's Dani Dexter's lover."

Johnnie stared at me and waited for my reaction.

"So," I shrugged. "What's so special about that? Happens all the time."

Bramble shook his head. "Not on Wall Street."

"Even on Wall Street."

"Not this way."

"This way? What does that mean?"

Bramble took a deep breath and prepared to deliver a lecture. I waited expectantly. "You can be a woman on Wall Street and be successful. You can be black and be successful. You can even be gay and succeed."

Annoyance flashed through me. "Spoken like a true white, male WASP."

Johnnie blushed; it was the least he could do. "Okay, it's hard. Not many break through to the top, but it can be done. There is one thing you can't do."

"Oh?" I asked dryly. "And what might that be?"

"You can be whatever you want to be on Wall Street. Just don't flaunt it. Show up every day in your white shirt and dark suit, toe the line, and do whatever the hell you want after the market closes. But don't ever tell anyone how you spent the night."

"Let me guess. Mariah Becco broke that rule"

Bramble nodded. "Exactly. Dani Dexter was successful. Believe me, Dani rubbed everyone's nose in her success, but she kept her personal life a secret. Mariah didn't. And Mariah made the mistake

of not being successful. That's what killed the ro-
mance. Dani thought Mariah was dragging her
down. So Dani moved on to someone who could
advance her career."

My cigarette burned down to the filter and singed
my fingers. I dropped the butt in the ashtray and
asked, "Who took over the role of Dani's lover?"

"George Walden."

"How convenient. A spurned lover is your
source. I'm disappointed; I thought you'd say Gary
Preston was the lover."

"Some say Dani started with Preston and worked
her way down."

"The woman is a success. Therefore, she must
be sleeping with the boss. Now, that's original." I
didn't try to hide my disgust.

"It's been done, Blaine." Bramble shook his
head. "You can't deny it."

Cursing out a would-be informant is never a
good idea. I clamped my mouth shut and swallowed
the urge to tell Bramble what I thought. After all,
I did want information from him. "Does Becco still
work at Kembell Reid?"

Bramble nodded. After realizing that he'd made
a big mistake by blurting out his informant's name,
he tried to make me promise I wouldn't contact
Becco. Of course I wouldn't make such a ridiculous
promise. We bickered for several minutes, not
reaching an agreement.

"Checkmate." I smiled at Bramble, who grew
more visibly angry with each breath. "I think we're
stuck. Any suggestions? It shouldn't be hard for
me to find Mariah Becco. After all, I know where
she works." I gave him another sweet smile and
waited for the explosion.

Bramble disappointed me. He growled, "Don't screw with my informant and don't tell your story to anyone else. Remember, we have an exclusive." He threw a twenty on the table, said, "Don't stiff Stella on the tip," and walked out.

I waited a few seconds before following Bramble out the door. It was Stella's lucky day. And my lucky day, too.

Chapter 14

I got to the office early the next morning. Earlier than anyone—except Grace Hudson. She was pacing up and down the hallway, impatiently glancing at her watch and then at the locked door to our suite. When I saw Grace, I stuffed the *Times* into my briefcase and tried to visualize my calendar. *Had I forgotten a meeting?*

Grace read my mind. She smiled to put me at ease and held out a white paper bag. "Breakfast? The bagels are still warm and the coffee's strong. Just the way you like it. Thought I'd better come bearing gifts—or bagels. Lox, too."

"Lox?" I dropped my briefcase and fumbled with the keys. "Am I having premature memory loss? Did I forget that we had an appointment? An appointment important enough for such a splendid breakfast."

Grace never backs down in the face of sarcasm; she ignores it. "I haven't been waiting long. I wanted to talk to you."

I managed to poke the right key into the lock and pushed the door open. "Telephones, Grace. Wonderful inventions."

I stood aside and let Grace past. As she walked by, I caught a glimpse of dark smudges under her eyes that hadn't been completely covered by makeup. This was not going to be a short meeting. Knowing that one cup of coffee wouldn't be enough, I ushered Grace to our small kitchen and started brewing a full pot.

Grace took a container from the sack and handed it to me. She pried the lid off the other one and took a dainty sip. She leaned against the water cooler and watched me. Her pose was anything but relaxed.

I grabbed two mugs from a cabinet over the sink and lined them up in front of the coffeepot. "Why are you looking so glum this morning, Grace? Did you think I might cheer you up?"

She shrugged. "It's been a while since we had breakfast. I miss our monthly meals."

"Bullshit." We'd known each other too long to sugarcoat the truth with politically correct platitudes. "Why are you darkening my door so early in the morning?"

Grace took another careful sip of her coffee. Recognizing the signs of a person in the midst of stalling, I waited; the silence might make Grace uncomfortable enough to blurt out the true reason for her visit. I pried the lid off the other cardboard container of coffee and tried it. It tasted like very hot water.

"You're looking glum yourself, Blaine."

"You're confusing tired with glum—and you're ducking my question, Grace. What brings you here at the crack of dawn?" I caught her eye and solemnly said, "The truth, Grace."

"Couldn't sleep. I kept thinking about George. Went to his funeral yesterday. I was hoping you'd come up with something." Grace smiled ruefully.

"Decided to harass you in person instead of over the phone."

The pot gurgled and spit—a signal that it had finished its work. I filled the mugs and gave one to Grace. "Dump that other stuff that's masquerading as coffee and let's go to my office. You can harass me in comfort."

We walked down the hallway, making idle conversation along the way. I flipped the light on and tried unsuccessfully to hold back a yawn.

Grace noticed and smiled again. "Why are you so tired, Blaine? Working too hard?"

As if on cue, another yawn escaped. I apologized and said, "I didn't get home until after ten last night. Dennis was still working. He's got some hot new case and it's driving me nuts because he can't talk to me about it. I decided to wait up for him and see if I could worm anything out of him. Of course, I fell asleep on the sofa. Eileen called around midnight and woke me up. She's worried about Sandy, so I let her talk."

"Sandy?" Grace had heard enough stories about my niece to feel intimately acquainted with her. "What's wrong with Sandy?"

"Nothing. The question should be: what's wrong with her parents?"

We entered my office; I pointed Grace to the small round table near the windows. As we tossed our coats on the sofa and settled down, I quickly summarized Eileen's dissolving marriage and her fears about Don and Sandy. Grace listened with a look of disbelief on her face. It matched the disbelief I felt at hearing the words said aloud.

"Do you really think Don's capable of something like that?"

I brushed Grace's question aside with a wave of my hand because I didn't want to think about the answer. "Eileen's not the only one headed for divorce court. I found out last night that George Walden was on his way there, too."

"George get a divorce?" Grace shook her head. "No way. He would have said something to me. Your information's bad."

I took a bite from a bagel, chewed, and quickly swallowed. "I don't think so. Parish priests don't usually lie."

"A priest? That's your informant?" Grace laughed. "Blaine, you've got to find better sources."

"Gimme a break; I just started." I crumpled my napkin and threw it at Grace. "I have been interviewing other people, you know."

"You talked to Preston. What did he say?"

I shrugged. "Not much. Gary's not very talkative. I talked to the neighbors; they didn't have much to say."

"That's all you have?" Grace couldn't, or didn't bother to, hide her disappointment.

"That's it." Or at least that's all I was prepared to tell. I never tell clients everything, not until the very end—when it's too late for them to interfere. Even though I'd known Grace for years, I didn't see any reason to break my long-standing policy.

I sipped my coffee and watched Grace over the top of the mug. She looked haggard and drawn. George's death—or something else—was causing Grace to lose sleep. To change the subject, I casually asked, "How's the market doing, Grace?"

It was the wrong question to put her at ease. Grace's body went rigid with tension. "You read the papers. It sucks. Market's going down. Clients are bailing out."

"Not all of your clients are panicking, Grace." I smiled reassuringly. "I'm still around."

"And I appreciate it. But I just lost a big one. A huge one . . ." Grace shook her head. "Shit, will you listen to me whine? I've been through this before. I'll survive."

The faint smile on her face made me wonder.

I put the mug down and said, "Tell me about Dani Dexter."

Grace's answer was noncommittal. "I don't know much about Dani. I've read the same stories you have; that's about all I know. Why? Have you talked to her?"

"I wouldn't call it talking. I *listened* to her." I laughed. "I was given the favor of an audience with her. She swept in here the other day—"

"She came here?" Grace grabbed my arm to stop me. "What did she want?"

"Dani?" I frowned. Grace, realizing that she had wrapped her fingers around my wrist, relaxed her grip. "She wanted to hire me to look into George's death. I told her that I already had a client."

Before I could ask why Grace sounded so alarmed, she looked at her watch and gasped. "Speaking of the market, I have just enough time to get downtown before it opens." She stood and struggled to put her coat on. "You'll call me?"

"As soon as I have something to tell you."

After Grace left, I dragged out my notes and a legal pad and settled back to plan my next attack. Gary Preston's call saved me the trouble.

Jona stuck her head in my office. She smiled

broadly and said, "Gary Preston's on the phone. He asked if it would be possible to speak with you for a few moments. Whatever you said to him yesterday made quite an impression. He said to tell you that he hopes he's not interrupting you."

Puzzled by the change, I picked up the phone and said hello. Gary's response sounded subdued, almost depressed. Expecting bad news about my request to meet with his daughter, I asked, "Did you talk to Carol?"

"Yes." Preston paused. The pause stretched out until I started wondering if he would continue. "Yes," he repeated. "I did. Carol and I had a long talk. She wants you to come down here to meet with her. Name the time; she'll be here."

I wanted to question Carol, but not under her father's controlling eyes and judgmental ears. People have a strange way of censoring themselves when they have an audience. If that audience includes a parent or spouse, the censor becomes even more overbearing.

"I'd prefer to meet her in my office. She can come up whenever she'd like."

Preston covered the mouthpiece. I heard the mumbling of a conversation with another person. After a few seconds, he came back to me.

"Carol said here or nowhere."

Telling myself to take what I could get, I asked, "Is Carol with you right now?" When Preston said she was, I promised to be in his office as fast as I could get there. I grabbed my coat and blew past Jona, calling over my shoulder that I'd be back in a few hours.

This time, Preston's guards didn't stop me. I was quickly escorted up to the top floor and led to the executive's office. Gary met me at the door and motioned for me to sit at the long conference table. Carol sat with her back to the door, oblivious to the magnificent views of the Statue of Liberty and the New York harbor.

I introduced myself and extended my hand across the table. Carol held out a limp, trembling hand, brushed my palm, and quickly pulled away as she recognized me. "You're the one who—"

"Yes," I quickly stopped her before she remembered how angry she'd been when I rang her doorbell. "I'm sorry. My timing could have been better."

Carol's eyes had the vacant stare of a soldier returning from a long, bloody battle. I wondered how much time I'd have before she broke down. As gently as possible, I said, "Carol, I really appreciate this meeting. I—"

"Don't tell me how sorry you are or that you know what I'm feeling. You already told me that."

"Okay." I sat back, pulled a legal pad from my briefcase, and uncapped my pen. "Why don't you tell me how you feel?"

Carol blurted out the words she'd been rehearsing. "I feel like people are blaming George for everything that happened around here. He's a handy scapegoat—can't defend himself." Preston gurgled, but didn't protest. Carol's rules undoubtedly included a gag order for her father. She continued, "George received a Wells notice the day he died."

Gary couldn't contain himself. He growled, "And I received one this morning."

Preston tried to sound angry, not worried, but I didn't believe him. Wells notices come from the Securities Exchange Commission, the SEC. It's their final notice before they pounce on you. It's your last chance to give them a reason, a good reason, to stop. Most of the time, your reason isn't good enough.

Carol's voice was slight, but determined. "George called to tell me about the Wells letter, but he wouldn't talk about it. He said he'd be home late because he had a late meeting. I shouldn't wait up for him because I need my sleep."

Carol's eyes misted. I didn't need psychic powers to know she was thinking of her unborn baby.

"I checked his calendar. It didn't have any appointments listed. George always wrote everything down. No matter how rushed, how upset, how angry he was, George wrote it down."

She smiled briefly. "Drove me crazy. Notes, notes, little notes all over the place. George would have written down the appointment—the time, the place, the person, the reason. Everything."

"Unless he had something to hide."

Carol glared at me. "You didn't know my husband, so don't jump to conclusions. If George had a meeting, it would have been in his calendar. Or his notebook. He always carried a small notebook to back up his calendar."

Sensing that Carol's answer would make me unhappy, I asked another question. "Do you have your husband's calendar and notebook? Or did the police take them?"

Carol shook her head. "Up until last night, I had them. I went to my parents' house for dinner last night—I had to get out. Someone broke in while I was away. George's papers on the dining room table—they're gone."

"How—" I almost said, *how convenient,* but

stopped myself. Sometimes I'm suspicious for no reason at all. "What did the police say about the break-in?"

"They checked the house." Carol's voice trembled. "It was empty. They said something must have scared the burglars away before they took anything of value."

"Was anything else stolen?"

"Nothing."

"How convenient." The words slipped out, surprising me more than Carol or her father. "I mean, who knew how convenient it would be to break in last night? What did Detective Hutchinson say?"

She glanced away from me to her father. I snapped, "The police did know about George's files, right?"

My question annoyed Gary Preston. He leaned forward and spat out his displeasure. "Don't be ridiculous. Of course they knew."

"Then what did they say about them disappearing?"

Carol shook her head with disgust. "That's the second reason why I told Daddy to call you. I tried calling the detective. He's not interested anymore."

On cue, Preston grabbed a newspaper from the floor and angrily read the headline aloud. "MASSIVE MANHUNT FOR COP KILLER." He flipped the paper open and read from the first sentence of the article. " 'All other investigations put on hold as Mayor Weigand promises all police resources will be put to work to track down—' "

I groaned. "Please stop. That paper is hardly the most reliable source in town. I don't think the NYPD would suspend a murder investigation—"

"Then why is Chris Hutchinson suddenly too

busy to return my phone calls?" Carol's voice rose.
"I'll tell you why. He's too busy looking for a dope
dealer who killed a cop."

"You have to understand—"

Preston exploded. "Understand this—the cops
are taking care of their family, just as I have to
take care of mine."

Carol ignored her father's outburst. She calmly
said, "I want to find out who killed my husband. I
want to end the rumors that accuse my husband of
being the cause of all the problems here at Kembell Reid."

I glanced at Preston. He grabbed the chair's armrest and held tight, but he didn't say a word. Carol
didn't notice her father's reaction. The words continued to rush from her mouth. "The two are con-
nected. George was murdered because he was
going to tell the SEC everything."

"What's everything?"

"I don't know." Carol's eyes blazed. "But it was
enough to get him killed."

"If you're right, everyone at Kembell Reid is a
suspect. Everyone. Even your father."

Carol said, "When you tried to force your way
into my house the day after George was killed, you
said you wanted to find out who murdered him.
Do you still feel that way?"

Without any prompting, the image of George
Walden's body sprawled across my front steps
flashed through my mind. I solemnly answered, "I
do."

For the first time since I'd met Carol, she smiled.
"Good. No one else will help me." From the corner
of my eye, I saw her father stiffen. Again, and with
great effort, he managed to keep from interrupting.

"I want to hire you."

Another name for the growing list of would-be clients. I shook my head. "Someone has already hired me to investigate the . . ."

Gary Preston watched his daughter's struggle and frowned. "Who hired you?"

"I can't tell you that." Preston's face reddened. Quickly, to defuse the tension that engulfed the table, I said, "Look, it's no big secret, but I don't have permission to use my client's name."

Preston smiled knowingly. "Grace Hudson. It has to be Hudson. She told me I should hire George in the first place. She told me to meet with you."

I shrugged. Gary relaxed slightly. "For a second, I thought that Dexter bitch was trying to screw me again. How long have you known Hudson?"

"Ten, twelve years." I turned to Carol. "Did George say anything else when he called to say he'd be late?"

"Nothing. Just that he'd be late."

"Did he say if his meeting was supposed to be in his office, or someplace else?"

"I assumed it would be at the office. George said he was going to get this thing cleared up, once and for all. Then he'd come home. That's all. That's the last time . . ."

The lurking tears resurfaced. I changed the subject. "Did George drink?"

"You mean, did he hang out in bars? Like the place they say he was in before he got killed? George never went to places like that." Carol's nose crinkled with distaste.

Bobby and Ryan wouldn't have been pleased to hear the View classified as a dump. Instead of telling Carol that the View was—still is—my favorite bar, I looked at Preston. "I'd like a copy of George's phone log."

He made a face that showed disgust with my request. "It won't do you any good. The police have been over all those numbers. Calls to brokers. Calls to Carol. Calls to friends. Nothing unusual."

"Even so, I'd still like to see the records for the past month. Maybe something obvious, or not so obvious, got overlooked. If not, it's my client's time I'm wasting—not yours."

Preston gave in too easily. He nodded. "You'll have them in the morning. What else do you need?"

"I have to talk to the people who worked with George. I need complete access."

Carol watched her father's jaw set in a stubborn line. She leaned over and touched his arm. "What if we hire Blaine to work in the department?"

"Hire her to snoop around?" Preston grumbled, "I don't think so. People will find out. They'll get all riled up again. Before we know it, no one's doing any business and the company's going down the tubes."

"No one will know. Just me and you. I run Personnel, remember?" Carol looked at me and asked, "Can you type?"

"Doesn't everyone? My parents made sure we all knew how to type."

The personnel director side of Carol showed itself. "What about computers? Do you know how to use one?"

"Same answer: doesn't everyone?"

"You'd be surprised. Most of our temps have trouble with the alphabet, let alone typing or using

a computer. They use the computer to play soli-
taire—and nothing else. There's a spot opening up
in George's department." She gulped. "You can
work for the new department head."

"Carol, don't you think you should ask Blaine if
she thinks this charade makes any sense? Maybe
she thinks it will be a waste of time."

They turned to me. Gary looked skeptical. Carol
looked hopeful.

Getting away from my world and into another
one where I could be whatever I wanted sounded
appealing. An undercover job would give me the
perfect excuse to disappear from Eileen and her
fears, real or imaginary. I agreed to start in the
morning.

Chapter 15

"They want you to start in the morning?" Eileen's voice rose. "And you agreed to it?"

"I did. But they decided it's easier to explain a new person starting on Monday, not Friday."

"Why did you ever agree to such a harebrained scheme?"

I sipped my coffee and let Eileen's sarcasm slide over me. Unless I managed to be uncharacteristically diplomatic, a major battle would erupt.

"Look, Eileen, it's no big deal. I want to find out what people are saying about George Walden, Dani Dexter, and the rest. I'll be there a week or two. Three at the most."

"I've heard that before. Three weeks will turn into three months. Things will go to hell around here."

"You're right." My grin didn't have much effect on Eileen's mood. "It has happened before. I promise I'll come in every evening, on the weekends, too, if necessary. We'll manage to stay afloat. I'm not completely indispensable—as you so often remind me."

"What about Dennis?"

I waved Eileen's objection away with the back of my hand. "Dennis will understand. Heck, he'll be relieved. He's on a big case himself and feeling guilty because he's never home."

Eileen instantly found another reason for me to stay in the office. "You've been down there—twice. Don't you think someone will recognize you and blow your cover?"

"I already thought of that, Eileen. But I'll be working in a different building. There isn't much chance of being recognized."

"What about Sandy?"

Patiently, ever so patiently, I said, "That's being taken care of. I don't see any need to change. Do you?"

Eileen wasn't able to come up with any objections, but she lingered, trying to think of another reason to chain me to my desk. I passed her a cigarette, then lit one for myself. After a long look at the unhappiness on her face, I gave in.

"I'm being stubborn—as usual. If you really need me here, I'll stay. I can make other arrangements with Kembell Reid."

Eileen carefully shredded the unlit cigarette. She pushed the tobacco into a neat little pile and stared at it. "Why can't we have normal lives?"

I blew a cloud of smoke into the air. "In our family, normal lives seem to skip a generation. Sandy's destined for a normal life; we're not."

Eileen stared at me, certain that I'd lost my mind. I shrugged. "Well, it's a theory. Still being tested, of course." Eileen didn't laugh; she didn't even crack a smile.

Humor was not going to work with my glum sister. I took another drag on my cigarette and tried unsuccessfully to blow a smoke ring. "So, what do you want me to do, Eileen? It's your decision.

Whatever you think is best. You want me to stay, I'll stay."

"And do what? Hang around here and be a high-priced babysitter? No, Blaine, go to Wall Street and be a trader for a week, or a month, or however long it takes."

"Ahhh . . ." I hesitated. Telling Eileen the truth would invite hours of teasing. If I didn't, and she found out on her own, I'd hear even more heckling. "There's just one thing, Eileen. I'm not going to be a trader at Kembell Reid. I'm going to be a temp."

"A temp what?"

I mumbled, "Secretary. The new boss needs a new secretary. I'll be filling in until he finds the perfect one."

Eileen couldn't control herself. She laughed until tears rolled down her cheeks and her aching ribs forced her to stop. In between bursts of laughter, she gasped, "You—a secretary?"

With great dignity, I said, "I've done it before, I'll do it again. It's a perfect job; I'll be invisible. No one pays attention to a temp secretary."

"Okay, if you say so." Eileen wiped the tears of laughter from her eyes. "You'd better spend the rest of the week practicing your typing."

Confident that she'd made the right decision, Eileen said good night and walked out of my office. At least I'd made her laugh.

When I got home, it was after nine. Dennis was stretched out on the sofa—sound asleep. He looked too comfortable to be disturbed. I covered him with an afghan, grabbed my coat and keys, scribbled a note about where I was going, and quietly let myself out again. This was a perfect time to visit the View.

I paused in the doorway and took a deep breath. The inside of the bar was smoky and dim—and felt just like home. I sat at the bar; Ryan, the shorter owner (Bobby's six-eleven), was on duty. He came over to me and slapped a coaster down on the bar.

"It's ladies night. Two for one." He stopped short and feigned surprise. "Blaine! Almost didn't recognize you, girl."

"Very funny. Speaking of not recognizing someone"—I reached across the bar and brushed the new growth on his chin—"why did you decide on this goatee thing?"

"Got to keep up with the times, hon. Seltzer?"

I nodded. "Start a tab, will you, Ryan? And can I borrow some change for cigarettes? I left mine at home."

"With your money?"

I nodded. Ryan filled a mug with soda, grabbed a handful of quarters from the cash register, and put both in front of me. He casually asked, "Where's Dennis?"

I propped my head up with my hand and grinned at Ryan. "You're such a gossip. Always looking for something. Sorry to disappoint you, sweetie, but my darling husband is home asleep on the sofa. I didn't have the heart to wake him and I'm feeling too restless to sit around and quietly read a book. So I decided to pay you a visit. I was halfway here when I realized my wallet is safely tucked away in my briefcase. Don't worry. I'm good for it. I left a note for Dennis to join me here when he wakes up."

Disappointed that he'd be unable to spread the

word that my marriage was on the verge of breaking up, Ryan grumbled.

I glanced around the nearly deserted bar. "Ryan, were any of these people here the night George Walden got killed?"

Ryan scratched his goatee and looked around. Nearly a dozen people were scattered throughout the bar. Some in groups, some solitary drinkers. I didn't recognize a single face—quite a feat for me. A few years ago, I would have been good friends with all of them.

"No. Those guys went to the game—or had a game. I don't remember what Bobby said." As Ryan said those words, another thought came to mind. "Shit, the half a brain I have left must have stopped working. Bobby left something for you in case you came in."

He turned to rummage through the stack of papers next to the cash register, found what he was looking for, and trotted back, triumphantly waving a dog-eared index card in the air. "Bobby said that if you came in I should give you this number. He said the cops asked him about it. It's the number your dead pal called. That's the one where he actually did some talking." He held the card out to me. "Recognize it?"

555-7554. I held my hand out, palm up. "Quarter, please."

Ryan turned to the tip jar and pulled out another quarter. As Ryan teased me about not hesitating to spend the View's hard-earned money, I dropped the coin in the pay phone and dialed. It rang twice before an answering machine kicked in.

"Hi." The slightly breathless voice reminded me

of Jackie Kennedy. "This is Dani. Leave a message—"

I hung up and slowly walked back to the bar. Ryan watched.

"Anyone you know?"

I nodded. "Do you have a phone book?"

Ryan reached under the bar and pulled out a dog-eared telephone directory. He slapped it down in front of me and watched with an amused grin on his face. I looked up Dani Dexter's name. Each year, the White Pages shrink as more and more people search for privacy. I'm always surprised when I find someone actually listed in the Manhattan phone book. Dani was one of the brave few who publicized their phone numbers—and their addresses.

When I returned to the bar, Ryan shook his head in disbelief but withheld his comments. I sat and swallowed the last of the club soda. "Ryan, I have one more favor to ask. It's a big one."

"I'm fascinated, dear. Go ahead and ask."

"I'd rather not stop at home because I'm so noisy I'll wake Dennis up. And he'll want to know why I won't stay home. And—"

"You need money." Ryan shook his head sadly. "I am crestfallen, Blaine. I expected you to ask to borrow my decoder ring. Will twenty do?"

"Fifty would be better."

"Shit, Blaine, why don't you just take a hundred?"

Without thinking, I accepted. "Okay. Since you offered . . . I'll bring it back tomorrow. I promise."

"You'd better. Bobby's gonna kill me if you don't. We didn't make a hundred dollars tonight."

Still complaining, Ryan pulled a handful of bills

from the cash register. When he held them out to me, I leaned across the bar, kissed his cheek, and said, "Thanks, pal." I grabbed the money and ran.

Dani lived on Park Avenue, where the stately buildings had unobstructed views of Central Park, four, five, or six bedrooms, terraces, fireplaces, maid's quarters, formal dining rooms, and doormen to ensure your privacy. The only difference between these doormen and those in the less exclusive buildings is that it costs more to get by them.

Eighty bucks is what it cost me that night. But I believe in installment plans: forty on the way in, forty on the way out—if he didn't call ahead to warn Dani.

He took the two twenty-dollar bills and pointed me to an elevator. "Twenty-seven," was all he said.

The elevator opened to a small lobby furnished with nothing but a large wall mirror and a small antique table. A large crystal vase filled with fresh exotic flowers sat on top of the table. If the doorman had sent me to the right apartment, Dani lived behind the wide double doors across from the elevator.

I rang the bell. A dog barked wildly. The noise should have been loud enough to wake anyone inside the apartment, but it took three more rings before the door opened. The man who stood behind it stared at me with annoyance. I stared at him with interest. About six feet tall, curly black hair, a dark shadow of growth on his chin. Thin and wiry; I saw ribs beneath his dark chest hair.

He felt my eyes examining his physique and quickly pulled the maroon bathrobe closed. "We didn't order anything."

"That's good, because I'm not delivering anything. I'm looking for Dani. I hope I didn't wake you"—I noticed the thin sheen of sweat on his forehead and smiled—"or interrupt anything."

He turned and bellowed "Dani! Company!" Then he turned back to me and said, "You might as well come in. It's going to take her a few minutes to put some clothes on."

Before he could change his mind, I darted inside. Without bothering to ask my name or how I'd arrived unannounced on the doorstep, he slammed the door behind me, yelled Dani's name again, and wandered away.

I stood in the vestibule and waited, listening to the dog's high-pitched barking. When no one came to invite me in—or throw me out—I walked down a narrow hallway, carefully lifting my feet so I wouldn't scuff the Oriental carpet. As I walked, I also admired the oil paintings on the wall. No paint-by-numbers for Dani Dexter; these had been created by Monet, Renoir, and Picasso.

Low bookshelves lined the walls. Almost every well-worn book told the story of a financial scandal. From Robert Vesco to Joe Jett, Dani's collection covered them all. I pictured her hunched over the books, studying them to learn which scheme had worked and which had failed.

The hallway ended in a stark and startling room. Chocolate-colored wooden floors gleamed, making the white walls and furniture as brilliant as an arctic glacier. Two kidney-shaped mirrors flanked a white marble fireplace, bouncing the light from the crystal chandelier back into my eyes.

Wishing I had my sunglasses, I blinked and walked over to the glass wall. Beyond the terrace, the city sparkled through the floor-to-ceiling windows. I saw the shadows of Central Park and the skyline of the West Side beyond it. I was trying to pick out the Dakota, the only building distinctive enough for me to recognize, when I heard footsteps behind me.

I turned. Dani's outfit, a shapeless green sweatshirt that hung to her knees and skintight pants with a horrible lime-green-and-orange-paisley print, was even more bizarre than my jerry-built disguise. Her makeup was smudged; her hair sweaty and rumpled.

I thought about offering her a cigarette, but settled on another apology for interrupting. Obviously I'd interrupted something more passionate than an evening of watching sitcoms.

Dani ignored my apology and rudely asked, "What do you want? Did you change your mind about working for me?"

"I came to find out why George Walden talked to you on the night he died. Very shortly before he died."

"You're too late. That sexy young detective has already been here. He asked questions remarkably similar to yours. Did you two consult before coming here?"

I took a deep breath and silently counted to ten.

"I'm not cooperative, am I?" Dani flashed a very insincere smile. "That's no way for me to convince you that I'm innocent, is it? I'll tell you what I told that cop: I don't know what George wanted because I didn't talk to him. I was in London, remember?"

Dani turned and pushed open the terrace doors; a blast of cold air rushed into the room. Motioning for me to follow, she stepped out. The faint wind carried the sounds of the traffic up from Park Avenue to where we stood. Dani rested her arms on the broad railing and stared out at the city.

"You see all this—I earned it. I worked hard to get into this building; I'm not giving it up without a fight. I was born in coal country, Pennsylvania. My parents never had an extra dime. They never went out to dinner. Dairy Queen was a treat for them. They never went to the movies. Never went farther than Niagara Falls—and that was on their honeymoon. You know where they are now? On the QE2, cruising around the world. I sent them away so they would escape this misery."

"How touching." I didn't feel the slightest bit of sympathy for her melodramatic tale. "I don't care about your parents, their vacation, or your rags-to-riches story. What about George Walden?"

Dani shrugged. I tried to shake her complacency. "I found out who turned you in."

Dani shrugged again. "It doesn't matter. I didn't do anything wrong. Those jealous assholes should have spent more time working and less time making up stories about me. I was successful. They weren't. Jealousy—that's why someone tried to frame me."

"A different type of jealousy motivated this person."

Dani stiffened. I waited to let her worry expand. "Jealous ex-lovers will do anything for revenge."

"What are you talking about?"

"Mariah Becco. She was angry because you tossed her aside for George Walden. Was George upset because you dumped him for your live-in doorman? Is that why George kept calling you?"

Enough light spilled out of the living room for me to get a clear view of the look on Dani's face. She looked amused, not stunned. It wasn't the effect I'd been hoping for.

"Mariah—my ex-lover?" Dani was having trouble keeping herself from laughing. "What a load of bullshit. You don't believe that, do you?"

"Should I?"

Dani turned away and looked downtown toward the Empire State Building. "Two women become good friends and people assume they're lovers. I thought you were smarter than that. Did you come here to ask if I prefer sleeping with men or women?"

The wind picked up; I moved back against the sheltering wall. "I don't care who you sleep with. I came here to find out why George Walden called you the night he died."

"George wanted me to save him." Dani shook her head. "Stupid fuck. No one could save him, not even his precious father-in-law."

"Save him from what? Why did Walden think you could save him? You don't look like a savior. You look like you'd flatten anyone who dared show a weakness."

Dani whirled around and glared at me. "Fuck you, too. George Walden was a pitiful jellyfish of a man. He got his job because he fucked the boss's daughter. Then he married that bitch just to guarantee lifetime employment."

I coldly said, "And this from a woman who once told me that George Walden was her friend."

"Walden was in over his head. He didn't understand the markets or the way I traded. I tried to teach him, but he was too stupid. Everyone took advantage of him and he didn't even know it. All George knew was that his department's profits were going down—when they should have been going up. He pushed me to take too much risk, to make questionable trades. When I wouldn't do it, George started trading on his own. He faked profitable trades in my accounts."

"I'm having trouble following you, Dani. The other day, you said that Gary Preston and his gambling debts were the cause of your troubles."

Anger flashed from Dani. "Are you calling me a liar?"

I didn't give Dani a chance to calm down. "So why do you suppose George was calling you?"

"Probably to beg me to change my mind."

"Change your mind about what?"

"I was heading a risk management committee. We were supposed to recommend ways to tighten up our trading policies."

How convenient for someone who's ripping off her company.

Dani didn't notice that I hadn't responded. She rushed on, "That's how I stumbled onto George's fake trades and huge losses. My mistake was not going to management. George got there first. He blamed everything on me." Dani shivered and folded her arms across her chest. "The bastards didn't have the nerve to confront me. You know how I found out they'd fired me?"

I don't mind playing the straight guy if it leads to useful information. I said, "I give up. How did you find out?"

"When I showed up for work, I got red-lighted."

"Red-lighted?"

"It's the modern version of the pink slip. The

building has one of those space-age security systems. You stick your pass into a slot, a little green light comes on and the door unlocks. Overnight, those bastards deactivated my card. When I stuck my card in the slot, I got a red light. Two security guards came out. They took my useless pass and told me they'd mail my personal effects."

Dani's voice shook with anger. "That's what they called it, personal effects. Like I was some stranger who'd died. Then they escorted me out."

Dani was either a great salesperson or I was too tired to be cynical. For the first time that evening, I believed her. "What did you do after that?"

"I went to a friend's office and wired all the money out of my accounts. I knew they'd freeze them—when they got around to thinking of it." Dani hesitated; I was supposed to believe that she was measuring her words. "I know it sounds cold, but I was only trying to protect myself."

That delicate hesitation didn't convince me. It had the opposite effect: my suspicious nerves started tingling. "How much money did you move, Dani?"

"About one point five million in cash. Another five or six in stocks or bonds."

"Trading is much more lucrative than I imagined."

"If you're good. And I was good. Very good," Dani said arrogantly. "Kembell Reid paid me a four-million-dollar bonus last year."

"Some people might think that draining your account of six, maybe seven million dollars is a sure sign of guilt."

Her composure remained intact. "You don't know how many times I've heard that. What would you have done—left the money at Kembell Reid so they could grab it and leave you penniless? Come on, I'm not an idiot. I'm Gary's easy way out. Think about it. Who would you throw to the SEC wolves? Your son-in-law or a trader? A woman trader."

My patience finally cracked. "Now you're going to toss discrimination into the fray. How about a little sexual harassment, too? Keep flinging excuses until you find one that sticks."

"Bitch." Dani's anger boiled over again. She took a loud, indignant breath. "Grace said you were good. She didn't tell me that you're worse than the men."

I grinned at her. "Thanks. You know, Dani, you're building a strong set of reasons why you hated George enough to kill him." I smiled again. "Got any sharp knives around here?"

Whoosh! Dani's story changed again. "George Walden knew his ice castle was melting. He didn't want to be the only one to go down so he tried to make a deal with the SEC. A lot of people had good reason to silence him."

My head spun from her quick reversals and sprints to a new theory. "A deal? Why would Walden need your help to make a deal?"

"Because I have proof that would clear him—and me."

I was cold, hungry, and tired of Dani's endlessly changing stories. I snapped, "And what might that be?"

"My proof will wait until you're working for me. Not Gary Preston."

"Keep your little secret, Dani. I'm trying to find out who killed George Walden. That's all I care about. Not you. Not Gary Preston. Not unless one or both of you killed him." When my heated sermon didn't impress her, I said, "If that's true, aren't you afraid that the same people who killed George might try to kill you?"

Dani turned back to her glowing city. I took a step closer to hear her soft answer. "I have protection."

Chapter 16

I gave the doorman the forty bucks I'd promised him and had just enough money for a cab ride home. I sat in the back of the taxi and rested my aching head on the back of the seat. *More motives than a barrel of monkeys.* That nonsense phrase kept running through my mind as the cab wove through the after-theater traffic to the Village. It would take me days to sift through the layers of bullshit and decide if anything Dani had said was true.

I didn't get home until a few minutes after midnight. I trudged up the stairs, put my key in the lock; the door swung open without warning. I nearly fell into Dennis's outstretched arms.

"Blaine, is everything okay? I went to the View and you weren't there. Ryan told me that you'd gone rushing out—"

I stood on my tiptoes and quickly kissed him. "Sorry, I should have called, but I didn't want to wake you up—again." I pushed Dennis back so I could get inside the house and kicked the door closed behind me. "I've been out lead-hunting, my dear. No time to inform my patient, long-suffering husband." I didn't give Dennis any more details. After all, he does work for the FBI. I kissed him again. "Ready for bed?"

"More than ready. You go on up; I'll lock up."

I slowly climbed the stairs, shedding clothes along the way. I walked into the bedroom and dumped my load of clothes in an untidy pile; a night on the floor wouldn't hurt them. I fell into bed and was asleep before Dennis made it up the stairs.

I started Friday morning by sleeping late. When Dennis left, I pushed myself out of bed and outside to run. Running usually clears my head, but this morning the fog only thickened. Dani and Eileen were too complicated to be sweated out on a five-mile run. After a few halfhearted miles, I gave up and slowly walked home, kicking at the leaves and the trash on the sidewalk.

I dressed in jeans and a turtleneck sweater. Shoes instead of sneakers were my only concession to Eileen's preference for more formal clothes. I was halfway down the subway stairs when I remembered the hundred dollars Ryan had loaned me. I wheeled around and hurried back up to the street to find an ATM. I withdrew enough cash to repay the loan and hurried down the street to the bar.

I expected to find Bobby or Ryan inside the View preparing for the weekend rush; I didn't expect to find the door unlocked. Cautiously pushing it open, I slipped inside.

The bar smelled of the previous night's beer, cigarettes, and greasy hamburgers. Some of the smoke still lingered, leaving behind the spooky atmosphere of a low-budget horror film.

The View isn't large, but it's filled with nooks, crannies, and small rooms that are used for private parties or storage. Voices floated out from the back of the bar, from the office, or maybe the kitchen. A prickly feeling ran across the back of my neck. Instead of calling out the guys' names, I quietly walked to the back of the bar, wishing I had a gun.

The voices moved toward me. I grabbed a pool cue from the table and stepped back into the shadows near the bathrooms. Gripping the stick like a baseball bat, I strained to hear what was being said.

I heard a deep voice, not Bobby's, but couldn't make out the words. As the voices came closer, my heart started pounding louder. I tightened my hold on the stick.

Bobby and another man, who was burly enough to play on any of the local pro-football teams, turned the corner and looked at me. No, they didn't look at me. They stared at me. Stared at me like I had escaped from a locked ward at Bellevue.

"Kinda early for a drink isn't it, Blaine?" Bobby glanced at my flimsy weapon; the questioning look on his face changed to a smirk. "Oh, I see, you came for a game of pool. By the way, this is Kurt. He delivers Budweiser."

I blushed. There's no way to unobtrusively put a cue stick down, especially when you've been caught ready to swing it at somebody's head. Both men were courteous enough to not comment as I casually lowered the rod and rested it against the wall.

"It's never to early to visit you, Bobby. I bet you'll look a lot happier when I give you this." I pulled the money from my jeans pocket and waved it in the air. Bobby snatched the bills and made a grand show of counting them.

"God bless you, dear. Ryan confessed to emptying the till for you last night. Poor boy couldn't sleep all night." He slapped the deliveryman on his

back and nearly sent him flying across the room.
"He kept worrying that this lady here had run off
with our money."

"He was probably more afraid that you wouldn't
stop hounding him until I paid up."

"So that's why you're here at the crack of dawn.
Good thing Kurt had an early delivery or you'd be
out in the cold."

Kurt mumbled something about having other
customers waiting and left in a hurry—like he was
afraid I'd grab that pool cue again and start whack-
ing him. Bobby went behind the bar and stuffed
the bills into the register. "You know, Blaine,
maybe we should start opening in the morning.
Business is good; we had another visitor this morning. If you'd been here ten minutes earlier, you'd
have met her." He sighed. "Problem is, none of
you bought anything."

"At least I gave you money." I pulled a stool
out and took a seat. Pointing to the hot plate next
to the cash register, I asked, "Is that coffee fresh?
I hope so. If you're going to tease me and tell
me riddles about your morning adventures, I need
coffee. Lots of coffee."

Bobby filled two thick ceramic mugs. One for
me, one for him. He hopped over the bar and sat
next to me.

I sipped the coffee and smiled. Strong and hot,
just the way I make it. "So, who came a-visiting
this morning?"

"Well, it wasn't a nasty robber like you thought.
Were you really going to bash that guy over the
head?" Bobby smiled and patted my arm. "Thanks
for the thought. Good thing you didn't have a gun."

"Good thing. What about your visitor, Bobby? Anyone I know?"

"Beats me; she didn't say. She wanted to know what we'd told the cops about your dead man. Blaine, honey, I get the feeling people are more interested in this guy now that he's dead than when he was alive."

"You may be right." I yawned and drank more coffee. It didn't help. I yawned again. "Who was this mystery woman? Cop or a reporter?"

"I dunno." Bobby shrugged. "She was waiting on the doorstep, pacing back and forth like I was hours late for an appointment. Wouldn't give her name, so I wouldn't answer her questions. Wouldn't even let her inside. Kept her rude, blond, bitchy, twitchy butt out in the cold."

I'd been slumping down until my head nearly rested on the bar, but Bobby's words made me sit up and look at him with interest. "Blond and bitchy? What did this bitchy lady look like?"

"Hard to tell. She was wearing a very expensive full-length mink coat and hat with bleached blond hair sticking out. Good thing those animal rights people weren't out or there would have been a riot." As an afterthought, he added, "Short. She was pretty short."

"Bobby, you're so tall, everybody looks short. How short?"

Bobby closed his eyes so he wouldn't see me laughing and blurted out, "Short. About an inch shorter than you."

"You call that short? Bobby, I'm five-eleven."

Trying to redeem himself, he quickly said, "Horrible makeup. Joan Crawford would have been proud."

Dani Dexter. It couldn't be anyone else. "Did she look like Faye Dunaway playing Mommy Dearest?"

"Yeah." A lopsided grin spread across Bobby's face. "That's exactly what she looked like. Anyone you know?"

I nodded and gulped down the rest of the coffee. Dani Dexter, who not quite ten hours earlier swore she didn't know who George had been calling or where he'd been calling from. Dani Dexter, who swore she'd been in London the night Walden was murdered. At least Dani didn't have a good night's sleep.

When I got to the office, Eileen was out. Before settling down to the paperwork, I called Grace Hudson. Calls to Grace never required small talk about the weather or the family. Grace doesn't have time; when you call her, you do your business and hang up.

This time, Grace surprised me. She said hello, then asked, "Your sister and your niece. How are they?"

"They're fine, thanks." I tried to turn the conversation to business, but Grace kept coming back to Eileen and Sandy. Where did they live? Who was watching over them? Did I still think Don was a threat?

I answered each question as briefly as possible. Grace listened and asked questions until she sensed my growing impatience. "Sorry, Blaine. Don't mean to pry. You were worried last time, that's all. I wanted to be sure everything was okay."

Instant guilt. I apologized and went back to business. "I called to—"

"—ask for money. You run through the retainer?"

"Well"—I made a quick calculation—"not quite, but give me a few more days and it will be gone. I have some expensive plans that we need to talk about."

"You're asking permission?" Grace sounded surprised. I hurried to explain.

"I'm about to run up the tab. You need to know what I'm going to do and agree to it."

"It's okay. Don't care about money."

Clients who ignore my reports and say they don't care about costs often turn into irate ex-clients. I protested, "No, Grace, that's not good enough. You have to close your door and listen to me for a few minutes. You're my client now. You follow my rules or I'll quit."

"I don't believe you'll quit. You don't give up."

I rubbed my forehead and wondered if I had any aspirin in the desk. "That's right, I don't quit. But giving up is different from firing an uncooperative client."

Without saying a word, Grace dropped the phone on the desk. I counted to three, heard a door slam in the background, and counted to three again before I heard Grace's voice. "Go ahead. Talk."

It took less than five minutes to tell Grace how little I'd managed to accomplish, how I hoped to learn more from being inside Kembell Reid, and how the police seemed to have lost interest in George Walden's murder. Grace didn't ask any questions until I finished.

"Dani Dexter?"

I've known Grace for so long that her habit of

speaking in short, clipped sentences doesn't bother me. I listen to her verbal shorthand and automatically fill in the blanks.

"I'm not sure about Dani. One minute she has me thinking that she's an innocent victim. Then she starts spinning around, trying out one story after another, hoping one will stick, and I'm convinced she's guilty. Have you ever met her, Grace?"

"No. Your plans sound good. You start Monday?"

I told her I did. Satisfied with my answer and my plans, Grace said calls were waiting and abruptly hung up. I sat with my hand on the phone for a few seconds, feeling vaguely dissatisfied with our conversation. It had been brisk, even by Grace's impatient standards. But I'd done my job; I'd kept my client informed. I could go on spending her money without worrying—at least for another week or two.

Dennis spent most of the weekend working—I spent most of the weekend alone. By Monday, I was anxious to start my new job.

Chapter 17

I pushed the heavy revolving door and spun into the John Street building where Kembell Reid's trading operations were housed. A man, too busy scanning the front page of the *Wall Street Journal* to watch where he walked, plowed into me. His briefcase snagged my panty hose. He yanked it away, leaving a little hole in the stocking; there'd be an ugly run by the time I reached my new assignment. No apology, just a jab in my back with his newspaper to move me out of his way—that's all I received from the short, balding man. Welcome to Wall Street.

I already had my pass; a temporary version of the one that had given Dani a red light. Mine worked. It got me past the security guards without them giving it, or me, a second glance, and in through the locked doors on the fortieth floor.

A buzz of noise engulfed me. The room, about the size of two football fields placed end-to-end, had long rows of counters running from one end of the room to the other. The chairs were filled with young men and women; only a few of them appeared to be more than forty years old.

Two, sometimes three, computer monitors were stacked in front of each person. Talking and yelling into telephones, or intently staring at a monitor, they ignored their neighbors and scribbled on pads. No one noticed me standing in front of the glass doors with a confused, uncertain look on my face. I asked one of the youngsters for directions. He snarled at me, grabbed a telephone, and shouted into it.

The woman sitting behind him crumpled a sheet of paper and threw it over her shoulder. A perfect shot. It hit him in the back of his head and dropped to the ground.

I picked up the paper and dumped it on her desk. "Bull's-eye. You have good aim."

"I get lots of practice. Jobey's a real pain in the ass—on a good day. And it's been a while since he had a good day. He's been losing money." She called over her shoulder. "Isn't that right, Jobey, darling? You're swimming in the toilet this morning."

He cursed and said, "Market's not open yet, Gretchen. Even you should know that by now."

Instead of making the sharp retort I expected to hear, she laughed. "That means you have half an hour before you go under. Get out the life preservers. Jobey's jumping in."

Jobey muttered another curse and picked up one of his ringing telephone lines. "It doesn't matter anyway. Give it another month or two and we'll all be out of work. Did you see the article in the *Journal* today? The SEC is going to close us down. They never should have let a woman handle big trades."

Gretchen's good-natured smile spread across her face, making her look much too young to be sitting forty floors above Wall Street, waiting for the market to open so she could trade bonds valued at millions of dollars. She swung her chair around, leaned over, and tapped him on his shoulder. Once again, I was surprised by her response.

"You'll pay for that, buster. Tonight could be the night the honeymoon ends."

"Honeymoon?" I nearly stammered with surprise. "You're married? To him?"

Gretchen's face reddened. "Six months. Jobey's a sweetheart—when he's not working. Speaking of work . . ." She glanced down at the telephone console in front of her; a half-dozen red lights were flashing. "Are you looking for somebody?"

"I am." I fumbled in my coat pocket, found an index card, and unfolded it. Gretchen watched, her patience stretching to the snapping point. I blushed. "Sorry. I'm looking for—" I glanced at the card and read the name, "Morley McGovern. Where I can find him?"

"Whorely? Just wait right here. He'll be around in a second or two to yell at somebody. Probably Jobey."

"There must be some mistake." I studied the paper. "Personnel told me to ask for Morley, not Whorely."

That naive comment instantly identified me as the new kid on the floor. "You must be Whorely's latest temp."

I nodded shyly. "Is it that obvious?"

"Anyone who doesn't know Morley and Whorely are the very same monster has to be new around here. The man's a prostitute. He'll do anything—oh, forget it. Complaining will only get me in trouble and get you fired before you even sit down."

Gretchen pointed to a man on the opposite side

of the room. "That's Morley. Be careful, temps don't last long around him."

Morley McGovern towered above the waist-high cubicles. His hair was as white as his crisp shirt. Even from across the room, I saw an angry gleam in his eyes. The irate glare swung at me. He hurried over and snapped, "Are you my new girl?"

"Temp. I'm your new temp."

"Yeah, whatever." Morley peered at me with suspicion. "You're not one of those libber freaks, are you? Because if you are, you can get the hell out of here. I don't have time for hysterics."

I started to answer, *not unless they're yours,* but clamped my jaw shut. Instantaneous dislike for the man swelled my temper, but I didn't say anything. Blaine Stewart, the temp, couldn't afford to lose her temper—and her job—before she even started it.

My silence encouraged Morley to bully me further. "You're late. I expected you here at eight-thirty."

I took a deep breath and tried to sound apologetic. "I'm sorry. The lady in Personnel said to be here by nine."

He muttered something that sounded like *temp time* and impatiently snapped his fingers. "Come on. We don't have all day."

I trailed behind him, trying to take it all in without looking too interested. We walked past more rows filled with clean-shaven young men and an occasional woman. They didn't watch our strange procession; they were too busy focusing their attention on the voice blaring from the tiny speakers on their desks—or maybe they were just trying to hide from Morley's venom. The voice rumbled on about interest rates, currency fluctuations, and other things that meant nothing to me.

Morley stopped in front of a large office. Through the flimsy curtain that covered the glass panel, I saw a large, gleaming desk—not quite as large as Gary Preston's—matching credenza, an oval conference table and chairs, and a few nondescript plants in gold buckets—standard Kembell Reid furniture. A gleaming gold nameplate identified it as Morley's domain.

"You know how to answer a phone?" I nodded. "Good." He pointed to the small cubicle. "Sit there and answer the phone. Tell people I'm in a meeting and I'll call back when I get a chance. Make sure you get their numbers right."

"Okay. I can do that." I tried to sound uncertain. "Is there anything else?"

He jerked his thumb toward an adjoining cubicle. "Kendra will be back in a few minutes. She'll fill you in on the other stuff. Just don't screw up those messages. Last temp couldn't get the phone numbers right."

Orientation over, my boss disappeared.

I looked at the cubbyhole that would be my home away from home. It wasn't much bigger than a large cardboard box and had even less personality. The previous occupant had stripped everything personal. A computer, telephone, message pad, and a handful of pens were all that remained.

The phone rang. I draped my coat over the low wall and got to work.

By the time my new neighbor appeared, I had answered a dozen calls, switched my sneakers for the heels that I had carried in a Macy's shopping bag, and scrounged a hanger for my coat. The woman who would be sitting beside me wasn't impressed. She stood about four-eleven, maybe five feet tall—in her two-inch heels. From the scowl on her face, I could only assume that her feet hurt. The bright red suit she wore matched the angry red flush on her cheeks and neck.

"Moved in already. That didn't take very long, did it?"

"Not really." I smiled the friendliest grin I could muster and introduced myself. "You must be Kendra. Mr. McGovern said you'd fill me in on everything I need to know."

"Oh, *Mister* McGovern said that, did he now? You can tell Mr. McGovern to kiss my ass. I told him I won't train a replacement."

I love unhappy employees—they're so anxious to talk about their mean bosses and their horrible jobs. All they need is a little sympathy. "I don't mean to pry, but is something wrong?"

Kendra said bitterly. "I'm fifty-five years old. Where do you think I'm going to find another job that pays this much money? Where do you think I'm going to find another job? I'm too old to start over again."

"So why don't you stay?" The frown Kendra shot at me made me wince. I wanted to apologize, but didn't. I continued prying. "They told me your old boss was gone. Is that why you're leaving?"

Tears welled up in her bloodshot eyes. I resisted the urge to comfort her and waited. Kendra didn't answer; she pushed her chair back and fled. The chair rolled into a filing cabinet and toppled over on its side.

Morley chose that moment to return. He scowled

at Kendra's disappearing figure, then at the over-turned chair. "Where's she going?"

"The ladies' room. Her stomach's upset. I think she has a touch of the flu or something." I handed Morley a neat little stack of messages and casually righted Kendra's chair. "Is there anything you want me to do?"

McGovern snarled, "Just answer the damn telephone and don't fuck up the numbers."

I stood waiting as Morley flipped through the message slips. He pocketed a few of them and dropped the rest on my desk. He went into his office and slammed the door behind him. I stood there watching him. My new boss was quite an ass.

The door was too thick for me to hear anything, but I watched McGovern pace back and forth as far as the cord would allow. He spent fifteen minutes on one call, then banged the phone down. McGovern slouched in his chair and sat staring at the shiny desktop until he sensed that I was watching. He stormed out and flew to my desk.

"What do you think you're doing?"

"I—"

"You listen to me." Morley leaned down until his face was inches from my ear, close enough for me to smell a trace of his aftershave.

"If you think you're going to sit here and spy on me, you'd better think again. They may have put you here, but I don't have to keep you. If you want to keep your job, you'd better remember that you work for me—not them."

I didn't try to defend myself. Satisfied that I was cowering under his attack, Morley walked away to attend to his very important business. I went back to waiting for the phone to ring.

It was nine-thirty. My boss hated me. The other secretary was hiding in the bathroom. When—if— she came out, she probably wouldn't talk to me. I had nothing to look forward to—nothing but another seven and a half hours of answering the telephone. I sighed and picked up the ringing phone.

All day long, I answered McGovern's damn telephone and scribbled names and phone numbers on Kembell Reid's carbonless message pads. Some of the messages he took, the rest got tossed back on my desk.

In between calls, I took the discarded messages and made a list of those names. Then I consulted the message pad and made another list of the people important enough to receive a return call. Each time I entered a new name on a list, I searched the corporate phone directory and tried to match a title to the name. By the end of the day, I had two tidy lists of names and not a single clue about what to do with them.

All day long, I made believe I didn't notice that Kendra ignored me, refused to answer my questions, and that she wished I would flee in tears. I didn't cry. I kept chattering away, seemingly too cheerful to notice her foul mood.

The first day of any undercover job is exhausting. You use a lot of nervous energy trying to make people believe your story. At the same time, you're watching and judging everyone.

Any excess energy I had went to reining in my temper. Whenever Morley walked by, he'd fling a snide comment at Kendra and pause to watch her reaction. Kendra ignored him—she was good at that.

By five, I felt drained and ready to go home to

bed, not to the office to face Eileen and whatever problems had erupted during the day. So I went home. But first I took the precaution of taking a subway to the Upper East Side, getting off and walking around Lenox Hill Hospital until I was convinced that no one had followed me. Then I took a cab home—I'd earned the luxury.

Hoping that Dennis was home and that we'd be able to have a quiet evening together, I unlocked the door and stepped inside. The lights were on; I smelled garlic. Dennis was home. Better yet, Dennis was cooking dinner.

I called out hello, threw my coat over the banister, and made my way to the kitchen. Dennis had his back to the door. Busy searching the spice rack, he didn't hear me—or pretended to not hear me—sneak up behind him. I wrapped my arms around his shoulders and kissed the back of his neck. I dropped my head on his shoulder and closed my eyes. His flannel shirt smelled like sunshine and warm fields.

"I'm home, dear."

"So I noticed." Dennis pried my arms apart to give him enough room to turn and kiss my cheek. "How'd it go today? You look tired."

"I am tired."

Dinner was on the verge of burning. Dennis pushed me to a chair and hurried back to the stove. He started stirring and said, "Tell me about it."

I slumped down and propped my head up with my hands. In between yawns, I said, "I have the most boring job on earth and a boss who's the biggest jerk on earth. And I have to go back in the morning."

"Will a big bowl of spaghetti with clam sauce help?"

I thought for a moment. "It could. Red or white sauce?"

"White. And plenty of garlic bread. You'll reek. Your idiot boss won't come near you."

"In that case, bring on the food."

Wishes can come true. We managed to have an evening without a single interruption—one of the last times that would happen for a long time.

As fall chilled to winter, New York City turned ugly. Or maybe it was my mood that caused me to see nothing but beggars, drunks, drug addicts, prostitutes and their pimps, rude people pushing and shoving me out of their way, and garbage— always garbage—filling the streets.

You need a sense of humor to survive in Manhattan and somewhere, somehow, mine had disappeared. Ground to bitter dust by my daily trudge from a cold home to a subway car packed door-to-door with commuters sweating in their heavy coats to a day filled with ringing telephones and mind-numbing chores to another subway and another office filled with stacks of messages and reports that screamed for attention to Eileen who grew thinner but didn't want my attention and back home to fall into bed for four or five hours of exhausted—but dreamless—sleep before it started again. I also learned WordPerfect's latest release and that Morley McGovern was an award-winning asshole.

Chapter 18

At first, Morley and Kendra kept me pinned to my desk, answering the phone and typing endless versions of memos. But eventually they loosened their grip. One day, when Kendra slipped away for lunch and Morley was nowhere in sight, I grabbed a stack of research reports and stuffed them into an interoffice mail envelope. With the envelope tucked under my arm, I started roaming.

My new friend Jobey, the hapless trader, noticed. He grabbed my arm as I walked past him, squinting at cubicles in my search for a nameplate.

"Hey, Blaine, my favorite temp. What are you doing so far from home?"

I tapped the envelope and frowned. "Trying to deliver wayward mail. But I seem to be having a bit of trouble finding a particular occupant. Perhaps you can give directions."

Jobey grinned, happy to be helpful. "To whom is this special delivery going?"

"Mariah Becco."

His grin deepened. "Alas, dear temp, your poor little feet will be unable to carry you to Ms. Becco's door. Unless, of course, you have a pair of water wings stashed in that envelope."

I shook my head. Keeping up with Jobey's conversations required a clear head. "What are you talking about?"

"She's gone. Across the pond to jolly ole England. Back to the home of the now-divorced Chuck and Di. The Queen Mum. London Tower. Scones and tea. The Rosetta Stone. Double-decker buses. The Changing of the Guard."

"Stop with the tour guide rap. So Mariah's in London. When does she get back from her vacation?"

"Not a vacation." Jobey shook his head but couldn't hide his glee. "The woman packed her bags and went back to her homeland. She didn't like the land of Yankee Doodle Dandy." He dropped his voice to a conspiratorial whisper. "We were mean to her."

I leaned closer and whispered back, "What did we do to her?"

"Blamed her for our troubles. Mariah didn't want to be our scapegoat, so she took her toys and went home."

"Oh." I turned the manila envelope over in my hands. "Then I guess she won't be needing this junk mail. When did this happen?"

"A few weeks ago, I guess. It's hard to say; no one made much of a fuss when she resigned."

"Mariah quit? She wasn't fired?"

"No, dear temp. No evidence that the brilliant trader did anything wrong." He leered and twisted an imaginary mustache. "Would you like to hear my brilliant thoughts on the subject?"

"I live for your brilliant thoughts on any subject, Jobey. What do you think?"

"She missed her mommy."

*   *   *

I should have been an actor. It didn't take McGovern long to decide I wasn't a spy. That I was too much in need of a job now that my fictitious husband had left me to survive on my own to risk losing my job by complaining about my boss. McGovern assumed I was too dumb, too scared, to be interested in his personal affairs—that's when I started to learn things.

I learned that McGovern was desperately afraid of losing his job—with good cause. Ever since he'd inherited the department, McGovern had lost a dozen of his trading stars to the competition. The department's profits and morale were plunging. As hopes of bonuses faded, the surviving traders openly polished their résumés and met with head-hunters. Gary Preston increased the pressure for McGovern to revitalize the operation. McGovern responded by throwing temper tantrums and loudly rebuking anyone who didn't meet his performance standards. The warlike atmosphere made the rest of my life seem like paradise.

It also didn't take long to make a few friends on the fortieth floor. It started when I crept into the bathroom one morning to sneak a smoke. Remembering my junior high school days, I checked the stalls to be sure the place was empty, then lit a cigarette and managed to smoke half of it before the door opened. Disappointed, I took one last drag and turned the water on to extinguish the cigarette.

Gretchen walked in and started laughing. That wasn't very unusual—she was laughing every time I saw her. "Gotcha. Don't you know those things are bad for you?"

"Yeah, I've been thinking about quitting, but . . ." I ran water over the butt and listened to the sizzle. "Smoking is better than punching Morley McGovern in the nose."

"That bad?"

"Yeah, he's worse than usual today. That little bastard thinks he's a god or at least a king. I'm getting tired of him and his ego." I sighed. "If I didn't need this job . . ."

"What's your story?"

I made sure the cigarette was out, then tossed it in the garbage. "I don't have a story."

"Yes, you do. Every temp who passes through here has a story." Gretchen leaned against the low counter and folded her arms across her chest. "Come on, I have time. Tell me your story."

Finally someone was interested in the new temp. Convinced that Gretchen was asking out of kindness, not suspicion, I sighed. "There really isn't much to tell. I was married for fifteen years. I'm not anymore. I need this job because my lousy ex had a better lawyer. His checks are barely enough to live on—when he bothers sending them."

Gretchen quickly calculated my age. "You got married pretty young, didn't you?"

"Right out of college. He was a few years older, just finishing law school, and landed a great job that paid more than we ever imagined. I never had to work." Echoing the bitter laugh Kendra had used on my first day at Kembell Reid, I laughed. "There aren't many jobs for someone with a fifteen-year-old B.A. in English Lit. That's why I'm here. It does pay more than Burger King."

"Why don't you do something about it?"

"Find a lawyer to sue a lawyer?" I let out another bitter laugh. "It would be easier to win the lottery."

Gretchen smiled sympathetically. "Well, maybe Whorely will hire you. You've been here longer than any other temp. After a day or two, most leave in tears. But, you know, you're screwing up the office pool."

"The office pool?" I raised my eyebrows. "You've got to be kidding me. You're betting on how long I'll last?"

"Don't take it personally, Blaine. We bet on everything around here. You're upsetting all the guys. Almost everyone bet on less than a week."

'How long did you say?"

A sly smile crept across Gretchen's face. "Three weeks. I liked your style when you walked in here and got between me and Jobey. So do me a favor? Hang on for another week before you quit. There's three hundred bucks in the pot. I'll buy you lunch if you stay long enough for me to win."

I almost believed Gretchen's offer, but the twinkling green eyes gave her away. I laughed. "Let me think about it. But you'd better tell the guys to drain the pool. I'm staying. I can't afford to leave. Do you know how hard it was for me to find this fucking horrible job?"

I paused to ask a hopeful question. "Do you really think Morley might hire me? It would be great to have medical insurance. It's so expensive. I . . . Oh, forget it. I'm tired of talking about my problems. Can I ask you a question?"

"Sure." Gretchen's dark hair bobbed up and down as she nodded her head. "Go ahead, ask."

"What's going on around here? One second everybody's happy. The next, it's a morgue.

Morley . . ." I shook my head. "I'll never understand that one. Anyway, what's going on around here? It's not what I expected."

Gretchen's smile was filled with pity for my innocence. "How do we disappoint you?"

"You guys don't strut around like you're masters of the universe. You just sit in front of your monitors, work all day, and then clear out after the market closes. You people are dull."

Anger burned through Gretchen's smile. "Sorry we're not exciting like some silly movie. We're trying to earn a living—that's all. And hoping that when we come to work in the morning we don't find out that the company's been closed down. Don't you read the newspapers?"

I was born with the ability to blush on demand. It came in handy when I was a child, when I started dating, and when I started doing undercover work. I shook my head and summoned up a blush. "Most of my newspaper reading has been limited to the want ads. I'm not following current events."

"If you were, you'd know that Kembell Reid isn't the most secure place of employment. If the government gets its way, we'll all be out of work."

Feigning ignorance, I gently questioned Gretchen. So gently that she never realized I had turned her into a fountain of information. Unfortunately, the information trickled out of her—it didn't flow. Gretchen didn't tell me anything I didn't know, except that most of the traders—men and women—blamed Dani Dexter. Only a slight handful felt otherwise.

Was Dani a sacrificial lamb or conniving bitch? The winner of that office pool had yet to be decided.

I went back to my desk feeling like I was banging my head against an unyielding, uncaring wall. The image of George Walden's body was fading. How much longer would Grace allow me to waste her money?

I also made some enemies. Actually, I only made one enemy: Kendra. For a reason known only to her, I became the evil that was driving her from Kembell Reid. Spending eight or nine hours a day sitting next to a person who hates you isn't fun. Kendra's mean-spirited slights, her petty insults, and the way she managed to get McGovern to chew me out for the slightest offense wore me down.

After one particularly trying morning, I casually rummaged through Kendra's desk while she was at lunch. I looked at her family pictures, pushed her spare house keys around to the other side of the drawer, and flipped through her checkbook and address book—just to be mean. I went back to my lifeless desk, feeling just a tiny bit happier.

And so the days dragged on.

"Stewart! Get in here." Before McGovern bellowed my name again, I grabbed a pad and rushed into his office. "Close the door," he ordered.

I did, congratulating myself for not slamming it. "Yes, Morley." He glowered at me. He insisted on being called Mr. McGovern. I refused.

I stood before his desk and waited. McGovern stared at me with distaste.

"Where's Kendra?"

On another day, I might have fabricated a story to cover for her absence, but not that day. Kendra had been ruder than usual to me that morning. In return, I didn't feel an obligation to protect her. "She hasn't come back from lunch yet."

"And when did she go to lunch?"

"About twelve." Morley glared at me. "Okay, she left a little early."

"How early?"

"About eleven-thirty."

Morley looked at his watch with an exaggerated movement. "It's almost two-thirty. Where is she?"

I didn't like Kendra, but my dislike wasn't strong enough to get Morley after her. I shrugged. "I imagine she's still at lunch."

"Come on, Stewart, don't be stupid. Kendra is never late for anything. She's too afraid she'll get fired. How long were you going to wait until you said something to me?"

All day, if necessary. I bit the inside of my mouth and held my smart answer back. Since it was obvious that McGovern wasn't going to ask me to sit, I dropped into a chair.

He frowned.

I frowned.

"Morley, I haven't seen you since ten o'clock this morning. Did you expect me to interrupt you—"

"Don't sit there. Go find her."

"What?"

"You heard me." He shouted, "Go find her. I called those idiots in Personnel to find out what to do about an AWOL employee. Spoke to the big bird herself. Carol said to send you to find Kendra. I don't know why she thinks you can do it, but that's what she said. Find Kendra and bring her back."

"Aren't you panicking over nothing? Maybe

Kendra's having a long lunch with friends and forgot to mention she'd be late."

McGovern's face reddened. He didn't like having a temp question his authority. "She missed a two o'clock meeting with the SEC. You don't miss meetings with the SEC to have a long lunch with a bunch of giggling old buddies. Find her."

Chapter 19

I didn't move.

"Jesus Christ, what are you waiting for? An engraved invitation? Get going."

"I'm not jumping at your command, Morley. Answer a few questions and I'll be on my way."

Morley's face turned crimson. Recognizing the signs of a grand tantrum, I quickly said, "I need to know Kendra's home phone number, where she lives. What do you want me to do when I find her? Simple stuff like that."

"Don't waste time calling her house. She's not there. I've been calling for forty-five minutes and getting nothing but her answering machine. That's all you need to know. Get going."

I waited patiently until Morley got the message that I wasn't moving until he answered my questions. Glaring with contempt, he grabbed a file and tossed it at me.

"Here's a copy of her personnel file. The U-5 form has Kendra's current address and where she's lived for the past ten years."

Now that the file was off his desk, Morley looked relieved. He sat back. I waited for him to rub his hands together with satisfaction, ridding himself of responsibility.

"Any idea of where she might have gone?"

"How the hell should I know? You're the one who sits next to her. You must have noticed shopping bags from the stores she goes to or heard her calling friends. Go ask around the area. See if anyone remembers seeing her."

"Who was Kendra supposed to meet at the SEC?"

Morley didn't like the confident woman who had inexplicably replaced his timid temp. He snapped, "You stay away from the SEC. I don't want you screwing around there while you're playing detective."

I flipped through the meager file. It had nothing but an application form and annual reviews inside—not much to show for Kendra's fifteen years with Kembell Reid. I closed the file and looked at Morley with suspicion. "This can't be the whole file. Where's the rest of it?"

"Stewart, for Christ's sake, I'm not asking you to investigate a murder. That gives you enough to go walk around the block and ask people if they've seen Kendra O'Donohue. You got that?"

I reluctantly let go of the file. "I guess so."

"Then get the hell out of here. Don't come back until you find her. I did some sweet-talking and managed to get her meeting postponed, but only for a day. Take the rest of the day. You have to find her."

"Okay," I said reluctantly. "What do you expect me to do once I've found her?"

"Call me. If I'm not here, I'll be at home." McGovern scribbled on the back of a business card and handed it to me. "Here's my home number. Call me, no matter how late it is. Don't call anyone else. Just me. You got that?"

"Don't you think—"

"Don't think, Stewart. Thinking will only get you in trouble. Just do as I tell you and you'll be fine."

I stared at Morley until he shifted uncomfortably, then I walked out of the room. McGovern followed me. I sat at Kendra's desk and fished her spare keys from their hiding place in the bottom of her filing cabinet.

Morley stood beside me with his hands on his hips. He quickly regained his nasty composure. "What are you doing? I thought I told you—"

"I know what you told me." I peeled a photo of Kendra and some friends from the side of the monitor where she'd taped it. "I thought it would help to show people a photo of Kendra."

I opened the top drawer of the desk and pulled out Kendra's address book. "I also thought it would help to have her friends' phone numbers in case I have to call them."

I searched for Kendra's calendar, but it was gone. I slammed the drawer shut with a lot more force than necessary. "Now I'm going."

For once, Morley was speechless.

I stopped at the row of telephones in the lobby and dialed Kendra's house. The phone rang five times before her machine answered. Feeling slightly foolish for having been sucked into Morley's hysteria, I left a brief message asking Kendra to call the office and hung up.

The absurd sensation increased as I started walking into the stores, delis, and restaurants that surrounded the building. After a few tries, I developed a routine. I'd walk in and patiently stand near the cash register until someone noticed me and asked if I needed help.

"Yes." I'd hold out the picture of Kendra. "I'm looking for this woman. Have you seen her? She never came back after lunch—we're worried."

No one remembered seeing her. By four, I admitted defeat—and apprehension. As much as I disliked Kendra, I couldn't imagine her just walking away from her job without a word of warning to anyone.

I called Morley. When he answered, on the first ring, I quickly asked, "Has she come back yet?"

"No, she hasn't. Does that mean you didn't find her?"

"That's right, Morley. I visited every store within ten blocks of the office. No one's seen her."

"Do you know what I think you should do?"

"I can't begin to guess."

"Go to her apartment. If she's not there, wait until she gets there. I want to know where she's been."

I had already decided that Kendra's apartment was my next stop, but I wasn't going to let him off that easy. "And what if I tell you that I have plans for this evening?"

McGovern's laughter grated in my ear. "Is that what they call a rhetorical question? I hope so. 'Cause if that's what you were really telling me, I'd be telling you to find another job."

Such an understanding man. I hung up the phone and hailed a cab.

Kendra's apartment was on Seventy-seventh Street, right around the corner from Lexington Avenue. Typical of the area, the brick building was short and squat. A row of garbage cans lined the front of the building; window boxes hung in each window; the skeletons of summer flowers swayed in the wind, gently brushing against each other.

As I walked up to the building's door, I heard sirens as ambulances pulled up to the emergency room of nearby Lenox Hill Hospital. The wailing noise reminded me to add hospital emergency rooms to my list of places to search.

With that cheery thought in mind, I fumbled with the keys until I found the one that unlocked the outside door. Kendra's secretary wages didn't give her the luxury of an apartment in a building with a doorman. As I went through the same routine to unlock the lobby door, I guessed that once inside Kendra's apartment I wouldn't find panoramic views of the city.

The aroma of freshly baked bread filled the stairwell. I climbed to the fourth floor, propelled by a fantasy of Kendra throwing aside her job to rush home to proof yeast, knead dough, and fill the oven with loaves of sourdough, rye, or pumpernickel bread.

I'd ring the bell. When Kendra answered the door, flour would be streaked across her forehead from when she had used the back of her hands to brush away beaded sweat. She'd laugh at my concern and invite me in for a slice of warm bread, fresh from the oven. We'd drink tea and laugh at Morley until it was time for me to go home.

I have a very vivid imagination.

Chapter 20

A thin sliver of light seeped from beneath the door to Kendra's apartment. She was home. A sigh of relief escaped from my lips, but the tension didn't leave my shoulders. It wouldn't until I saw Kendra's face.

I rang the bell long enough to rouse even the deepest sleeper. Telling myself that maybe Kendra wasn't home—and not believing it—I dug in my purse for the keys, unlocked the door, and stepped inside to a long, narrow kitchen.

Kendra either loved to cook or she was a compulsive shopper. Every inch of the room was filled with cooking equipment. Neat glass canisters filled with rice, beans, spices, and pasta lined the counter. Gleaming copper pots and sauté pans dangled from hooks on the wall. Two blocks of professional chefs' knives stood between a cappuccino machine and a food processor. A coffee bean grinder, pasta machine, chrome salad spinner, waffle maker, stainless steel toaster, bread machine, and other gadgets took up the rest of the available space.

The kitchen was coldly spotless and sanitary. I shuddered. I couldn't imagine any joyful feasts being prepared here.

"Kendra?" I strained to hear an answering voice over the soft guitar music coming from deeper inside the apartment, and added, "It's Blaine. From the office. Kendra?"

I didn't waste time conjuring up images of Kendra napping on the sofa. Squaring my shoulders, I quietly walked through the small dining area to a large room that served as Kendra's living room and bedroom. A sofa and two chairs were crowded in front of the windows. A tall divider ran through the room, hiding Kendra's bed and giving the appearance of a separate room.

Kendra sat in an old-fashioned wing chair, the type my grandmother used to have in her parlor, a place we could go into only on Christmas Day to admire the tree. Grandma would gather up our presents and walk out of the room to the huge kitchen where she spent every waking hour. She never had to tell us to leave the living room because we'd follow, squealing with delight.

Kendra was the type of woman who had never, ever squealed in delight. She never would, either.

The knife that had been drawn across Kendra's throat decided that. Rivulets of blood dripped from beneath the scarf that had been neatly wrapped around her neck. The front of her white blouse was soaked with blood.

I brushed Kendra's cheek with the back of my hand. The skin was cold; I couldn't find a pulse or any sign that air was moving through her lungs. For a brief moment, I considered starting CPR, but didn't—it would be a futile gesture, done more for my benefit than hers.

"Kendra." I dropped into the chair opposite hers and stared at the body. Too late again. How many times had I been too late? How many more times would it happen before I decided that I couldn't—wouldn't—do it again?

I sat there for a few seconds, rapidly spinning from guilt for my mean-spirited thoughts about the living Kendra to anger at another meaningless murder. Anger won.

I jumped out of the chair and quickly searched the apartment. The rumpled bedspread and black glove on the floor next to the bed were the only things out of place in the apartment. The rest of the place was too spotless, too neat for me to search without leaving noticeable signs of snooping. Too neat for Kendra to have been overpowered by an uninvited guest. Too neat for the body in the chair to be the handiwork of a burglar surprised in the act.

With all my suspicious nerves tingling, I left the apartment and locked the door behind me. In the elevator on the way down to the lobby, I dug through my wallet to find Chris Hutchinson's card.

"Chris, it's Blaine Stewart." I pictured Hutchinson frantically trying to place my name and prompted his faulty memory. "The woman who tripped over George Walden, remember?"

Much too quickly, he said, "Of course I remember. How could I forget? Did you come up with something—or somebody?"

"Not somebody. I found a body."

"Another one?" He sounded incredulous. "Where's this one, in your backyard?"

"It's not your precinct. But I called you because it's related to your case."

"Oh, yeah." Suspicion colored Hutchinson's

voice. "And which one might that be? Wait, let me guess—George Walden."

"Right."

He sighed with resignation. "Why is this one related to Walden? And has the medical examiner said it's murder? By the way, Blaine, who's dead?"

"First of all, it's Walden's ex-secretary. It sure looks like she was murdered. Unless, of course, she slit her own throat."

"It's been done before."

I ignored his cynical comment. "She was scheduled to meet with the SEC today. She left her office at noon and never went back. Never showed up at the SEC, either."

"How do you know that?"

I sighed. "It's a long story, Chris. Do you want me to tell it to you now or wait until you get here? After all, there is a body that needs to be picked up."

"Where's here?"

I gave him the address and asked, "Do you want me to call anyone else?"

"Don't bother. Stay right where you are; I don't want to have to go scouring the neighborhood to find you."

After promising that I wouldn't move, I called Dennis and told him I didn't know when I'd be home. I was fighting off the urge to light a cigarette when Chris Hutchinson's car pulled up at the curb. He ignored the sign warning that it was a no-parking zone and climbed out.

He had on the same worn leather coat that he'd been wearing when we first met. He was still without a partner. His partner's flu must be an especially powerful strain; I briefly thought about calling Dr. Mabe for a flu shot.

Hutchinson didn't say hello. He impatiently snapped, "Come on. Show me the victim."

I repeated my fumbling at the door while Hutchinson fidgeted beside me. I led the way to the elevator, feeling Hutchinson breathing on my neck. As the elevator moved up to Kendra's floor, he pulled his tattered notebook from an inside pocket and flicked it open. "You called at five thirty-seven. When did you find the body?"

"Somewhere between five-fifteen and five-thirty. I didn't look at my watch."

Hutchinson grunted that I should have and stopped asking questions. When we reached the fourth floor, I led him around the corner to Kendra's apartment. I pulled the key chain from my pocket and held it out to him. The lucky rabbit's foot swayed back and forth.

"Where did you get the keys?"

"From Kendra's desk. In her office." His eyebrows raised. I gently dropped the key ring in his outstretched palm and said, "I work in the same office. That's part of my long story."

He slid the key into the lock and opened the door. "Wait here."

I leaned against the wall and did as Hutchinson ordered: I waited.

It took Hutchinson only a few minutes to confirm my diagnosis. The detective came back out in the hall and said, "She's dead, all right."

After that, I was on my own. He pulled a cellular phone from his jacket pocket and started making calls. I continued leaning against the wall. When

Hutchinson finished, he turned the phone off, stuck it back in his pocket, and turned to me.

"What did you touch? You had enough time between finding the body and calling me to take a good look around. I'm sure you didn't waste any time pawing through everything."

"Give me a break. I know enough to not disturb a crime scene." I shook my head. "I touched the door on the way in and out. I touched her to see if I could do anything. . . . I sat in the chair across from her; I probably touched the chair's arms. That's about it."

"So tell me your long story. We have time."

And so I told my story, interrupted by the Crime Scene Unit and the others who arrived to investigate and, eventually, remove the body. Hutchinson would leave me for ten, fifteen minutes at a time to go inside for a consultation, then return to me. He always picked up exactly where we'd left off.

When I finished, Hutchinson stared at his notebook and asked, "Tell me something. Did you lose an earring inside?"

My hand involuntarily moved to my ears. Both earrings were where they belonged—but then Hutchinson could see that with his own eyes. I didn't answer.

"We found an earring under the chair the victim was sitting in. She had two earrings on. So it can't be hers."

The detective's easygoing tone set off alarms in my head. My eyes narrowed. "You're not suggesting that I slashed Kendra's throat, lost an earring in the process, and just happened to be carrying a spare pair, are you?"

"Not when you put it that way. It sounds too

stupid for even me to believe. Can't blame a guy for trying, can you?" The detective laughed and rubbed his forehead with the back of his hand. "Now you're thinking I'm nuts, right?"

"Well . . ."

"My sense of humor sucks—that's what my wife says. It's really bad on nights like this."

I must have been overtired, because I gave into Chris's attempt to wring sympathy, and cooperation, from me. I made an offer I couldn't believe. "Chris, you once suggested that we work together. Now, I'm not in the habit of offering my services to the NYPD—"

"I know, I know. You told me that. You've done your duty." The detective pushed an unruly strand of hair from his eyes. "So what changed your mind?"

"I'm already inside the company. If you don't blow my cover, I'll sign on as your partner—"

"—unofficial."

I nodded. "Very, very, very, very unofficial. As long as the public record continues to show that I'm a struggling temporary secretary."

Hutchinson didn't even stop to make believe that he was considering my offer. "As long as you share information and don't try to hide it from me, I'll keep your real job out of the reports. Don't fuck me or I'll be looking for work. And that will make me a very unhappy man. You see, all I want to do is get through my twenty and retire to a cabin in the Adirondacks. The only things I'll shoot at are deer that don't shoot back. I don't want to be some jerk who once had a promising career and threw it—and his pension—away on some asshole P.I."

The long speech surprised both of us. He blushed and stuffed his notebook into his coat pocket.

Still feeling uncharacteristically kind, I said, "I gave up heroics years ago, Chris. I just don't want to flush the work I've done in the past couple of weeks down the toilet. Keep me out of your investigation—and the papers—and I'll fill you in on everything I learn. I promise. No holding back."

I don't know why, but Detective Chris Hutchinson decided to trust me. "I think we're done for now. Want a ride home? We've got more than enough guys in uniform standing around gawking. I can get a car to chauffeur you." Hutchinson grinned. "It's the least I can do for my new partner. I'd take you myself, but it's gonna be a while before they remove the body. Of course, you could hang around and wait until I'm done."

Remove the body. I didn't want to hang around and watch. "Thanks, but I'll find my own way home."

Chris nodded. That unruly lock of hair fell across his eyes again. He impatiently shoved it aside. "I'm going to have to interview the people Kendra worked with. I assume we'll cross paths."

I said good night, walked around the corner to Lexington Avenue, pulled out my phone, and dialed Morley's home number.

A mild-voiced woman answered. Before I could say hello, Morley snatched the phone away. He growled, "What took you so long? Where's Kendra? Did you find her?"

I started to answer. Morley's voice buzzed in my ear. "Speak up, will you? What are you doing, calling from the street?"

"As a matter of fact, I am. Shut up and listen

for a change. I just left Kendra's apartment." I rushed on, without attempting to cushion the news. I wanted to hear Morley's reaction. "I found her, all right. She's dead, Morley. Dead."

Watching over a floor of traders who dealt with hundreds of millions of dollars each day makes you calm in the face of bad news. Morley didn't sound shocked or surprised. "Are you sure? Did you see the body?"

"Yes. I saw the body. And the blood that flowed out of her slit throat."

At last, Morley was stunned into silence—for only a few seconds. When he spoke, his voice was shaky, but still nasty. "I'll see you in the morning. Get in early, will you? We'll have lots of calls to make."

I walked down Lexington Avenue, finding strange comfort in the cold, numbing air. Without thinking about anything, not even the cold, I tramped from the Seventies to Grand Central Station before my aching calves and frozen nose screamed at me. As if waking from a coma, I blinked and looked around.

Forty-second Street was bustling, but it's always crowded. The daytime commuters and early evening theater-goers had come and gone, leaving the street to hustlers and people searching for a warm spot to sleep. I shivered. The ragged man standing behind a folding table covered with books noticed and grinned.

"Cold night, ma'am. Sure you wouldn't like to take a good book home to your warm bed?"

I looked at him. He was in his thirties; the old army parka he wore was held together with patches and tape. I smiled. "It's a cold night to be out selling books."

"Better to be working in the cold than living in it. Believe me, I don't mind putting in a few hours in the cold, then going home. Least I got a home. Books got me off the street. You wanna buy one before I pack them up for the night?"

I couldn't resist his sales pitch. I grabbed a battered Julia Child cookbook for Dennis, stuffed it in my pocket along with my change, and flagged down a cab.

Dennis was lying on the sofa, watching another basketball game and reading the newspaper. He called out a welcome. I grunted a response and trudged up the stairs to the bathroom. Nothing but a scalding hot bath could wash the smell of death from my skin.

While the tub filled with steaming water and bubbles, I stripped, balled up my clothes, stuffed them into the laundry basket, and pushed it into the back of the closet, far away from my sensitive nose. The sound of the water rushing furiously into the tub drew Dennis upstairs.

I slid down the tub until the soap bubbles touched my chin. Dennis walked into the bathroom and sat on the edge of the sink. "That bad?"

I brushed Dennis's concern away—for the moment—and said, "I brought you a present. It's in my coat pocket."

Dennis gave me a quizzical look and wandered away to find my coat. By the time he returned, the dog-eared book in his hands and the puzzled expression still on his face, I was frowning and swatting at the mountains of bubbles.

Chapter 21

Dennis came back, flipping through the pages of the worn book, ready to tell me how to make a soufflé of something. He stopped short, uncertain about what he should do. "Hey, don't get mad. I like Julia Child."

"That's good. I can't get a refund."

Dennis tucked Julia Child into his pocket, crossed the room in one long stride, and knelt beside the tub. "What's wrong? What kept you out so late? You're not hurt, are you?"

"Not hurt. Just sick of tripping over bodies." I slapped at the defenseless bubbles again. "I'm frustrated."

I told Dennis about searching for Kendra and finding her body. I finished with, "Morley McGovern is such an asshole."

Dennis started to say something wise, but I interrupted him. "Do you know anyone at the SEC? I need someone who can put me in touch with the people working on Kembell Reid. I want to find out why Kendra was going to meet them."

"Nope. I can't think of anyone." Dennis rose to his feet and started to the bedroom. "But I'll bet a dinner with Julia Child that your sister does."

He came back with the phone. I grabbed a towel from the floor, dried my hands, and dialed Eileen's house. Sandy answered. After a few minutes of chatting about school, I asked for her mother. Sandy said okay and handed the phone over.

Eileen didn't sound quite as happy as Sandy. "Hi, Blaine. I missed you at the office. I wanted to stick around until you showed up, but Sandy got impatient."

"Good thing you left. I never made it there." Quickly, before Eileen asked why and I had to tell the story about Kendra again, I said, "It's a long story. I'll tell it when I see you. In the meantime, I need to talk to someone at the SEC about Kembell Reid. My wise husband thought you'd be able to get me a name."

Eileen's address book is thicker than my unabridged dictionary. It rarely lets me down, but Eileen was reluctant to start making calls at eight in the evening. "Can this wait until tomorrow?"

"No." After taking a deep breath, I briskly said, "A secretary from Kembell Reid was supposed to meet with the SEC this afternoon. She never made it to that meeting. She got killed instead. I found the body. I need to know what the SEC hoped to learn from her."

"Give me an hour or two." Eileen sounded doubtful. "Maybe I'll be able to come up with a name for you. Are you staying home tonight?"

"Home in the bathtub. That's where I am now and where I intend to stay for a while longer. After that, I'm not going anywhere except bed. Do me a favor? If I've gone to bed, leave the name and phone number with Dennis."

"What makes you think—"

"Because I know you, Eileen. You'll stay up all night waking people up if you have to because it's a challenge. Just don't make me one of those people you wake up."

Eileen laughed, promised to do her best, and hung up. While I was on the phone, Dennis had wandered away with Julia Child, too engrossed in reading recipes to listen to my conversation. The radiator clicked; the soft hiss of heat rising from the furnace filled the room. I added more hot water to the tub and thought about Kendra.

The sterile apartment didn't have any family pictures on the dresser, or paintings from a young niece or nephew hung on the refrigerator. I didn't remember overhearing any calls from friends or lovers, never heard her mention an evening out with an old friend from college. Who would mourn for her?

Even though Morley had taken extra care dressing that morning, he still had the furtive air of a man who expected to be tapped on the shoulder and accused of stealing the fancy pinstriped suit off the rack. To be honest, he looked like a thug. He stood in front of my desk, for once fumbling for something to say. I didn't help him.

"Stewart," I refused to acknowledge his presence. Morley cleared his throat. "Stewart, did you—I mean, are you okay? Tell me what happened, but tell me fast. The police are on their way over here. They want to talk to people who worked with Kendra, probably you too. I couldn't think of any reason to keep them out."

Suspicion raced through me. "Why would you want to keep the police away? I'd think you would want to do whatever you could to help the police."

"Don't misunderstand me. I want to help." Insincerity colored Morley's voice; I didn't believe anything he said. "I just don't want cops wandering around here upsetting everyone. . . ."

That old line again. I wondered if Gary Preston had put out a memo telling all managers to use that excuse.

"Don't worry, Stewart, we'll do what we can to help. I've got a sales meeting to run. You keep an eye on the phones."

"That's it?" I still held hopes that Morley could act like a normal human being. He kept crushing those misguided hopes beneath his sleazy heel. "That's all you're going to do, run a sales meeting? Aren't you going to tell people what happened? Shouldn't you notify someone? After all, Kendra was an employee."

"The markets don't close just because somebody died, and I don't have to answer to you." Morley's jaw hardened into an angry line. "Keep it up and you'll be an ex-employee, too."

I clenched my fists and clamped my mouth shut. Morley watched until he was satisfied that I would cower and obediently follow orders. He gave me a smirk and turned away. My palms itched to slap him. Instead, I reached for the telephone.

Morley started to the conference room for his sales meeting. He was halfway down the hallway when he whirled around and shouted, "Hey, Stewart, call Personnel, will you? Tell them we need to start interviewing people—unless, of course, you want a permanent job." He laughed, turned the corner, and disappeared. I waited until the sound of his laughter faded, then dialed Carol Walden's office.

"What happened?" Carol Walden's voice rose to

a hysterical pitch. "Are you telling me that some-one in this company was murdered last night? Why didn't someone tell me?"

I calmly said, "I'm telling you now, Carol."

"You're telling me?" Her voice rose to a higher, disbelieving tone. "You are supposed to be a tem-porary secretary. Why are you calling me? Where's Morley?"

I ignored the disdain in Carol's voice and cheer-fully told her, "Morley's running his morning sales meeting. The police should be here soon."

"The police?" Carol's voice dropped to an icy hiss. "Get Morley. Now."

"He told me he didn't want to be interrupted."

"I don't care. Get him. You tell him I want to talk to him. Now."

A shadow fell across my desk. I looked up at my visitor. "Carol, maybe you should come down here instead. The police just arrived."

Carol ordered me to say nothing and slammed the phone down. I replaced the receiver and smiled at Chris Hutchinson. "At last, a human being. These people are nuts. Every single one of them."

"I take it a bigwig is hustling down the stairs to intercept me before I can interview the underlings. I love the cooperation." Chris pried the lid off the cardboard cup in his hand and took a long swallow of coffee. "Stuff's not bad. I got it from the truck parked outside. Would have brought you one, but I didn't want to look too friendly."

I muttered, "Friendly doesn't do a damn bit of good around here. Did you come up with any-thing new?"

"In the ten hours since I saw you? Well, I wasted several hours by sleeping. The rest of the time has been wasted waiting for an autopsy report. It was a bloody night in the Big Apple—they've got a line of corpses. So they only had a preliminary report. But I don't need an autopsy to tell me she bled to death." Chris took another sip of coffee and switched to a different topic. "How long you been here, three, four weeks?"

"Longer than that. I've been here for an eternity."

Chris's grin cheered me more than a cup of coffee and cigarette could have. "In that eternity, did you ever see Kendra wearing this—and its mate?"

He laid a small plastic bag on top of the computer monitor. I picked the bag up and shook it. The large pearl earring inside bounced around. "I don't remember seeing this. But that doesn't mean a thing. I spent most of my time avoiding Kendra."

"What about the scarf? Did you ever see her wearing that?"

I closed my eyes to visualize Kendra's wardrobe. "The woman had a lot of clothes."

Hutchinson reached inside his coat and pulled a Polaroid snapshot from his breast pocket. He slapped it down on my desk. I glanced at it and saw the scarf—still wound around Kendra's neck. "Take another look."

I flipped the photo over to hide the gruesome image. "Nice. You sure know how to ruin a day."

The detective ignored my sarcasm. "The scarf has a weird design on it. Kind of like an abstract thing. Some kind of intertwined symbols. Not the type of thing you'd buy from a street vendor for five bucks. We're trying to track down the manufacturer, but the label seems to have been removed."

I tapped the photo. "Are you going to show this to everyone? If so, bring some barf bags. This is a pretty brutal thing to be showing the woman's coworkers."

Carol Walden and Morley McGovern appeared at the same time, ending our discussion about the photo. I slipped it into my pocket before anyone noticed. Carol glared at Morley. Morley glared at Hutchinson, then at me. I folded my arms across my chest and sat back to watch.

Morley started the battle. He looked at our visitor and snapped, "Who the hell are you?"

"Detective Christopher Hutchinson. I'm investigating the murder of Kendra—"

"Yes, yes. We know about that. Tragic. If there's anything I can do, you just let Blaine here know."

Chris didn't like the interruption. "Who are you?"

Morley disappointed me. He introduced himself and moved the group to his office. The door closed firmly behind them, ruining all chances of eavesdropping. While they were busy, I pulled the note Dennis had left on the nightstand from my wallet and dialed the number that Eileen had left. The man answered immediately, as if he expected my call. We made plans to meet at lunch and hung up.

The conference in Morley's office continued. The reddish tint on Morley's neck and cheeks told me that things weren't going well for my boss. The heavy door muffled the sounds of the raised voices inside. Suddenly, the discussion ended. The trio filed out, silently, unhappily. Carol Walden nodded at me. Morley ignored me, but hovered within earshot. Chris Hutchinson stopped in front of my desk.

"Your boss said I could use the conference room

to interview people. He said you'd set it up and
fetch people as I need them. To save time, we
might as well start with you."

Morley protested. "Wait a minute, she's got work
to do. Didn't you ask her enough questions last
night?"

Hutchinson turned his official glare on Morley.
He didn't have to say a word; the look said enough.
After warning me to not be gone for long, Morley
stomped back into his office and slammed the door
behind him.

The more contact I had with Chris Hutchinson,
the more I appreciated his subtle sense of the absurd. He shrugged his shoulders and said, "Okay,
Ms. Stewart. Why don't you show me this conference room and we'll get started? The sooner we
start, the sooner we'll finish and you can get back
to your exciting job."

"Jealous? You know, Chris, I have some influ-
ence with Personnel. Just say the word, you can
start in the morning."

He laughed. "Tempting, very tempting. But, you
see, I have this pesky murder case to solve."

I stood up and stepped away from my desk.
"Well, then, follow me. We'll find a nice, quiet
place to talk about it."

To get to the conference room, you have to walk
the length of the trading floor. I'd gotten used to
the commotion and barely noticed the bedlam
caused by ringing telephones, shouted orders and
instructions, and raucous celebrations after a
profitable trade. Chris walked beside me, taking in
the action with interest.

The markets weren't doing well. We passed rows
of glum faces. One distraught trader sat in front of

his monitors shouting *fuck* over and over again. The people at the stations surrounding him paid no attention; neither did I.

Chris stopped as if to offer solace. I grabbed his arm and pulled him along. "Bad day," was the only explanation I offered.

The quiet and opulent conference room was a world away from the high-tech clamor of the trading room. The long table and its twenty chairs didn't come close to filling the room. A sideboard, made of the same gleaming wood, took up one wall. The windows on the opposite wall opened up on a spectacular view of lower Manhattan.

I shut the door and leaned against it. "Okay, let's talk."

After an appreciative glance at the view, Chris collapsed into a chair. "Kendra wasn't awake when she was killed. She had swallowed a dozen or more sleeping pills."

I carefully studied Chris's face for a hint of his thoughts. "Overkill?"

"I've seen it before. Someone wanted to make sure that the woman was dead. Dead without any of the messy, noisy struggling that happens when you try to cut someone's head off. Her windpipe was partially severed, so were her vocal cords. The fatal wound came when the blade sliced an artery. She bled profusely until she died."

Hutchinson politely waited for me to respond. But there wasn't anything to say. I rested my head in my hands and waited for him to continue.

"Another funny thing. The visitor either wore gloves or took care to not leave any fingerprints behind. We found two fresh tea bags in the trash. Maybe they had tea—"

"And the guest slipped the drugs into the tea?"

"We also found a wine bottle in the trash. You know much about wines?"

"Used to. Why? What kind of wine was it?"

"Opus One. It must cost at least fifty bucks a bottle. Pretty expensive stuff to be swilling on a secretary's salary, don't you think? You know what else?"

Since he seemed to be waiting for a response, I said, "No, what?"

"We didn't find any other booze in the house. No sherry, no beer. Not even cheap cooking wine."

"How much alcohol was in her bloodstream?"

"No more than what you'd expect after a glass or two. Of course, she could have dumped the rest down the drain."

"No way." I shook my head adamantly. "That woman was frugal. I sat next to her for weeks. I watched her take home bagels that were left over from the morning meetings. If she couldn't finish her lunch, she'd leave it in the refrigerator—even if it was only a few bites—and eat the rest the next day.

"Kendra was terrified that she'd retire and not have enough money to live. She was convinced she'd be a bag woman wandering the streets and sleeping in Central Park. Kendra would not have spent fifty dollars on a bottle of wine. If she did, she wouldn't have wasted a single drop."

Chris never got a chance to answer. The door flew open. It bounced off the wall and back into Morley's face.

Chapter 22

"Listen, officer—"

"Detective."

Chris's voice held an unspoken rebuke for the interruption. Morley's bluster faded, but didn't disappear. "Okay, detective. How long are you gonna keep her tied up? She's a valuable member of my staff. I need her at her desk."

"I'll be done when I'm done. If she's so damn indispensable, you ought to give her a raise. I'm sure she's underpaid. Let me tell you one more thing." Chris laid into Morley; I watched with enjoyment. "If you keep interrupting, I'll close this place down for a month or two while I complete my investigation. I'll bring in busloads of cops. I'll wrap yellow crime scene ribbons around the building until it looks like a Christmas package. Think of what that will do to your precious profits. And while you're closed, I'm going to put everything under an electron microscope. How much do you want to bet that we find something the district attorney, the attorney general, and the SEC will want to explore?"

Morley's expression didn't change; only the slow twitch of his left eye gave away his feelings. Chris rammed his point home. "If you think I'm taking up too much of your staff's time, I'll be happy to ask your boss for permission. I'm sure he'll resolve this problem."

"There will be no need for that, detective. As I told you before. I will do everything I can to cooperate."

I avoided Morley's eyes. If he saw the slightest hint of the amusement I felt, he'd retaliate. He'd be bastard boss for at least a week, complaining about everything I did.

Morley's apology flew out in a rushed, run-on sentence. "I'm just concerned that you're using too much of your valuable time with someone who might not be able to contribute anything of lasting value."

"In other words, talking to Blaine is a waste of time."

Morley backed down without appearing to retreat. "Of course not, Detective Hutchinson. I don't mean anything like that, I simply want you to have the opportunity to question everyone. I want to ensure that one person does not monopolize your time. I know the city's resources are strained in this time of budget cuts."

"How kind of you to be so concerned." Hutchinson sounded like he truly believed what he was saying. "Next time I have lunch with the mayor, I'll pass your budgetary concerns along to him."

A man after my own heart. I bit the inside of my cheek and bowed my head so Morley wouldn't see my grin. I didn't dare lift it until I heard the door close behind Morley.

"Chris, these people are insane. Morley isn't the least bit upset about Kendra. He's more concerned about having his damn telephone answered so he doesn't have to do it himself. I can't wait to hear how the others react."

Chris folded his hands behind his back. "Do you really think you're doing any good here? Have you learned anything useful?"

"That's not a fair question." Despite Chris's smile, I felt angry. "I've only been here a few weeks. I'm working my way in—it's not something that happens overnight. If I can keep myself from punching Morley McGovern, I should be okay."

The easy smile didn't leave Chris's face. "Yeah, but what have you learned? We never got around to that last night."

Wishing I had a cigarette, I gave him a brief synopsis. "It's a pretty lax atmosphere around here. People don't pay much attention to the rules, especially if they're making money. Dani was making a lot of money for the firm—"

"Or so they thought."

"Right." I nodded my agreement. "They *thought* Dani was pulling in buckets of money, so they left her alone. People who make money for Kembell Reid don't get questioned about how they do it. To make matters worse, Dani got herself appointed to run a committee that was set up to investigate weaknesses in the system. 'Risk management,' they call it. She got to set up the rules that guided her trading practices."

Chris whistled. "The crook wrote the rules?"

"Something like that. Of course, Dani denies everything. She says she's a scapegoat."

"For what?"

I was doing too much sharing of information and not enough receiving. I answered quickly so the hesitation I felt wouldn't be noticed. "I don't know that yet."

"What about Kendra? How does she fit in?"

"Did Morley tell you about Kendra's meeting at the SEC?"

"He did not." Chris unwound his hands and leaned forward. "Funny how your boss forgot to mention that to me. Do you know who she was meeting?"

"No." I grinned, enjoying my head start. I couldn't tell him *everything*. "But I am meeting with a source who should be able to tell me. I'll let you know the results."

"You work fast."

I nodded at the compliment and hoped it was clear that Hutchinson was not invited to tag along. He read my mind. "Maybe I should come along."

"That's not a good idea. If I show up with a cop at my side, I won't learn anything."

The skeptical look on Chris's face worried me. I immediately added, "You're investigating murders, not trading scandals. You don't have a reason for being there."

"Nice try, Blaine, but what if the trading scandal is the reason for the murders? A murder wave is striking this building. It's more than coincidence, don't you think?"

The Stewart stubbornness reared up. If Hutchinson pushed, I'd cancel my meeting instead of bringing him along. "Why don't you follow official channels? I'll keep on working on the unofficial side."

Chris stared at me, trying to gauge the soundness of our relationship. "I don't have any reason to trust you."

"I could say the same about you." I pushed back from the table and stood up. "I'd better get back to my desk before Morley comes barging in with reinforcements."

Hutchinson stood. He casually blocked my way to the door. Leaning close to my face, he stared into my eyes as if they would tell him the truth about my intentions. "You'll call me?"

I solemnly nodded. "I will."

But I didn't promise to tell him anything when I called.

I ducked my head and pushed the tinted glasses up higher on my nose. The man standing in front of my desk stared at me with puzzlement. "How long did you say you've been working here?"

"Three, maybe four weeks."

"And we haven't met?"

"No." I vainly prayed to be interrupted by a ringing telephone. "I don't think so. Mr. McGovern needs me to stay close to my desk."

"We've met." Harold Wisekopf continued staring at me. "I know we've met."

"Well, you know they say everyone has a twin somewhere on earth. Maybe you met my twin." I smiled. "Now that we've taken care of that problem, can I help you with something else?"

The scrawny, nerdy-looking man couldn't let go of the idea that had gotten into his head. He scratched his wiry hair and wrinkled his forehead. "I don't know . . ."

I scowled. "Look, I've got work to do. If you want to talk about my imaginary twin, come back after five."

In answer to my prayers, the phone rang. I

grabbed it and bowed my head to focus on the message pad. Harold impatiently threw the stack of computer printouts he'd been cradling under his arm on my desk. I put the caller on hold and waited for an explanation.

"Tell your boss that's the stuff he wanted. It's the best we could do on twenty minutes' notice."

Before I had a chance to answer—or scan the pages—Morley showed up. Without saying a word to Wisekopf, Morley grabbed the papers and scooted into his office.

After another lingering look at my face, Harold left, but he didn't leave the floor. He stopped near a row where some of the newer traders sat. Three rookies who always arrived together in the morning and left together at night dropped their phones and warmly greeted Harold.

As they talked, the back of my neck tingled, warning me that I was the subject of their conversation. They talked for a few minutes and sealed the talks with a round of high-fives. After flinging a malevolent glance in my direction, Harold disappeared and quiet descended on the floor.

The calm lasted thirty seconds. It ended when Morley burst out of his office and screamed Jobey's name. Everyone on the floor cringed—Morley was about to deliver another public spanking.

Jobey came running and stood at attention in front of my desk, giving me an unwelcome ringside seat. Morley planted himself about a foot away and breathed fire. Jobey tried to look cool; the thin line of sweat on his forehead betrayed his nervousness.

Morley snarled, "How's your month going, son?"

Jobey undoubtedly grew up cursing his blond hair and light complexion. The flush that appeared

on his face was obvious—even Morley noticed it.
Jobey stammered. "It's going okay. I've a really
strong finish planned."

"Don't tell me what you're gonna do, son. You
worship in the Church of What's Happening Now.
What are you doing now to help the church?
Today. Don't give me any more gonna-dos."

Jobey hung his head and stared at his shoes.
"Morley, I'm—"

"I'll tell you what you're doing. You're losing
money."

"I'm not."

Disagreement only made Morley's temper tantrum more severe. Just like a little kid, he turned
red, stamped his feet, and wailed out a string of
unchildlike obscenities. I watched to see if he'd
hold his breath until he got his way.

Morley waved a sheet of paper in Jobey's face.
"Don't try to bullshit me. I just got the report, had
it printed out 'specially for you. It's right here in
black and white. You're in the red."

"Your report is wrong. Let me take a look at
that. I'll show you where it's wrong."

Jobey held his hand out for the paper. Morley
jerked it out of reach. "Prove to me that you know
how to make money—not lose it. Now get away
from me before I fire your lazy ass."

Jobey turned pale and walked away, his back
stiff and proud. I added Jobey's name to the list of
suspects for the day Morley turned up dead.

With Jobey gone, it was my turn to feel the wrath
of McGovern. Morley glared at me. "Stewart, that
picture in my office—"

"What's wrong with it? Isn't it the one you told
me to order?"

Morley had decided that his new office required brand-new art. For a week, I watched him agonize over the choices. The painting had to be bold—but not bizarre. Corporate—but not stuffy. Classic—but not cliché. Most important, it had to prove that Morley was a man of taste.

Just as I was tempted to order a velvet Elvis, Morley settled on a bright abstract that gave me a headache. But there wasn't anything unusual about that—everything Morley did gave me a headache. The painting had been delivered late the day before and hung that morning while I was with Chris Hutchinson.

"The painting, Stewart. Who hung it?"

A Morley headache started throbbing. "I don't know. Someone from Facilities came while I was away. Why, did they hang it upside down?"

I grinned; Morley didn't. "Yes, there is something wrong. It's crooked, that's what's wrong. Find out who did such sloppy work and fire him."

Morley McGovern had to be from another planet. One filled with primitive, rude, insane life forms. "Wouldn't it be easier to just straighten the picture? I think I can do that without any trouble."

The alien life form snapped. "Don't think. Just do what I tell you. I don't pay you to think."

A thousand replies flooded my head. Morley stomped off in search of his next victim a second before I lost the struggle to keep my mouth closed. I went to Morley's office and straightened his picture.

And then it was time for lunch.

Chapter 23

I went to lunch at the McDonald's on Water Street, the one that's practically across the street from the terminal where the Staten Island ferry docks. Following directions, I bought lunch and climbed the grimy pink stairs to the dining area. The tables were packed, which was okay because I didn't want to sit at a table. As instructed, I sat on one of the stools at the island in the center of the floor and waited. I unwrapped the hamburger and took a bite. My queasy stomach gurgled. I dropped the burger on the tray and sipped the soda. How thoughtful of them to sell me a flat soda. I took another sip and hoped it would calm my stomach. I also hoped Dennis would get home in time to cook dinner—I'd be starving by then.

The man sitting next to me glanced up from his *Daily News* and smiled sympathetically. "Not quite the same as lunch at Bouley, is it?"

"Not quite the same prices, either."

"You wouldn't be Blaine Stewart, would you?"

"I am. And you?"

"Jeremy Ray. You look a lot like your sister."

"I'm glad you spotted the family resemblance. Eileen didn't give me a clue about how I was supposed to recognize you." I stopped short of adding that he had hurried off the phone before I'd been able to ask for a description.

"Closemouthed." The man's smile was warm and genuine as he remembered happier times. "Even way back in law school, Eileen kept everything to herself—unless . . ."

"—unless it's something urgent. She hasn't changed."

Jeremy smiled. "I must say, I was surprised to hear from Eileen last night. It's been a while since we spoke." He paused; the smile dropped off his face. "I don't have much time, so if you don't mind . . ."

I took a bite of a french fry and tossed the rest on top of the burger. "Yeah, I've got one of those clock-watching bosses, too. I have only a few questions. Eileen said you're a staff attorney at the SEC."

Jeremy nodded cautiously. Sensing that he was questioning his decision to meet me, I barreled on. "Is the SEC trying to put Kembell Reid out of business?"

The twinkle in Jeremy's dark eyes hinted that a sense of humor was buried beneath his bureaucratic skin. "No, we're not going to put Kembell Reid out of business. Why should we? They're putting themselves out of business faster than we could."

"How does a trader lose five hundred million dollars without anyone noticing?"

"Welllll . . ." Jeremy reluctantly dragged the word out. "I can't really say. I'm not supposed to discuss that particular case. Our investigations are not a matter of public record."

I waved his limp protest away with an equally

limp french fry. "But you have been working on it?"

Again, my lunch companion nodded cautiously. I gently pressured him to continue. "Hypothetically speaking, how could one trader rack up losses that large? Shouldn't someone have caught it?" I don't understand why people feel more inclined to talk after I mutter the magic word *hypothetically,* but it worked again.

After stirring two containers of cream and three packs of sugar into his coffee, Jeremy patiently said, "You know Dexter was trading government securities, right?"

I nodded. "Yes. I always thought government securities were nice and safe. The type of thing conservative investors buy."

"That's what Kembell Reid thought, too. It made it easier for Ms. Dexter to do her thing."

"Just what was her thing, Jeremy? I'm getting stonewalled by everyone at Kembell Reid."

"This is kind of technical."

"I'm strong; I can handle it. How did Dani Dexter blow half a billion dollars without anyone noticing her, or helping her?"

"It's more complicated than writing a fake ticket for a few thousand bucks for a Treasury bond. That department did more than a billion dollars' worth of transactions last year."

I dryly said, "Half of which were fake."

"Exactly." Jeremy shook his head vigorously. "Dani Dexter put together an intricate scheme. It started when her trades lost millions of dollars."

I knew that. I impatiently asked, "How? I thought Dexter was a savvy trader."

"Not as savvy as she—and everyone else—

thought. Dexter was convinced that interest rates were going up, so she made some pretty big bets. Rates went down; she lost millions. But Dani Dexter, the Wall Street hotshot, couldn't admit that she had been wrong. She buried the losses, faked some winners, and trumpeted those fakes as profitable. When that worked, she realized she was onto a good thing. She started to make hundreds of fake trades that happened to look extremely profitable."

Professional curiosity made me ask, "How did Dani hide the fake trades from her bosses? Weren't there any warning signs?"

"Sure, there were signs. There was one great big sign: the government securities trading desk made too much money."

"That's a warning sign? Wouldn't Kembell Reid's management think that was good news? It proved Dani was a great trader." Even though I knew the answer, I played dumb—I learned more that way.

"Profits were way out of line with the rest of the Street. Other government securities desks of that size didn't come close. It should have flashed a warning signal, but supervision isn't a high priority at Kembell Reid."

Jeremy leaned closer; his voice picked up speed. "It's bottom-line management. If someone's making money, leave him—or her—alone. Don't ask how the money's being made. Let her make all the money she can. Fire her if she stops making money or if she screws up—and gets caught."

I nodded and chewed another french fry. "How convenient."

"Exactly." Jeremy paused to tear open a pack of ketchup.

While he struggled with the plastic, I said, "Dani told me Kembell Reid encouraged her because they needed to keep the shareholders happy by showing good profits. Dani also claims to have proof that Kembell Reid approved her trades—all of them. What do you think?"

Jeremy opened his mouth, then closed it. He was caught between the desire to share and the desire to be circumspect. I gently prodded him. "Eileen thought you would give me some insight into the problems at Kembell Reid. I really need your help. I'm investigating a murder—two murders."

Surprise flickered through his eyes. I pressed harder. "Everything you tell me will be kept confidential. It might help me turn a murderer over to the police."

He bit into his Big Mac and carefully chewed—twenty-three times. I counted.

After glancing around to be sure no one seemed to be too interested in our conversation, he softly said, "Kembell Reid paid hush money to its employees. In exchange for a special payout, these employees agreed to not make any statements to us about the firm. Payments reached a million dollars, sometimes higher."

I whistled softly. "That's a lot of money to buy silence. But what's to stop someone from taking the money and then telling all?"

"Those folks were too smart for that. They didn't pay all at once. Special accounts were set up." He grimaced; heartburn had finally struck. "Deferred compensation, they called it. Violate the terms of the agreement and the account reverts to Kembell Reid."

"Has anyone talked to you?"

Jeremy's eyes darted away to look nervously over my shoulder. "We're running an informal investigation. That means we don't have subpoena power. No one *has* to talk to us. Of course, cooperation is encouraged."

"Has anyone at Kembell Reid cooperated?"

"Oh, of course." Sarcasm filled his voice. "Everyone at Kembell Reid has done everything they can to cooperate. Everything except tell us the truth about what went on. They tell just enough to make my bosses reluctant to grant me the power to go in and take what I want from the files."

"You spoke to George Walden?"

"Walden?" Anger replaced sarcasm. "Do you know he made twenty million dollars last year for running that department? He talked to us. He claimed no knowledge of the fictitious trades. All sixty thousand of them."

"Sixty thousand trades. Must be some kind of record. Is that possible?"

Jeremy snapped, "What do you think?"

"They knew."

"George Walden said he had no knowledge. That's a direct quote."

"Did Walden manage to keep a straight face when he said that?" Jeremy nodded; his eyes sparkled with amusement. "How did he explain his lack of knowledge?"

"Walden told me he gave Dexter an opportunity, a chance of a lifetime. She took advantage of his goodwill." I swirled a fry in the ketchup and thought. If Walden hadn't cooperated with the investigation, why was he killed? Was someone afraid he'd change his mind? "Did you believe him?"

Jeremy's eyes narrowed. He quietly answered, "I

have no reason to believe or disbelieve him. We're still investigating."

"If you had to guess . . ."

"I don't guess about anything."

Jeremy folded his arms across his chest and sat back. He would not allow anyone to force him to guess. I went back to my magic words. "Hypothetically speaking, what penalties does a firm like Kembell Reid face from all this?"

The rule book in Jeremy's mind popped open. "Negligent supervisors could be barred from the securities industry for life."

"Barred for life means no more Wall Street job, right?"

"Not at Kembell Reid. Not anywhere. You're back to flipping burgers, hustling for minimum wage." Jeremy grinned. "Unless, of course, you write a book telling how you were victimized."

"What about Kembell Reid itself?"

Jeremy's grin disappeared, replaced by a grim seriousness. "The firm faces huge fines, suits by shareholders, and lots of bad publicity that could send its customers to other, more reputable firms. Each state's securities division could start looking at them and maybe ban them from doing business in that state. There could be mail fraud charges—"

"In other words, lots of problems." Millions, possibly billions of motives for killing anyone who threatened Kembell Reid's cover-up.

Jeremy nodded and took another bite of his Big Mac. I watched him chew his food, just like his mother taught him, and felt misgivings stir deep inside my stomach.

"I assume you have proof." Jeremy probably lost a lot of poker games; his eyes gave away too much of what he was thinking. I watched those eyes narrow and asked, "You do have proof, right?"

Jeremy hesitated long enough to make me worry. "I'm reconstructing Dexter's trades. I'm hoping that will—"

The remainder of my appetite disappeared. I interrupted. "You don't have proof. You're afraid your investigation is going to die."

"You don't understand how difficult this case has been." His voice rose defensively. "The payoffs I told you about—they stopped a lot of people from talking. Hell, they stopped everyone. Name, rank, and serial number is all I get. And that's from the talkative ones."

I thought of the inane correspondence I'd typed for Morley and asked, "What about files? There must be memo after memo."

"The files have been Hooverized. Vacuumed clean. There's nothing left but take-out menus and football pool results."

I saw the government's case sliding down a shredder. Jeremy did too. He shook his head. "We were hoping to have definitive proof. Unfortunately, our source suddenly became incommunicado."

I took a not-so-wild guess. "Kendra O'Donohue was your source?"

"*Is* my source." Jeremy's voice became heated; he was trying to convince himself that Kendra would still appear and resurrect his case. "We had a meeting scheduled for yesterday; she never showed. I've been calling her all morning; I can't seem to locate her."

"Try the morgue."

The cool bureaucratic facade cracked. "That's not funny."

"It's not funny, but it's true. Kendra O'Donohue was murdered yesterday afternoon. Probably right around the time she was supposed to be in your office."

Jeremy didn't react. I pulled a fry apart and asked, "Was your meeting with Kendra supposed to be secret?" When Jeremy's face showed nothing but confusion, I impatiently asked, "Did Kendra's boss know she was meeting you yesterday?"

Jeremy's voice mirrored my impatience. "Blaine, people who want to be an inside source rarely announce their intentions to their bosses. I assume Kendra did not inform anyone at Kembell Reid about our meeting." Jeremy raised his hands and shrugged. "Why would she? They'd only try to talk her out of it. Whistle-blowers often go through hell as a result of their actions. They may get ostracized or fired. They do not get killed."

"You mentioned a report." Jeremy's big brown eyes grew wary. Had he been hoping that I had forgotten the report? "What happens once it's finished?"

"We make a recommendation to the five SEC commissioners. If they decide to continue, we continue. If not, the investigation ends with no further action."

Jeremy ran his fingers through his close-cropped hair. He didn't look convinced that his report would persuade the commissioners to take further action.

"They may also decide to forward the report to the U.S. Attorney's office. She'll read it and decide if she wants to bring criminal charges."

I wistfully said, "I'd love to see that report when it's finished. Is there any way I could get a copy?"

"You're wondering if I could make you a copy of a nine-hundred-page confidential report?"

"Something like that." I smiled and instantly regretted it. My dazzling smile wouldn't sway this man.

Looking as if he regretted ever meeting me, Jeremy crushed his coffee cup. "Look, you're a nice lady and I respect your sister, but you have to understand something. I'm fifty-eight years old. This job has been good to me; I earn more than I ever dreamed possible when I was a poor black kid growing up in Newark. Better than that, I *like* my job. Don't ask me to jeopardize it by leaking sensitive material to you."

I could argue for a day and not loosen the stubborn set of his jaw. I backed down and tried to sound friendly. "Fine. I'll give you a call in a few days. Maybe you'll see a way to get a copy to me."

"You don't understand. I'm under tremendous pressure to wrap this up. That's what I'm doing, I'm wrapping it up. Don't call me. I won't take your calls."

I wanted to hiss, *Civil servant,* but I didn't. Instead of hissing, I thanked him for his candor, gave him a business card—just in case—and picked up my tray.

I dumped the garbage and headed back to work. After paying six bucks for a minuscule hamburger billed as a quarter-pounder, limp fries, and a soda, cleaning the table was the final insult. For six bucks you should at least get someone to clean up after you.

Chapter 24

I hurried back to Kembell Reid, wondering if Dani Dexter had worked alone. Wondering if George Walden had been murdered to keep him from telling—

A southern drawl interrupted my musing. "Now, that's a mighty deep scowl on your face. Must be the thought of seeing our boss again."

The voice snapped me back to the present. Blushing at being caught in another world, I looked at the man huddling in a little alcove near the building's revolving doors—the smoking section.

Extending my lunch hour suddenly seemed to be a good idea. "Hey, Jobey. I didn't see you behind that smoke screen. Got an extra cigarette handy? I sure could use some nicotine before facing Morley again."

Jobey pulled a pack of cigarettes from his pocket, shook one out, and politely struck a match for me. I lit the cigarette, took a deep drag, and said, "You're the one who should be scowling. Morley was way out of line this morning. He shouldn't be allowed to talk to people that way."

"Around here, when you're the boss, you can talk any way you like."

"Funny, that's not what I hear." I waved the cigarette in the air; the faint smoke track quickly blew away. "I hear prima donnas can do whatever they want. Their bosses don't dare say anything about it."

"Yeah." Jobey shook his head. "Look where it got us. Aboard a sinking ship, fighting to get a life jacket."

I took a quick, nervous puff on the cigarette. "There's one thing that puzzles me about all this."

"What's that?"

"How did Dani Dexter rip off the company without anyone noticing? I read the newspaper articles." I grinned sheepishly. "At least the ones that have been written since I started working here. How could one person do so much damage?"

"It's very simple." Jobey took a hit on his cigarette and watched the smoke drift away. "Speed kills."

"Drugs? That's a new twist."

"Nope, you got it wrong. It's not drugs. It's computers. They've speeded everything up. A trader can write lots and lots of bad orders and *shazam!* The company's gone belly-up before anybody knows what's happening. In a slower world, our esteemed management would have caught her about four hundred and fifty million dollars ago."

"Hey, Jobey, it's too easy to blame our woes on those plastic boxes—I know, I've tried. Isn't there some kind of oversight system to catch bad trades?"

He grinned. "You ask very perceptive questions, my dear naive temp."

When Jobey smiled, I caught a glimpse of a carefree youth now saddled with a lunatic boss who constantly screamed about slipping profits. I laughed and motioned for him to continue. An appreciative audience deepened Jobey's southern drawl.

"However, Kembell Reid is not nearly as perceptive as you. Controls cost money. You have to hire a bunch of people who don't make any money. You have to spend money hiring programmers to write your suspicious little programs. You have to listen to your traders screaming that you don't trust them. Then you start worrying that you're about to lose those big-time traders. Know what happens next?"

I flicked my cigarette butt out to the sidewalk. It bounced once and rolled down the curb. "You dump the oversight."

Jobey sucked as much nicotine into his lungs as he could and ground the butt out with the heel of his tasseled loafer. He quickly lit another one and passed a fresh cigarette to me. I took it just to keep the discussion going.

"Precisely, dear temp. You dump the oversight. Speaking of dumps . . ." Jobey jerked his thumb in the direction of the building behind us. "This dump is going to be filled with pissed-off people next Thursday, all because of Dani Dexter. Good thing they don't carry guns."

I'd heard enough gossip to know that next Thursday was Bonus Day. *Everyone* knew next Thursday was Bonus Day; it was impossible to escape the speculation. Secretaries discussed bonuses in the bathroom. The guys from the mail room delivered the latest rumors every time they dropped packets of mail on my desk. The man who went from desk to desk, shining the shoes of traders too busy to leave, stopped by to share the bonus tidbits he'd overheard.

"How bad do you think it will be?"

Jobey's face reddened; his breath came out in short, angry puffs. I waited for a violent eruption. He kicked a soda can out into the street and smiled happily when a bus flattened it.

"Bad, bad, bad. Worse than bad. That bitch got twelve million dollars last year. This year, I'll get shit because of her. Morley will tell us to be thankful that we're getting anything at all. For once that bastard will be right."

"What was it like before Morley took over?" I dropped my half-smoked cigarette on the sidewalk and ground it out. "Was it better working for Mr. Walden?"

"You've probably heard this a lot, but George Walden really was a nice guy. Too nice to work here."

"What's that mean?"

"Cutthroat land got too rough. Walden was getting his throat cut and he was too nice to fight back."

"Who was cutting his throat?"

"Morley."

Even though it didn't surprise me to hear that Morley had been doing something despicable, I asked, "Why?"

"He wanted to be the boss." Jobey paused to decide if he wanted to continue. "It's common knowledge that Walden was on his way out."

"I thought everyone liked Walden. I've heard so many people say he was doing a good job."

Jobey snorted. "You've got to be kidding. Everyone, me included, walked all over him. Gretchen yelled at me for taking advantage of good old George. But that wasn't the problem."

He stopped and stared out at the street. I followed his gaze but didn't see any familiar faces. Softly, to keep the confessional mood alive, I asked, "What was the problem?"

"George Walden was too honest. Too honest for Kembell Reid. Maybe too honest for the Street." He blushed. "Now, that sounds too stupid for even a romantic southern boy like me to say. Gretchen tells me I'm Faulkner reincarnated." He blushed again and continued, "They say they brought Walden in to clean the place up. He tried. When the big boys—and girls—complained, George was told to lighten up. Or else."

Or else. Was that Kembell Reid's euphemism for murder?

Jobey glanced at his watch. "Break's over. It's time to journey back to Morley-land before he dumps our asses."

Morley was standing in front of my desk, glaring at his watch. I snuck up behind him and cleared my throat. He whirled around and snapped, "Where have you been?"

"Lunch, Morley. I've been at lunch."

"For an hour and a half?"

"Sorry, I got hung up. I didn't think you'd mind."

"Well, I do. Gary Preston's office has been calling."

My stomach turned. I was sick of Kembell Reid and everyone in it. I was sick of being a submissive temp. Or maybe I was just sick to think that Morley stood to make millions of dollars from badgering and belittling the people who worked for him. I couldn't hold back a smirk.

"What's the matter, Morley? You sound frantic. Has answering your phone been too much of a strain?"

"Frantic? When you're out looking for another job, you call me and tell me about frantic. Preston wasn't calling me. He was calling you. He wants you in his office. Now."

I pulled my coat on again and said, "Guess I'll be gone for a while. Is there anything you'd like me to tell Mr. Preston?"

Caught by surprise, Morley blurted out, "You tell him that what happened to Kendra wasn't my fault. You got that, Stewart, it wasn't my fault."

Undisguised fear colored Morley's face. Suddenly, I knew why Kendra had hung on to her job—even after Morley had discarded as many reminders of George Walden as possible. It also explained how Morley knew about Kendra's meeting with the SEC.

Instead of answering, I walked into Morley's office and stood beside his door. Morley followed me in. I slammed the door shut and glared at him. "You were sleeping with her."

Morley tried to look brave. The slight quiver of his eye betrayed his nervousness. "No, Stewart. She was sleeping with me."

I folded my arms across my chest and waited.

"Kendra knew what she was getting into. She—"

"She was trying to save her job. You knew that after George died, Kendra was deathly afraid she'd be fired. You bastard, you took—"

"I took nothing Kendra didn't want to give."

Morley stared at me, trying to convince me of his innocence. He could have stared at me for an hour—I still wouldn't have believed him. "Think whatever you want, but I loved Kendra. She loved me."

Disgust pushed my temper way beyond the breaking point, close to a complete meltdown. "Is that what I should tell your wife the next time she calls? How about your kids? Did they know about the new love in their daddy's life?"

"That's it. I don't want to hear any more of this crap." Morley clenched his jaw—and his fists. "You just remember that you work for me—no one else. You play your cards right and I'll make you permanent. Benefits. Paid vacation. A nice raise. Year-end bonus. You'll make so much money here that you can tell your ex-husband to go fuck himself. Just keep your mouth shut, that's all you have to do."

"And if I don't?"

"Then don't come back here when Preston's done with you." He leaned closer until I saw every red streak in his bloodshot eyes. "It's your choice, Stewart. You don't tell Preston anything about anything that you've seen down here and you'll be a happy woman. Or you can go home and just try to find another job."

Bribery is an effective persuasion device. Even though I didn't know why Morley felt it necessary to buy my cooperation, or what he was afraid I'd seen, I flashed a greedy smile. "There's nothing to choose. I'll do anything for a real job. Especially one with a good salary."

"And benefits."

I echoed Morley's words and mirrored his knowing smile. "And benefits."

Morley smiled, treating me to another view of

his perfectly capped teeth. "Now get your ass out
of here before Preston calls again."

Gary Preston and Carol Walden were sitting at
the conference table, waiting for me. Deep frowns
creased the faces of father and daughter; my appearance did nothing to lighten their frowns. I
paused in the doorway, took a deep breath, and
confidently strode into the room.

Gary waited until I took my coat off and draped
it over a chair before speaking. "It's been another
tough day around here. You seem to be at the
center of this. I want to hear your side of it."

"My side?" I sat and casually crossed my legs.
"I don't have a side. I can tell you what I know.
Then I have a few questions."

"Wait." Preston held up a well-manicured hand.
"I'll ask the questions. Then I'll decide what we're
going to do."

I got up and walked around the room. The pictures on the wall behind Gary's desk drew my attention. I walked around the huge piece of
furniture to look at them.

Horses, horses, and more horses. Horses and
jockeys accepting congratulations from a jubilant
Preston. Horses breaking out of the starting gate.
Horses rounding the turn and heading for the tape.
Horses with celebrities standing next to them.
Horses grazing in a meadow.

"I see you're a horse fan."

"Fanatic is more like it. Daddy's never met a
horse he didn't like."

"I own a few horses. It's my only vice. You
oughta come out to the track some night. We're at

the Meadowlands for the next few weeks. Give me a call, I'll show you around the stables."

"It's more than a vice. He spends almost every night there." Carol wrinkled her nose. "Personally, I don't see any fun in wading through the muck."

I scrutinized the photos and murmured, "Horses are such an expensive hobby."

"I'm a wealthy man." Gary wasn't bragging, just stating a fact. Preston abruptly veered back to the reason I had been summoned to his office. "Do you think Kendra's death is related to George's?"

I turned to him. "I'm surprised that you asked that question, Gary. Of course the two deaths are related."

Carol spoke up. "How can you be sure? Maybe it's just some awful coincidence."

I glared at her. When she finally looked away, I turned my scowl to her father. "I'm too tired to go through this. If you want to have a realistic discussion, let's have it. If not, let me get back to my desk."

Preston's cooler head prevailed. He filled three cups with coffee from a carafe that sat on a table near the door. I went back and took my seat between them. After bringing the coffee, creamer, and sugar bowl to us, he sat and calmly sipped his coffee. Carol and I did the same.

"Okay, Blaine, let's try. How is Kendra's death related to our troubles here at Kembell Reid?"

Not wanting to ruin Jeremy's investigation—and because I'd stopped trusting anyone who worked at Kembell Reid—I hesitated. "Both people worked for the same company, in the same department. A department that is under investigation for major fraud. Both were killed with knives."

Carol wasn't convinced. "That doesn't prove a thing. A lot of people in New York City get killed with knives."

I sipped more coffee and stared at her over the rim of the Wedgwood mug. She looked dubious and disgusted.

"If that's what you want to believe, it's fine with me, Carol. I'm not trying to convince you of anything. I'm telling you what I know."

Preston studied my face and quickly came to a conclusion about my report. "You're not telling us everything."

I shrugged. "And you haven't told me everything, either. I'm having trouble getting a clear answer on how Dani Dexter worked her magic without any help. I'm having more trouble believing that these murders weren't committed to cover up deeper, more extensive problems."

After a lifetime in sales, Gary had learned to keep his face and his eyes neutral. Carol had trouble controlling hers. Fear? Anger? I couldn't decide.

Preston calmly said, "Problems? What kind of problems?"

His suave voice started warning bells clanging inside my head. I shrugged nonchalantly. "Morley McGovern is a bastard. He mistreats everyone. Everyone hates him. Morale is probably higher on Death Row."

Preston casually dismissed my complaints. "Morley's department makes money. He must be doing something right. Is that all you have?"

"Who's Harold Wisekopf?"

"I don't know."

"He works for you."

Preston shrugged. "I can't be expected to know the name of everyone who works here."

I looked at Carol. As she mimicked her father's shrug, I snapped, "Aren't you the director of Personnel?"

"We have thousands of people working here. I can't be expected to know the name of every employee. Is it important? I nodded. "I'll pull his file. Call my office in the morning and I'll tell you what I find."

Preston leaned back in his chair and folded his arms across his chest. "So, is that it? That's all you have to report?"

"For the moment. I—"

"How much longer will it take for you to turn up something useful? Something that will help Carol rest easy. I'm beginning to agree with Carol. These tragedies seem to be random, horrible acts of violence. I don't think you're going to find a Kembell Reid connection, no matter how hard you look for one."

Preston cut off the protest I was about to make. "Blaine, you're working very hard, putting in lots of hours. I realize that—and I appreciate your efforts. But you're on the wrong course. I've been doing a lot of ruminating about this situation. Going forward, things will change."

"Daddy—"

"No, Carol, you can't stop me. You know I'd do anything to help you get over George, but I will not let my company be destroyed—"

"*Get over* George?" Carol's voice rose with anger. "You make it sound like I have a cold or the flu. George was my husband, the father of your future grandchild. His death is not something I'll get over in a week or two."

"Honey, that's not what I meant." Gary squirmed, his embarrassment heightened by my presence. "I'm trying to keep things under control. Tell you what I'll do. I was going to have Blaine clear out today. For you, I'll give her a little more time."

Carefully keeping my voice nonjudgmental, I asked, "How much more time did you have in mind?"

"It's Thursday, right?" Carol and I nodded. "Fine. Take the rest of this week and the two weeks after that. Which brings us to the end of the month. If you haven't turned up anything by then, I'm pulling the plug on your little masquerade. You understand?"

Gary was right—I hadn't accomplished more than improving my typing and wasting Grace's money. Mixed feelings of relief at being able to give up my double life and anger at being fired ran through me. I nodded without saying a word. Carol was more vocal about her feelings.

"I won't allow it. I won't . . ."

Listening to a family squabble wasn't in my contract. With a quick nod to Gary Preston, I rose, grabbed my coat, and hurried out of the office. Carol kept haranguing her father. Her voice followed me out of the room.

". . . I won't let you brush George aside . . ."

I walked onto the trading floor. As always, tension skipped and crackled above the low cubicles, hopping from station to station as millions of dollars in bonds changed hands. No one paid the slightest attention to the breathtaking views of the

Statue of Liberty and the Verranzano-Narrows Bridge—the sights on the monitors were breathtaking enough.

Not everyone was on the phone. Jobey and the three younger guys I'd come to think of as the Three Stooges were huddled outside the men's room, deep engrossed in their conversation. I brushed past them to get to my desk. Jobey smiled and waved, Larry, Curly, and Mo ignored me.

When he caught sight of me, Morley popped out of his office. He waved me inside and closed the door so no one could listen to our conversation. "Well? What did Preston want?"

I sank into one of Morley's plush chairs and slumped down. Weariness made my voice hoarse. "Not much. I told him exactly what I told the police. He asked that we tell him about the funeral arrangements."

"Good work." Morley patted my shoulder. "You did a fine job. Take the rest of the day off. Go home and catch up on your sleep." He smiled; I had become a co-conspirator. "Don't worry about your time sheet. I'll take care of it."

He didn't have to repeat his offer. I said thanks and good night and dashed out before Morley changed his mind. I stopped outside the building and took a deep breath. More sensitive noses may have smelled exhaust fumes from the passing traffic or the salty air blowing in from the harbor; I smelled freedom.

A movie matinee, a trip to the Museum of Natural History to look at the dinosaurs, a long, hot bath, and other pleasurable ways to spend the afternoon ran through my mind. The pleasant interlude ended when I thought of my office, my real office. I hailed a cab and headed uptown.

I hurried past everyone, even Eileen, to my office. After dumping my coat on a chair, I grabbed the phone and dialed. It was time to give Grace Hudson a progress report—and ask a question that had been bothering me for days.

Grace sounded relieved to hear my voice. "Blaine, I was going to call. Any progress?"

I sighed. "Grace, it's not going very well—"

"Not that. Your niece. Sandy. How is she?"

Surprised by Grace's question, I sat back. "Sandy?" I stammered a little. "She's fine. Everything's fine."

"Still worried?"

"Of course I'm still worried, Grace. Wouldn't you be?"

"Yes." Her answer was forceful. "You still have somebody doing guard duty?"

"Yeah," I sighed. "Unfortunately, I do. I have a skeleton crew keeping watch."

"Skeleton crew?"

"One person hanging around outside and following them around the neighborhood. It's not great coverage, but it's enough to keep Don from breaking in." I added silently, *and to keep Eileen out of my hair.*

"Kembell Reid? What's happening there?"

I wanted to sigh again, but managed to stifle it. "Nothing good. Do you have a few minutes?"

Grace said she did. I lit a cigarette and quickly told the story of finding Kendra's body and about Gary Preston's ultimatum. When I finished, her only comment was, "Is that all?"

I hesitated, searching for a diplomatic way to ask my question. Grace sensed my uncertainty.

"What?" She sounded impatient. "What else?"

"You gave George Walden my home phone number, right?"

Grace snapped, "Right. So what?"

"I found the number George kept calling the night he was killed. The number's no good; it just rings and rings. What number did you give him, Grace? It wasn't mine."

I wish I could have seen Grace's face. Instead, I had to rely on my ears to judge the truth. Grace sounded incredulous. "You must be kidding, Blaine. Are you accusing me—"

"Just asking. Did you give George a wrong number so he wouldn't be able to get in touch with me?"

"I gave George several phone numbers when he called. An attorney I knew. A therapist. Maybe one of them wasn't working." Grace's icy voice suddenly warmed. "Blaine, how many years have we known each other?"

Guilt formed a thick lump in my throat. "Ten, maybe twelve years."

"Have I ever given you bad advice? Have I ever misled you?"

Feeling thoroughly and completely ashamed of myself, I mumbled, "No. I'm sorry for asking. As you can tell, I've reached the point of grasping at straws. I suspect anyone who comes near me."

"Want more advice?" I didn't, but Grace gave it anyway. "Go home and sleep. Exhaustion breeds bad judgment. Sleep it off."

I rubbed my dry, gritty eyes and considered

Grace's advice. "You might be right. But I have one more question."

"What?" Grace spat the word out and instantly tried to soften it. "Sorry. I'm feeling a little stressed today. The market's been diving again. My clients are screaming. . . . Screw it, I'm not crying. What's your question, Blaine?"

If my own day had been going better, I might have asked Grace about her troubling day. Instead, I stuck to business. "Do you want me to stay on this case? I'm not making much progress. Hell, I'm not making any progress. It's your call. I don't want to waste your money."

"Do you want more money?"

"That's not what I asked, Grace. I—"

"I heard you. Stay on the job. We'll reevaluate when Preston throws you out."

I hate to quit almost as much as I hate to lose. I agreed. Grace quickly said, "Great. Call me when you have something." With that, she hung up.

When I walked in the door, I found Dennis sprawled on the sofa watching the ten o'clock news. He bounced up and rushed over to me. "Hey, I was wondering when you'd get in. I managed to pry myself away before midnight for a change."

"Hey, yourself, Dennis."

I pulled my coat off and tossed it over the banister, where it would spend the night, as usual. I dragged my sagging body to the living room. Dennis followed. He kissed my cheek. "You're late."

"I went to the office. The stack of papers on my desk is about two inches from the ceiling." I collapsed on the sofa and stared at the television. My eyes were closing when two familiar faces appeared on the screen.

The earnest face of Johnnie Bramble held a microphone up to the equally earnest face of Dani Dexter.

Chapter 25

I sat up, grabbed the remote control from Dennis, and turned the volume higher.

"In an exclusive interview, former Wall Street trader Dani Dexter tells a shocking tale of sexual harassment, discrimination, and, ultimately, betrayal."

"Now I know why Johnnie Bramble's been too busy to return my phone calls." I didn't bother mentioning that the last time I called Bramble I'd left a rude message. Something short and sweet, telling him that his source had fled the country, and accusing him of using me to keep his story on the air.

"Double-crossing bastard. He's afraid to talk to me." I hit the mute button. "I don't believe it."

"What don't you believe?"

"That bitch. She hired a public relations firm to make her look good. Betrayal?" My voice rose. "She ripped them off for millions of dollars and has the nerve to go on TV, bat her eyelashes, and whine that she's the victim of discrimination."

Dennis stroked my hair. "Why are you getting so upset? What did you expect her to do, make a tearful confession?"

"No, I didn't expect a confession. I'm pissed because people like her"—I pointed the remote at the silent, talking head—"women like her cheapen the problem. When a real victim of sexual harassment comes forward, people will remember Dani Dexter, shake their heads, and say this woman's a fraud, too.

"And people like him," I waved the magic wand at Johnnie Bramble. "Leeches sucking the blood of anyone who comes near them with a story that might capture our attention for ten or twenty seconds. Who the hell cares if they're guilty or innocent? Get them to cry on camera and you've got a story."

I shook with anger. "And do you know what's the worst thing about all this? I gave her the idea."

"Give me that." Dennis reached over my shoulder and pulled the remote control from my hands. "You've had enough for one night. So have I." He stabbed the power button; the earnest faces disappeared. "I'm going to bed."

I went to bed with a headache and woke up with a headache.

Friday, the working stiffs favorite day, started off on a depressing note. As always, I stayed in bed until the last moment, then hurried to shower and dress. I stepped outside and glowered at the overcast sky. Rather than go back inside to search for an umbrella, I decided to take a chance. Of course, the rain started pelting me blocks before the subway station. The morning paper didn't provide much shelter from the stinging rain, but it kept my hair dry.

The day dragged on. From the packed subway to the crowded elevator to the balky computer to Morley, who was more surly than usual, nothing went right. I broke fingernails, put runs in my panty hose, and made more mistakes than usual on everything Morley asked me to do. At the end of the day, I was tired and desperate to go home and hide for the weekend.

I made it to five. Telling myself that I would go to my office, my real office, and stay there no longer than an hour, I bent to fish my sneakers out from under my desk.

Jobey appeared just as I dragged them out. "Can you do a little favor for me, Blaine? Please?" He leaned over my desk, gently slid a folder in front of me, and whispered, "Pretty please. Big prospect coming in. I need to have this presentation ready first thing in the morning."

I flipped the file open. Charts and tables—two word processing skills I hadn't mastered. "I find it hard to believe that you, of all people, are planning to work on a Saturday."

Jobey hung his head and shuffled his feet. "Got to make my month or Morley's gonna bounce my ass out of here. If I get fired, Gretchen will kill me." He begged, "Please save my life. Say you'll do this for me. Please?"

I held my arm up. "Look carefully. What do you see on my wrist?"

"One slightly battered watch."

"That says it's time for this temp to go home."

"It also says this deal could be worth hundreds of millions of dollars." Jobey polished my watch crystal with the tip of his wild tie, which had more colors than a rainbow. "If I land this account, it'll make my month. No, it will make my year. I'll buy you a new watch. Something fancy. Something befitting your status as a lifesaver."

I protested, "It's five after five. It's Friday."

"So? Pardon me for sounding rude, Blaine, but haven't you been complaining that your social life is . . . well, that it sucks."

"Yeah, it sucks." I closed the file and smashed it against his chest. "Working late on a Friday night isn't going to improve it, either."

Jobey refused to touch the file. He backed out of reach and grinned. "Would this little favor be keeping you from an incredibly hot date?"

I thought of Dennis, who was probably stuck working late on his case, and blushed. "Noooo, but—"

Jobey sensed victory. He tried dazzling me with his smile. "But this won't take long. You'll be out of here in an hour. I'd do it myself, but I'm such a klutz with the computer. I'll pay you fifty bucks—cash."

"Up front?"

"What's the matter, don't you trust me?"

"I trust you, Jobey, my pal. But if you don't land this client, your I.O.U. won't be worth shit." I laughed and tossed the file on my desk. "I'll do it. After you pay me."

"You, my dear temp, you have been working here too long. You have lost all faith in humanity."

"You got that right, buddy. I don't trust humanity—especially you. Pay up or I'm out of here." I held out my hand, palm up.

Jobey pulled a few bills from his shirt pocket and gently placed them in my hand. "Here's sixty—I thought you'd be a tougher negotiator. Be a sport, leave two copies on my desk where I can find them in the morning." He patted my shoulder. "You're a pal. Thanks, Blaine."

He disappeared. Everyone disappeared, everyone but me. I struggled through the presentation, cursing every chart, table, and graph in the fifty-page report.

Jobey's hour-and-a-half estimate was optimistic. Three hours later, I had eradicated the last typo, printed out two perfectly beautiful copies, and left them neatly stacked on his desk.

The quiet floor, normally a scene of bedlam, was spooky. Most of the overhead lights had been turned off. Computer monitors flickered in the darkness. A lonely telephone rang. I listened to the forlorn sound and wondered who'd be calling this late at night. The ringing stopped and quiet blanketed the floor again.

Although I wanted to go home, I didn't want to waste the great opportunity. I took the key to Morley's office from my desk, unlocked the door, and started thumbing through his files. Morley was very organized—and very stupid. Within minutes, I uncovered a thick file with a label written in Kendra's precise script. *Dexter.* I opened the file and flipped through confidential memo after confidential memo. The initials at the bottom showed that most had been typed by Kendra.

For the first time that day, a big smile crossed my face. The smile stayed there as I copied the thick stack of paper. I knew that file would disappear—or be Hooverized—when Morley realized that Kendra's death would bring another swarm of curious investigators.

After being sure I wasn't leaving any stray pages behind, I turned off the machine and went back to my desk. After packing my copy in an envelope and stuffing it into my bag, I replaced the file.

Pleased with my evening's work, I sat in Morley's chair and whirled around to look out the window. I watched the falling snow swirl around the street-lights and started feeling lonely and guilty for not calling Dennis.

Pulling Morley's phone into my lap, I called home. I barely had a chance to say hello. Dennis quickly interrupted me. "Blaine, where are you?"

"I'm sorry, I should have called. I'm in the office. The Kembell Reid office. You sound like you've been pacing back and forth waiting for my call."

"Not pacing, but definitely waiting impatiently. It's after nine. Pacing starts at ten."

"Well, did you have something special in mind? Something that would make me rush home?"

"As a matter of fact, I did. I cooked a special dinner. I thought it would be nice to spend a ro-mantic evening together—we've hardly seen each other lately. I've been missing you."

"You have?" I laughed. "Well, Dennis, you con-vinced me. I'm leaving here in a few minutes. I have to go to the office first, then I'll come straight home. I'll be there in an hour."

"Why are you going there? Can't whatever it is you have to do wait until Monday?"

I started feeling as impatient as Dennis sounded. "No, it can't wait. I have to pick up a financial report. I promised Eileen I'd look at it over the weekend. Then I'm on my way home. I promise."

"Promises, promises. You'll see a stack of work on your desk and forget all your promises. Come straight home. You can pick up that report in the morning."

I teasingly said, "We probably won't get out of

bed until noon. I'd better get that blasted thing tonight. I promise I won't stay."

Sensing that he was losing, Dennis tried another argument. "Blaine, you can't make it to Fifty-fourth Street and back home in an hour."

"Especially if we keep arguing about it." I sighed again, louder this time. "Okay, I'll be home in an hour and a half. *I promise.*"

"Sorry." Dennis laughed. "You win. I'm an idiot. I promise to have dinner waiting when you get home. Hurry—but be careful. I love you."

"I will and I do. I mean, I will be careful and I love you, too."

I hung up and quickly put on my coat and left. With luck, I'd get to the office and home before dinner got ruined.

Sometime in the early evening, the rain had changed to snow. About half an inch covered the ground, transforming the narrow streets to snowy, slippery canyons. I walked around the corner to Pine Street and stood there for a few minutes, vainly hoping a taxi would appear.

Stewart's Law of Travel: the worse the weather, the longer the time between vacant cabs. I thought about going back up to the office to find an umbrella but remembered the slow elevators and the sound of Dennis's voice. I didn't want to waste any time.

I turned my collar up against the howling wind and trudged up the street. I decided to cut across Gold Street to Fulton. Hopefully, I'd find a cab that had just dropped off a fare at the South Street Seaport.

No luck. There weren't any cabs. There weren't any people. The snowy streets were deserted. I shivered. The feeling of having wandered onto the set of a Hitchcock movie came over me. I glanced over my shoulder, and through a filter of fine snow, saw a desolate street. Expecting to have a flock of birds swoop out of the clouds and attack, I put my head down and walked faster.

Early in my career at Kembell Reid, I'd discovered a shortcut—a narrow alley between a coffee shop and an office building. A perpetually overflowing Dumpster sat in the middle of the alley, but if you squeezed past it and made your way to the end, you'd be two blocks away from Broadway—and a better chance of finding a cab. I walked through it every night. The alley wasn't pleasant, but it cut three minutes off the trek.

I turned into the alley. A light dusting of snow covered the icy pavement and the plastic garbage bags piled around the Dumpster. It didn't cover the smell of urine and rotting garbage. I wrinkled my nose and quickened my pace.

The men appeared out of nowhere. Two stood in front of the Dumpster, blocking my way. I quickly glanced over my shoulder. Two stood at the mouth of the alley.

I stopped. My muscles tightened, preparing for battle. The men closed in and formed a tight circle around me. The shadows hid their faces. The unmistakable smells of beer, whiskey, cigarette smoke, and sweat drifted past my nose. Drunk muggers. My heart pounded harder.

In New York, and too many other places in this country, people die every day because they fight to hang on to their wallets, their jewelry, their leather coats, and their sneakers. My heart started pounding furiously. I understand the desire to not give in to a bum who decides he wants what's yours, but I wasn't ready to be killed for the seventy-seven dollars in my wallet or the Seiko watch on my wrist.

"Here." I thrust my bag at the man closest to me. "Take it. Take whatever you want."

The guy on the left took it and fumbled with the zipper. He impatiently pulled off his gloves, yanked the zipper open, and pulled my wallet out. He tossed the bag to the ground, took the money from my wallet, and fanned the bills out.

"Not much here."

"It's all I have."

He threw the money on the ground. The bills landed in a slushy puddle at my feet. He stuck my wallet in his coat pocket and rasped, "Maybe you should find another job."

"I like my job."

A hand flashed and struck my face. A heavy college ring caught my lower lip. Blood dripped from the split and rolled down my chin.

"I said, maybe you should find another job. It's good advice—take it."

Four against one—horrible odds. I forced down the urge to strike back and said, "Maybe you're right. Then again, maybe you're wrong."

It was the wrong thing to say. A switchblade knife clicked open—my cue to get the hell out of that alley. I elbowed the man behind me, feinted to the right, and spun to the left around the two men in front of me.

Nice move. It might have worked—if the alley wasn't coated with snow-covered ice. Doing a bad imitation of a drunken Hans Brinker trying to control his silver skates, I slid, flailed my arms, and fought a losing battle to keep my balance. I toppled over. On the way down, my head smacked against the side of the Dumpster. My ears rang; my head filled with a sharp pain. I landed on top of my seventy-seven dollars in an ice-encrusted puddle. The last thing I remember is the sound of my head hitting the pavement.

Chapter 26

Loud footsteps and louder voices clanged in my ears. The noise bounced off the brick walls of the buildings, booming through the alley. I winced; the noise made my head ache.

I heard voices but couldn't force my eyes open. I was too cold to move anything—even my eyelids. My mind wandered off.

"Jesus, this place stinks. How long do you think this garbage has been here?"

The smell? What smell?

"I don't fucking know and I don't fucking care. Let's check this out and get the hell out of here."

"Friday night drunks. Jesus, what did we do to deserve this call? If I get puked on . . ."

"Then stand back and shine the light so I can see. Hey, lady, wake up. Rise and shine. The neighbors are complaining. You'll have to sleep it off someplace else."

Something round and hard prodded my back. I moaned and tried to tell the man to stop. Hands grabbed my shoulders and rolled me over.

My head spun. A white-hot, blinding flash of pain ran across my forehead. I heard, "This ain't your ordinary bag lady. Better call EMS." I didn't hear anything else until later, much later.

*   *   *

Even before I recognized the voices or tried to open my eyes, I knew I was in a hospital. The bed felt stiff and uncomfortable—just like a hospital bed. The smells, the noises—they all belonged to a hospital. A frightening thought ran through me: why was I in a hospital?

I moved. The bed bobbed up and down and spun in a tight, frantic circle. I couldn't enjoy the circus ride; my head spun in the opposite direction. I clamped my jaws shut and cautiously opened my eyes.

Dennis's blurred face—and its twin—anxiously watched me. I blinked. The faces didn't go away.

Rather than try to figure out which face belonged to Dennis and which one didn't, I closed my eyes. The bed spun again. I grabbed the mattress and hung on with all my feeble strength.

Dennis whispered, "Blaine?"

Another ghostly voice answered from somewhere in the fog on my left side. I concentrated on deciphering the words. "Your wife kept us busy— as usual. Hypothermia, a concussion, a gash on the side of her head that took three stitches to close, assorted pavement scrapes, a split lower lip with one stitch—that's the bad news."

The list frightened me. I groaned, but no one noticed.

"There's more good news. None of the injuries are permanent. The scrapes, the headache, blurred vision, and nausea will all fade in time."

A name suddenly attached itself to the voice. *Dr. Mabe? How did she get into my nightmare?* Some of the fog lifted. With eyes shut firmly, I mumbled, "I want to go home."

"Not today, Blaine. Let's see what kind of night

you have. If you're a good patient, I'll let you out tomorrow."

The doctor's cheerful voice pounded inside my head. My stomach rotated faster and faster. I hung on to consciousness and disagreed. "I'd rather go home tonight."

"I'd rather have you stay."

Dr. Mabe's voice turned serious. "Blaine, listen carefully. Your body temperature had dropped to ninety-four point six by the time EMS brought you in. A lot of things happen to your body when it gets that cold. You stop shivering. Your pulse and breathing slow. Your blood pressure drops. Then you die. Rewarming is a slow process. That's why you need to stay here. I have to keep an eye on you."

I muttered something about a hot bath. Dr. Mabe angrily replied, "Go too fast and your cardio-vascular system could collapse. I'd rather not lose a patient tonight. So stay put and keep those blankets pulled up around your chin. You've been fortunate up to now—don't push your luck."

I listened to Dr. Mabe's footsteps as she walked away and tried to feel fortunate.

Dennis's whisper thundered in my ears. "Dr. Mabe's right, honey. You're not in any shape to go anywhere." I couldn't disagree. I clenched my jaws until the urge to vomit passed. When my stomach was under control, I whispered, "How did you find me?"

"Dr. Mabe spotted you in the emergency room. She called me."

"There's something else . . . I can't remember . . ."

Dennis squeezed my hand. "Don't worry, it'll

come back. You've got scrambled brains. You'll start feeling better soon; just don't push it."

"What happened?" I wrinkled my forehead and tried to focus on the hazy images. "All I remember is bouncing around in the back of an ambulance."

"The cops found you about two o'clock this morning. A guy who lives in a shanty near the Fulton Fish Market waved down a patrol car. He was scavenging in the Dumpsters in Theater Alley."

"And found me."

Dennis squeezed my hand. "We're lucky. He had the sense to do something and not just leave you there."

"How did I get here?" Here, St. Kitt's, is on the Upper East Side—that much I remembered.

"The nearest emergency room was packed— some kind of subway derailment. EMS routed you up here. Dr. Mabe was going off duty, but one of the interns mentioned that an interesting case had come in. She wandered in to take a look and there you were. She called me. Solved a mystery for the cops, too. They didn't have a clue as to who you were."

I opened my eyes and blinked at the harsh light. "I can't remember anything. Nothing."

"It's the concussion. You're going to be okay. That's the important thing. . . ." As Dennis talked, my eyes closed. I fell asleep.

On Saturday, I slept while the hospital bustled around me. On Sunday morning, Dr. Mabe gave me a stern lecture about the danger of repeated blows to the head and sent me home. I stayed awake long enough to dress, check out, and get into a cab.

Dennis gently woke me when the taxi stopped in front of our house. Hobbling along like an old, arthritic lady, I dragged myself from the cab and propped myself up against the wrought-iron railing while Dennis unlocked the door. I stumbled inside, body aching for rest, and stopped at the stairs leading to the bedroom. They looked too steep to attempt. I stubbornly shook off Dennis's supporting hand and headed to the sofa.

As much as I wanted to, I couldn't sleep.

Dennis instantly picked up on my restless mood. He sat on the floor in front of the sofa and grabbed my hand. "Do you remember anything unusual? Anything that doesn't seem right?"

I stopped, unwilling to put myself back in that dark alley. "They weren't your average muggers. They didn't want money. They took my wallet—and made a point of throwing my money back at me."

"So they wanted your credit cards."

"Or maybe they were checking to see if I'm who I say I am. The stuff in my wallet won't tell them anything. I always carry fake ID on a job, just in case somebody gets too suspicious."

Dennis followed with another quick question. "How did they know where to find you? They didn't follow you. You said the streets were empty."

I shook my head and winced again. The sudden movement instantly brought my headache back to life. Reality made the pain worse. I groaned. "I'm so stupid. They knew where to find me. I cut through that alley every night on my way to the City Hall subway station. It's less crowded than the Fulton Street stop."

"You settled into a routine and made it easy for them." Dennis's words held no judgment, he simply stated a fact.

"Stupid. I was stupid."

"You were human."

Dennis's attempt to comfort me failed. I closed my eyes and slid down to rest my head on the lip of the tub. An image flashed through my mind. "My bag. Dennis, where's my bag?"

He shrugged. "I don't know. I'll call the precinct in the morning, but I'd imagine it's long gone. Did you have anything valuable in it?"

"I found something." The memory faded as fast as it had come. I closed my eyes and tried to pull it back. "Something important. I think I put it in the bag." I grimaced. "Damn. It comes to the edge of my mind, then jumps back into the fog. Why can't I remember?"

"It's okay." Dennis patted my hand. "Just take it easy. Post-concussion syndrome goes away with time."

"Post-concussion syndrome? Have you been reading medical textbooks?"

Dennis sheepishly said, "I've been reading the sports pages. You and Boomer, the quarterback, have something in common."

I laughed and groaned at the same time. "We're both losers?"

'Guess again."

"What could I possibly have in common with a quarterback? I didn't throw an interception."

"But you got knocked down and you got a concussion. Remember how that kept happening to Boomer during his last season with the Jets? You're both prone to concussions."

Laughing made my head ache. I nodded gingerly. "And . . ."

"And I've been reading about postconcussion syndrome. You have the same thing. You don't remember what happened. You have headaches and nauseous feelings." Dennis smiled proudly. "The symptoms might linger for weeks."

"Thanks, doctor dear, for the optimistic prognosis. If you don't mind, I'll stick with Dr. Mabe's opinion."

Dennis took my hand. "Blaine—"

The concussion didn't affect my ability to read Dennis's mind. "I'm going back."

"Blaine, listen to me. Someone—four of them, people who might work at Kembell Reid—left you in an alley to freeze to death. Think about that while you get dressed in the morning."

I woke minutes before the alarm sounded, aching, exhausted, and straining to match a face, a name, with the raspy-voiced man in the alley. Dennis was still peacefully asleep; I shut the alarm off and tickled his chest. Dennis, a morning person, woke smiling just as he does every morning. "How do you feel?"

"Better. A lot better." I sat up. My head gyrated from the sudden movement; my stomach performed a slow-motion sympathy roll. I held my breath, hoping I'd feel better in a few minutes. I sank back on the bed and said, "Go take a shower. I'll wait."

Dennis rolled over on his side to look at me. His eyes were bleary—and worried. "I really think you should stay home for a few days. Dr. Mabe said—"

"I'll be fine. Don't nag, please."

Dennis didn't argue. After another long, worried look, he got out of bed and went to take a shower. When the bathroom door was safely closed, I decided to experiment. I sat up, swung my legs to the floor, and tried to stand. My legs were shaky, but they didn't crumple. I walked to the closet to pick out some clothes.

After standing in front of the closet for what seemed like an hour, but unable to remember why I was standing there, I admitted defeat. I stumbled back to bed and curled up in a tight ball. That's where Dennis found me when he came out of the shower.

"Blaine, what's wrong?" Dennis knelt by the bed. I opened an eye and squinted at him. He looked ready to call an ambulance.

"Scrambled brains, I guess. Kembell Reid will have to limp along without me today."

Dennis's eyes were filled with worry. "I'll stay home with you. You shouldn't be alone."

"Please, don't. I've had a concussion before. I need another day, that's all. I'm going to lie in bed all day. I promise."

"You promise?" Dennis raised his eyebrows. "Now that sounds familiar. Haven't I heard that line come out of your mouth once or twice before?"

I groaned and cradled my head between my hands. "Don't tease your invalid wife. Go to work. Let me sleep."

Dennis rocked back on his heels and studied my face. I tried a brilliant smile. "Please. I'll be fine. Go to work."

While he considered my request, I closed my eyes and drifted off to sleep. The smell of perfume

woke me. Either Dennis had spent the time dous-
ing himself with my perfume, or I had acquired
a nurse.

Without lifting my head from the pillow, I
opened an eye. Eileen was sitting in a chair,
frowning as she scribbled on a legal pad. Bright
sunlight flooded through the windows, stabbing
at my eyes.

"What are you doing?"

"Writing a letter to the Supreme Court."

Irritated, I snapped, "Very funny. Why are you
here?"

"Dennis called and asked me if I would keep an
eye on you until he got home. So, I packed up my
briefcase and headed over here."

I muttered, "It's a conspiracy."

"A conspiracy to keep you alive for another year
or two. You're getting too old for this, Blaine. How
many more lumps can your thick head absorb?"

"How many more of your lectures can my aching
head absorb before it explodes?" I closed my eyes
and tried to concentrate on the hazy images bub-
bling in my mind. "What time is it?"

"Eleven. You were asleep when I got here."

"When was that?"

"Around eight."

"You've been sitting here since eight o'clock
this morning?"

"In the house, but not right here." Eileen tried
to sound patient, but patience isn't one of her best
features. "I stayed downstairs for a while, but I got
tired of climbing the chairs to check on you. So I
figured I'd sit here and do some work until you
woke up."

Work. My eyes flew open. I pushed myself up with my elbows. "Where's the phone?"

"Here on the nightstand." Eileen warily asked, "Why?"

"I have a day job, remember? Someone's going to wonder where I am."

Eileen smiled; she looked so pleased with herself. "It's already taken care of, thank you very much. I called Carol Walden."

"What did you tell her? You didn't get me fired, did you?"

"Blaine," Eileen made a face, "I know what I'm doing. I told Carol you'd been mugged and that you'd be out a few days. She was very concerned and worried that it might be related to your investigation. I think she's worried that you'll sue."

"And having a lawyer call didn't make her feel any better."

Eileen grinned again. The phone rang. Eileen grabbed it and said hello. Without any prompting, my eyelids started closing.

"Who is this?" The sharp tone caught my attention. I forced my droopy eyes open. "Larry? Larry who? You found what? A bag? You think I might be interested in a bag?"

I hissed, "Give me the phone." Eileen ignored me. I snapped my fingers. "Come on. Come on. Give me the phone."

"Wait a second, Larry. Here's somebody who is interested."

Eileen held the phone out and said, "He's drunk, or stoned. Maybe drunk and stoned."

I pulled the receiver out of her hands and put it to my ear—just in time to hear my caller hang up.

"Shit." I dropped the phone on the bed and

glared at Eileen. "He hung up. Why did you have to harass him?"

"I didn't harass him. What was that all about anyway?"

"That was the sound of my evidence disappearing."

Chapter 27

"I want a cigarette."

"You can't smoke in bed."

I tossed the comforter back and sat up. "Fine, hand me my robe. I'll go downstairs to smoke. Besides, I'm hungry."

"Suit yourself. I've heard that concussions make people act weird—I guess it's true." Eileen pulled a bathrobe from the back of the chair and tossed it at me. "Here, suit yourself."

"Stop complaining. I don't remember inviting you to babysit."

"You didn't. Dennis did."

I fumbled with the robe. My struggles amused Eileen. She grinned but didn't offer to help—she knows better. More angry with the robe than Eileen, I snapped, "You can leave if you'd like."

"Oh, no. I'm not falling for that. The second I leave, you'll rush out to do something stupid. Anyway, I'm having too much fun to leave."

Eileen finally stood and yanked the robe from my hands. "Give me that."

As she briskly pulled the sleeves right side out, she said, "You're worse than Sandy. At least she dresses herself. Here." She tossed the robe on my lap. "Stop fighting with me and put this on. If you're a good girl, I'll make grilled cheese sandwiches for lunch."

"With tomato soup?"

Eileen patted my shoulder and handed me a pair of slippers. "Yes, Blaine. If you put these on, I'll make tomato soup, too."

I did—without complaining. I walked slowly down the stairs, clutching the banister for support. Eileen hovered behind me like a protective hen. I turned toward the kitchen. Eileen pushed me to the living room and told me to get comfortable while she cooked lunch.

The journey wiped me out. I fell asleep without having a cigarette, without asking a single question about Sandy or Don.

By Wednesday, the worst of the aches had faded and the world didn't spin every time I moved. It was time to get back to work. Makeup would have covered the bruises, but I left them uncovered. I walked out of the bathroom, dressed for the Wall Street wars, bruises flying proudly like a battle flag.

Dennis, who'd been carefully knotting his tie, noticed. He stopped and gently kissed my forehead. "Hoping to shock a confession out of someone?"

"Something like that. I want my scrapes and bruises visible to even the most nearsighted, or farsighted, person in the office."

"Good luck with the near- and farsighted. Just don't scare the neighbors. They can't take much more."

I felt a pang of guilt. I missed Ida, the elderly woman who used to live across the street. Ida acted as the unofficial grandmother for the block. She kept watch over the neighborhood, picked up garbage, took in deliveries, and chased noisy ruffians from our stoops. Ida scrutinized everything. She would have seen George Walden approach my doorstep. She would have called me. Now, Ida was gone and our small block lost its spirit. I missed her more than I ever thought possible.

Dennis watched my eyes and read my thoughts. "Blaine, are you going to be okay? Maybe you should take the rest of the week off and just take it easy."

"I'm not good at this invalid stuff. I want to go back to Kembell Reid and see who's surprised when I walk in the door."

He sat on the edge of the bed and watched as I rummaged in my jewelry box for earrings. "I'd feel better if you took a gun with you."

I laughed. "I can't do that, Dennis. I'd be tempted to shoot Morley. Of course, everyone would testify that it was self-defense. The jury would find me not guilty in seconds."

When Dennis didn't smile, I sat next to him and put my hand on his thigh. "Come on, buddy. That's a joke. I'll be fine, really."

"Really? Do you promise to be careful and not take any unnecessary risks?"

I kissed his cheek and hoped I wasn't lying when I said, "No unnecessary risks. I promise."

Dennis didn't know that I had a secret mission: to track down Larry and my missing bag. If I had mentioned my plan to search among the ramshackle huts near the East River, he would have locked the door and refused to let me leave the house.

That's why I didn't tell him. I kissed him again and left.

*   *   *

Everyone, starting with the people on the subway, noticed my bruises. Even Morley noticed. He walked out of his office, snarled hello, and did a double take. He stepped over to my desk and examined my face. "Hey, Stewart, you really did get mugged! I thought you were trying for a few extra days off."

My hand strayed to my lip and brushed against the stitch. I winced. "There are easier ways to get a vacation."

"Well, I'm glad you made it back. I had to hire a temp to temp for you. She doesn't know shit."

I sarcastically thanked Morley for his concern. After giving me his customary order to mind the phones, he swaggered off to torment his traders. The phone started ringing; I opened the top drawer of my desk for a pen—and froze. The phone continued ringing. I didn't notice. My head started pounding. My heart raced.

The new temp, a woman much too young and much too nice to stay at Kembell Reid for longer than a week, intervened. She quickly answered the phone. As she wrote on the message pad, she kept watching me as if she expected me to topple over onto the floor. She got rid of the caller and rushed over to my side.

"Do you feel okay? You look awful."

"I'm fine. Really."

"I don't know." The woman's concern lingered, not at all eased by my halfhearted response. "You look shaky. You should go home. I can last around here for another day or two. Morley's not so bad—now that I've learned to ignore him."

She followed my gaze and looked down into the

open drawer, expecting to see a rat or a snake. When she saw nothing but my wallet and the usual assortment of paper clips, pens, and rubber bands, the woman backed away.

I repeated, "I'm fine. Look—I'm sorry, I don't even know your name."

"Sally."

"I'm Blaine." I slammed the drawer shut and quickly scanned the room to see if anyone had been watching my reaction. No one appeared to be interested.

"Sally, I really need this job. I can't afford to go home."

Sally instantly understood—people don't take temp jobs for the high pay. Temps have sympathy for the financial woes of other temps. "Let me get you a cup of tea. It'll make you feel better. Look, I'll cover everything today. You just look busy so Morley doesn't bother you."

Hoping to use the time to clear my head—and move the evidence—I let her go. I resisted the urge to pick the wallet up with my bare hands. After putting my gloves back on, I placed the wallet into a thick envelope and stuffed it into my purse.

By the time Sally returned with a Styrofoam cup of weak, lukewarm tea, I had a plan. I sipped the tea and grimaced. "Maybe I did come back too soon. . . ."

Sally nodded her head in agreement and even tracked Morley down and dragged him back to my desk. The generous Morley McGovern is much harder to take than the miserable Morley. After much winking and grinning, he generously gave me the rest of the week off—with pay. I hurried away before he came to his senses.

*   *   *

Jobey gallantly sprang up from his chair and held the door open for me. "Leaving so soon? You just got here. I haven't even had time to stop by and see how you're doing."

"Take a good look." I stepped through the door. "Because I'm out of here. I'm not strong enough to spend another second in this nuthouse."

"What happened?" The mocking smile Jobey usually wore disappeared. He followed me out the door to the elevators. "The rumors say you got mugged. Are the rumors true?"

"Yeah, they're true." I punched the elevator button. "I got mugged."

"When? Are you okay?"

"Do I look okay? And you know what, Jobey, it's all your fault."

"My fault." The blood drained from Jobey's face.

I snapped, "Yes, your fault. I stayed late to do your little project, remember? Well, it took longer than expected. The streets were dark and empty— no one but the muggers were out in the snow."

"And you thought this would be a cushy assignment. Maybe you should find another job before we manage to do you in."

A chill ran down my spine. "What did you say?"

"I said, maybe you should find another job." Jobey blushed. "Hey, what's wrong? I was only joking. . . ."

By the time the elevator touched down in the lobby, I felt like I should crawl back home to bed. But sometimes I won't listen to anyone—not even myself. I buttoned my coat, wrapped my scarf securely around my neck, and walked toward the East River.

The South Street Seaport area that most tourists know covers only a few blocks. From Water Street to the East River, you can find the same stores as in any mall, shipbuilding museums, and tall-masted schooners that once sailed across the oceans and survived the trip around Cape Horn. Now they lazily bob up and down in the river.

Most tourists end their tour of the Seaport at Pier 17, a three-story mall that juts out into the water, where they can buy mediocre but expensive food and enjoy breathtaking views of the Brooklyn Bridge. Few of them wander north beyond the fish market. If they do, they're surprised and slightly unnerved by the rapid change in the neighborhood. In less than a block, the tony shops and souvenir stands are replaced by brick warehouses and semi-abandoned tenements. An occasional gem, an art gallery or restaurant, brightens the squalor.

Just north of the market, a village of shacks has sprouted beneath an elevated stretch of the FDR Drive. Made out of scraps of cardboard, wood, and aluminum, they withstand the winter snowstorms and the summer thunderstorms. They aren't strong enough to survive the political storms. Every few years, a vengeful mayor orders the structures demolished. As soon as the media attention evaporates, or the mayor is voted out of office, the shacks return.

A chain-link fence surrounds the lot in a futile attempt to keep the squatters out. I squeezed through a small hole that had been cut in the fence and approached the huts. Suspicious eyes followed my progress. A man's voice called out from one of the sheds, "Go away. There's nobody here."

Picking my way across the patches of ice and snow, I cautiously approached the hut. "Can you help me? I'm looking for Larry."

"Go away."

That phrase doesn't slow me down—I've heard it too many times.

"I won't go away. I have to talk to Larry."

"I told you he's not here." The voice quavered. "Go away."

The timid voice encouraged me to press on. "I can't go away. I have to talk to Larry."

"Why?"

"He saved my life the other day. I want to thank him—and give him a reward."

The voice gained strength—and interest. "A reward? How much?"

Ever philosophical, I asked, "Who can put a price on life?"

"Life ain't all beer and skittles, and more's the pity; but what's the odds, so long as you're happy?" The blanket covering the doorway moved slightly. "Come on in."

Chapter 28

The tarp that served as a door moved; the man who peeked out looked at me with wild-eyed fear. I backed away and waited for him to charge out swinging an ax.

He wore a New York Mets baseball cap, the worn insignia nearly invisible after years of daily wear. He could have been twenty-five or sixty-five. The stubble that covered the bottom half of his face and the oversized, mirrored sunglasses that covered the top half hid all signs of age. He giggled and in a singsong voice repeated; "Life ain't all beer and skittles—"

He turned and disappeared back into the hut. Pushing aside the nagging misgivings I felt, I followed him inside.

"I know, life ain't all beer and skittles—did you make that up?"

"George du Maurier."

"Are you George?"

He shook his head impatiently. "I'm George, but not the 'Life ain't all beer' George. The other one wrote that. I read it in the library. It's warm there and they can't throw you out. If you've come for the money, it's gone."

I stood on the cardboard floor and looked around the hut. I saw a neat stack of blankets on a wooden palette, a kerosene lantern, a stack of newspapers, and a pile of empty soda cans. No furniture, no refrigerator, no bathroom. No heater.

The cold seeped through my boots and my coat. The shivers started running through my body, bringing a flood of unpleasant memories. I innocently asked, "What money?"

"Don't ask." His eyes darted away guiltily. "I'm not supposed to talk about the money."

"I'm trying to find Larry. Do you know where he is?"

"Life ain't all beer—"

"—and skittles. I know that." How well I knew that.

He rocked back and forth on his heels. "The money's gone."

A complete waste of time—I decided to get out before my unbalanced poet lost control. "Tell Larry to call me." I scribbled my home phone number on the back of a card and handed it to him. "I'll give him more money if he does."

"How much?"

"It depends on Larry. I lost something. He found it." The card didn't move from my outstretched fingers. "There's a reward."

"How much?"

I flapped the card up and down. "Larry will have to call me to find out."

He grabbed the card and stuffed it in the pocket of his grimy jeans. I watched with dismay. That little card—and my bag with Kendra's file—were gone forever. Reluctant to let go of my slender lead, I said, "Does Larry live here with you?"

The head wagged back and forth. "No room for Larry at this inn. No siree." He lowered his voice and in a stage whisper, said, "Larry lives next door. But don't you go poking around. He left me to watch over it. Are you going to give me money?"

The isolation pressed in on me. Very much aware that no one was within shouting distance—even if I could be heard over the highway noise—I edged away from him.

"Not unless Larry calls me. If he calls, you get ten bucks. That's your reward."

I spent the afternoon marching up and down the streets around the Seaport asking all the street people if they knew Larry. My nose turned red with cold and then went numb. My achy brain stopped working; I navigated on automatic pilot.

Promising myself that this would be the last stop on my tour, I stopped in the seediest of the seedy bars. The grime didn't stop this bar's patrons. Every seat was filled with men, young and old, silently nursing boilermakers.

Most were too engrossed in their drinks and their private agonies to notice me. Only a few heads turned to watch my entrance. The bartender noticed. He motioned for me to stop and ducked under the counter. After two steps he was standing in front of me, blocking my way.

About thirty-five years old, he was obviously both bartender and bouncer; the muscles rippling under his tight shirt would discourage the most rowdy patron. He wiped his hands on a dirty towel and glared at me. "This ain't your kind of party. Get out of here."

"This is a public bar, isn't it?"

"Not for people like you. Get out."

My temper sizzled. "People like me? What's that supposed to mean?"

He leaned forward and rested the palm of his hand on the door. "Look around, lady. See anyone you might like to sit next to? Why don't you go to the Rusty Staub's or Sparks and pick up some rich guy who wants to cheat on his wife?"

I was tired of being thrown out of places most people would never dream of entering. "I'm looking for a homeless guy who came into some money recently. I thought he might be spending it here."

"You a cop?" I shook my head. "Don't tell me, Larry mugged you and you want your money back."

"You're right about one thing and wrong about another. I got mugged all right. But Larry helped me. I wanted to thank him."

"Larry the Loon helped you?" He stroked his goatee and smiled. "That sounds like Larry. He never does what you expect."

The bartender impatiently looked over his shoulder at his bar. The glasses were still full. Quickly, before he used his customers as an excuse to walk away, I asked, "Can you tell me what this guy looks like? I really want to thank him."

"Guilty conscience?"

"Appreciation. Tell me what he looks like and where he hangs out and I'm gone. Your clientele will never notice my disruptive presence."

The bartender snorted and shook his head with disgust. "Larry looks like a bum and smells like a bum. They all look alike."

Another man in love with his job. Determined to find out as much as possible before he practiced his bouncing skills on me, I fired questions at him. "White or black?"

"White. Not just brothers come in here."

"Short or tall?"

"About an inch taller than you."

"That makes him about six feet?" The bartender nodded. "What kind of coat does he wear?"

"Coat? One of those beat-up army jackets. Larry went to 'Nam. He never got over it, especially the drugs. Man came home and couldn't do a thing. Couldn't hold a job, couldn't stay married. Drifted down here about five years ago. He's been living in that box he calls home for about a year now."

"Where does he spend his days?"

He snorted again. The rude sound matched the rude set to his mouth. "Larry certainly doesn't spend his days in the office and his nights at the opera. He's homeless, lady. What the hell do you think he does all day? He scrounges for cash and looks for a meal—just like the rest of the guys who come here when they hit the jackpot or score enough for a boilermaker or two."

He pushed me out the door. "Why don't you try the soup kitchens?"

I let him push me out. The door slammed behind me. Even after only ten minutes inside that hell-hole, I felt greasy and dirty. I took a deep breath and felt the cold air sting my lungs. The headache that had never completely disappeared roared back. Larry would have to wait. I hailed a cab and headed for home.

I kicked my boots off, draped my coat in its customary spot on the banister, and stretched out on the couch. The sound of footsteps woke me. I blinked at the unexpected light from the table lamp. The afghan that Dennis had flung over me while I was sleeping slid to the floor.

He crouched down and smiled at me. "So you're finally awake. When did you get in?"

"Around four." I stretched and rubbed my eyes. "What time is it? How long have you been home?"

"Seven-thirty. I got in a little after five. You were sound asleep, so I didn't wake you. Tough day?"

"Life ain't all beer and skittles, and more's the pity; but what's the odds, so long as you're happy?"

"What?" Dennis stared at me. I knew he was wondering if he should call Dr. Mabe to report that I'd finally lost my mind.

I smiled and rubbed Dennis's shoulder. "Don't worry, I'm fine. Yes, it was a tough day. A very tough day. But it wasn't all bad. My wonderful boss gave me the rest of the week off. I promise to sleep late every day."

"Good." Dennis leaned over me and kissed me. "Now if only I could convince you to stay out of Aldridge and Stewart for a few more days."

"Not a chance. I haven't been there for a week. Eileen's probably buried my desk with papers." I sniffed and didn't catch any scent of food. Surprised, because Dennis usually heads right to the refrigerator when he comes home, I asked, "Did you eat?"

"No time. I've been busy in the darkroom."

"The darkroom?" My fuzzy head slowly cleared. I sat up and made room for Dennis to sit next to me. "You developed the film?"

"Yeah." Dennis picked up a stack of photos from the floor and laid them in my lap. "I've been feeling guilty about having it sitting down there in the darkroom collecting dust. I decided to sneak off for a few hours to take care of it. I found you on the sofa, checked to be sure you were still breathing, and went to the darkroom."

Dennis draped the afghan over my shoulders. "Look at the contact sheet first and tell me if you want any others enlarged." He gave me a small magnifying glass.

I didn't see anything extraordinary, just your average photos of a corpse. I flipped the sheet over and looked at Dennis. "Let me see the ones you blew up."

"These are more interesting." Dennis was proud of his work, so I didn't hurry him along. "They're pictures of the street."

"And," I pulled a cigarette from the pack on the table, "what do they show?"

"Someone who looks very interested in what you were doing."

I lit a cigarette and blew out the match. "Nothing unusual in that, Dennis. After all, I was standing in the middle of the street."

"And what do average New Yorkers do when they see someone acting weird?"

"They take a quick look and keep on walking."

"Right." Dennis picked up an eight-and-a-half-by-eleven photo and held it out to me. "What's this lady doing?"

I glanced at the grainy picture and reached for an ashtray. "Walking her dog. Why do people think it's cute to clip poodles? It makes the dog look stupid."

"Look again, Blaine," Dennis said impatiently. "She's doing more than walking a dog."

"She's standing in the street staring at me."

Dennis picked up another picture. "And here, four frames later?"

"She's still watching."

"Now, two frames later. She's moved to the curb because a car was turning the corner, but she's still watching you." Dennis laid the photo on top of the others and leaned back, satisfied with his findings. "Look, even the dog lost interest; it's straining to pull his mistress away. This lady is a little too interested. Recognize her?"

I took a drag on the cigarette and squinted at the picture. "The woman's wearing a long coat, a scarf, and sunglasses. How could I recognize her? That could be Eileen, for all I know."

"Yeah," Dennis sighed, "that's what I thought." He gathered the pictures into a neat pile. "It's been an interesting exercise, but not very fruitful. I'll try to blow them up even larger and hope for a better look at the face."

"Yeah, and we can hope to win the lottery, too." I grabbed a photo. "Let me hang on to one of these. Maybe I'll get a brainstorm."

Dennis put the photos aside, draped his arm over my shoulders, and ran his index finger across the back of my neck. I sat quietly for a few seconds and wondered if a great clue was hidden in the photos. All that came into mind was that it had been a long time since lunch. "Are you hungry? We could go out."

Dennis continued running his finger up and down my neck. "Or you could stay here while I go back to work."

I groaned and crushed the half-smoked cigarette in the ashtray. "You're not staying home?"

"Can't." Dennis stroked my cheek with the back

of his hand. "But I suggest that you take a nap while I'm gone so you're wide awake when I get home. . . ."

I smiled at the warmth of his touch. As much as I wanted to, I couldn't complain about Dennis's late hours—I have too many of those late nights myself. After a kiss designed to make him hurry home, Dennis left. With a huge smile on my face, I stretched out on the sofa again and pulled the afghan up to my chin.

My eyes closed.

The doorbell rang.

I peeked out the window. My visitor looked so uncomfortable, so out of place, that for a split second I thought about not opening the door. He rang the bell again. The rotund man was slightly out of breath and stamping his feet to keep warm. I dropped the curtain, hurried to the door, and pulled it open.

I swung the door open. "Bobby, when did the View start making house calls?"

"Ever since Ryan came across this." Bobby held out a wrinkled envelope. As I reached for it, he exclaimed, "What happened to you? You look like shit."

"Thanks. And you guys wonder why I haven't been hanging out in your bar lately." I opened the door wide enough to let him in. "Come on in. What's so important that you had to jackass down here in the middle of the night?"

Bobby followed me into the living room and thrust the envelope at me. "Ryan said to bring this down here ASAP. He said to tell you that he was going through the receipts and found this. It's from the guy that was hanging out in the bar the night that other guy got killed."

Despite all the "guys" in Bobby's explanation, I knew exactly what the message meant. I eagerly ripped the envelope open and pulled out a credit card slip. The receipt was from the View—on the day George Walden got killed.

I smoothed the paper and squinted at the smudged name. Harold Wisekopf. The man who answered the door the night I visited Dani Dexter. The man who worked at Kembell Reid—in the systems department, where it would be easy to rig false trades. The man who probably engineered the mugging in the alley.

Talking more to myself than Bobby, I sat and stared at the receipt. "This doesn't put him in the View at the same time that Walden was there. It's not time-stamped. A clever lawyer would say it's an uncanny coincidence."

I rubbed a corner of the paper, seeking inspiration. "Wait a second, this bill is for thirty-five dollars."

Bobby, who was watching with interest from his comfortable seat in the rocking chair, prompted me, "And . . ."

"And Ryan would have called for authorization. You know Ryan doesn't trust people with credit cards—he likes cash."

I tapped the little box where an authorization code had been scrawled. "I bet there's a record of when this call was made. Unless Harold happened to report his card stolen that day, this proves that he was there."

"Wow." Bobby rocked the chair forward. "What are you going to do now?"

"Make a phone call."

Before doing that, I dragged Bobby to the door, ignoring his entreaties to let him eavesdrop. I kissed his cheek and told him to thank Ryan—then I pushed him out the door. Then I found Chris Hutchinson's card and started dialing. I dialed his office. I dialed his pager. I dialed his home. I didn't get an answer.

Chapter 29

I dialed the numbers a second, then a third time, leaving messages each time, before giving up. The long day caught up with me, but I was too stubborn to give in to my aching head and go to bed. Intending to wait up for Dennis, I turned the TV on and stretched out on the sofa.

My peaceful sojourn lasted less than ten minutes. As I was trying to find something funny in the latest hit sitcom, the telephone rang. Thinking it was either Dennis telling me he was on his way home, or Chris Hutchinson returning my calls, I eagerly answered it.

"This is Larry."

My nerves started tingling. I forced myself to sound calm and friendly. "I'm glad you called, Larry. Thank you for calling the police the other night. You saved my life."

My caller grunted. I quickly said, "You said you found my bag. I'd like to get it back as soon as possible. When can I pick it up?"

"I hear there's a reward."

"There is." I hesitated, torn between the desire to retrieve my file and unwillingness to finance an alcoholic's binge. But I wasn't a social worker—I brushed my doubts aside and asked, "When can I get the bag?"

He giggled. "How fast can you get here? You know where I live. Bring money."

"I'm leaving now."

Larry grunted again and slammed the phone down. I jumped up to grab my coat—and my wallet.

The ghostly voice of Jeff, my first husband, usually spoke to me, but lately it was Dennis's voice that rang in my ears. I heard him say, *Don't go without backup.*

I didn't want to ignore that little voice, but Larry was waiting for me—and my money. Going alone could be suicidal; ignoring his call could kill my case. I briefly thought of running after Bobby and asking him to accompany me, but the idea of sweet, naive Bobby protecting me from the bad guys made me giggle.

Brad was my best, and only, hope; no one else was close enough to get to the Seaport in time. I dialed Brad's number and impatiently paced around the living room. My stomach dropped with each unanswered ring. Brad's answering machine came on and invited me to leave a message. I muttered a curse, hung up—and made a decision that I hoped I wouldn't regret. I'd go alone.

Not completely alone. I did have one reliable backup handy: my gun. I ran up to the bedroom, grabbed the pistol and extra ammunition, and hurried out to find a cab.

Most of the bars had closed and the fish market hadn't opened yet, leaving the area around the Seaport dark and quiet. After asking for a third time if I was sure I wanted to get out in that deserted spot, the driver dropped me at the corner of South

Street and Peck Slip, and sped away as soon as I cleared the door.

There's a time for misgivings and a time to act. I pushed the worries about being alone away and hurried to the squatters' field. Without a second thought about the isolation, I scrambled through the hole in the fence. The streetlights, those that worked, gave the lot the eerie air of a battlefield, strewn with torn concrete and the litter from a million litterbugs, maybe even a body or two. I picked my way through the wreckage of discarded tires and decaying furniture.

Taking a deep breath, I turned the flashlight on and shone it on the center shack—the fancy one made of wood with a plywood door and corrugated tin roof. I called out, "Larry, it's Blaine."

The door opened slightly. A husky voice said, "You came about the bag?"

"Yes, I did. Let me ask you something. How did you find my phone number?"

"Sometimes I find good stuff in that Dumpster. Stuff I can sell. Instead, I found you. Found your bag. I looked inside. Found this." He slipped a grimy strip of paper through the crack.

I shone my light on the paper and smiled. The obsessive part of me, the one that I try to keep hidden, surfaces every so often. When it does, look out. This time it had led me to fill out the little emergency card that came with the bag. Name and telephone number—at least I'd been smart enough to skip the line for my address.

"I'm glad you called. Can I have the bag?"

The door creaked as he opened it wider. "It's cold out there. You come in while I look for it."

Don't. The word rang in my head. *Don't. Don't.*

Don't. But sometimes you have to take a chance. I put my hand in my pocket, wrapped my hand around the pistol, and walked inside.

Larry had lived there long enough to collect an odd assortment of junk. He had rigged a bed by stretching an abandoned mattress on makeshift boards so it didn't rest on the cold floor. The floor, made of small squares of carpet samples, was laid down on the dirt in a hideous design of competing colors and patterns. An electric lantern, fed by an illegal tap on a nearby light pole, sat atop a rickety chest. Boxes and plastic milk cartons stuffed with clothes, newspapers, and junk covered nearly every inch of floor space in the minuscule hut.

My host looked fearsome. Larry's bushy white beard and eyebrows reminded me of drawings of Santa Claus. He stood about six-six and outweighed Santa by at least fifty pounds. But Larry didn't say ho, ho. He scowled and snarled, "You bring the money?"

The stench of fish, garbage, and ripe body odors made me gag. I leaned against the door to let in some fresh air and heard footsteps crunching on the ice. Once again, the sensation of time being wasted pressed down on me. The longer I stayed inside that shed, the greater the risk of being ambushed.

I sternly asked, "Where's the bag?"

The steely tone of my voice cut through Larry's bluster. He bobbed his head up and down in a movement that was supposed to signify his embarrassment. "I'm not trying to rip you off. It's just—"

"That you could use the money. How does fifty dollars sound?"

We had a deal. His eyes brightened, then narrowed suspiciously. "You got it with you? I don't give credit."

"The bag, Larry." I threatened, "Give me the bag now, or I'm leaving. My money's leaving too."

Larry stared at me with glazed eyes. I froze, afraid that even the slightest movement would send him into a frenzy. My heart pounded. I tensed and got ready to dart outside.

He blinked and shook his head. The manic look disappeared as fast as it had come over him. He grinned and said, "Geez, gimme a second to find it. It's here somewhere."

Larry knelt and dug through one of the cartons under his bed. He tossed papers and crumpled bags on the floor. "I know I put it in this one. Didn't want anyone to steal it."

I watched impatiently as he rummaged and muttered. My heart continued to pound, advising me to get away before the maniac returned. But I was too close to getting that file to slink away like a coward.

"Hey, wanna help?" Larry looked over his shoulder and gestured at a box at the foot of the bed. "Look in there. Maybe I put it there."

Suspicion mingled with impatience. I didn't want to abandon my relatively safe position by the door, but I didn't want to stand there, watching him go through box after box—and leaving without my bag wasn't an option.

I followed Larry's direction and opened the box. Keeping a careful watch for needles, I gingerly pushed aside the top layer of old clothes and didn't see anything that resembled my bag. Larry uttered a triumphant cry. He pulled my worn bag out from beneath a pile of clothes on the bed. It dangled from his huge fist and swung back and forth. "Here it is."

I stood and reached for it. He swung the bag out of my reach and stepped between me and the door. "Money."

Taking five ten-dollar bills from the pocket of my jeans, I waved them in front of him and grabbed the bag. He took the bills and laboriously counted them.

I opened the zipper and stuck my hand inside—and felt sunglasses, tissues, makeup, pens—no file. Disappointment cascaded over me; suspicion that Larry might be holding out for a larger reward followed. "Are you sure this is everything?"

Too many accusations of stealing had been flung at Larry for mine to go unnoticed. His face turned purple; his hands shook with anger. "I don't steal. You accusing me of stealing? My fucking pride is all I have. They took everything else. Everything but my fucking pride. You say I steal and you know what I got left? Nothing. No fucking pride. No nothing. No fucking pride—"

Slinging the bag over my shoulder, I tried to calm him. "Hey, Larry, I'm sorry. I wasn't accusing you of stealing. How could I do that? You helped me. Maybe there's something I can do to help you."

Larry flapped the bills in my face. "All the help I need, I got right here. You want to help, you give Larry more money. You got more money?"

The white-haired giant took a giant step toward me. I held my ground and put my hand in my pocket. As soon as my fingers brushed the cold metal, I knew I couldn't use it. Pulling the gun out would make him completely berserk.

I calmly said, "Larry, I gave you all the money

I have. Just like I promised. Now let me by so I can go home."

My words didn't register. The sound of my voice enraged Larry. He started panting with anger and clenched his fists. He solidly planted his feet, blocking the way to the door. A glob of drool ran from the corner of his mouth. "Come here, you motherfucking bitch. . . ."

All the football games Dennis and I watched paid off. I lowered my shoulder and drove it into his stomach. He swung his fist, narrowly missing my jaw. I shoved him against the bed, spun away, and sprinted for the door.

He bellowed and lumbered after me. I burst through the door—and into another set of arms. I slapped them aside and kept moving. Hands grabbed my bag, yanking me back. I pulled my gun from my pocket and whirled around. I smashed the barrel across my attacker's knuckles. He yelped; I jammed the pistol into his throat, instantly silencing him. Recognizing Larry's friend, George, I yelled, "Life ain't all beer and skittles, pal. Touch me again and I'll kill you."

Chapter 30

The next morning, I walked into my office feeling sorry for my colleagues who don't have the resources to maintain a full staff of investigators. While I was wasting my time at Kembell Reid, Brad and the others were searching databases, talking to credit bureaus, and bribing bank clerks.

Eager to see what they had turned up, I hurried to Brad's office and knocked on the open door to get his attention. He had a stack of manila files on his desk and a smug grin on his face. He patted the files and said, "Just about everything you asked for, Babe."

"What's missing?"

"Dexter. We should have her stuff in the morning. We've been having a little trouble getting hold of her financial records. But never fear, Babe, you won't miss it. That other stuff will keep you busy for a while."

Brad sat back and crossed his legs. "Let me give you a time-saver tip. Start with Gary Preston. The rest are so normal, they're boring. Preston's different. He's got a very expensive hobby."

"Horses?"

Brad nodded. I laughed at the disappointed expression on his face. "You got it. Horses. That guy is throwing buckets of money at the horsies. I think the ungrateful creatures are eating it instead of their hay, 'cause nothing seems to be coming back." Brad flipped the top file open. "Look at these PFM statements."

PFM—Personal Finance Manager. Kembell Reid's answer to the cash management systems that are in vogue at every brokerage firm. Checking, credit cards, investments—everything wrapped up in one neat package. Convenient for clients—and nosy private investigators lucky enough to get their hands on a statement.

I glanced at the column of withdrawals and then looked at Brad. "This has to be wrong."

"It's not wrong, Babe. I checked it myself. Like I said, everyone else is N-O-R-M-A-L. Normal." Brad smiled and gleefully pushed the files across the desk. "You have a bit of reading to do, Babe. Why don't you get started and leave me to do my work?"

Brad saluted. I gathered the files in my arms and slowly walked toward my office. ATMs at the Meadowlands. Cash withdrawals of fifteen, twenty, thirty thousand dollars a month. Could it be going to the horses? Or had Gary Preston found a way to launder money? And why?

I walked past Eileen's office and abruptly wheeled around as the thought struck: she'd been avoiding me.

Eileen was sitting behind her desk, looking grimmer than ever. I threw myself into a chair and stared at her. After about thirty seconds, she tossed her pen down and snapped, "What are you doing?"

"Trying to figure out why you're in such a bad mood and why you're avoiding me. How's Sandy? Jeannie working out okay?"

"She's fine. They're both fine. I have work to do. Don't you?"

"Nope." I smiled sweetly. "I'm taking it easy. Recovering from a concussion, remember?" I re-arranged the files that threatened to slip off my lap and casually asked, "So, sis, how's Don these days?"

Eileen glared at me. "Don't you ever give up?" I smiled again and shook my head. Eileen patiently explained, "Don is also fine, Blaine. He's really trying. He's going for counseling."

"So things will be different this time?"

I'm not the only one in the family with a temper. Eileen's flared. "Maybe they will. What makes you an expert on all this?"

I waved her objections aside like a puff of smoke. "Has Don moved back in yet?"

"Don't you have people watching my every move? Haven't they told you when Don visits—and when he goes home?"

I shrugged. "Maybe I'm not keeping up with my report-reading. I'd rather hear it from you."

The look Eileen threw at me would have melted mere humans, but I was immune to her glares. Her eyes sparked with barely contained anger. Rather than let her give me a tongue-lashing, I picked up my files and headed to my office.

As I walked past Jona's desk, I saw a gleam of amusement in her eyes. I stopped. "What?"

"What what?"

"Everyone's a comedian today—even my secretary. What's so funny?"

Jona smiled. Or maybe she smirked. "Nothing's funny. I just thought you'd be in a better mood."

I shifted my cargo to my other arm and said, "No one's making any sense. It must be the concussion. What are you talking about?"

"Your secret admirer." She gestured at my office. "The one who sent you the gorgeous roses. Long-stemmed. Two dozen. Does your husband know?"

"Roses?" The night before, I'd been asleep before Dennis finished climbing the stairs. I never even heard him come into the bedroom—certainly I'd done nothing that deserved flowers.

Curious about the reason for the flowery display of affection, I hurried to my office. Jona followed, mumbling a flimsy excuse about forgetting my messages.

A large vase overflowing with blood-red roses sat in the center of my desk. I ripped the envelope open, read the card, and dropped it on my desk. "They're from Grace Hudson. Wishing me a speedy recovery."

I don't know who was more disappointed, me or Jona.

"How does Grace know that I'm recovering from anything? That's not the type of thing I like to tell clients." Especially since I was embarrassed about being caught in the alley.

Jona blushed. "It's my fault. Grace called late yesterday afternoon. I told her that I wasn't sure when you'd be in. Then I explained what had happened."

"No need to apologize." I put the roses on the credenza behind my desk. "I was going to call her anyway. Now I can start with thanks instead of bad news."

Grace tried to sound delighted to hear my voice,

but my ears picked up a note of tension. I let it pass as Grace said, "Blaine—how's the head?"

I told Grace that my hard head was fine, thanked her for the flowers, and sat back to wait for her to fire questions at me. She did fire questions, but not about George Walden. Her questions were about Eileen and Sandy.

I impatiently answered that both were doing fine and said, "I wish I could say the same about George Walden."

"Progress?"

"Slow progress." I fingered a cigarette. "Which I guess is better than no progress. I just got the financial records of Gary Preston and some of the others in that company. I should have Dani's tomorrow."

"Financial records?" Grace sounded puzzled. "Why?"

"Just looking for something unusual. Something that might give a person a connection to Walden— or a reason to kill him."

I heard a phone ringing. Grace abruptly put me on hold. I looked at my watch: 9:35. The market was open; Grace had orders to take. After waiting a few minutes, I hung up.

Chapter 31

The rest of the day disappeared in a flurry of dead-end leads and paperwork. Still shaky from what Dennis had diagnosed as post-concussion syndrome, I went home and crawled into bed. It was another one of those late nights for Dennis; I never heard him come home.

I tossed and turned all night and blamed it on the lingering aftereffects of my concussion—not the sinking feeling that I had to go back to the Seaport. Dennis, worn out from the late hours he was working, slept through my restless night. At five, I gave up and carefully crept out of bed. I pulled a pair of jeans and a sweater from the closet, quietly dressed, grabbed my pistol, and tiptoed down the stairs. After leaving a note for Dennis in the kitchen, I was on my way.

The early morning fog gave the Seaport a sinister appearance. I smelled fish. I heard the trucks revving their engines and pulling away from the wholesalers. All I saw were the ghostly facades of the buildings. People materialized out of nowhere, walked by, and immediately disappeared in the mist. It was a perfect morning for waiting and watching.

Hoping that Larry was an early riser, I bought the largest cup of coffee I could find and the local papers. By the time I got to the field where Larry had built his shed, most of the fish merchants had hosed down their concrete floors, rolled down the iron gates, and gone home—leaving me a choice of doorways to lurk in. I picked one directly across from the field and made myself as comfortable as possible.

As the sun rose, the fog started to burn off. I inched back deeper into the shadows and started reading the *Times*. Midway through the Business Section, I encountered a small bit of luck: Larry scrambled through the hole in the fence. Without even a glance in my direction, he ambled down South Street, carefully searching through the piles of garbage for anything he could salvage or sell.

I dumped the newspapers and hurried across the street. Once again, I slipped through the fence and quietly approached the center shack. Hoping that the residents of the other shacks wouldn't notice, I opened the flimsy door and slipped inside.

I didn't waste time searching the room; I knew exactly where to look. I crossed the room to the rattan chest, knelt in front of it, and swung the lid open. The stuff crammed inside bounced up like a jack-in-the-box suddenly set free. A file, my file, was nestled in the center beneath a worn flannel shirt. I grabbed the file and stuffed it into my knapsack.

The problem with acting alone is that no one guards your back. Most of the time, it's not a major problem—not unless you open a door and are greeted by a madman swinging a crowbar.

The not-so-jolly giant stormed inside, filling the tiny space. I backed away. I could have dealt with the anger in his eyes—it was the long black steel bar in his hands that worried me.

The iron hook lashed the air. I ducked and backed away until my calves brushed against the chest.

With the instinct of a street fighter, Larry carefully positioned himself in the center of the hut, leaving me no way around him. His voice thundered in the small room.

"The Bible says, *Rob not the poor.*"

The crowbar lashed out again, whistling in the still air. "Why have you come to rob me? I've got nothing. I told you that. Nothing. No fucking pride. Thou shall not steal."

Larry punctuated his anger by waving the crowbar back and forth, mesmerized by the power it held. He stepped forward and swung again. The distance between the bar and my head narrowed.

"Listen to me, Larry." I spoke in a calm but forceful voice. "I'm not stealing from you. You forgot to give me everything the other night. All I'm taking are my papers. That's all. Nothing else."

My feeble logic didn't make an impression on the enraged man. I made it worse by saying, "I'll pay you."

He shrieked, "Pay me! Pay me! You'll pay, you bitch. You'll pay!"

Larry bellowed that I was a godless bitch. Wrapping his hands around the crowbar as if it were a baseball bat, he swung like a homerun slugger. The bar whooshed over the top of my head, missing my skull by inches. I dove to the floor and slid into Larry's legs. Off balance from his mighty swing, he fought to stay on his feet. On my hands and knees, with my backpack dangling beneath me, I scrambled to get away.

I didn't move fast enough. Larry tottered and fell. And landed on my back, smashing the air from my lungs.

I fought to catch my breath and untangle myself from the fallen giant. Larry's fists pounded at me. The heavy coat absorbed most of the blows, but the man's weight pinned me down. I swung my arms behind my back and jabbed at him, managing to land ineffective blows that only made him madder.

My gun dug into my ribs, mocking my efforts to protect myself. Even if I could have reached beneath me to grab the pistol, it would have been useless—I risked having him pull it away and turn it on me.

Sensing that his fists weren't having any effect, Larry grabbed my hair and pulled my head back so he could smash it into the floor. Knowing that my concussion-prone head couldn't take another beating gave me an extra ounce of strength. I squirmed and rocked around until I was lying on my side.

Larry yanked harder on my hair and shouted about godless bitches invading his home. I made a fist, swung, and hit the side of Larry's head. He grunted and pulled my head back; the bones in my neck crackled.

Closing my eyes, I swung again. My fist pounded against Larry's nose. Blood spurted as the cartilage gave way. Larry shrieked. Clutching his nose, he bellowed curses at me—and the rest of the world.

But I still wasn't free. Larry rocked back. Just

enough for me to bring up my knee and smash it into his groin.

He crumpled and fell over on his side, moaning with pain. I didn't stop to check his condition. Grabbing my knapsack, I half crawled, half ran from the shed and didn't stop until I was blocks away from the squatters' field. I spotted an empty doorway.

After being sure Larry hadn't followed, I bent over and gasped for air. In those minutes as I waited for my heart and my breathing to get back to normal, a sobering thought ran through my mind. I was going to have to stop smoking.

Chapter 32

Feelings of shame dogged me all the way to the office. The file weighed me down, reminding me that I was a despicable thief. *The end justifies the means.* I kept repeating that cliché, but didn't convince myself.

I walked into the office and the guilt followed. Marcella, our receptionist, started to say good morning, but I blew past her desk before she finished, waved at Jona, who was busy on the telephone, and rushed into my office. Jona called after me, "It's Grace Hudson. Do you want to talk to her?"

"Yeah, give me a second." I tossed my bag on the desk, tossed my coat over a chair, and rushed to grab the phone. I picked it up and said hello. Grace has even less patience than I do, so her abrupt questions don't bother me. "I called for a report. Any progress?"

At least some good would come from my morning's excursion. I fingered the strap of my bag and said, "A key to the whole mess might just be sitting here in the middle of my desk. It might even be *the* key."

"What do you mean?" Grace couldn't keep the excitement from her voice. "Can you tell me?"

"Sure." I leaned back in my chair and absentmindedly pulled a cigarette out of the pack that I had in the drawer. Remembering my pledge to quit, I crumpled the entire package and tossed it in the trash can. Quitting didn't bother me. I didn't need cigarettes. Victory was hovering over my desk. I could smell it. I could taste it—and it tasted better than any cigarette I'd ever smoked.

"Remember Kendra? She was George's secretary. Well, Kendra kept a file of everything that went on down there—and I found it."

"You found it? Where?"

"Doesn't matter." No one, not even Dennis, would hear that tale. "The important thing is that I've got it. I haven't had time to go through it yet, but I think it will provide answers—a lot of answers. I'm not leaving this office until I've carefully examined everything."

"You'll call me?"

That's not the way I usually operate, but Grace sounded worried. The lengthy, fruitless investigation was taking its toll on her nerves. The nose-diving market only increased the stress. "Sure, I'll call—if I come up with anything."

"Great." Relief lightened her voice. "Gotta go. Clients are calling."

Grace didn't waste time on good-byes. She hung up. I turned my attention to Kendra's file.

Everything happened at once. I opened Kendra's file, only to be interrupted by Marcella calling to tell me that a messenger had arrived with a package from Dennis. As I passed Brad's office, he jumped from his chair and ran after me, waving a thick file in the air.

"Hey, Babe. I got the goods on Dexter. Here you go." He thrust the file at me. "Read all about it."

"Thanks, Mr. Cliché Man, for 'getting the goods.'" I tucked the file under my arm and walked away, ignoring Brad's questions about why did I look so tired and how did I get the bruises on my hand.

I got to the lobby just as Eileen walked in the door. I looked at my watch with an exaggerated motion. "Ten-thirty. Late by even my night-owl standards."

Marcella giggled; Eileen didn't. She stared at me with an icy glare that would have terrified most people and walked past me without a word. I shrugged and smiled at Marcella. Then, with Brad's file and Dennis's package under my arm, I followed Eileen down the hallway to her office.

Without removing her coat, Eileen had plopped down in her chair and turned it around to face the window. She could have said she was admiring the view—if she had thought of opening the blinds. I stood in the doorway and brightly said, "Good morning, Eileen. Why are you so late? Did you decide to sleep in this morning?"

Eileen refused to turn her chair around. "Will you leave me alone?"

"No." I sighed loudly for effect and walked in. "You know I can't do that until you tell me what's wrong. Is it Sandy or Don that's giving you grief this morning?"

"Don."

"Did he call or show up on your doorstep?"

"Called. Several times. Then he threatened to show up if I didn't put Sandy on the phone."

When Eileen decides to hold back, it's nearly

impossible to drag information from her. But I'm a master—I've had years and years of experience. I strode across the room and sat on the edge of her desk. Eileen glanced at me out of the corner of her eye.

I smiled sympathetically. "So counseling isn't working. Is that what you're telling me? What did he have to say?"

"I know you don't believe me, but something's going to happen. Something bad. I can feel it." Miserable was the only way to describe Eileen's voice. "I wish Don would just leave me alone."

"What do you want me to do about it?"

Eileen swiveled around and glowered at me. "Nothing. I don't want you to do a thing. Just keep out of this. It's my problem—not yours."

Don Quixote I'm not. Nobility does not run through my veins—I'd already proven that to myself earlier that day. I awkwardly patted Eileen's shoulder, hopped off her desk, and headed back to my office.

I started with Dennis's package. I ripped open the envelope and shook out four eleven-by-fourteen photos. Dennis had scrawled an apologetic note and stuck it on top. *These are awful—sorry. I'm working on an enhancement. I missed you this morning!!*

With growing dismay, I flipped through the pictures. The woman's face had been enlarged to an unfocused, unrecognizable, grainy mess. Useless. I stuffed the pictures back into the envelope and tossed it on the floor.

The bulging envelope with the copies of Kendra's file seemed more promising. I pulled out a thick stack of spreadsheets, copies of memos from Dexter to Wisekopf on requirements for a new computer system, memos from Walden to Dexter questioning trading practices, memos from Walden to Preston warning of impending doom if Dexter wasn't stopped, memos from Preston to Walden telling him to leave Dani alone, and memos from Kembell Reid's compliance and legal departments as they belatedly tried to impose control. The smoking file. Everything the SEC needed to put Kembell Reid out of business. Nothing to prove who murdered George Walden.

I turned to the file Brad had shoved in my face. Credit card statements, bank statements, credit reports, and brokerage account statements spilled out. I browsed through them with a familiar voyeuristic pleasure that left me feeling slightly unclean.

I turned the pages with deepening dismay. As much as I wanted to connect that despicable woman, Dani Dexter, to George Walden's death, I couldn't find a link.

The last stack of papers slapped me out of my lethargic state. A black clip held together a year's worth of statements for an account at Gardner Norvill & Burnett—Grace Hudson's firm. The account belonged to Omega Enterprises, Incorporated, care of Dani Dexter. The balance made me sit up and pay attention: seventy-five million dollars.

My stomach dropped. I whispered to myself, *Coincidence. Look carefully. Grace's name isn't listed as the broker in charge of the account.*

Too much of a connection to ignore, my intuition thundered back.

Corporations have to file their incorporation papers with the state. The names of the corporation's owners, officers, agents, and any corporations they may own are listed. Unless Omega's owners used fake papers and ID numbers to open the account, I'd be able to track them down.

In the past, I would have been forced to tramp through acres of dusty records and endure the rudeness of a thousand surly clerks. The search would have taken days, maybe weeks. Those days, I'm happy to report, have ended. After a few minutes searching the Internet's version of dusty records, I had Omega's incorporation papers.

Beta, Inc., owned Omega.

I spent three hours running through the Greek alphabet from shell company to shell company, hopscotching from corporation to corporation, from state to state, until I reached the end of the deception trial. I punched the print key and waited for my printer to disgorge the damning evidence.

I was rubbing my eyes, hoping to rub away the names dancing in front of me, when the phone rang. Grateful for the interruption, I hit the speaker button and let Dennis's voice fill my office.

"I called in a favor." Dennis sounded excited, but unhappy. "We worked some magic on the computer and got a good image. I just sent it to you."

"I could use some help right about now." I massaged my forehead and wondered if my head would ever stop aching. "I hope the messenger makes me the first stop."

"Messenger?" Dennis chuckled. "We messenger bad news. Worse news goes by modem. Turn your computer on."

I was one step ahead. As Dennis talked, I logged onto my E-mail and retrieved his message. A fuzzy, ghostly image appeared on my monitor. It took only a few moments for the picture to come into focus. It may take me a lifetime to get over it. Shock, then anger struck.

"Blaine? Blaine, are you still there?"

"Yes." My breath caught in my throat. "I'm here. I got the picture. . . ."

"Is it—"

"Yes. Yes, it is. I'll call you later." I quickly added, "Thanks," and hung up. I instructed the printer to add that image to my stack, carefully placed everything in my briefcase, and rushed from the office.

Chapter 33

Ignoring the receptionist's squawking protests that I must be announced, I stormed past her to Grace's office. She looked up from the phone and motioned for me to sit. I slammed the door in the face of Grace's irate assistant and leaned against it.

Grace quickly ended her conversation and hung up. She put down the glass of ice water she'd been sipping and calmly asked, "Blaine, what seems to be the problem?"

"I've come to make my final report." I crossed over to her desk and threw the photo down on top of a stack of order tickets.

"What's this?" Grace glanced at the photo and pushed it aside. "You come charging in here to show me photos? Really, Blaine, don't you think this could have waited?"

"I took that picture the morning I found George Walden's body. Why were you standing on that corner watching?"

Grace shrugged. "I don't know what you're talking about. That's not me."

"Let me guess. You have an identical twin sister." I shook my head with sorrow. "I expect my clients to lie to me, Grace. They do it all the time. But I've known you for what, twelve years? Naturally—foolishly—I assumed you were telling the truth."

Grace sipped her water and loudly chewed on an ice cube. The smug grin on her face infuriated me.

"I've been spinning off in the wrong direction— the direction you wanted me to take."

"You give me much too much credit." Grace frowned. "I'm not that devious."

"That's right. You never lied to me." Bitterness gave my voice a harsh edge. "You never asked me to find George Walden's killer. You asked me to keep you informed on what the police were doing. You schemed with Dani Dexter and used me as your window into the investigation."

"So?" Grace sat back in her chair and casually crossed her legs. "Dani and I have a working relationship. I wanted to protect it."

From the moment I saw Grace's name on the incorporation papers, I knew the answer. But I wanted to hear the words come from Grace's mouth. I dropped into a chair and asked, "What kind of work were you doing together? Why the secrecy?"

"Information, Blaine. This is the information age. Knowledge is power—and money. Everyone's on the information superhighway. I had to get into the express lane."

She was working a little too hard to hang on to her casual poise. Sensing that Grace was having trouble holding her cool facade together, I snapped, "Why?"

"Grow up, Blaine." Grace shook her head with false pity. "How long would you have been my client if I didn't get you in on the hot stocks, the winners? Did you honestly think that a kid who

grew up in Staten Island and went to a cheap state
college could acquire the financial savvy to consis-
tently pick winners? Of course I needed help. I
needed an edge."

Her matter-of-fact admission of guilt sickened
me. "How does it work, Grace?"

"Simple. Dani made friends with the editors of
the research reports and the writers for one or two
financial columns. It's not hard. Broadway tickets.
Dinners at Tavern on the Green. A night at the
Rainbow Room. Cash for birthdays. Cash for
Christmas. Lots of cash."

"And what did you get in return?"

"Not much. An advance look at a report or an
article. A call if an analyst was about to change
a recommendation." Grace shrugged nonchalantly.
"It's a competitive world."

I took a wild guess. "Your quest for a head start
soon led past Dani's friends, right? You found Harold Wisekopf and he found a way to create trades
on his computer system."

Another chip fell from Grace's veneer. She
twisted her pearls around her fingers and nodded
slowly.

Since guessing was working so well, I tried again.
"George Walden finally had enough proof to stop
Dani. But he had one fatal flaw: he was a nice guy.
Too nice to turn Dani in without giving her one
last chance to go to Preston and confess. That's
when you and Dani killed him. I don't know how
Dani managed to do it, but she convinced Harold
Wisekopf to do the dirty work."

"I don't know anything about that." Grace shook
her head vigorously. "I drew the line at murder.
The minute Dani started talking crazy like that, I

broke off all contact with her. I didn't want to get drawn in."

"Too late. You stood on the corner and watched as I found the body." I stared at Grace and felt my body stiffen with anger. "You were involved from the moment you knew about Dani's plans to get rid of her little problem. There's one thing I don't understand. Why did you insist on hiring me?"

"I didn't trust Dani. I wanted to know what she was telling the police so I could protect myself. I was afraid she'd blame me for everything." Grace raised her hands, then let them drop in her lap in defeat. "That's all. I only wanted to protect myself."

"You wanted advance warning if the SEC or the police got too close to you."

Grace coldly said, "If that's the interpretation you want to make, make it."

"You said you broke off all contact with Dani."

"I did."

"Then tell me something." I put my briefcase on my lap and opened it. Grace watched anxiously as I slowly pulled out the statements. I fanned them out on her desk and circled the name on the account. "Who's taken your spot on the board of directors for Omega Enterprises?"

In a split second, Grace's self-assurance deflated—then roared back stronger than ever. She looked at me with admiration and murmured, "Fast. I expected this to take longer. There is a way out of this mess, you know."

"I'm sure the SEC will think of something."

"We don't have to go to the SEC." Grace tapped the statements with her manicured fingernails.

"You looked at these?" I nodded. "Lot of money, isn't it?"

I've lost track of the number of bribe offers I've received—and declined. Bankers, lawyers, doctors, husbands, wives, employers, employees. Murder, fraud, gambling, addictions. Bribe offers from everyone for everything. I nodded and carefully answered. "It certainly is a lot of money."

Grace's eyes narrowed. The money's lure had wiped away every trace of the woman I used to know and replaced her with something not quite human. "Even if it's split four ways, instead of three, it's still a lot of money."

"Just like that? I agree to go away and suddenly I'm nineteen, twenty million dollars richer. Don't you have to consult with your partners before making an offer like that?"

Grace backpedaled slightly. "I'm not suggesting an equal share, but an amount commensurate with your contributions." Grace hesitated and rapidly tried to calculate how much it would take to win me over. "Say, ten percent. I think that's fair. What do you think?"

"Almost eight million dollars to walk out of your office—"

"And leave your little file behind."

It was my turn to look at Grace with admiration. Her offer made all the others look like what Brad would call chump change.

Like a good salesperson, Grace pressed to close her deal. "That's a big payday. We could set it up in a Swiss bank, or offshore if you'd like. Tax-free, of course. You and Dennis can retire and enjoy life."

I couldn't believe the matter-of-fact offer. I repeated, "Just like that?"

Assuming she'd bought herself out of another problem, Grace nodded. "Just like that. What do you think?"

"I think you're out of your mind." My anger built to a nearly uncontrollable level. I bit down on it and coolly said, "As far as I'm concerned, Grace, you're dead inside. Deader than George. Deader than Kendra. I don't want your money."

With the aloofness of a waiter asking for my dinner order, Grace said, "That's your final answer?"

"It is."

Grace shrugged. My refusal did nothing to shake her poise. She had something else in mind. I didn't have much time to worry; Grace moved in to make her final point.

"Now, about Omega Enterprises. Look carefully, Blaine." Grace leaned forward and rested her fingertips on the account statements. "See those stocks? Do they look familiar? Wait, let me save you the trouble. You own the same stocks. You bought them at the same time."

"On your recommendation."

'That's not what the headlines will say. The headlines will say you made the same tainted profits. That's what your corporate clients will remember. By the time you prove your innocence, you'll be out of business." Grace laughed derisively. "Maybe you'll get over your aversion to divorce and adultery cases—because that's all the work you'll be able to get when the media finishes dragging you through an insider-trading scandal."

My anger passed and left me feeling exhausted. "Bribes and threats don't intimidate me."

Once again, Grace's reaction puzzled me. She said, "They should."

She wasn't worried, not even slightly nervous. I was missing something, something vitally important. Being careful to not let my puzzlement show, I said, "You know I'll have to take this to the SEC."

My former friend shrugged again. She made a stack of my papers and held them out to me. "So, I'll lose a few million dollars in fines."

"And get thrown out of the business forever."

"That didn't bother Mike Milken. He spent a year or two in a federal country club and then got out. I haven't seen him panhandling on the subway."

"Milken didn't murder anyone."

"Neither did I. People don't kill over insider trading, Blaine. It's not worth it."

Maybe it was.

Chapter 34

The beeper I carry to avoid having my cell phone ring at awkward times vibrated. I squinted at the display and saw Eileen's home phone number. My stomach rolled; the color drained from my face. I knew it was more than Eileen calling to invite me for dinner.

A stricken look came over my face. Grace instantly offered assistance. "Blaine, what's wrong? Do you feel okay? Can I get you a glass of water or something?"

Without acknowledging Grace's concern, I grabbed my phone and dialed. Eileen answered immediately.

"What's wrong?"

"Blaine," Eileen's ragged voice teetered on the edge of hysteria, "Sandy's gone."

I tried to project calmness even though my heart pounded wildly. "What happened?"

"I took the afternoon off. Sandy and I went to the supermarket around the corner. We were going to cook a special dinner. I turned my back to get some lettuce . . ." Eileen's voice faltered. "I told Sandy to wait by the carriage."

I felt sick; I couldn't imagine what Eileen felt. "How long were you gone?"

"A minute or two." Eileen's voice rose. "It's not

like I abandoned Sandy. I went to the end of the aisle to grab a head of lettuce for our salad. I pointed out watercress to a man who asked for help. I left Sandy standing at the front of the aisle near the cash registers. When I turned around, she was gone."

"When did this happen?"

Eileen took a loud, shaky breath and spoke in staccato sentences. "About forty-five minutes ago. I searched the store and the neighborhood. I asked the clerks and the other people in the store. I stopped people on the streets around the store. No one saw anything. I called 911. A patrol car showed up a few minutes later. They think she just wandered off. They brought me home so I could give them a picture of Sandy. . . ."

Eileen's voice broke. She took another deep, shaky breath before continuing. "I called Don's apartment; there's no answer. I called to find out his schedule—they told me he's on vacation for the next two weeks. He called in and said he needed time off. . . ."

I looked at Grace. She mouthed, *What's wrong?* I scowled at her and glanced at my watch. How far could Don get in forty-five minutes?

I didn't tell Eileen to calm down because she sounded calm. Much too calm. "Eileen, I'm down on Wall Street; I'm leaving now. I'll be at your house as soon as I can."

"What about Brad?" Eileen sounded bewildered. "I didn't think of calling him. Should I?"

"Don't do anything, Eileen. Sit tight and wait for me. I'll call everybody who needs to be called." I ended with much more confidence than I felt. "Don't worry. We'll find Sandy."

I slammed the phone down. Grace came around the desk and put her arm around my shoulder. "Blaine, did I hear right? Your niece is missing? What happened?"

I slapped Grace's hand away. I didn't want her insincere sympathy. "I have to go."

"Blaine, what can I do? Do you want me to call a car service?"

"No, Grace. You've done enough. This isn't over."

Grace measured me as if we were meeting for the first time. "You have time to change your mind."

"You have time to look for a good lawyer."

Sadly, Grace said, "As do you. Insider-trading charges will ruin your reputation and bring your business crashing down. Why don't you think about that before you do anything?"

I didn't think about Grace. My business was the last thing on my mind as I hurried from the building. Fear about Sandy overtook everything else. I stopped a cab, dove in, slammed the door hard enough to rattle the car, and snapped out Eileen's address. As the cab bounced up the FDR Drive from lower Manhattan to the Upper East Side, I didn't pay any attention to the barges on the East River or the view of Brooklyn. I pulled my cellular phone out of my briefcase and started dialing.

To my relief, Dennis, not his voice mail, answered my call. I quickly relayed Eileen's news; Dennis said he'd meet me at Eileen's. Before hanging up, he quietly assured me that everything would be fine. For a brief moment, I almost believed him.

My call to Brad brought the fears back.

                    *   *   *

"Who's on duty at Eileen's?"

We had recently expanded the crew to give Jeannie a break. Brad had willingly taken over the duty of coordinating coverage. He wanted to ask why I was calling to ask that question, but recognized the warning edge in my voice.

"Jeannie had babysitting duty this afternoon. But I'm getting kinda worried. Whoever's on duty is supposed to call in every hour. Jeannie missed the last two check-ins and doesn't answer her phone. I was just about to head over there to be sure everything's okay."

My stomach turned sour. Jeannie was more than capable of trailing behind Sandy and making sure nothing happened. Even though she was often mistaken for a petite, carefree coed, Jeannie was a tough ex-cop who had spent half a dozen years on the street.

"It's far from okay, Brad. Sandy's gone. She's been missing for about an hour now."

I allowed Brad a few seconds of stunned silence, then briskly said, "Dennis and I are on the way over to Eileen's. You find Jeannie." I repeated the details Eileen had given me and said, "Start at the supermarket. While you're looking for Jeannie, you might as well ask if anyone saw Sandy—and Don."

"Do you think Don snatched the kid?"

"Who else would it be?" I watched a tugboat struggle to push a garbage barge down the East River. "It's not like Eileen's prosecuting some sex offender, or serial killer, or someone who's out for revenge. Let's eliminate Don from the list of suspects before we start looking for others."

We were silent for a second. Horrible thoughts

ran through my mind; I couldn't stop myself from speaking them aloud.

"Because if it's not Don, then we're dealing with a stranger. An unknown kidnapper." I shuddered. "Let's not mention that to Eileen, okay? She has enough to worry about."

Trying to make his voice ring with confidence, Brad told me he had everything under control. Knowing that was a lie and that it would be a long time before we had anything under control, I said good-bye.

My next two calls were less successful.

Jeremy Ray refused to talk to me. He answered his phone and listened to me say my name. He hissed, "I told you I would not talk to you," and slammed the phone down with all his strength.

Undaunted, I called back three times. Each time, the phone rang and rang and rang. I had visions of Jeremy fleeing his office to escape any career-breaking contact with me.

I hoped the NYPD would be more interested. It wasn't.

At least Chris Hutchinson didn't hang up on me. He patiently listened to my quick summary of the mugging, the lost file, Grace, Dani, the secret account, the photo, and the credit card receipt. His response infuriated me.

"So that's where you've been. When I didn't hear from you, I assumed you'd found a more lucrative way to occupy your time." Before I snapped out a rude rejoinder that I had called and left several messages, he continued. "In a way, I wish you had found something else to do. Then I wouldn't feel so bad about you wasting your time on this."

"Wasting my time?" Aware that the cab driver

understood enough English to be keenly interested in my conversation, I lowered my voice. "What do you mean?"

"Cases—cases—closed. Two arrests. Both in Riker's Island because they can't make bail."

My poor head had taken too many blows for one day; it spun out of control again. "Who did you arrest?"

I heard papers shuffling as Hutchinson looked through his reports. "For the murder of George Walden, we picked up one Alan Ramirez. He tried to pull the same stunt last night. This time he jumped a woman who had just left the View with her date. Guess the homeboy figured it was a good hunting ground."

Hutchinson chuckled, taking great pleasure in the outcome. "Only problem is, he jumped two plainclothes cops we had working down there. See, there've been a dozen robberies in that area; we thought maybe . . ." Hutchinson laughed again.

Nothing felt right about Hutchinson's report, but I didn't have any solid facts to challenge him. "What about Kendra?"

Hutchinson proudly said, "Solid police work took care of that one. We arrested the super, Peter Hewlett. He was new to the building. New because he managed to bust his way out of a jail in Montana. He made his way to the Big Apple and tried to start a new life. We think Kendra found out and made noises about turning him in."

"Did you get a confession?"

"Not yet. But don't worry, Blaine. We have enough to keep him in jail until a trial starts. And we'll get a conviction, you can bet on it." Hutchinson paused. "Now, I know you're thinking that we're on the wrong track, but we're not. Hewlett and Kendra were seen arguing in the lobby on the morning she was murdered."

"Why was he in jail in Montana? Was it murder?"

"Car theft. He's what the papers call a career criminal. Car theft is what they managed to get him on."

I knew Chris had that one wrong too. Once again, I didn't have any proof; I couldn't argue. Chris sensed my discomfort. "Blaine, trust me. There is no conspiracy here. Just a couple of incredibly unlucky people who happened to work together. But I appreciate your willingness to help. Thanks."

With that quick brush-off, he was gone. I muttered a curse and put the phone away. At least I had tried. The cab picked up speed; I sat back and tried to make plans.

Sammy, the doorman at Eileen's building, has incredible psychic powers. He senses when he should talk to the people passing through his door and when he should simply wave as they hurry by his lobby station to the elevator. Tonight, Sammy tipped his hat. His eyes were solemn, almost mournful. He knew.

I had the elevator to myself. As the car glided to the fifteenth floor, I rehearsed my scene with Eileen. When the elevator reached its destination, I was torn between running down the narrow corridor to Eileen's door and stepping back into the elevator and punching the button that would take me to the safe lobby. I let the elevator go and hurried to Eileen's apartment.

Nerves stretched to the limit, I knocked on the door. As I waited, I took a few deep breaths and tried to remember everything I could about kidnapping. When the door opened, the face that greeted me was one that had been through a thousand hells and saw no way to escape.

My world changed the night Jeff, my first husband, died. A gauzy shade fell over my eyes, blocking out the sunlight, the happiness, and the people who surrounded me. I wanted to die, too, so I could join him. Since I couldn't bring myself to commit suicide, I drank and drank and drank until I couldn't feel a thing, couldn't cry another tear. Dennis pierced that veil. Slowly, the brightness had returned to my world.

That same veil had fallen over Eileen. Except it was worse. Darker, heavier. Uglier. Her child was missing.

My stomach twisted. Despite my promise to protect her, Sandy was gone.

Eileen didn't utter any words of greeting. She let the door swing open and walked away. I locked the door behind me and followed her—to Sandy's room. I stood in the doorway and watch Eileen mechanically fold clothes and stow them away.

Icy coldness radiated from her. *Keep away* was the unspoken message. My sister often calls me stubborn, but she's just as bad—sometimes worse. When Eileen doesn't feel like talking, she doesn't talk. But I know how to goad her out of her angry silence.

I folded my arms and prepared for battle. "Is that what you've been doing since you called, sorting laundry?"

Eileen snapped, "What did you expect me to do, bake a cake?"

"A cake might have been more useful than moping around here, creating a shrine."

"I've been busy."

"Doing what?"

"If you have tears, prepare to shed them now."

"Who's that, some old Greek guy?" Eileen's love of Greek myths had started early and grew more intense over the years. Naturally, I assumed she was quoting from one of the more obscure myths.

"Shakespeare, you dummy." Eileen attempted to smile. She failed. "Did you cut every lit class you had in school?"

"As many as I could. Come on, Eileen, let's make some coffee. You can tell me all about Shakespeare—and everything else."

By the time the doorbell rang to signal Dennis's arrival, we had finished our coffee and rehashed the disastrous supermarket trip a half-dozen times. Eileen struggled with the guilt of having turned her back on her daughter; I struggled with the guilt of inadequacy. The ringing bell was a welcome interruption.

Afraid to leave Eileen alone for more than a moment, I answered the door, gave Dennis a quick hug, and led him to the living room where Eileen waited. They embraced; Dennis settled Eileen on the sofa and started to ask the same questions I'd been asking for the past half hour.

Eileen didn't notice that she was repeating the words, telling the same story. I sat back, lit a cigarette, and watched Dennis with professional interest. His horn-rimmed glasses, dark suit, and short brown hair that showed faint traces of silver gave him a professorial air. Dennis's calm concern helped relax Eileen.

We moved to the living room. I sat beside Eileen on the sofa as she repeated her story. Dennis leaned against the piano and listened.

Eileen didn't hear the soft knock on the door; Dennis and I did. Looking at him over Eileen's head, I nodded, patted my sister's shoulder, and said, "Be right back."

Casually, as if going to the bathroom, I stood and walked down the hallway to the door. I quietly undid the locks and pulled the door open. Brad stood there; his face was ashen and worried. He grabbed my arm and yanked me out into the hallway.

I immediately thought he was bringing news that Sandy's body had been found. Warning myself that I had to be strong for Eileen, I whispered, "Sandy?"

"No." Brad gulped. "It's Jeannie. The cops found her in Central Park, in the Ramble area near the lake. Someone attacked her and beat her up pretty bad. She's in surgery. Her skull was fractured. There's bleeding and pressure's building up."

Shock made my stomach tumble. I felt sick. Our staff had become a tight family; an attack on one of us hurt everyone. Rage instantly shoved the shock aside. *How could Don . . .*

I pushed my anger away until I had time to do something about it. In the meantime, we had more important problems to face. "Is someone at the hospital with Jeannie?"

Brad nodded. "I sent Jona. I thought she was the best one."

"What about her family?"

"Notified and on their way. What about Sandy?"

"Still gone. No word from anyone about a ransom. Or anything." I shook my head. The day had taken an ugly spin—and it was still spinning. "What happened to Jeannie?"

It didn't take Brad long to tell me the few details he knew. When finished, Brad sagged against the wall and waited for my reaction. For a second, I thought he would cry. Instead, Brad made a face that looked more like a grimace than a grin.

I hugged him and said, "It's not your fault. Jeannie knew what she was doing. Let's get busy finding out what went wrong—and who's responsible. Okay?"

Brad nodded mournfully. I'd never make it as a cheerleader. I tried a bright, confident smile and said, "Give me a few minutes to talk to Eileen. Then we'll go to the hospital and then the office. You ready?"

Brad nodded. I hugged him again and opened the door. When we walked into the living room, Eileen and Dennis's quiet conversation ended abruptly.

Dennis sprang to his feet, torn between protecting Eileen and hurrying to my side. Eileen sat on the couch, frozen by fear. In voices that blended into one, they asked, "Brad? What's wrong? Did they"— Eileen stopped, too horrified by the image in her mind to put it into words.

"It's not Sandy." I sat next to Eileen and took her hand. Her skin was cold; she seemed almost lifeless. Brad, who clearly wanted to be anywhere else, hovered in the doorway.

"It's Jeannie." Eileen stiffened. Her hand flew to her mouth as if to hold back a moan. "She was found in Central Park. She's alive, but she's in surgery."

Eileen's eyes darted to Brad. "What happened?"

Brad looked at me, silently pleading with me to change the subject. I shrugged and told him to go on. He jammed his hands in his pockets and stared at his feet as he spoke.

"A senior citizen out walking his dog found Jeannie. Actually, the dog found her and started barking. This senior is a hip guy. He had a phone in his pocket, so he called 911. That's all I know."

A heavy, gloomy silence grew until it threatened to suffocate me. Dennis gently caressed my shoulders.

"Was Sandy there when it happened?"

Gently, as gently as possible, I said, "No one knows that, Eileen."

Eileen moaned. "Don did this? And took Sandy, too . . . It couldn't be Don. I can't believe it. Don wouldn't—couldn't—do something likc that."

No one answered. Brad, Dennis, and I had seen too many monsters. We'd stopped believing that people wouldn't—couldn't—do things like kidnap their children—or attempt to kill. . . .

Brad broke the silence. "The police think Jeannie put up a hell of a fight. Whoever did it has more than a few marks."

"Were there any witnesses?"

Shaking his head, Brad said, "Eileen, it gets dark early these days. People stay out of the park. No one was around."

Eileen's eyes went blank—shock. Her imagination was busy filling in the details. I tried to nudge her out of it. "Eileen, Brad and I have to go to the hospital and the office. I'll be back as soon as I can."

"I'll go with you."

I looked over my shoulder at Dennis for help. Without acknowledging my silent appeal, he turned to Eileen.

"I don't think that's a good idea, Eileen. You have to stay here in case there's news—or a call. You have enough to take care of here. Let Blaine handle everything else. I'll stay with you."

Dennis's calm was infective. Eileen didn't have the strength to argue. She went to the window and stared out at the street, looking for her daughter. While Brad awkwardly tried to comfort Eileen, Dennis walked me to the door.

We stopped near the door for a quiet conference. "Dennis, I'm afraid this is going to be written off as a domestic dispute. A custody battle."

Dennis nodded. "Don *is* Sandy's father. Legally, he has the right to be with her."

I finally voiced the fear that had nagged me from the moment Eileen had called. "What if Don didn't take Sandy? What if it's someone else? We're losing time. Valuable, precious time."

"My FBI credentials have some pull. I'll do what I can to shake up official interest. We'll find Don, wherever he is, and see if Sandy's with him."

"And if she isn't? What then?"

"Let me worry about that, Blaine. You have other things to deal with right now." Dennis pulled me against his chest and wrapped his arms around me. I wanted to stay there until I woke up from this nightmare.

Dennis broke the fantasy I was building about

never moving from his arms. "Are you going to be okay?"

"Okay enough to get through this. Really okay? I don't know." I tried to shake my head but wound up rubbing my cheek against his tie instead. "I never thought . . . Brad didn't tell Eileen, but Jeannie might not make it."

"Blaine, stop." Dennis kissed the top of my head. "You don't have time to be upset. We'll talk later."

From the moment I walked in the door and saw the tears on Marcella's cheeks, I knew the news had gotten to the office before I did. I hugged her and asked, "How did you find out?"

"The newspapers." Stress made Marcella's French accent stronger. "They called to ask our comment. They keep calling. Word spread. It is true?"

I cursed myself for not being there sooner, but my stop at the hospital was hardly a pleasure trip. "Yes, Marcella, it's true. Do the others know?"

"There has been talk . . ."

I patted her back reassuringly and said, "We'll get through this. Let's get everyone together. The service can answer the phones. Tell them to say, 'no comment.' "

I grabbed a can of seltzer from the pantry and headed to the conference room. No one had to call a meeting; a procession formed behind me. I stood outside the door, quietly talking to Brad as Marcella, my investigators, and Eileen's attorneys filed past.

I cleared my throat. The thirty people gathered in the room fell silent and waited expectantly. "I understand the rumors are flying. I also know how inaccurate rumors can be. Let me clarify things." I paused for a sip of soda, then rapidly, and without emotion, repeated everything Brad had told me.

I stopped abruptly and swept the room with my eyes. Shock and anger were visible on every face. "Brad's going to run the investigation from Jeannie's side."

Surprised expressions appeared on the faces of those who expected me to take charge. "Unfortunately, the bad news doesn't stop with Jeannie. As many of you know, Jeannie was on surveillance. What you don't know is that she was following Eileen's daughter, Sandy. This afternoon, Eileen and Sandy went to a D'Agostino's to buy some groceries. Eileen turned her back for a minute. Sandy disappeared—and there's been no word since."

Chapter 35

I waited for the sounds of surprise to fade before continuing. "I'm convinced that the two incidents are related. If we find Sandy's kidnapper, we'll find the person who attacked Jeannie."

"Kidnapping?" A voice rose from the corner of the room. "Are you sure Sandy didn't just wander away? My kids do it all the time."

"It's a kidnapping. I'm positive."

Now I knew what shell shock looked like. All I had to do was glance around the room—it was on everyone's face.

"Let's talk about what we're going to do." I spent a few minutes laying out a very sketchy plan to keep only the essential cases operating. The rest would be put on hold while our dual investigations ran their courses.

Brad quickly asked, "What about the undercover job you've been on?"

I managed a weak grin. "I guess I just quit." I turned away from Brad. "That's it. Anyone who wants to volunteer for a task force should see me. Above all, this is a time for grief; anyone who needs to take some time, should."

People stirred, ready to move out and get to work. I held up a hand and raised my voice over the noise. "There's one more thing. We are going to do this the right way. No hotheads. No Lone Rangers out for revenge. Anyone who gets out of control gets permanent desk duty—at the unemployment office." I smiled apologetically. "And no more lectures from me—I promise."

I spent half an hour setting up three squads: one to handle ongoing cases too critical to be dropped, one to work with Brad, and one to work with me. My squad had two assignments: scour the neighborhood to find witnesses. More important, they were to find Don.

I wanted to be in a dozen places at once, searching and digging for anything that might lead to Sandy. Instead, I went to Eileen.

I left Eileen lying in her bed, wide-eyed, tense, and alone, waiting for a call, as we had waited all afternoon and all evening. I closed her bedroom door and stood in the quiet, forlorn living room. It was too quiet, too empty.

Sandy's toys were scattered around, painful reminders that she was missing. I spent a few minutes picking up the dolls, the clay, and the books and carefully stacking them in a corner where they wouldn't be the first thing Eileen saw in the morning. Chores done, I turned off the light and stood in the darkness, wondering if Sandy was safe and remembering Jeannie's first day in the office.

Dismayed at the corruption scandals rocketing through the precinct where she'd been stationed, Jeannie had finally accepted my offer to leave the NYPD behind and join the firm. She'd shown up for her first day wearing a new navy blue linen suit

and crisp white blouse, tottering slightly on unfamiliar heels. Very corporate, very nervous.

Jeannie hadn't done anything special that day;
she followed me around on a quick tour, tried to
remember everyone's name and how to find the
ladies' room. In less than a month, Jeannie had
become one of the most popular, most reliable, and
most successful members of our staff. She'd been
a good investigator who quickly endeared herself
to our most demanding clients.

And now . . . I shook those fears off. No sense
in adding to the worries that would keep me tossing
and turning. Hoping Dennis was still awake, I
walked down the hallway to the guest room.

Dennis was sitting in bed, flipping through the
pages of a *National Geographic* magazine. When I
walked into the room, he gladly dropped the magazine and pulled the covers back for me. "How's
Eileen?"

"Making believe that she's going to sleep. You
know Eileen. She won't talk about what she's
feeling."

I dropped my borrowed robe on the floor,
yanked my socks off, tossed them on top of the
robe, and sank back on the pillows. "I wish she
had some sleeping pills in the house. I think I'll
call Dr. Mabe in the morning and get some. I don't
know how long Eileen will be able to last if she
doesn't sleep."

"What about you? How are you?"

I slid down and drew the covers up to my chin.
"My body aches and my head feels like it's being
squeezed in a vise. Other than that, I'm fine.
Thanks for asking." I tried to laugh, but the laughter caught in my throat. "I want to go someplace

where we can hide and be alone for a week or two."

Dennis rolled over on his side and stroked my hair. "When this is over, we'll go away. We'll find a place where no one can find us and stay for a month—or two. Three if we want."

"Sounds good." I suddenly felt old and weary. "They'll find us, Dennis. They always find us."

"Then we'll have to find a really good hiding place." Dennis pulled me to him and continued to gently rake his fingers through my hair. "Where can we go? Let me think about this. I know." He kissed me. "We'll go to Bulgaria."

I looked at him in disbelief. Now my rational husband had gone insane. "Bulgaria? I was thinking of a Hawaiian island. Or maybe the Greek islands."

"No, Bulgaria. It's perfect, Blaine. No one will think of looking for us there. I was just reading about it. Bulgaria's a beautiful country. We can dip our toes in the Black Sea and wander through the streets of Sofia. What do you say?"

I snuggled against Dennis, fitting perfectly into the hollow of his chest. "Let's buy our tickets in the morning."

The thought of the morning broke my pleasant Bulgarian fantasy. Dennis felt it shatter. His hands moved down my back and gently massaged the tense muscles. "We're going to have to rev up the publicity machine in the morning. Let's use the press to our advantage for once."

"Eileen won't want to do that."

"She doesn't have any choice, Blaine. It's the best thing we can do for Sandy. You'll have to convince Eileen. She'll listen to you."

I quietly said, "You'll have to convince me first."

Dennis took a deep breath and started his lecture. "One out of every seven kids featured in photo distribution programs is returned as the direct result of a lead that came from that photo. We'll plaster the city with pictures and get the story out all over the country, set up an eight hundred number in your office. Sooner or later, someone will spot Sandy and remember seeing her picture. Or someone will see the picture and realize they witnessed the kidnapping. Sure, we'll get a lot of crank calls, but we may also get a good lead. One good lead is all we need, Blaine. What about a reward?"

Dennis's conviction overcame my hatred of publicity. I named the first figure that came to mind. "A hundred thousand? We can raise that much without too much trouble."

"Blaine . . ."

My shoulders stiffened. I knew Dennis too well. The way he said my name and the slight hesitation that followed told me that Dennis was carefully choosing words that wouldn't hurt.

"I think you should double the reward."

"And? Come on, Dennis. Don't make me drag it out of you. What?"

"A two-hundred-thousand-dollar reward for information that gets Sandy back—and finds Jeannie's attacker—should get some results. Call your friend Johnnie Bramble. He'll put on a good show. And a good show is what you need."

I rolled over on my back and stared at the ceiling. Not a cobweb in sight—they were all inside my head.

"Eileen won't like it one bit."

"Convincing her is your job, Blaine. She'll listen to you—if you yell loud enough."

I closed my eyes and tried to block out everything. "You know, Dennis, the reporters won't be happy with Eileen, Don, Sandy, and Jeannie. They'll come after me—and you, too. Are you ready for that?"

Dennis wrapped his hands around mine. His grip felt strong and confident. "Are you kidding? They won't even look twice at us."

"Don't be naive. We could be the First Family of tragedy. My first husband died a heroic death in a gun battle while fighting the war on drugs. Then I have a miscarriage and try to drink myself into a premature grave. After spending years in a drunken stupor, I sober up. And then you come along."

Dennis gently kissed my hands. "Nothing tragic there."

I opened an eye and looked at Dennis. He had propped himself up on his side and was watching me intently. Instead of mentioning any of the things that worried me about our marriage, I smiled. "At least you can cook. You saved me from the tragedy of starvation."

"Now I'm going to save us both from the tragedy of exhaustion. Good night." He gently kissed my cheek and turned off the bedside lamp. "Try to get some sleep. Tomorrow's going to be a hell of a day."

Dennis is a master of the understatement.

I didn't sleep much that night. I kept remembering how I tried to explain to two worried parents how their only daughter gave up the dangerous job of patrolling the New York City streets for a much safer corporate job—and then wound up in the intensive care unit with a skull fracture and dangerous blood clots in the brain. I kept remembering Eileen's face when I walked in the door and heard her say out loud that Sandy was missing. I kept remembering how I promised that Sandy would be safe.

Chapter 36

Dennis didn't get much rest that night either; my tossing and turning kept him awake. He finally gave up on sleep and rolled over to face me.

"Blaine, we've done everything we can for one day. We can't do anything else until the morning. You won't be any help to Eileen or Sandy if you keel over from exhaustion. Neither will I."

The dark always makes it easier to talk. I slid closer to Dennis, close enough for the skin of his thigh to brush against mine. I moved closer; the warmth of his body didn't offer any comfort.

"Do you think she's dead?"

Another man might have tried to talk me to safer ground, but Dennis knew he wouldn't be able to pat my fears away. He reached out in the darkness and grabbed my hand.

"She could be," he said quietly. "Blaine, we can't rule it out. Random kidnapping and murder. It's been done—too many times." He squeezed my hand. "We have to be ready. We may never find her."

"Or we may find a body." I shuddered. "I don't know how Eileen—"

Dennis squeezed my hand tighter. "Stop. Don't say it. Don't even think it."

I didn't say it, but I couldn't stop thinking the worst. It was Don. It had to be Don.

We were up at dawn. Dennis called his colleagues and set an unofficial investigation in motion. I called Brad to tell him I had nothing to report and listened to him say that he had nothing to report either. Fear and anger kept our conversation short. We agreed to meet later at the office and hung up.

Eileen refused to leave her bedroom. I allowed her an hour to brood, then burst into the darkened room.

"You've had enough time to feel sorry for yourself. What about Sandy? Don't you think—"

"Get out of here."

"No." I walked to Eileen's closet, pulled out a handful of clothes and threw them in her face. "We have work to do."

"You have work to do. What am I going to do? Work on a brief? Maybe I could catch up on my correspondence." Eileen tossed the clothes on the bed. "I'm staying here."

Dennis, who'd been listening outside the door, stepped in with a suggestion. "Blaine, you go to the office. I'll stay here. Some of my buddies from work are coming over. We're going to get set up in case Eileen gets a phone call."

Eileen nodded her approval. Relieved that Eileen appeared ready to follow Dennis's suggestion, I moved to the next item on my list.

"I'm going to meet with Johnnie Bramble. Dennis and I think you should do an interview with him." Eileen stiffened. I interjected, "I know you don't want publicity, but I think you should do this."

"No." Eileen shook her head adamantly. "No. I won't do it. I won't put Sandy through that."

"Put her through what? Sandy's missing, for God's sake. Stop fooling yourself. You can't hide out here and make believe nothing's wrong. Wishing won't bring Sandy home. You should do whatever it takes to find her—and not waste time worrying about too much exposure."

Dennis murmured a warning. "Blaine, ease up a bit."

I glared at him for interfering and snapped, "No, I won't. Publicity is our best hope—maybe our only hope. Isn't that what you said?" Dennis nodded reluctantly. "Then don't tell me to go easy on Eileen. Help me make her understand how important this is."

I swung back to Eileen; childhood fights stirred in my memory. I pushed and prodded. "Help us find Sandy."

Eileen's temper blazed. "Why don't you look for Don instead of wasting time with your television buddies? You don't really care about finding Sandy. You just want to get yourself on TV."

During my drinking days, I'd flung enough angry, hurtful curses at Eileen to recognize what she was doing. I let her comments pass over me without responding.

"Don's still missing. The story may flush him out." I crouched down in front of Eileen. "If we're wrong, and Sandy isn't with Don, then we have a bigger, much bigger, problem. The publicity could uncover someone who saw Sandy leave the grocery store."

Eileen's eyes went glassy with shock. Cursing

myself for throwing new fears at her, I rocked back on my heels. "Eileen, this interview can only help."

"No." Eileen jumped to her feet, nearly knocking me over. She took a deep breath as if getting ready to shout.

Dennis grabbed my arm to steady me. "Leave her alone for a little while. She'll see it's the right thing to do." Before I could answer, he pulled me from the room and quietly closed the door.

Hoping Dennis would restore calm and reason, I left.

Bramble made a little tepee with his fingers and frowned at it. "You're trying to use me."

"Yep," I grinned. "That's the only good thing about this whole mess. I get to use you for a change. How does it feel, Johnnie?"

Bramble ignored me. He pulled the cap off his expensive fountain pen and shuffled through the papers on his desk to find a clean pad. "Okay, give me the details."

I told him about the kidnapping. He didn't write any of it down. Instead, his frown deepened. "I can read that in any newspaper. In fact, I read that in this morning's *Post*. I want details. I want the parents."

I grimaced. "There might be a little problem with that, Johnnie. The mother's not in any condition to cooperate with the media."

"Not cooperate? Her daughter's been kidnapped and she won't cooperate." Bramble carefully replaced the pen's cap. "Your sister doesn't have to talk to the *media*, she has to talk to me. If she won't, we can't do business. There's no story without the mother. Come back when she's ready to talk."

I wouldn't beg Johnnie Bramble to do the story—I wasn't having much luck with pleading. My attempts with Eileen had been disastrous. My mind wandered back to Eileen's apartment; I started wondering if Dennis had been successful.

Johnnie Bramble cleared his throat; the noise dragged me back to his shabby office. He looked sincere, but I've learned to not trust his earnestness.

"I'm sorry, Blaine. It's a touching story, but nothing special. Nothing that doesn't show up on the evening news at least twice a week—in a slow week. I want to help, but my producer would never let me put it on the air. Having the mother on camera would make it special."

I leaned across his desk and fiercely argued my point. I wanted to shake him until his perfect hair got mussed and his perfect smile vanished. "We are talking about a little girl's life. We are not talking about ratings, about selling more commercials."

"No," Johnnie shook his head vigorously. "You're wrong. It is about ratings. Without ratings, we're gone. I know you and your sister are going through hell. I'd like to help. But let me be honest—if you want my help, I need a sexy story. One that will make people eating dinner during the news drop their forks and pay attention. Bring your sister in and I'll get you all the time you want. Missing kid, critically wounded bodyguard, missing husband. You'll get airplay. Guaranteed."

With as much sarcasm as I could summon from my tired body, I asked, "Does my sister have to cry on camera, too?"

Over the years, Johnnie Bramble covered thousands of cases of murder, mayhem, deceit, and betrayal. Most people who hover that close to the edge of civilization develop a sense of humor—it's the only way to reconcile the horrors of life and death. Johnnie Bramble never developed that cynical skin; he took everything, especially my anger, personally.

For a guy who's on camera a lot, Bramble also has trouble hiding his anger. His jaw tightened. "That's it. You have my offer. It's the best you're going to get. Take it or leave it."

"You disappoint me. Clichés are so unbecoming to a suave anchorman like you." I stood and ignored Bramble's outstretched hand. "Thanks for your help. I'll be in touch."

As I slammed the door behind me, I knew I was being unfair. My wrath should have been directed at Eileen. No, at Don. But Bramble was handy and I knew he wouldn't fight back—he was too interested in getting the story. I trotted down the stairs to the street, determined to find my brother-in-law.

But first, the office. Subdued activity is the only way to describe the feeling in the air. Interview requests were piled on my desk. I flipped through them, regretting Eileen's adamant refusal to speak out. Since returning the reporters' calls would violate Eileen's demands that this be kept private, I put the stack on the credenza behind me where they'd be out of sight, but easy to reach—just in case. . . .

By eleven, an 800 number had been set up; we were ready for the calls. All we needed was a reason for people to call. Another group was scouring Eileen's past cases, looking for a forgotten threat to get even—just in case. . . .

Johnnie Bramble called at 11:02. Two minutes later than I'd expected.

His voice was silky smooth and supremely confident. "Blaine, I have a camera crew standing by. Just say the word and your niece's story will be on the noon news. Live."

I interrupted Bramble's sales pitch. "Your station doesn't have a noon news broadcast."

He chuckled. "It doesn't, but the local NBC affiliate does. You know, I used to be their anchor. They'd welcome me back for this. I know because I already checked."

I hesitated, just long enough for Bramble to pounce. "We're out the door. Where should we meet you?"

Knowing that Eileen would slam the door in Johnnie Bramble's face, I happily gave him the address. Bramble claimed to love challenges; maybe he could charm Eileen into giving an interview. If not, she could vent her frustration by slamming the door in his charming face.

I called Dennis to warn him that Bramble was on his way—and that I wasn't. If I showed up, Eileen wouldn't yell at Johnnie or Dennis, she'd yell at me.

And the waiting started.

The combination of Bramble's charm and Dennis's calm reasoning convinced Eileen. As Bramble promised, the kidnapping did make a good story. Good enough to make the noon news, as well as the five, six, ten, and eleven o'clock evening broadcasts. Good enough to get picked up on CNN. Good enough to make me feel light-headed every time I watched Eileen repeat the story of Sandy's disappearance. Although I've often wondered, I never asked Eileen how she made it through the interview without dissolving in tears.

Every crank in the country took advantage of our toll-free number. When the crazies gave up, the reporters started. Solid tips never arrived. By midnight, we were all ready to give up. I chased everyone out, leaving behind only a skeleton crew to deal with the late-night calls.

Dennis was waiting at Eileen's, where we planned to spend another sleepless night. I hailed a cab and gave the driver Eileen's Upper East Side address. As the cab drove up Park Avenue, I found myself thinking of Don. Not Eileen, not Sandy. Suddenly, I knew where to go.

I've been in the business long enough to trust those lightning bolts of inspiration or instinct. I pulled my notebook from my briefcase and flipped through the pages until I found the address of the apartment Don had been renting. I leaned forward and gave the driver the new address.

The driver grumbled something about making up my mind. I serenely pointed out that grumbling wouldn't change the destination, but it damn sure would change the tip. He stopped complaining and drove faster.

We were two blocks away from the Chelsea address when my cellular phone gave off the strange burping sound that announces an incoming call. Dreading the news I would receive from this call, I cautiously said hello.

"Blaine?" The familiar voice held a faintly triumphant note. "It's Dave. Dave Magayna."

Dave, who had started working with us only a few weeks before Jeannie, had volunteered for the overnight shift in front of Don's apartment. "I'm not positive, because I didn't get a close look, but I'd bet a paycheck that our subject just stepped out of a cab and walked inside the building."

"Did he have—"

Dave quickly said, "No, sorry. He was alone. He had a garment bag—nothing else. What do you want me to do?"

"Nothing." I looked out the window at the street sign. "Believe it or not, I'm about thirty seconds away from you. If Don tries to leave before I get there, follow him. Better yet, delay him until I get there."

The building didn't have a doorman. Dave had been quick enough to follow a careless tenant inside and grab the door so we wouldn't be locked out. We ran up the two flights to Don's second-floor apartment. Dave hovered behind me while I pounded on the door.

Don opened it wide enough to tell me to go away.

I jammed my foot into the narrow opening. "Either let me in or I'll stand here and shout loud enough for you—and your neighbors—to hear."

He muttered a curse, but let me inside. As planned, Dave slipped in behind me. While Don tried to force him out, I tried to scoot down the hall to check out the rest of the apartment, but Don blocked the way. He snapped, "What the hell do you want? Did Eileen send you to harass me again? You should know that my attorney isn't going to let you two keep playing these crazy games. He said he'll get a restraining order to keep you away."

Raising my voice so Sandy, if she was in the apartment, could hear me, I said, "Eileen doesn't know I'm here—"

"Great." Don groaned. "So you took it upon yourself to do some midnight marriage counseling. Do me a favor? Come back in a year or two— maybe I'll feel like listening to your bull."

My almost-ex-brother-in-law was many things— but he wasn't an actor. Don's eyes and face always give away his thoughts and feelings. His face showed irritation and fatigue, but no sign of hiding something—something like kidnapping his daughter.

The rage I wanted to let loose on Don cooled slightly under a wave of misgiving. "Then you don't know what's been going on around here?"

"I don't know and I don't care. Do you want to know what I've been doing lately? Well, I'll tell you." Don glowered at me with bloodshot eyes. "I've been stranded in Heathrow Airport, sitting out two days of foul weather. Since I was dead-heading back, I had nothing to do but sit in the bar. When I finally got on a flight, I tried to sleep off a hangover. When I got back to the good old U.S. of A., I was greeted by an hour-long line at Customs and spent another half hour finding a cab. Then we got stuck in a traffic jam because of road-work. Frankly, Blaine, I'm not in the mood for you tonight."

Thinking he'd be able to get rid of me, Don took my arm. "Why don't you take your guard dog and let me get some sleep. My attorney will be happy to call you in the morning."

I refused to move. "You haven't seen the news or read a paper?"

"I've been drinking and sleeping." Don increased the pressure on my arm. "I'd like to get back to the sleeping part."

"Why were you in London?"

Exasperated by my persistence, Don shot back, "Who said I'd been in London? I said I was in Heathrow Airport. It's none of your damn business where I was or why I was there. What the hell is wrong with you, Blaine? What do you want from me?"

"Sandy's gone." My lack of sugarcoating had been intentional. I wanted to slam Don across the face with the news and watch his reaction.

Jet lag and the remnants of a hangover dulled his response. He stifled a yawn and said, "Gone? What do you mean, gone?"

"Don, unless you have her hidden away inside, Sandy's been kidnapped."

First Don's face crumpled, then his entire body sagged. All the color leaked from his skin. He leaned against the wall to steady himself. Don's response was the universal response to tragedy. "You're kidding, right? This is a sick joke, right?"

There was no easy way to tell the story. I didn't try to soften my words; it would have been impossible to make kidnapping sound any better. "It happened yesterday. They were in a supermarket. Eileen looked away for a second; when she turned back, Sandy was gone."

Any doubt I had about Don's innocence vanished. He trembled and asked all the questions I couldn't answer. Nothing I said satisfied him. As Dave shifted uncomfortably, Don said, "I'm not going to sit back and let you and Eileen run the show. I'm—"

"What are you going to do on your own, Don?" The little inner voice that usually nags at me made a brilliant suggestion—one that I hoped Eileen would second. "Dennis has the FBI involved. We're running down a list of leads—"

"—now that you've eliminated me." Anger sparked through Don. "Haven't you wasted a lot of time hoping to blame me?"

The only way to deal with his anger was to meet it head-on with the truth. I looked him squarely in the eyes and said, "Yes, Don, I did want to blame you. In fact, you've been my number-one suspect— with good reason. But we haven't been wasting time; I'm too smart and too mad to do that. And I didn't want to believe that you would try to kill someone—"

"Kill?" Don shouted. "Kill someone? Over Sandy? You thought I could . . . I would . . ." Don's mood abruptly shifted. Sounding bewildered, he murmured, "Kill someone . . . What happened?"

Without apology, I quickly told him about the twenty-four-hour watch and Jeannie. Then I finished my brilliant suggestion. "I think it might be a good idea to go see Eileen."

Don eagerly agreed. Hoping Eileen wouldn't blast me for sending another unannounced, and possibly unwelcome, visitor, we left. Dave, his work done for the evening, followed us outside and went home to sleep. With a pang of jealousy, I said good night to Dave and watched him go.

*   *   *

While Eileen and Don held a tearful reunion in Sandy's bedroom, Dennis and I held a conference in the kitchen. I slumped down in a chair until I was about to slide under the table. If I had cigarettes, I would have lit one after another until the pack was gone. Instead, I closed my eyes and dreamed of smoking.

Dennis, who looked as tired as I felt, slumped on the chair next to me. The day had been just as hard on him—maybe harder. At least I hadn't been forced to try to keep Eileen's spirits from crashing completely—and deal with her when Johnnie Bramble showed up on the doorstep.

Quickly, while we were still able to function, I repeated Don's story.

"And you believe him?" Dennis wasn't judging; he only wanted my opinion. Dennis's opinion wouldn't jell until he talked to Don.

"I don't believe anyone's story anymore. Everyone lies, that's my conclusion, Dennis. Everyone lies to me—everyone except you, of course."

Dennis found the energy to smile. "Such a cynic. But thanks for the exemption. What are you going to do next?"

"It's almost two a.m. We've been up since six. My brain stopped working about five or six hours ago." I propped my head up with my hand and squinted at Dennis. "Unless you have a better idea, we're going to have to beat the truth out of Don. Maybe truth serum or hypnotism. Or we could just go to bed."

"You private guys have all the fun." Dennis paused.

I yawned. "Stop trying to think of a nice way to say whatever it is you want to say. If you have an idea that might help find Sandy—and Jeannie's attacker—I'd love to hear it."

"Let me handle Eileen, Don, and any ransom demands. Officially, I'm on a leave of absence until this is settled. Unofficially, I've been assigned here. That way, if the Bureau does get called in, we're ahead of the game. You run down the ghosts from Eileen's past—"

"We're already doing that. We're creating a database of her cases and checking on the whereabouts of the key players." I yawned; my body was starting to ache from lack of sleep. "It's slow going. Most of Eileen's weirder cases happened more than a dozen years ago when she was with the DA's office."

Dennis's interest perked. "Some of those weirdos could be getting out of jail about now."

"Yeah, but it's a long shot. I don't ever remember her getting any threats."

"Sometimes the bad guys don't send threats. . . ."

I yawned again. "Where are we sleeping? I'm about to crash."

Fatigue darkened Dennis's eyes. "I'd like to go home, but I think we should stay here."

"What about Don and Eileen?"

Dennis pushed his chair back, stood up, and held out his hand to me. "They're adults. They can do what they please."

We stumbled to the guest room, drunk with exhaustion. Even the thought of Sandy's empty bed couldn't keep me awake.

Chapter 37

So Don didn't kidnap Sandy. As much as I wanted to blame him, I couldn't. Not after listening to him. Not after seeing the wreckage of a father who believed his only child was dead. Sandy was gone—without a trace. No ransom demands. No sightings. No credible leads. No hope?

I sat in my office with the door closed, refusing all phone calls, getting up only to refill my coffee mug. I turned the radio up, thought a dozen times about lighting a cigarette, and idly doodled on a pad. On the surface, I did everything to keep from thinking about Eileen, Sandy, and Don. Meanwhile, I subconsciously considered and discarded suspects.

It didn't take long to reach the only logical conclusion. I grabbed my coat. It was time to get proof.

On impulse, I ducked into Brad's office. He didn't try to make believe he was working. He simply glanced at my coat and asked, "Going somewhere, Babe?"

"As a matter of fact, I am, Bubba. I came in to see if you were busy."

"Naw. I'm having trouble concentrating. Shit, I'd love to cream that bastard. . . ." Brad shook his head slowly, almost mournfully. "I'm pushing this stack of papers from one side of the desk to the other and back again. Sometimes I leave them sitting in the middle for a few minutes."

"Bubba, Bubba, Bubba." I shook my head in mock pity. "What a pathetic creature you've become. I am going to take you away from all this. Want to come play with me? I'm going to terrorize somebody."

"Who's our target? Anyone I know?"

"Someone who is going to be very surprised to see me—and be very intimidated by the giant standing beside me." I pulled Brad's coat from the hanger on the back of the door and threw it at him. "Come on, get moving. We have to be downtown by four."

During the ride, I told Brad what I expected of him: Look big. Look mean. Look angry. Look rabid. Look ready to attack.

As Brad listened, his smile grew deeper, until it finally reached his eyes. For the first time in days, his eyes shone with amusement.

When we got out of the taxi, I grabbed Brad's arm and whirled him around to face me. I leaned close to him and warned, "Remember, keep your hands in your pockets and off this guy. He's mine. You're here as a prop, not an avenger."

"Babe, are you telling me that you want me for my body, not my brains?"

"You got that right, Bubba. I want your big, brawny body to scare the shit out of this guy."

The wild look in Brad's eyes and his bulky body would have scared most people. Not me; I knew better. I linked my arm with Brad's and dragged him to the building.

*   *   *

I couldn't help myself. I had to have a cigarette.
I took out the emergency pack I was carrying and
lit one. Brad stood beside me, impatiently stamping
his feet to keep warm, waving at the smoke that
drifted past him, and complaining about my bad
habits. Fortunately, for his sake, we didn't have to
wait long.

The stock market closes at four. By four-fifteen,
the trading desks at Kembell Reid are deserted.
By four-eighteen, the traders are hitting the street,
heading to the bars for a nightcap or to Grand
Central Station to catch the Long Island Railroad's
four thirty-seven to Huntington.

Jobey belonged to the drinking crowd. He and
Gretchen burst out of the revolving doors, looking
happy to escape the stifling atmosphere of Morley's
shop. I nodded at Brad. He casually stepped forward, blocking their way. I grabbed Jobey's scarf,
pulled him away from his wife, and slammed him
into the small alcove used by the daytime smoking crowd.

The anger on Jobey's face turned to surprise and,
briefly, to fear. He tried to cover it up by slipping
into his trading bravado. "Blaine! How nice to see
you. Where have you been? Morley said you'd quit.
Did that old bastard finally get to you?"

"You know what got to me, Jobey. I came here
to talk about it."

Gretchen tried to move around Brad, but didn't
succeed. Brad shifted his weight and blocked her
from getting near her husband.

The young trader reddened and tried to push
me aside. "You have no reason to come here and
threaten me—"

I held my ground and smoothly said, "Stop blubbering. I haven't threatened you—yet. You made two big mistakes, Jobey. One: you got into bed with Harold Wisekopf. Two: you set me up."

His voice lost a bit of its self-assurance. "What do you want from me?"

"I came to give you an opportunity to atone for your sins. If you don't confess, my friend here will be happy to jog your memory."

My words sounded like dialogue from a bad movie, but they worked. The flush disappeared from Jobey's face; it turned whiter than the snow that wouldn't stop falling. He fumbled in his pocket for a cigarette, lit one, and took a series of short, nervous puffs before speaking.

"I never thought you'd get hurt."

"Jobey." Gretchen squirmed through Brad's arms and went to her husband's side. "What's going on?"

I glared at her. "Your husband is about to tell us why his trading profits have suddenly picked up."

I glanced at Jobey. For a moment, I thought he might faint or throw up on my shoes. I kept guessing. "Isn't that right, Jobey? Haven't you suddenly gone from goat to hero? Does Morley go around saying how bright you are? How everyone should take a lesson from you?"

Gretchen gently touched Jobey's arm. "What is she saying, Jobey?"

"I'm saying that your charming husband dreamed up a bogus assignment that kept me here late so he and his three buddies could mug me in an alley." My anger rose. "Your husband set me up. In return, Harold Wisekopf set up some fake trades for him—just like he did for Dani Dexter."

Even though my accusations unnerved her,

Gretchen kept her cool. Her hand dropped to her side; she whispered, "Is that true, Jobey? Is what she's saying true?"

He swallowed and nodded. If Gretchen was tempted to walk away, she didn't show it. She turned to me. Brad hovered in the background, forgotten for the moment.

"What do you want from us?"

I admired Gretchen's loyalty to her husband, but I wasn't about to let her take control. In a cold voice, I said, "I don't want anything from you. I want your husband's story."

"I want a lawyer."

"For what?" I sneered at him. "I'm not a cop. I don't have to follow any of that Miranda garbage."

I glanced at Gretchen. Her face wore a mixture of puzzlement and foreboding. Her husband's face held the same expression. He shrank away from me and stammered, "I don't know what you're talking about."

Gretchen vainly took up his cause. "Leave him alone. He didn't do anything wrong. He couldn't."

I resumed my tirade. "He couldn't? You got that wrong, lady. Your husband has done more than let a pal cook the trading books for him. He's two seconds away from being implicated in a murder. No, make that two murders, one attempted murder, and one kidnapping."

My words bounced off the wall and echoed in the small alcove. I stabbed Jobey's chest with my index finger. "If you think Harold Wisekopf and Dani Dexter are going to keep your ass out of jail, you're dumber than dumb. This case has death penalty written all over it, and I bet they already figured out a way to dump the blame squarely on your ass. The guys at Riker's are going to have fun with that cute white butt of yours. Better learn to enjoy it, because you're never going to get out of jail."

Brad put a warning hand on my shoulder and gently squeezed it. Moving aside, I let him into the angry circle. He offered a reasonable way out. "If you cooperate, we'll try to get the district attorney to recognize your help. But that's all we can promise."

"Doesn't he have the right to an attorney before he tells you anything?"

"Shut up, Gretchen. As far as I'm concerned, this piece of shit you call a husband barely has the right to keep living. No one bothered to tell your husband that the little girl he helped kidnap is my niece."

Jobey watched me from the corner of his eye. The short, angry breaths of air coming from my mouth did more to convince him than anything I said. In an instant, Jobey made up his mind.

"I'll tell you what I know—it's not much. But let's go someplace where it's warm."

I wasn't about to let Jobey get comfortable. I snapped, "We'll stay right here. I don't give a fuck about the money you've been ripping off from Kembell Reid. I don't even care about how George and Kendra got killed. I only want to know two things: Who kidnapped the girl? Where is she?"

Jobey shook his head. "I don't—"

"I think you do, pal," Brad intervened. "Don't make us drag it out of you. Who took the kid?"

Jobey shook his head helplessly. Sensing that his confidence was shaking and cracking, I moved closer to him, until I was inches away from his face. "You have thirty seconds to start talking."

Jobey blurted out, "Harold said we had to do it or he'd turn us in. We'd all go to jail."

"We? You and who else?"

Jobey reeled off three names. The Three Muske-teers. I nodded. "How did you do it?"

"Harold planned it. He said he'd . . ." Jobey swallowed hard, the newspaper headlines were probably too fresh in his mind. "He said he'd take care of the lady guarding her. Harold said he knew what to do. He's always bragging about the stuff he learned in the army."

Brad murmured, "Special Forces. It's in his file."

"How did you get Sandy to go with you?"

Jobey started to say it had been easy to lure Sandy away, but wisely changed his mind. "We said her daddy wanted to see her—and move back into the house. We had to hurry and we couldn't tell her mother because it was a surprise. She rushed out without a sound. . . ."

Jobey's voice faded to guilty silence. I felt a rush of anger. Brad grabbed my arm and held me back. Without a hint of judgment, he asked, "Where did you take her?"

"To Dani's co-op."

As Jobey realized that he'd thrown away his charmed life, disbelief, guilt, fear, and finally shock ran through him. I watched those emotions cross his face, but didn't feel victorious; I felt exhausted.

With great effort, I said, "You're smart enough to know that you'd better go find yourself a good lawyer. You're also smart enough to know that if you tell Harold or any of your pals that you talked to me, I'll be back—and I won't be so nice next time."

I spun around and walked away. Brad gave the shaken couple one last word of advice, then hurried to catch up to me.

"What did you tell him?"

"That you're a mean son of a bitch and you carry a gun."

"And don't you forget it."

Nothing like a little terrorism to lift the spirits. I grinned at Brad; he grinned at me. We swaggered to the street and hailed a cab.

As we climbed into the car, I said, "Bubba, we've got one more stop to make. Do you mind?"

Brad squeezed himself in and slammed the door. "Let me guess. Dexter's place?"

"Another wild goose chase, but . . ." I gave the driver the address.

"Did you get what you wanted, Babe?"

Too tense to relax, I sat on the edge of the seat and anxiously waited for the cab to pick up speed. "More than I thought possible. Much more."

Brad blew out a long sigh of relief and started to giggle. " 'I'll be back and I won't be so nice'— what kind of crap was that, Blaine?"

I protested, "Hey, it worked. It's a good thing you didn't laugh; you would have blown the whole thing."

"Laugh? No way." Brad shook his head. "Hell, you had me scared. I thought I was going to have to pull you off that guy. It's a wonder he didn't shit his pants. Do you think he'll run?"

"Jobey? No, he doesn't have the nerve to disappear. He'll go home and break into a cold sweat every time the doorbell rings. He won't be able to

eat or sleep and his wife won't talk to him. Gretch-
en's probably already planning the divorce. Getting
arrested will be a relief."

I sat back against the seat and stared out the
window. "You did a good job back there. I almost
lost it."

Brad shrugged it off. "Good cop, bad cop gets
them all the time, Babe. How much of that was
guesswork?"

"All of it. Lucky guess. Now all I have to do is
make another lucky guess and figure out where
Dani's hiding. You . . ." I looked at Brad. His eyes
were excited, but sorrowful. "You are going to nail
that bastard, Wisekopf, for trying to murder Jeannie. He probably murdered Kendra and George,
too."

The savage look of determination on Brad's face
took my breath away and sent a pang of fear
through me. Had I unleashed Brad's taste for revenge? Worse yet, had I done it to satisfy my
own cravings?

"Brad? Brad, are you thinking of doing something stupid?"

"Not stupid, Babe. I'm thinking of doing something that needs to be done. I may not have done
fancy time with the Special Services, but I learned
a lot of good moves on the football field. That
motherfucker needs to go up against someone
who'll give him a fight—a fair fight."

Aware that the cab driver might be worried by
what he overheard, I quieted Brad with a warning
frown. When we got out, Brad headed toward the
front door. I hurried ahead of him and blocked
his path.

"Do you remember the warning I gave on the day Jeannie was attacked?"

Icy calm sparkled in Brad's eyes. "I do."

"I meant every word, Brad. For you, for me, for everyone. If Harold Wisekopf gets killed and you're responsible, you're out."

My kindergarten friend didn't have to question my seriousness, he felt it. With equal seriousness, he said, "I'll try, Babe. But this time I can't make any promises. I'll do what I have to do. You'll do what you have to do."

We didn't stay long at Dani Dexter's building, just long enough to bribe the doorman into telling us that Dani had gone away. Where she went and who went with her were questions he couldn't, or wouldn't, answer. When she'd be back was also left unanswered.

Our swaggers long forgotten, Brad and I hailed yet another cab headed to the office. I stared out the window and wondered what I'd tell Eileen. Brad stared out the other window and thought about what he'd do to Harold Wisekopf.

Chapter 38

We soon became oblivious to the parade of lunatics that floated through our lobby in the days after the story first appeared. Cranks who felt compelled to confess their role in Sandy's kidnapping. Well-meaning, but nearsighted, citizens who had spotted Sandy in a dozen different places—at the same time. Psychics with visions and publicity seekers. Marcella became an expert at sizing them up and throwing them out.

The crowd swelled every time an article or TV interview appeared. When the number of people in the waiting room dwindled, I knew it was time to call Johnnie Bramble and feed him another story. I didn't like the publicity—I hated it. I did it, hoping and praying that one sane person with a real lead would walk through the door as a result.

When I walked in early one morning a few days after Sandy disappeared, I found Marcella sitting behind her desk, chatting with a young woman as if they'd known each other for years. I nodded as I walked past. The musical mixture of Marcella's French accent and her visitor's faint British accent followed me down the corridor.

Almost every office was occupied by people talking on phones, typing reports, and frowning at computer screens. In normal times, the buzz of activity would have made me happy. That morning, it made me sad—all the activity was focused on Jeannie and Sandy.

Jona was in early too. I found her sitting behind her desk, softly talking into the telephone. Jona looked up, smiled at me, said into the phone, "Give me a few minutes and I'll tell her," and hung up.

I waited. "Tell me what?"

"Blaine, aren't you even going to take your coat off before you start interrogating me? I made coffee. Do yourself a favor, sit for a minute before you jump into work. You're still supposed to be taking it easy, remember?"

Jona doesn't often play mother, but when she does you can't ignore her, because she never gives up until you give in.

I surrendered. Jona followed me into my office and hovered around me, making sure I hung my coat up and poured two cups of coffee. I passed one to Jona and took a sip from the other. Strong, hot, and black. The caffeine rushed to my head and blasted away the cobwebs.

I put the mug down. "Break's over. Who was that on the phone?"

"Marcella." Jona isn't much of a coffee drinker. She took a sip, grimaced, and put the mug on my desk. "There's a lady outside. She claims she has information and won't talk to anyone else. Marcella thinks you should listen to her."

"Marcella's judgment is good enough for me. I'll go get her."

Before I could move, Jona jumped to her feet. "I'll get her. Here," she pulled a stack of message slips from her pocket and dropped them on the desk. "These should keep you busy for a few minutes."

My nerves tingled with anticipation. I left the messages where they had fallen and waited impatiently for Jona to return.

The woman that Jona ushered into my office had curly brown hair that was long enough to brush her shoulders. She wore a navy blue suit, sensible pumps, and flawless makeup. Slender and petite, she looked like a teenager. When she got closer, I realized that her skillfully applied makeup hid fifteen or twenty years.

"Blaine, this is Hazel Conklin." With that brief introduction, Jona backed out and quietly closed the door behind her.

I led the woman to the less-formal corner of my office. After making sure she was comfortable on the sofa, I sat in a chair opposite her.

"I hope you weren't waiting long. Can I get you something to drink? Coffee, tea?"

"Your staff has been most attentive. I could not possibly drink another drop of tea."

She nervously plucked at a stray hair on her skirt. To put her at ease, I idly asked, "Do you live here in New York?"

"Sometimes."

Another crank. I stifled a groan and thought about lighting a cigarette—that's guaranteed to drive most cranks away, and it would be reason enough to break my no-smoking pledge. "Where do you live the rest of the time?"

"London. I grew up in this country. We moved overseas when I was in junior high. I hated my parents for dragging me away. Now when I'm here, I want to be there. When I'm there, I want to be here. Americans tell me I'm too English. The Brits tell me I'm too American. I'm a mess."

Impatience made me want to shout, *Get on with it!* I bit down on my eagerness and gently hurried her along. "You said that you had information about my niece. Have you seen her recently?"

Hazel opened the large shoulder bag she'd been tightly clutching and took out an old copy of the *Daily News.* I knew the crumpled paper was old because it had a picture of Sandy on the front page.

The woman carefully unfolded it so I could see the front page. Sandy's smiling face mocked me, the great protector. "I have seen this little girl. I'm positive. I have seen her."

"Where?" I prepared to listen with skeptical ears. I'd heard too many fruitless tales to be excited by the prospects of another.

"I work for British Air as a stewardess—flight attendant, they call us these days. Newark to Heathrow. Heathrow to Newark. Been doing it for nearly ten years now. I've seen thousands of passengers and forgotten most of them as soon as they got off the plane. This girl, and the woman with her, stuck in my mind."

"Why?"

"I can't explain. There was an aura of unease about them."

An aura of unease. Stifling a groan, I gestured at the photo. "You obviously know what Sandy looks like. Can you describe the woman she was with?"

"Rather tall, blond hair. The woman wore rather garish makeup, that's the first thing I noticed. Before we even got off the ground, she started demanding royal service like she was a direct descendant of the Queen Mum. Bring me food, bring me wine, bring me a pillow, bring me a blanket. On and on. I felt sorry for the little girl. She looked like a little cherub. I couldn't imagine her wanting to be with that woman."

The woman Hazel described could have been Dani Dexter. Excitement stirred, but I kept it hidden. "Could that woman have been the girl's mother?"

"No." I raised my eyebrows at Hazel's forceful answer. "I heard the little one say she missed her mum and dad."

"What about the girl? How did she act? Was she scared or frightened?"

Hazel twisted a strand of hair around her index finger. "She didn't seem quite right. Seemed a bit off to me."

"Off? Was she upset? Crying?"

"She didn't cry or cause a fuss; she slept most of the time. When she was awake, she was sluggish. Peculiar. I thought maybe she'd been fed tranquilizers. People do that, you know. Bloody imbeciles. Feed their babies a lot of sleeping pills so they won't be a bother. I pay special care to those poor tykes. Can't trust the adults to do a proper job."

I casually asked, "Do you remember what day it was?"

Hazel leaned forward and used her index finger to draw an invisible line under the date. "They were on the flight the day before this article appeared."

I tried to dampen the excitement I felt growing inside my chest. We'd had too many promises turn to ash. "Are you sure about the day?"

"Positive." Hazel frowned. "I share a flat with a very untidy friend. Newspapers all over the place.

The photo caught my eye." She tapped the photo with her finger; the polish was chipped and peeling. Hazel needed a good manicure. "Has she been found yet?"

I grimly shook my head and studied the woman's face. She met my gaze with clear, decisive eyes. "I have nothing to gain from telling you anything other than the truth."

"There is a sizable reward. Didn't you read that in the newspaper article?"

My question did not offend. Hazel nodded. "That's a fair question. Your receptionist said your lobby has been filled with people who wanted to join the reward queue. It would be a lie to say the reward didn't interest me—it does. . . ."

"But? There's more, isn't there?"

"My friends told me to stay out of it. But I couldn't sleep last night. I kept looking at that paper and thinking about that sweet little angel."

After asking a few more questions, I took down Hazel's New York and London addresses and phone numbers, as well as her schedule. Promising to be in touch with news—good or bad—I walked her to the door.

I went to visit Brad. Tapping on his open door, I said, "You busy?"

Brad stretched and yawned. He didn't look any happier than he had the day before. "To tell you the truth, Babe, I'm having trouble getting started this morning. When I get home at night, I'm so tired I can't keep my eyes open. Until I put my head on the pillow. Then all kinds of crazy thoughts gallop through my mind. Maybe breakfast will help. Want to go downstairs and grab a bite to eat?"

I understood how Brad felt—I'd been having the

same nighttime troubles. Brad's yawn set off a chain reaction. I yawned in response. "No, thanks. Too much to do. Maybe you'd better order in—I need a little help." Quickly, before Brad complained again about his empty stomach, I added, "I'll spring for the bagels if you'll tap into the computers of your credit card friends. I need to know if Dani's cards are getting a workout. I also want to know where she's using them."

I dropped into a chair. While Brad worked, I amused myself by looking at the photos, trophies, footballs, and other memorabilia scattered around the office. "This place looks more like a sports bar than an office. Are you planning to hold a Super Bowl party here?"

Brad kept his eyes on the computer screen and grunted. "If I do, you won't be invited, Babe. You're too rude."

Laughing, I went to get two cups of coffee from the pantry. I got back in time to watch Brad pump his fist in the air. "We got her! She's spending the living daylights out of her credit card."

I walked around his desk and squinted over his shoulder at the monitor. "Where is this shopping spree taking place?"

Brad pointed to some lines at the right side of the screen. "London."

I leaned against the filing cabinet behind Brad's desk and stared at the screen. I didn't feel like celebrating. Dani's credit cards might be in London, but was Dani there with them?

My face showed my doubts. Brad groaned. "Now what's wrong?"

"It's too easy." I took a quick sip of coffee and

tried to articulate my uneasiness. "I have a funny feeling about this Hazel Conklin."

"You're looking a gift horse in the mouth, Babe."

"Gift horses scare me, Brad. I'm afraid they're going to kick me in the ass."

Three days had gone by; we were no closer to finding Sandy. Even though I wanted to believe the lead that had wandered in my front door, I couldn't. Not without confirmation.

"Brad, don't you know some kind of investigator in London?"

Affection and fond memories filled Brad's smile. "You mean Leah Hunter. She's a tax inspector with the Inland Revenue in Yorkshire—not London. Why?"

"Have you talked with her lately?"

Brad shook his head. "We went out for dinner a few times while I was in England. That's all—it was nothing special."

That wasn't what I remembered. I remembered Brad coming home from his vacation, unable to talk about anything but the woman he had met while jogging in a park.

"Why don't you call her?"

"Now?" Brad looked at me with mock concern. "It's been almost a year since we talked. Why should I call her?"

I laughed. "It's simple, Brad. I'm not playing matchmaker; I need info. If I call British Air and ask about an employee named Hazel Conklin, they won't talk to me. I bet they'll talk to your friend, Leah, the tax inspector."

Grinning mischievously, I continued, "If you don't want to talk to her, that's okay. Just give me Leah's phone number. I'd love to ask her a few questions."

Brad flushed and muttered an obscenity about my nosiness. I winked at him.

"Too bad I can't stay and eavesdrop, Brad, but I have to make a few calls of my own. I'll be in my office. Let me know if Leah was able to help."

By the time Brad came in hours later, I already knew that Hazel Conklin did not live on West Fifty-second Street. She did not have a New York State driver's license or a credit card. She had never registered to vote and never served on a jury. Hazel Conklin didn't exist.

The grim set to Brad's jaw confirmed my fears. He stood in the doorway and shook his head. "We struck out, Babe. British Air never heard of Hazel Conklin. Leah couldn't do more than that without running into problems with confidentiality. She wanted to do more, but Leah kinda likes her job. She'd like to hang on to it a little longer."

"Damn. I was hoping . . ."

Brad perched on the corner of my desk and listened to me recite my fruitless efforts. "Somebody went through a lot of trouble to make us think Dexter took Sandy to England."

"Or maybe the woman was afraid to use her real name."

"And pass up the reward?" Brad shook his head. "I don't think so, Blaine. So, what are we going to do? Ignore it or go to London?"

I had already made up my mind, but thought Eileen and Dennis should have a chance to disagree. "Let's go have a conference."

*   *   *

We gathered in Eileen's living room. Dennis hovered in the background and watched as Don and I nodded at each other from across the room. Oblivious to the tension, Eileen fell into a huge wing chair that immediately swallowed her up. Don sat beside her on a straight-backed chair he'd dragged in from the dining room. Dennis and I settled on the sofa. Brad loosened his tie and casually sat on the floor as I told the story of Hazel Conklin.

Skepticism filled Dennis's voice. "Are you telling us that you're planning to wander around London looking for them?"

"No."

Eileen snapped, "Why not?"

"There are a few things that make me uncomfortable with this. I have some questions and I want some answers before I go flying overseas."

"Questions?" Eileen leaned forward for a closer look at me. "What kind of questions?"

"To start, there's the passport question. How did Dani get out of the country with Sandy?"

Eileen frowned. "That's a stupid question. If Dexter could figure out a way to tip off Kembell Reid for half a billion dollars, she could figure out a way to get a counterfeit passport."

"Maybe. You know, Eileen, I'm not as stupid as you think." I paused and tried to find a way to explain my misgivings. "Dani knows a lot about ripping people off, but I'm not convinced that she knows how to buy a forged passport."

Dennis's skeptical mind had been quietly working. He interrupted with the results. "Blaine, we've been getting faked out every step of the way. How do we know this gem is genuine?"

"That's the problem. It's not. According to British Air, they do not have an employee named Hazel Conklin."

Eileen and Dennis know how difficult it is to get this type of information. They looked impressed. Dennis whistled. "That was fast. How did you do it?"

"Brad's responsible for the quick response. He has a . . ." I hesitated just long enough to make Brad blush. I grinned and said, "Brad has a friend in England, Leah Hunter, who's with the Inland Revenue. She graciously did some checking for us. The airline has never heard of our Good Samaritan. The people at her New York address never heard of her, either."

"Forget it then." Disappointed at seeing a solid lead vaporize, Dennis sat back and crossed his legs. "Blaine, why are we wasting time with this war council if your lead is bogus?"

"Blaine didn't tell you about the part that does check out." Brad didn't give me a chance to explain. He looked at Dennis and said, "The great god, American Express, told us Dani is in London. Never mind about how we know, but we know Dani's been using her credit cards in London. Her latest charge was this morning, in Harrod's."

Eileen interrupted. "Do you have any idea of where she's hiding?"

"Dani's financial records don't show payments for any properties in England," I said. "Knowing Dani, I'd say that if she is in London, she's in a top hotel."

Brad quietly interjected, "Don't forget, her friend Mariah Becco is supposed to be living in London these days. That would be a perfect place to hide out."

I nodded. "Brad's right. We have somebody working on that and the hotels right now."

"Who?" Dennis wanted to know everything.

Brad answered. "My friend Leah has a friend, Tom, who's an investigator. We're going to put him on a retainer as our English investigator. I'm going over as soon as I can to help out. Maybe it will turn up something useful. At the very least, I'll be able to have a chat with Ms. Dexter."

Hope is such a fragile thing. No one wanted to utter a discouraging word.

Chapter 39

Day four in what I feared had become a death-watch started on the same lousy note as the others. Dennis and I spent another night tossing and turning on the lumpy bed in Eileen's guest room. Don stretched out on the sofa for his sleepless night, the reconciliation not having progressed as far as the bedroom. Eileen's sleepless night passed in her king-sized bed, which was filled with nothing but fear.

We all woke up grumpy and groggy. I was happy to escape the oppressive atmosphere and go to work. Icy rain and snow pelted me as I vainly tried to find a vacant cab. I trudged toward the subway and fantasized about moving to a warmer climate.

Having decided that we couldn't afford to ignore Dani's credit card activity, Brad had left early that morning for London. He called once from the airplane because he couldn't resist the appeal of the phone stuffed in the armrest. I told him not to include the cost of the call in his expense report and laughingly wished him success on his trip.

The day passed in a blur of busywork, none of which brought me closer to finding Sandy. I tried calling Jeremy at the SEC but gave up after a half-dozen tries. I tried to talk Chris Hutchinson into reopening the murder investigations, but he wasn't interested. I tried to get Johnnie Bramble to do another story, but Eileen and Sandy were old news.

By noon, I was frustrated and angry because I was spinning around in circles, unable to break through. That's when Eileen walked into my office and dropped into the chair opposite my desk.

Surprised by her sudden appearance, I searched her face for a sign. "What's wrong?"

"Nothing's wrong. Does there have to be something wrong?" Eileen sighed and smiled wanly. "I couldn't spend another minute sitting in that apartment, waiting for the phone to ring. I wanted to scream and keep screaming. Dennis suggested that I get out for a little while. I decided to come here. I thought I could distract myself with work."

I dryly said, "God knows there's plenty of that around here. Can you type?"

"What?"

"I could use the help. Jona's been sick all week, but she's been dragging herself in. She finally got sick enough to spend a day in bed. I really need a secretary; a lot of letters have piled up."

Eileen gave me her *you-are-an-idiot* look.

I grinned because I was happy to see Eileen thinking about something other than Sandy. "Okay, you don't have to type. You could just answer the phone and take messages. You can do that, can't you?"

The phone rang. I looked at Eileen and raised my eyebrows. "This is a perfect opportunity to show your skills." The phone rang a second and a third time. I laughed. "Don't blow it. This could be your big chance to start a new career."

Eileen gave me the finger and leaned over my

desk. She grabbed the phone and sweetly said, "Blaine Stewart's office. Can I help you? Your name?" She listened a moment and said, "I see. Please hold; let me see if she's available."

She punched the hold button and dangled the phone by its wire. "Ms. Anonymous has to talk to you. Right now, before it's too late. Do you get a lot of calls like that?"

"More than you'd think. Three quarters of them come from people who've been skipping their medication. One quarter of them are genuine." I plucked the phone from the air, where it had been swinging back and forth. "I can't afford to let any of them get away."

Shaking her head, Eileen gave me the phone, released the hold button, and sat. She listened with a bemused smile on her face.

"Hello." Nameless callers tend to be skittish, so I tried to sound calm and friendly. "This is Blaine. Can I help you with something?" I waited and listened to the loud voices in the background.

"I hope you don't mind my calling. I had to do something." The woman stopped talking and laughed with embarrassment.

"Go ahead, I'm listening. You had to do something—about what?"

"My husband—he's the one who should be calling you."

"Gretchen?" I deliberately kept my voice level, but Eileen knows me too well. She recognized the edge that crept in. "What do you have to tell me?"

The silence in my ear stretched to an unbearable length. I firmly said, "You have to help him, Gretchen. And the only way to help Jobey is to tell me everything you know."

"It's the girl."

"Go on. I'm listening."

"I just saw her."

I wanted to shout. Instead, I calmly asked, "Where?"

"Downstairs in the lobby. She was with . . ." A voice murmured in the background. Gretchen answered, then whispered into my ear. "She was with someone. Look, I can't talk long."

I urged her to continue. I could picture Gretchen looking over her shoulder to see if her husband was listening.

"She came to give Jobey money. Cash. For his work. We fought about it. I want him to give it back. He won't." Gretchen's voice shook with disillusionment and unshed tears.

"Gretchen, listen to me. You're doing the right thing. Just remember, you're helping Jobey out of a deep mess." I felt like a counselor at a suicide hotline talking to someone standing on a thin, shaky ledge. "How long ago did you see them? Do you know where they were going?"

The woman took a deep breath. "About five minutes ago. I've been so worried—"

"Gretchen," I interrupted what promised to be a long monologue, "where were they going?"

'She said they had to run one more errand in the neighborhood. Then they had to catch a two o'clock ferry."

"A ferry? Which one?"

The urgency in my voice propelled Eileen out of the chair. She mouthed, *Sandy?* I waved her away and concentrated on Gretchen. I repeated, "Which ferry? Staten Island or New Jersey?"

"Staten Island. She laughed about going to Staten Island. I have to go."

Gretchen slammed the phone down before I could ask how Sandy was. Missing Brad more than I ever thought possible, I swung my chair around and hung up. The hope on Eileen's face wrenched my heart.

"That was about Sandy, right?"

I nodded and looked at my watch. "Eileen, get your coat. We're going to Staten Island."

Chapter 40

I ran up the escalator, rudely pushing people out of the way; Eileen followed on my heels. People snarled and cursed. I pushed them aside and kept going. As I ran, my eyes stayed fixed on the sign suspended from the ceiling. The red digital number flashed and dropped from three to two. Two minutes until the ferry left. I reached the top and paused.

The ferry terminal is really one large open room with high ceilings. Snow blew against the large windows that make up the outer wall, hiding lower Manhattan's skyscrapers. Large sliding doors, one at either corner of the far wall, blocked the entrance to the ferry. The doors, which look remarkably like barn doors, would soon roll back, allowing the long line of passengers to march aboard.

A sign above the doors on the left was lit, indicating that the next boat would leave from that spot. I didn't need the sign. The crowd would have told me where to go. Even though it was midday, several hundred people milled around, waiting to board the ferry.

I found it nearly impossible to push through the thick mass of people. Luckily, I'm tall enough to see over the top of most heads in any crowd. I caught sight of a head covered by a scarf with a familiar, colorful pattern—one that I'd seen around Kendra's throat.

The crowd parted slightly. I caught a brief glimpse of Sandy, her hand tightly grasped by her escort. Eileen doesn't have the same height advantage, but she sensed Sandy's presence. She frantically tried to ram her way through the tightly packed bodies. The hardened commuters welded together and refused to let her through.

The doors opened; the mass started moving. That's when Eileen spotted her daughter. She gasped. Before she could shout Sandy's name, I yanked her arm harshly and warned, "Don't. She's liable to do something stupid."

Eileen's face lost the little color it had. Eileen stared ahead with icy determination and pushed harder against the person in front of her.

As we shuffled down the passageway, unable to make any progress in our race to catch up, I'd catch a tantalizing glimpse of the woman and child. Seconds later, the crowd swallowed them up.

By the time we set foot on the ferry, the *Governor Herbert H. Lehman,* they had disappeared. A deckhand closed the wrought-iron gates behind us. After a short whistle blast, the ferry slowly crept from its mooring. The rough water took hold of the boat and smashed it against the towering wooden walls that flanked the boat. The logs wailed and splintered. The captain fought to straighten the boat. After much bumping and grinding, the ferry cleared the dock and steamed out into the harbor.

Eileen looked around helplessly, her eyes wild with panic. "It's too big. Where do we start?"

"At least we know they're on board. We have

about twenty minutes to find them before they try to get off in Staten Island."

I lied. I figured we had about ten minutes to find Sandy, not twenty. As soon as the ferry was out of sight of those on shore, Sandy would fall overboard. . . .

It was simple: a woman and a child board in Manhattan. A woman walks off in Staten Island—alone. After discarding the scarf and sunglasses that hid her face, she'd walk around to the boarding area and take the *Governor Herbert H. Lehman* back to Manhattan—alone.

No one would remember the woman. No one would remember the well-behaved little girl who thought she was going to see her mom and dad. Maybe someone would remember after the girl's body washed up in Manhattan, or maybe New Jersey or Staten Island. But it would be too late to find the woman. She'd be long gone.

I didn't share my fear with Eileen; I didn't mention that there was no reason for the two to be on their way to Staten Island. No reason except to be sure the little girl disappeared without a trace. Without a witness.

I grabbed Eileen's arm and dragged her into the sheltering cabin. "Come on. We don't have any time to waste."

The ferries have three levels. Eileen and I stood on the upper deck, which is really the one in the middle. The top level, or bridge deck, was above us. The bottom level, which for some reason is called the main deck, is a floating parking lot. You drive on in Manhattan and park, then drive off in Staten Island.

Most people stay on the upper deck, which has

rows of wooden benches and large windows so sea-faring commuters and tourists can watch the Statue of Liberty, Ellis Island, Governor's Island, and other sights float by. The more adventurous can stand outside, close their eyes and dream of their immigrant parents or grandparents steaming along the same route to their new life.

Those preferring solitude can climb up to the bridge deck and sit in the wind, or climb down to the bottom level and sit in the narrow cabins that flank the cars. On this cold and snowy day, the outside decks were empty. The crowd was more interested in buying hot chocolate from the concession stand on the upper deck than remembering their ancestors.

Eileen wanted us to split up and cover twice the ground. Afraid of what she'd do if she came upon Sandy, I refused. Instead, I slammed Eileen down on one of the wooden benches and sat beside her.

"Listen to me." I put my arm around Eileen's shoulders and pulled her close to me. Feeling like a liar, I confidently said, "We're going to find Sandy. She's going to be okay—if you do what I tell you. You have to be ready to go for help."

"Help—that's a good idea." Eileen tried to get to her feet. "Let's tell the captain. They'll stop the ferry and help us search."

I had already thought of doing that—and re-jected the idea. I tightened my hold on Eileen's shoulder. "Look outside. It's like a blizzard out there. If the engines stop or she spots a search party, she'll know something's wrong. Sandy will be in the water before we even see her. Before we can do anything."

"We'll start at the top and work our way down.

Okay?" Eileen nodded; I patted her shoulder reassuringly. "Great. Let's get going."

We walked to the bow stairs, carefully searching
the faces along the way, slowing down when we
approached a woman and child—only to speed up
when we didn't recognize them.

We climbed to the top to the bridge deck, the
narrowest of the three. It took only one quick
sweep of the interior cabin to see that they weren't
there. Hanging on to Eileen's arm so she wouldn't
run ahead of me, I strode to the Brooklyn side of
the ferry and stuck my head out the door.

A long bench, painted the same hideous shade
of orange as the walls, lined the outside wall. It
was empty. No one, not even the regulars who ride
the ferry back and forth because they have nothing
else to do, was foolish enough it sit outside in the
driving snow. The other side was just as empty.

We ran down to the upper deck and searched it
inside and out—with no luck. Down was the only
way to go. Down to the most deserted deck, the
spot where the homeless shuttle back and forth between the two islands until the ferry is taken out
of service for the day. Down to where a person
could stand on the stern, out of sight of everyone,
and neatly slip a defenseless child into the water.
The rumbling engines and the waves crashing
against the hull would neatly muffle any screams
the frightened child might make.

Narrow cabins flank the side of the floating parking lot that fills the center of the deck. The decor
is simple, just like the rest of the ferry: wooden
benches and doors at either end that give access to
the outside. The large windows also give anyone

huddling outside a clear view of who's coming down the stairs.

Before starting down the stairs, I pulled my phone out and jammed it into Eileen's chest. "They've got to be down there—probably out on the back deck where no one else would go today. Call Dennis. Tell him to get a police boat out here. Then go find the guy who's piloting this thing. Tell him we have a hostage situation, but not to make a fuss. He should slow the engines down a little— but not stop completely or she might panic. Then you stay put—up here. Don't come down. We don't need a scene."

Eileen clutched the phone to her chest. I wasn't sure how much got through. I shook her and said, "Understand?"

She mumbled that she did.

I ran down the stairs, confident that Eileen would follow my directions. I forgot that I'm not the only one in my family who routinely disobeys orders.

Chapter 41

The woman picked Sandy up and sat her on the wide ledge at the top of the railing. To the casual observer, she looked like a mom pointing out the sights to her young daughter.

The casual observer might not have the heart-stopping fear that she'd pull her hands away, letting Sandy topple over into the harbor. Sandy would die in seconds. If the giant screws that propelled the ferry didn't kill Sandy, the frigid water, with the small icebergs bobbing up and down, would.

With those horrible images dancing before my eyes, I opened the door and walked out. The wind, the sight of Sandy's precarious seat on the railing, or maybe the confirmation of my unspeakable fears about who had kidnapped Sandy, took my breath away.

"Disposing of evidence, Grace?"

"Stay back. If you come any closer, I'll let go of her."

"What?" I cupped my hands around my ears and shouted, "I can't hear you. What did you say?" I also took a step closer; Grace didn't seem to notice.

Sandy whimpered. I smiled reassuringly. "Everything's going to be okay, kiddo. Your mother's up-stairs waiting for you. Did you have fun with your aunt Grace? Wasn't it nice of her to take you on a boat ride?" Sandy whimpered again, but didn't move.

I unobtrusively studied Grace. She looked determined—and resigned. My stomach rolled with the ferry. "Grace, it's freezing out here. Let's go inside and talk."

"Too late, Blaine. Too late to talk."

"It's never too late, Grace." I inched closer. "You can make a deal. Tell everything you know. Agree to testify against Dani." Still hoping to find that Grace wasn't completely responsible for the deaths, the kidnapping, I said, "She's the one who planned all this, right?"

An ugly smile twisted Grace's face into that of someone I barely recognized. "You may be the only person in Manhattan who believes that."

Still searching for a way to prove to myself that Grace wasn't evil, I said, "What about Harold? He'll confirm everything—right?"

"Harold's dead."

The emotionless admission terrified me. Grace had decided there was nothing left to lose, a decision that would make it much easier for her to let go of Sandy.

The wind blew away part of Grace's confession. What I heard increased my terror. ". . . shot him. Weeks before he's missed. His boss thinks he's on vacation."

"That was the errand you had to run?" Grace nodded. I shook my head in disbelief. "Why did you kill him?"

"He got greedy." Grace missed the irony. She calmly said, "Wanted more than his share. Said he took most of the risk. Deserved most of the profits."

Desperate to keep her talking—and because I was curious—I said, "I don't understand. What kind of risk was he taking?"

"Harold ran the systems department. Programmed the computers to report Dani's trades as real. Programmed the computers to settle the trades and send the proceeds to our account."

The three had carried a nice, simple scheme to unimaginable levels. "So Harold made the cash flow possible. Whose idea was it, Grace?"

She beamed with pride. "Dani and I had a 'what if' discussion one night in a bar after a conference. Just a game. How easy it would be to rip off the companies we worked for. Before we knew it, we were doing it. When George found out about the trades . . ." Her face clouded. "We had to stop him before he stopped us."

"George Walden trusted you. He came to you for help." Every time I said *trust,* my stomach heaved. Bile rose in my throat. "It got easy after that, didn't it? Killing was easier than giving up your money."

Sandy squirmed and shook snow and ice from her curly hair. I held my breath, afraid Grace would use the movement as an excuse to drop her. I looked at my niece and silently prayed for her to settle down. "Aunt B, can we go in? I'm cold. My hair's wet. . . ."

"Soon, kiddo. I know you're getting bored. We'll go inside real soon—I promise."

Grace ignored Sandy's plea. She angrily said, "Then Kendra took up the fight."

"So you killed her, too. Just like you killed George."

"Not me. I didn't kill him. Harold learned those things in the army. He did it."

The lack of remorse sparked my temper. With great effort, I held it back and managed to keep from sounding like judge and jury. "At your suggestion."

Grace shrugged, but didn't take her eyes off my face.

The last, faint hope I'd held that Grace was innocent crumbled. "But taking Sandy was your idea—not Dani's."

"You were too fast." For the first time during the whole incredible confession, Grace sounded angry. "You uncovered more than I thought possible. I couldn't stop you without making you more suspicious. We had to distract you long enough to clear out the account."

Distract me? I stared at the woman who'd once been a friend and saw a monster. A money-loving ghoul. "The woman who showed up in my office and claimed to have seen Sandy and Dani on their way to London. She was another distraction?"

Grace nodded. "An actress."

"And she was your idea?"

Grace nodded again. "Don't see why you need to put a name to everything that happened. It happened. It's done. End of story."

"Humor me, Grace." I shook my head in confusion. "I'm trying to find out what happened—and why. Speaking of why," I smiled. "Why did your actress describe Dani as the woman with Sandy? Wouldn't it have made more sense to throw me off by describing a complete stranger. It would have taken the heat off you."

"Off Dani. Not me." Grace stared at me defi-
antly. "Dani thought she was in control."

Double-crossing, lying, thieving murderers. With
Harold out of the way, Grace had undoubtedly
started thinking about getting rid of her other partner. I hid my real emotions and casually said,
"We've tracked Dani's credit cards. She's in London, isn't she?"

Grace smiled and nodded, proud of herself. I
thought, *with no idea that her partner dissolved the
business.* Ignoring the feeling that nothing I said
would make Grace change her mind, I kept smiling.
Smiling like nothing I heard surprised me or
sounded too bizarre to believe.

Grace was a willing subject. I started hoping I
could keep her talking until the *Governor Herbert
H. Lehman* reached Staten Island—or until help
arrived.

"One more question, Grace. Then we'll talk
about straightening this mess out. Who tried to
kill Jeannie?"

"Jeannie?" Grace sounded puzzled. "I don't
know—"

I shouted over the wind, "The woman who
nearly got killed when you kidnapped Sandy.
Who—"

Embarrassment, not remorse, flooded Grace's
face. "It was an accident. Harold underestimated
her. She followed us from the supermarket. We led
her to the park. Harold . . ." Grace had been
watching the expression in my eyes and it frightened her. "Blaine, believe me. I didn't know . . . I
wish you hadn't interfered. The end would have
been different."

Sensing that we were getting closer to land, Grace gritted her teeth and dropped her hand from Sandy's shoulder to her wrist. The movement was a warning: time was running out. Grace was nearing the end of her confession.

"Stop, Grace. Let me help you. There's still time for us to clear everything up. There's still time to clear your name. You can't punish an innocent child because I messed up your game."

Her voice rose and took on an angry tone. "Why not? You ruined my life. This will ruin yours."

Grace's hands shook—mine did too. Taking advantage of a violent roll of the ferry, I slid closer. I was two steps away when the cabin door flew open behind me.

Eileen burst out and shouted at us. Her words barely carried over the droning engines and the howling wind. "Move, Blaine, I—"

The wind snarled and whipped away the rest of her message. It didn't matter; I didn't need to hear the words. The revolver in Eileen's hands said everything.

Desperate to get her to put the gun away, I yelled, "Kidnapping and three murders. You don't have to kill her, Eileen. The state will do it for you."

"Get out of the way."

"Where did you get that gun?"

"It's easy to get guns, you know that. I got this after Sandy disappeared, just in case." Eileen waved the gun, motioning me to move aside. "Get out of the way, Blaine."

Hoping that Eileen wasn't crazed enough to actually shoot, I turned my back on her. Grace's eyes fixed on the gun. Slowly, she moved her hands.

There wasn't time to take a deep breath or have a second thought.

With both hands extended, I lunged and snatched Sandy from Grace's hands. I knocked Grace back against the fence that stretched across the stern.

Wheeling around, I pushed Sandy into Eileen's open arms like a quarterback handing off the football to a running back. As Eileen grabbed her daughter, I yanked the revolver from her hands and threw it over my shoulder into the water. One less gun to worry about.

I turned back to Grace and watched in horror as she hoisted herself up and over the railing. I dove toward her. My fingers brushed across the soft wool of her coat and grabbed a handful of air. I bounced off the railing and fell to the deck.

On my hands and knees, I scrambled to the corner and desperately yanked the orange life preserver from its hook. I stood and awkwardly threw it at the spot where Grace had entered the water. A gust of wind blew the light float back into my face. Grabbing it with both hands, I flung it again. The ring hit the choppy water and quickly rolled over; I saw the blue lettering of the ship's name—but no sign of Grace.

While I struggled to keep my footing on the icy deck, Eileen scooped Sandy up, clutched her to her chest, and dashed inside the cabin. In the background, I heard her frantically shouting for help.

I impatiently pulled my coat off and dropped it on the deck. The engines shuddered and whined to a halt. Eileen appeared out of nowhere. She grabbed me and shouted, "Blaine, don't! You'll drown. Or freeze."

I wrestled with Eileen, stopping only when a crew of deckhands flew down the stairs from the upper deck. They pushed us aside and quickly pulled down the orange lifeboat that hung from the ceiling. Shouting at us to point out where Grace had gone in, they lowered the boat over the side and cast off.

Eileen waited until the lifeboat touched the water, then turned her attention to Sandy. They sat inside the cabin and huddled together, laughing and crying. My watch was more somber. Shivering and praying the search party would be successful, I leaned on the railing and watched the lifeboat troll the vicious water. I didn't move until the search was called off.

Two days later, Grace Hudson's body washed up on Staten Island.

Epilogue

The house was dark and quiet. Dennis had gone to bed, probably hours earlier, leaving the small porcelain lamp on the hallway table glowing to welcome me home. It had been glowing a lot lately— I'd been spending too much time in the office, with the SEC, or with Eileen as her marriage unraveled. The brief reconciliation faltered, then exploded. Don's willingness to negotiate custody of their daughter was the only bright spot in the mess.

Every tired bone in my body ached. I shrugged out of my coat and tossed it over the banister. I kicked my shoes off. They hit the wall beneath the coatrack with a satisfying clunk. Ignoring the stack of mail, I picked up the small paperback Dennis had propped against the lamp.

Dani Dexter: A Trader's Story. "A brilliant story of power and betrayal . . ."

Disgust coursed through me. I dropped the book and wiped my hands on my skirt, trying to rub Dani's slime from my skin. I walked away and grabbed a can of seltzer from the refrigerator. Intending to sit in the comfort of my rocking chair for a last moment of quiet before going to bed, I detoured through the hallway and grabbed the book.

The embers of a fire glowed in the dark living

room. I opened the grate and tossed the book on top of them. The pages immediately flared up. I dropped into the rocking chair and watched the flames.

I missed the telltale squeaks the stairs make when someone steps in the wrong place—something Dennis does every time he goes up or down. He stood in the hallway and called my name.

"In here." I couldn't take my eyes from the fire. Dennis walked over, bent down, and kissed the top of my head. Since there wasn't room in the rocking chair, he sat on the floor in front of me.

Dennis leaned back to rest against my legs; his terry cloth robe felt like a comfortable blanket. "I see you're having a party. I didn't think you were into burning books. Anything I've read?"

"Dani Dexter's book. I hope you didn't waste time reading that piece of shit."

Dennis bent his head back to look at me. "I thought you'd be amused."

"The legal battles are over. Three people are dead. At least, thank God, Jeannie's going to be all right. Dani Dexter bargained her way to a slap-on-the-wrist sentence in a federal country club. Kembell Reid is still in business. Preston is a little poorer after paying all those fines, but he's managed to hang on to his horses."

I stopped and brushed Dennis's hair with my fingers. "Do I sound bitter? I'm not bitter. I'm not burning books. I'm burning garbage."

"That's what the book-burners always say, Blaine."

I gently rapped Dennis's head with my knuckles. "Don't start a fight, buster. I'm not plucking books like *The Catcher in the Rye* from the library shelves and throwing them on a bonfire. Did you pay good money for that Dexter trash?"

Dennis grabbed my hands so I couldn't pound his head again. "I bought it from a street vendor for a buck."

"Then it's cheap kindling—not a book."

We sat there until the fire burned itself out. Without saying a word, Dennis got up and pulled me out of the chair. Hand in hand, we walked up the squeaky stairs.